Josie Day
Is Coming Home

Also by Lisa Plumley
in Large Print:

Perfect Switch

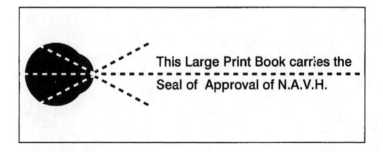

This Large Print Book carries the
Seal of Approval of N.A.V.H.

Josie Day
Is Coming Home

Lisa Plumley

Thorndike Press • Waterville, Maine

Published in 2005 by arrangement with Zebra Books, an imprint of Kensington Publishing Corp.

Thorndike Press® Large Print Americana.

The tree indicium is a trademark of Thorndike Press.

The text of this Large Print edition is unabridged. Other aspects of the book may vary from the original edition.

Set in 16 pt. Plantin by Carleen Stearns.

Printed in the United States on permanent paper.

Library of Congress Cataloging-in-Publication Data

Plumley, Lisa.
  Josie Day is coming home / by Lisa Plumley.
      p. cm. — (Thorndike Press large print Americana)
  ISBN 0-7862-7969-9 (lg. print : hc : alk. paper)
  1. Showgirls — Fiction. 2. Arizona — Fiction.
3. Large type books. I. Title. II. Thorndike Press large
print Americana series.
PS3616.L87J67 2005
  813'.54—dc22   2005015634

For John, with love.

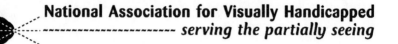

National Association for Visually Handicapped
-------------------------- serving the partially seeing

As the Founder/CEO of NAVH, the only national health agency solely devoted to those who, although not totally blind, have an eye disease which could lead to serious visual impairment, I am pleased to recognize Thorndike Press★ as one of the leading publishers in the large print field.

Founded in 1954 in San Francisco to prepare large print textbooks for partially seeing children, NAVH became the pioneer and standard setting agency in the preparation of large type.

Today, those publishers who meet our standards carry the prestigious "Seal of Approval" indicating high quality large print. We are delighted that Thorndike Press is one of the publishers whose titles meet these standards. We are also pleased to recognize the significant contribution Thorndike Press is making in this important and growing field.

Lorraine H. Marchi, L.H.D.
Founder/CEO
NAVH

★ Thorndike Press encompasses the following imprints: Thorndike, Wheeler, Walker and Large Print Press.

One

Some days, a girl just didn't feel like shimmying into her rhinestones, feathers, and spandex, and going to work. For Josie Day, the first Friday in April was one of those days.

Maybe it was because it was April Fool's Day. On a day like that, living in Sin City — aka Las Vegas — felt like one big "gotcha!" Maybe it was because, as a showgirl at Enchanté, she was required to hand out comped tickets on the casino floor an hour before each show — decked out in a full headdress, false eyelashes, and the rest of her regalia. Appearing offstage in costume was not her favorite thing. It only attracted trouble — not to mention stares, whispers, and drunken, pinching bozos who found her butt a prime target.

Sure. Those were likely reasons for the weird feeling of discontent she'd been experiencing all day. So were raging PMS and the high-heel blister on her big toe. But it was more than that, Josie thought as she gazed wistfully across Enchanté's glittering, flashing, noisemaking gaming floor. For months now, she'd been battling a niggling sensation of . . . restlessness. Of uneasiness. Even, at times, of loneliness.

Which was ridiculous. She was surrounded by people all day *and* all night. At the moment there were approximately one thousand gamblers, gawkers, and wide-eyed tourists all around her. She couldn't possibly be lonely. Especially in the midst of the glamorous life — so purposefully removed from her old life — she'd always craved and had finally made for herself.

But there it was. Undeniable. Inexplicable. And only partly drowned out by the clatter of slot machines shooting quarters into their payout trays nearby. No matter how hard Josie tried to ignore this edgy feeling, it always came back.

Lately it grew in ferocity each time it returned. Sort of like the Snickers cravings she tried to quash with fat-free Chocolate Fantasy frozen yogurt (the fantasy being that it actually tasted like chocolate) in order to meet her show-mandated, contractually binding weight range.

Was it unhappiness?

Nah. Instantly, Josie shot down the thought. She couldn't possibly be unhappy here in the glitzy Las Vegas life she'd worked so hard for. It had to be something else. Something like . . . a constant G-string wedgie. She'd had one for the past six years, ever since she'd made the cut to join the cast of the Glamorous Nights Revue. That would've gotten on anybody's nerves. Right?

Right. So Josie put her worries out of her mind. She handed out her last pair of show tickets to two fanny pack–wearing tourists, then headed backstage to the showgirls' communal dressing room.

As usual, everyone was getting ready for the seven o'clock show — the first of two back-to-back performances for the night. Some dancers stood nearby talking. Others limbered up, wearing track pants and zip-up hoodies over their costumes. The rest lingered in front of their assigned "stations" — lighted makeup mirrors and chairs arranged along a shared Formica vanity. They'd all been lucky enough *not* to have been assigned rope-in-the-tourists duty in the casino today.

Josie's spot was a small one, wedged beside a rack of shimmery beaded costumes. She squeezed onto the chair in front of her Hollywood-style makeup mirror, glad to have "pinch duty" over with. Once men entered a dark casino and knocked back a few cocktails, they all felt entitled to grope a showgirl.

Sure, it was all in keeping with Vegas's new tourism slogan: "What Happens Here, Stays Here." But it was galling, all the same. She was a regular person. A normal person. A person who recycled, who wore sunscreen, who treated people with respect and occasionally told knock-knock jokes. When she was grocery shopping off The Strip, men didn't feel compelled to reach in her cart and squeeze her melons. But at work . . . At work it was a different story.

Sighing, Josie elbowed aside a jumble of eye shadows, hairpins, and roll-on body adhesive used to secure costumes. The sharp smells of hair spray and false eyelash glue hung in the air. She inhaled deeply, trying to bolster her spirits. Those unique fragrances — along with the bustle back-stage — reminded her she'd really done it. She'd made it. She'd escaped Donovan's Corner and become a professional dancer. Just as she'd always dreamed.

Beside Josie, Parker Yates plopped breathlessly onto the nearest vanity chair. Late, as usual. She grabbed her waist-length ponytail fall.

"What did I miss?" she asked as she

10

pinned on the fake platinum hair — a near perfect match for her own — then wound it in a topknot. "Give me the whole scoop."

"Okay. But first . . . knock, knock."

Parker rolled her eyes. "You and your jokes. Okay. I might die of gossip deprivation in the meantime, but . . . Who's there?"

Josie loved this routine. After the day she'd had, she needed it. With relish, she said, "Dwayne."

"Dwayne who?"

"Dwayne the tub. I'm dwowning! Ha!"

They both giggled. Josie was a sucker for a cheesy knock-knock joke, and Parker . . . Parker was her most frequent audience.

"Better than the last one you came up with," she said, nodding. "Okay. On with the dirt-dishing. Is Jacqueline on the warpath? Did Ashley make her weigh-in? Are Marco and Ty still fighting? Tell me *everything.*"

"In the ten minutes between now and show time?"

Parker rolled her eyes impatiently. "I had time for that joke, you have time to fill me in. Hit the highlights. I feel as if I've been lost in the wilderness for a month."

"You were only gone for a week."

11

"Tell that to my ass. I think it's gone numb. Turns out, Thad suckered me into a fishing trip in disguise. I *still* smell like trout."

Parker and her boyfriend Thad, another Enchanté dancer, had been vacationing on a rented houseboat at Lake Mead. Josie couldn't quite picture her elegant blond friend "roughing it." But apparently when it came to true love, all bets were off.

Josie made a sympathetic face. "A little tomato juice in your next bath and that smell will come right out."

Parker looked at her oddly. "Should I add a celery stick and a hit of Worcestershire, too? I'm not a Bloody Mary."

Whoops. Sometimes Josie forgot to keep up with her new life. Showgirls in Las Vegas were glamorous. They didn't bathe in tomato juice, like her childhood mutt Squeegie had when he'd bumped into a backyard skunk. Literally.

"I'll just pop into the spa later," Parker continued, fiddling with her fishnet stockings. "A nice aromatherapy scrub will fix me right up." She grabbed her costume's headpiece and a mouthful of hairpins, then set to work anchoring the red feathered contraption to her head. "So, what's the dirt?"

"Okay." Settling in for a good dish session, Josie ticked off the answers to Parker's questions. "Yes, that new choreography has everybody tied in knots. Jacqueline isn't happy. Yes, Ashley made it with two pounds to spare. And yes. The latest drama happened yesterday. Marco completely freaked out when Ty cut off the fringe on his chaps. You know, the faux leather ones for the 'Way Out West' number?"

Parker's guileless blue eyes widened. She was, Josie noticed for the zillionth time, effortlessly beautiful in a way Josie could never hope to be. Not with her rambunctious red hair, affection for enchiladas, and big feet. But hey — all those things made her who she was. She wasn't complaining.

"No!" Parker said. "All the fringe? Marco must have been *crazed!*"

"He was. But he retaliated by putting Super Glue on Ty's prop cowboy hat. Since then, nothing." She shrugged. "I guess they feel as though they're even."

"*Super Glue?* That explains Ty's new buzz cut."

Josie nodded. "Mmm-hmm." Thanks to the mishmash of showgirl and showboy personalities, things were never dull behind the scenes.

"Ahhh. It's so nice to be back in the bosom of our own little dysfunctional family." Looking satisfied, Parker squinted in the mirror. She applied more lipstick. "It's sweet, really. Back home I never —"

"Five minutes, everybody!" the show's producer yelled.

"Yikes. I've got to change." Parker scrambled for her costume — all three feathers, four triangles of fabric, and six gazillion rhinestones of it. Matter-of-factly, she got herself outfitted. There was no point in modesty backstage. "Toss me my shoes, will you?"

Josie handed over the gold high-heeled Mary Janes all the girls wore in the first number — a Busby Berkeley–style routine with singing, dancing, and lots of feathered fan waving. She wished Parker had finished whatever she'd been about to say.

Back home I never . . .

Never what? Although they were friends, Parker never confided much about her past. She changed the subject whenever Josie asked. In fact, when it came to talking about herself, Parker was nearly as closemouthed as Josie was.

Oh, well. If there was one thing Josie understood, it was not wanting to revisit the past. She'd left hers behind her. That was exactly where she intended to keep it.

The moment the music started, Josie's spirits lifted. By the time she heard her cue and stepped onstage beneath the brilliant lights, her earlier troubles were forgotten. She didn't know what had been wrong with her. She *loved* this life. The dancing, the singing, the patented sideways showgirl walk with arms extended to show off her sequin-spangled costume. She couldn't get enough of any of it.

Getting here hadn't been easy. It had taken her grueling months of practice — on top of years of dance instruction — plus nearly a dozen auditions before she'd landed her first chorus position. Now, at Enchanté, she'd worked her way up to second-lead dancer. She had better costumes, more singing parts, and a prime piece of spotlit real estate at the edge of the stage. It didn't get much better than this.

High-kicking through the first number, Josie scanned the audience. Their smiling faces bolstered her; their energy pushed her to kick even higher. She adored performing. There was nothing else like it. On stage, nothing else mattered except the next step, the next turn, the next burst of applause. Nothing else really *existed* except this moment. Right now.

And some sort of commotion in the front row.

Shimmying sideways, twirling in time with a jazzy Gershwin tune, Josie looked curiously toward the premium seats. There, a half dozen audience members were on their feet. They clustered around the velvet-upholstered banquette that stood third from the left. Some pointed. Others looked around as though for help. A low murmur rose from the spot.

Josie's heart rate kicked up. None of the other dancers seemed to notice the hubbub. For most of them, the audience was a blur . . . a sea of faces. She was the unusual one. She liked to connect with the people watching the show. But tonight something was clearly wrong.

Probably it was a just a passed-out gambler, she told herself as she swished her enormous feathered fan. She issued her trademark showgirl smile. Chuck and Enrique, the security team, would take care of the problem.

Except they didn't seem to have noticed it yet. As Josie executed a perfect step-ball-change, she glanced back to the banquette again. The clump of onlookers parted. Just for an instant, Josie glimpsed an elderly woman at the center of all the attention. A woman with her eyes wide and her bejeweled hand at her throat.

Josie knew what that meant. A hand at the throat was the universal choking signal.

Quickly, she estimated the distance between the stage and the floor. Too far. If she leaped offstage in these shoes, she'd break an ankle for sure. Heart pounding, Josie broke rank with her fellow dancers instead and headed for the stage-left stairs. She moved in double-time with the music, smiling widely . . . and doing her high-stepping showgirl walk the whole way.

Hey, old habits died hard. The choreographer, Jacqueline, had threatened to cut any dancer who dared to walk normally while onstage. Doing a showgirl walk was second nature to everyone. Josie figured she probably lapsed into it in the supermarket without realizing it — while selecting a can of peas or carrying ramen noodle packages to her cart.

She reached the floor and scrambled to the banquette, feathered headdress streaming behind her. Shocked faces turned toward her. Josie only had eyes for the white-haired woman.

"Are you choking?" she asked.

By now, the woman was on her feet. Gesturing toward her martini glass on the table in front of her, she nodded. Her eyes widened with alarm.

"Let me help you."

Decisively, Josie maneuvered her way behind the woman. She apologized hastily as she whacked a few onlookers with her costume's booty frill. Music clamored all around. Show lights flashed. She wrapped her arms around the woman and caught a whiff of expensive perfume. Dimly, she realized the show was still going on above them in all its glitzy glory. Then there was no time to notice anything else. She concentrated on performing the Heimlich Maneuver.

The last time she'd practiced it, she'd been working on a plastic dummy in first-aid class. Squeezing a real live woman was a lot different. With frantic intensity, she kept at it.

Two-handed fist, below the rib cage, quick upward thrust. Again and again. She had to keep going. This woman was somebody's grandmother, somebody's sweet elderly wife, somebody's sister. Feeling panicky, Josie thrust upward again.

"That's enough!" the woman barked. "One more thrust and I'll cough up my spleen along with that damned martini olive."

Roughly, she twisted away from Josie's arms. In shock, Josie watched as the woman rounded on the onlookers.

"And *you!* Standing there like a bunch of idiots while an old woman chokes to death. Shame on you!" Even in competition with the music of the Glamorous Nights Revue, her husky voice carried. "I got up to Heimlich myself on the table edge, but this nincompoop" — she gestured to a gawking businessman — "wouldn't get his lard ass out of the way."

Red-faced with fury, she snatched her cocktail. Drained the whole thing. Winced. She banged her empty martini glass on the table, then swiveled her luxuriously clad, barrel-shaped body in a hasty arc. Looking for a fresh target.

Never one to cower in the face of a challenge, Josie lifted her chin. "You should sit down."

Calmly, she reached for the old woman's arm to help her.

"Mind your own business, Red!" the woman snapped. "I'm not decrepit."

But she wobbled slightly as she leaned in the banquette. Her wrinkled hand trembled as she retrieved her envelope-shaped

19

silk purse from the velvet cushion. Clearly the martini olive incident had affected her more than she wanted to admit.

All around them audience members murmured, getting resettled at their own tables. The show lights flashed. The music from the opening number reached its crescendo.

"I'll call security for you," Josie said. "You shouldn't be alone right now."

The woman stiffened. For an instant, her demeanor softened — as though she'd glimpsed a friend in the crowd. Then she morphed back to her curmudgeonly self.

"Look. They're continuing the show without you," she pointed out, eyeballing the stage knowingly. "It's almost as though they never even noticed you were gone."

Stricken, Josie glanced up. It was true. Parker and Thad and all the rest of the dancers posed in perfect position on the darkened stage. One by one, the spotlights popped on, illuminating the principals in the second number — a *Chicago*-style jazz routine.

The show was all she had. If she lost her place there . . .

"I'll comp your drinks and your show ticket," she blurted, hastily straightening her headdress. "Dinner, too, if you want.

Just leave your name at the door and I'll take care of everything. And next time, I recommend a cosmopolitan." She couldn't help but grin. "No olives, plenty of kick."

The woman *hmmph*ed. Taking that as her exit cue, Josie left her behind. Awash in a sea of curious gazes, she hurried backstage to rejoin the show. It wouldn't be the first time she'd bailed out on an awkward situation.

Given her track record, it probably wouldn't be the last, either.

Tallulah Carlyle had seen a lot of things in her sixty-seven years. She'd done a lot of things, too. Crazy things, wild things, happy and sad things . . . including losing her beloved Ernest. But somehow, watching the redheaded duplicate of herself who strode backstage toward Tallulah's chair right now, none of that mattered quite as much as it had a few hours ago. Because she'd found a way to do it all over again. By proxy, of course. But what the hell. A woman had to take what she could get.

Or at least to maneuver things the way she wanted them.

Patiently, Tallulah waited for the redhead to reach her. Dancers streamed through the dressing room, trailing short sequined capes and shedding parts of their costumes. There was only an hour-long break between shows, Tallulah had discovered. Then all the dancers would go back onstage for almost two more hours, until midnight.

"Omigod, Josie! You're like, a hero, or something!" a nearby showgirl said, grabbing the redhead's arm in excitement. "Can you *believe* it?"

"Yeah, you were amazing," another dancer added, crowding into the group. "You really saved that old lady."

Still unnoticed, Tallulah stiffened. *Old lady, my ass.* She'd been sitting backstage pretty happily until now. But if this kind of nonsense was going to continue . . .

"When you leaped offstage like that, I thought Jacqueline was going to have a cow." This from a statuesque blonde carrying a Dietrich-style black top hat. She slung her arm over the redhead's shoulders. "Way to go, Josie."

"Settle down, Parker. I didn't do it just to aggravate Jacqueline."

"*Sure,* you didn't."

"I'm serious." Josie widened her eyes. "Aggravating Jacqueline was just a happy side benefit."

They exchanged a mischievous look — borne of long-standing camaraderie, Tallulah would've bet — then went on chattering. The dancers neared the long row of makeup mirrors where Tallulah sat, unpinning headdresses as they came. Then, from amid her cohorts, the redhead spotted Tallulah.

To her surprise, the girl broke into a grin. It was a gaudy grin, brightened with stage makeup on a face streaked with sweat, but it looked authentic. That was good enough.

"You're all right!" The girl hurried closer. She peered at Tallulah as though checking her condition, then straightened with crossed arms. Her expression turned suspicious. "Hmmm. That's weird. You look almost happy. What'd you do, terrify a few slot machines into paying out?"

She was cheeky. Tallulah liked that. She liked her name, too. Josie. It suited her. She'd thought so from the minute she'd learned it — along with the showgirls' dressing room location — from the producer. It was amazing what throwing her weight around — not to mention her true identity — could do.

"No," Tallulah said. "I came to talk to you."

Wariness leaped into the girl's eyes. As though hiding it, Josie angled herself sideways. She didn't look at Tallulah as she dropped her spangled prop umbrella on the vanity, then set to work dragging pins from her rainbow headpiece. For a tall girl, she moved with surprising grace.

She carried herself with surprising nerve, too. She set down her headpiece. Then, rather than wait for Tallulah to take the lead, Josie swiveled suddenly to confront her.

"Look, about what happened out there. If you're thinking of siccing your lawyer on me, you'd better think again."

At that, Tallulah felt more encouraged than ever. The girl was tough, despite her loopy smile. Probably smarter than those tarted-up looks of hers would suggest, too.

"Because I only wanted to help you. If you can't handle that, then —"

"Is that your real hair color?" Tallulah interrupted. "Or a wig? If it's a dye job, it's a good one."

Obviously confused by the abrupt change of topic, Josie touched her hair. Her mouth opened slightly. Then, as though realizing she'd let herself be distracted, she shook her head.

"None of your business."

Tallulah nodded approvingly. In Josie's

shoes, she'd have said the same thing.

She heaved herself upward, cursing the snap, crackle, and pop in her knees as she went. Getting old was for the birds. She remembered when she'd been as lithe and limber as these pop tarts backstage were. No kidding — that shopworn cliché was true. Youth really *was* wasted on the young.

But maybe not on Josie. Not if Tallulah could help it.

"Well?" the girl demanded. "Are you going to sue? For overly enthusiastic Heimliching or something? I mean, I don't know why you wouldn't — everybody's lawsuit-happy these days." She flung up both arms in exasperation, showing off the sinuous gold costume bracelets on her wrists. "I might as well warn you, though. You won't get much out of me. I share a double-wide trailer with two other dancers from Bally's. The most valuable things I own are my dancing shoes. So unless you plan on cha-cha-ing your way back to the old folks' home —"

A pair of dancers lingering nearby gasped.

"— you'll be wasting your time." Clearly wound-up, Josie plunked both hands on her hips. She examined Tallulah with a de-

25

fiant expression. "What's so funny? Why are you smiling like that?"

"Because you remind me of myself. Which is why I'm here." Straightening herself to her most regal five-foot-two, Tallulah pulled a business card from her purse and handed it to Josie. "Also, to thank you. For saving my life tonight."

As she said it, the reality of the situation struck again. Immediately after Josie had Heimliched out that damned martini olive, Tallulah had been too shaken to think clearly. She knew she'd acted badly. But now she wanted to make amends.

She wanted to fire up a fresh pack of Winston Lights, too. However, like so many other things, her smokes were off-limits. She'd have to settle for this.

Gruffly, she added, "I might have to go eventually. But I'll be damned if my obituary will read: 'Done in by an extra-slippery martini olive. May she rest in peace.' "

Josie blinked at the card in her hand.

"I didn't plan on telling anyone this." Tallulah paused, glancing around the ever-quieting dressing room. Showgirls nearby puttered with their false eyelashes or their false ta-tas, pretending not to listen. "But you might as well know. I'm . . . Tallulah Carlyle."

She waited for the inevitable shriek of recognition.

And waited.

And . . . screw it.

"Hello? The owner of this dump! Tallulah Carlyle. Widow of Ernest Carlyle, Carlyle Enterprises. You mean to tell me nobody notices the name on the bottom of their paychecks?"

Muttering ensued. The lanky blonde stepped forward. "It's just a stamp. It's pretty unreadable, actually."

Tallulah frowned. "Don't you have somewhere else to be?"

"Not if you're causing trouble for Josie." Loyally, she edged closer to the redhead. "I'm sticking right here."

"It's okay, Parker." Josie shook her head over the business card, then gave it back to Tallulah. "Look, I don't know who put you up to this . . . Chuck and Enrique, probably. Or maybe Jacqueline. But the joke's over. I get it. April Fool on me, ha, ha."

"I'm serious," Tallulah insisted. "You deserve something for helping me."

"Yeah. A joke, apparently." Josie held up her hands, signaling for attention from the other showgirls. "Okay, you got me. Very funny, everybody. Just wait till next year."

Her playful expression promised retribu-

tion on an April Fool's Day yet to come.
But when she turned again to face Tallulah, her eyes were troubled.

"You probably weren't even really
choking, were you?" She smacked her forehead with the heel of her hand. "Geez, am
I a sucker. I bought the whole thing. Hook,
line, and sinker."

"It's no joke." Flummoxed by Josie's unexpected resistance, Tallulah crossed her
arms over her chest. "I intend to reward
you. So . . ." She leaned conspiratorially
toward the girl. "If you could have anything in the world you wanted, what would
it be?"

Josie rolled her eyes. "World peace."

"This isn't a beauty pageant, Miss
Spandex. Be straight with me."

"So you can report back to Chuck and
Enrique about how gullible I was? No,
thanks."

"Fine. You won't tell me what you want?"
Tallulah huffed. "I'll decide for myself. It'll
be a surprise. Here. Take this card."

Again she shoved it to Josie. The girl
stubbornly refused it. Determined, Tallulah marched to the redhead's vanity space.
She jammed the business card beneath the
edge of the light bulb-bordered frame.

"It's my attorney's," she announced to

the room at large. "When you're ready to get in touch with him, he'll tell you what your reward is."

"Thank you, Don Pardo," Josie said in an exaggerated game show–host voice, sweeping her arm to the left. "And thanks for playing, 'April Fool'!"

Tallulah tilted her head. All at once, she felt old. It wasn't a welcome sensation.

"Someday, young lady, someone just might surprise you."

Then she picked up her purse and swept from the room.

Two weeks later, Josie was leaning toward the mirror to draw on a fake beauty mark for the Glamorous Nights Revue's Fosse-inspired number when the business card caught her eye. Printed on expensive-looking ivory card stock, it bore a name and address she'd already half memorized. It also seemed to mock her every time she glanced its way.

Stupid old woman. Tallulah Carlyle. *Right.* She was probably crazy. Or an actress hired to play a joke.

Okay . . . so she did resemble the owner pictured in Jacqueline's office. Vaguely. And her portrayal of a choking victim had been pretty darn convincing. But that didn't mean that card was authentic. Or that "Tallulah's" offer of a reward — especially "anything in the world you wanted" — could be believed.

Josie snorted, then went back to penciling in her beauty mark. She wasn't cynical, exactly. But she'd learned a long time ago not to put too much faith in what other people promised. When push came to shove, the only person you could count on was yourself.

Leaning back, she adjusted the fringe on her fuchsia flapper-style costume. She already had everything she needed, she assured herself, rearranging the navel-length strand of imitation pearls around her neck. She had lots of friends, a good job, a place to live, a car . . .

. . . an ever-increasing feeling of restlessness.

Damn it. Why did that have to keep resurfacing?

Plunking her elbow on the vanity, Josie put her chin in her hand. She tapped her fingers on her cheek, thinking, as the other dancers bustled around her. Then she snatched the business card and grabbed her cell phone.

Time to find out what the score really was.

Two

Thirty-six hours later

She should have known there'd be a catch.

After all, when it came to second chances, there usually was. But somehow, Josie had managed to forget that. She'd road-tripped all night from Las Vegas, powered by Big Gulps and Twinkies and fueled by dreams of returning in triumph to Donovan's Corner. Now that she'd seen what was waiting for her — what Tallulah had "rewarded" her with — she couldn't believe she'd been so naïve.

Prompted by Tallulah, Josie had worked up the nerve to confront her past. She'd packed everything she owned in her beat-up Chevy convertible. She'd made her way through the twisty, mountainous roads that divided her old life from her new one. And for what?

For a tumbledown pile of an "estate" — a term she used *very* loosely — at the edge of a town she'd thought she'd left behind forever. That's what.

But this particular estate was hers, she reminded herself. Every last ramshackle inch of it. That made all the difference.

It was a good thing, too. According to her lawyer, Tallulah had thought she'd been doing Josie a favor by bringing her back to Donovan's Corner. If only she'd known the truth. For Josie, having her big second chance plunked down here, of all places . . . It was like a big cosmic joke. Fortunately, Josie was always up for a laugh.

Squinting through the springtime sunlight at the two-story shake-shingled house in front of her, she felt a surge of optimism. Despite the discouraging reality of peeling paint, crumbling stone chimneys, and overgrown weeds, she could make something of this place. She knew it.

The thought energized her. Or maybe that was just the Twinkies talking — she'd polished off the last of her stash upon rounding the circular gravel drive. Either way, it was time to get started. Through an unbelievable twist of fate, she finally had something to call her own — something bigger than a blow-dryer and more durable than a sequin-spangled G-string. Unreal as it seemed, she'd gotten a lucky break. She intended to make the most of it.

Pulling her duffel bag from her convertible's duct-taped vinyl passenger seat, she palmed her keys and headed across the drive. Her platform wedgies crunched against the gravel. Her hair swung across her shoulders, bared in her requisite post-show outfit of terry cloth track pants and a strappy tank top.

If she'd been smart, she'd have dressed for the chill in the mountain air. But she'd been too eager to start her new life to bother with anything but hauling herself out of Vegas the minute the curtain fell on last night's show. A part of her still didn't quite believe this whole thing was real. She half expected to find the house key in her hand didn't work at all.

Her gaze fell on the "Blue Moon" sign nailed to a porch post to her left. Josie smiled. It was a fitting name for the place. "Once in a blue moon" was about how often a girl like her made good. At least that's what people in town might have said . . . had they known she was coming back.

"Whatever you're selling, I don't want any."

The voice — a masculine one — came from someplace above her head. Startled, she glanced up.

A dark-haired man gazed steadily down at her from the porch roof, a hammer in one hand and a fistful of cedar shingles in the other. Clearly he'd been hired to do much-needed work on the place. Or to serve as eye candy for the newly arriving new owner: her. Either way, Josie relaxed.

Thank you, Welcome Wagon. Some old houses came with bats in the attic. Apparently, hers came with a resident hunk on the roof. One with dreamy blue eyes, whisker shadow, and muscles galore. Her opinion of the dilapidated estate went up a notch.

An impatient look crossed his face. "Did you hear me? I said I don't want any. Thanks, anyway."

He stuck a nail between his lips, pursing them to hold it in place. Then he peered at the roof as though preparing to get back to work — as though their conversation were finished. Just like that. Did he seriously think she could let a statement like his go unchallenged?

"Unless you find out what I'm here for," Josie told him, "you can't possibly know you're not interested."

"Oh, I know."

He looked as if he did, too. He looked as though he was always certain about every-

34

thing around him. He also looked as though he'd been working up there, belly-down, for at least an hour. Dust streaked his face. Wind tousled his hair. And some kind of black smudge decorated his biceps. But there wasn't enough grime in the world to hide his chiseled features, work-hardened shoulders, and ease in his own skin.

"You must be the handyman. I didn't know the place came with a handyman." Tallulah's lawyer hadn't mentioned him.

He ignored her guess. Instead, he rolled his eyes and removed the nail from his pursed lips, like a man forced to take seriously something that was really ridiculous. Killer bunnies. Fat-free cookies. Male pattern baldness.

His speculative gaze touched her pink-polished toenails, then her bare midriff, then her face and hair. Josie's skin tingled. Too late, she remembered that while she'd tissued off the brightest of her stage makeup, she hadn't yet ditched her trusty false eyelashes or her auburn ponytail hair extension — the one she'd affectionately dubbed "Frank." As in frankly fake.

He frowned. "You look as if you can probably read. But maybe you need glasses or something. I can see why you couldn't

35

get them on. You know, with all that fringe on your eyelids."

She gawked, speechless.

"And it looks as though maybe you're having a little trouble talking, too," he continued good-naturedly, "so I'll help you out. That sign over there says 'No Trespassing.' That means —"

"I know what it means. It doesn't apply to me."

He cocked his head, new speculation in his expression.

"A maverick, huh? I'll bet you beat your sales quotas all to hell. Good for you." As though doing her a favor, he nodded toward the acres of ponderosa forest surrounding them. "Try peddling your wares over at the Petersens'. About a half-mile that way. They'll buy all kinds of crap. If you've got some of those useless knickknack things to sell, you're in."

She crossed her arms. "I'm not selling knickknacks."

An *aha* look flashed over his face. He shook his head.

"Sorry. I can't help you with putting this place on the market. I'm just here to make repairs."

He thought she was a real estate broker? Josie opened her mouth to contradict him, but he was already off and running.

"On the other hand, you're the hottest agent they've sent out here yet." Another once-over . . . this one, entirely complimentary. He even put down his hammer and shingles. "So I'll listen if you want to try to change my mind."

She should have been offended. But a grin like his — masculine and cocksure and friendly, all at the same time — somehow made that impossible. With that remarkable grin, he could have tempted a nun into taking up sin. Josie couldn't help but respond to it. On the inside. On the outside, she merely shrugged.

"Your generosity is mind-boggling."

"So is my memory of the women in town." His gaze lingered on her face, then meandered to her legs. "You're new here."

He didn't know the half of it.

"I'm wearing track pants. You can make a positive ID just by ogling my calves?"

"I prefer thighs." A wider grin. "And yeah. I can."

"Remind me to avoid miniskirts."

With a shrug, he slid to the edge of the porch roof. His movements were steady and practiced. "Doesn't matter. In a pinch, I'm willing to ID using other means."

His gaze traveled north in demonstration, then zipped up to her face. A cheerful expression lit his features. It was clear he was teasing. It was just as clear he was flirting. Josie wished that fact didn't perk up her morning quite so readily.

She really shouldn't have slurped through all those Big Gulps. Caffeine was a stimulant, after all.

"I'll be in town for quite a while," she said, forcing herself to move things in a more businesslike direction. "Depending on how my plans work out, maybe indefinitely."

"Good. We have a serious shortage of frivolous shoes here in Donovan's Corner. You ought to fill the gap nicely."

She frowned at her rainbow-patterned cork-soled wedgies. When she glanced up again, it was to see him dangling from the edge of the porch roof. The muscles in his arms and shoulders bulged with the strength required to hold him suspended. Nimbly, he dropped the short distance between his booted feet and the new spring grass.

Standing on a level with her, he was both taller and bigger than she'd thought. He swiped his forehead with his forearm.

Without her permission, Josie's libido automatically tallied up the new information his nearness offered. This was a man who didn't care how he looked — and was all the more appealing for it. His jeans and black T-shirt were the uniform of careless bad boys everywhere . . . but the way they hugged his body seemed entirely new. So did the cryptic tattoo encircling one taut biceps. Probably it was a set of ancient symbols, all their inky blackness representing one simple warning: *think twice*.

It was advice she doubted any of the local ladies heeded. Around here, they probably watched his every move. Fortunately, Josie had sworn off inappropriate men. Especially the dangerously appealing ones. She'd dated way too many of them to be lured by the homegrown version now. Especially with so many other things she needed to focus on.

Mmm-hmmm, her conscience jabbed. *Tell me another one.*

She frowned, enjoying one last look as her new handyman bent to retrieve something from beside the toolbox at his feet. So she'd flirted back a little bit. Big deal. Could she help it if there was something about a guy with talented hands? Not to mention a backside so fine it could have incited a riot?

He turned. Caught her ogling. Grinned

again in that same swaggering fashion. She would have given anything to dump the water bottle in his hand all over his know-it-all expression.

"See anything you like?" he asked.

Josie envisioned water dripping from his prominent nose. "All the time. Admiring the view doesn't mean staking out a piece of it for yourself."

"It doesn't?"

"No."

Absently, she watched him drink. He did so greedily, his tanned throat working to drain most of the bottle. When he lowered it again, he lifted one thick brow in surprise.

"Especially when we're going to be working together from now on." She shifted her shoulder to keep her duffel in place, then extended her hand. "I'm Josie Day. The new owner."

"Of . . . ?"

"This place. Blue Moon."

With his hand clasping hers, he stilled. A strange expression crossed his face.

"I've got the key to prove it." She withdrew from his grasp and dangled the newest addition to her Enchanté key ring with a feeling of satisfaction. "Right here."

A frown. "You'd better let me see that."

"I'll do you one better. I'll demonstrate it in action."

"Yeah?"

With a skeptical snort, he set his bottle on the grass, then folded his arms. The gesture made his biceps flex in a way Josie wished she hadn't noticed. Unfortunately, she'd have to have been made of stone not to notice.

He nodded to the front door. "Good luck. I'll wait here."

Puzzled, she rubbed her thumb over her key. Her handyman sounded as though *he* had his doubts about it working, too. Sheesh. If this was the kind of prove-it-to-me reception she could expect in town, she had a lot of work ahead of her. Even more than she'd thought.

Josie glanced up at him. He jutted his chin toward the door as though inviting her to prove him right. The look on his face activated every rebellious instinct she possessed.

"Fine." She lifted her nose in the air. "After I take a look inside, we'll discuss the work that needs to be done around here. There seems to be plenty of it."

His dubious expression didn't waver. "Red, you get that door open with that key

41

of yours, and we'll talk about anything you please."

Generous as his words seemed, his tone clearly communicated something more. Something along the lines of: *You have about as much chance of opening that door as you do of growing a goatee.* Josie didn't have time to let it bother her.

"Watch and learn," she said instead, then headed toward the door.

With interest, Luke Donovan watched the redhead climb his porch steps in those ridiculous shoes. Too bad the most interesting trespassers were also the craziest.

There was no way in hell Josie Day owned Blue Moon — his aunt Tallulah wouldn't have done that to him. Not again. Josie had to be another in the long line of local real estate agents, all with dollar signs in their eyes, who wanted him to sell out. She was new in town — and more determined than most. That was all.

"If it's any consolation," he called, "I admire your willingness to take this all the way. You must be a hell of a poker player."

As he'd predicted, she couldn't resist answering.

"Poker?"

"Because you're willing to bluff. Do they

42

teach you that in Realtor school? Along with wheedling, finagling, and pushing the hard-sell?"

"Hey, watch it. My mother is a real estate agent."

"Then we've probably met." Idly, he admired the curvaceous shape of Josie's backside as she bent to examine the house's old-fashioned lock. Yeah, too bad she was crazy. Or determined to get him to sell Blue Moon. Either way, it wasn't good. He had plans of his own for the place. He wasn't ready to sell yet. "No hard feelings."

"You keep that in mind. *After* I prove you wrong."

He grinned. She had spirit, he'd give her that. Also, a jumble of ponytailed red hair he could easily picture spread across his pillow. Some men had a weakness for gambling or drinking or working ninety hours a week — like his father. They found those things completely irresistible. Luke felt that way about redheads. Especially, suddenly, the real estate–selling variety.

"Bluffing your way into hundred-year-old houses must be hard work. When you're finished, I'll get you a cup of coffee," he offered.

Given the circumstances, he thought that was pretty magnanimous of him.

Given her rolled eyes and the impatient jangle of her keys, she was less than bowled over by the gesture.

"Don't do me any favors."

He already had. Ordinarily, he'd have given her the boot — nicely — from the get-go. But something about her intrigued him. Either that, or he was bored with nailing shingles to the roof. He'd been working on that damned splintery cedar for three days now. He wasn't half done yet.

Another sound came from the porch — this time, jiggling hardware as Josie rattled the doorknob. He'd have sworn he heard her grinding her teeth, too.

"Having trouble?" he inquired innocently.

"Yes." An over-the-shoulder glare. "Someone won't shut up long enough for me to concentrate."

He guffawed. This was a lot more fun than shingling.

"Come on, Josie. Give it up. We both know why you're here."

"To hire myself a new handyman?"

"Ouch." As though wounded, he put a hand over his heart. "Take it easy. If you *were* my boss, I'd be filing a workers' comp claim right now."

"What, for hurt feelings? Please. You're obviously not keeping up with the job. You need to fix this lock." She jangled the doorknob again. "There's something wrong with it — like so many things around here. All things considered, I know I shouldn't complain. And I obviously haven't seen the whole place yet. But it looks as though I've got a regular money pit on my hands. I was really hoping . . . oh, never mind."

Her critical glance took in the house's weedy flower beds, the run-down split-log siding, and the hole in the porch roof he'd been repairing when she'd arrived. Her obvious disregard for the last piece of Luke's former legacy stung his pride.

"Yes, ma'am." He shoved both hands in his back pockets, then gazed up at the springtime skies. "Whatever you say. I'll get right on fixing things."

Josie *hmmph*ed and got back to the lock.

She was inventive, he admitted to himself. Pretending to own the place — probably in the hope that he, as caretaker, would open the door for her himself — was a new one. Unfortunately for Josie, she didn't have all the information Luke did. Beginning with the fact that *he* owned Blue Moon. And ending with the fact that he had no intention of opening the place to strangers until he was damned good and ready.

Especially strangers who dissed the place.

The estate had been closed up for a long time. His arrival in Donovan's Corner had incited a certain amount of interest — there was no doubt about that. But Luke had plans of his own for the property. It was the key to everything he needed. Not even a va-va-voom redhead was changing that.

No matter how cute she looked kicking the shit out of his front door.

"Why is this locked, anyway?" she demanded. "You're right here! Nobody's getting in without you knowing it."

He shrugged. "I can't always see who's here when I'm up on the roof or out in the carriage house. Locking up when I'm working helps keep away trespassers."

Her glare suggested she thought he meant her. Luke couldn't quite explain why he wanted to change her mind — or why he wanted to see her smile at him instead.

"I get quite a few. Mostly local teenagers who used to use the place for keg parties. Before I got here." Having revealed more

46

than he meant to, he frowned. "Ready to give up yet?"

"I never give up." She bent and rubbed her toe, grumbling under her breath. "You probably changed the locks since Tallulah had the keys made, that's all."

Josie straightened, glowering accusatorially at him for an instant. Then, as though fighting for patience, she swept her gaze over the pine forest bordering the house's neglected grounds. A thick carpet of ponderosa needles buried what had formerly been a grassy lawn. Scrub oak seedlings encroached on the old croquet turf. Weeds — always the first to sprout when the sun turned warm — dotted the wide expanse like unruly cowlicks.

Seeing the place through her disapproving perspective bugged Luke in ways he didn't want to consider. So he swung his attention back to Josie instead . . . and was shocked to see tears gathering in her big green eyes.

Considering what he knew of her so far, he guessed they were tears of frustration, not sadness. Still, he felt sorry for her. Maybe he should've shared the secret jiggle-turn-jiggle method of opening the front door. She was only trying to do her job.

Her chin wobbled. Her fingers clenched harder on her key. She blinked — once, twice, several more times in succession, as though trying to hold back the waterworks. If she wasn't careful, her fake eyelashes would cause a forty-mile-per-hour wind gust.

"Hey, hey —" Alarmed, Luke covered the distance between them in three long strides, his steps loud on the porch's floor-boards. He touched her arm. "It's not that bad. Look, who's your boss? I'm betting it's Linda at Round the Corner Realty. I'll tell her you browbeat me into giving you a tour."

He reached past her to open the door.

Sniffling, she whapped his arm out of the way. Then she dashed the tears from her eyes and elbowed in front of him.

"I can do it," she croaked.

"Okay." He held up both hands in sur-render. Clearly, Josie wasn't ready to admit defeat. "But it's only fair you know going in. I'm not changing my mind about selling the place."

"How could you? *You* don't own it. *I* do."

He rolled his eyes. "Look, determination is all well and good. But this is ridiculous."

She scoffed. Then she shoved her key in

place one last time. Luke didn't even try to stop her. What was it with him? Sure, she was cute. But cute didn't compensate for crazy.

Or did it? Reconsidering, he took one last look at the curve of her hips. Maybe if she was just a *little* nuts . . .

At that instant, he remembered what Josie had said a minute ago — while he'd been distracted by all the cleavage on display as she bent to rub her toe: *You probably had the locks changed since Tallulah had the keys made.*

He froze. Oh, shit. It was happening again.

The lock clicked. For a heartbeat, Josie only stared at it in apparent disbelief — right along with Luke. Then she pushed open the door and breezed inside. Turning, she grinned in triumph.

"Never mind. It looks as though I've got that tour covered." She dropped her duffel bag from her shoulder — the one he'd *thought* contained cheesy knickknacks for sale or real estate contracts — and slung it possessively in the foyer. "Thanks, anyway."

Stunned, Luke watched as she gallivanted into *his* house, clearly intent on taking possession of the place. And that was how he discovered that, for the third time this year, his eccentric aunt Tallulah had apparently given away his one remaining estate to a total stranger.

And it didn't look as if this particular stranger was bailing out anytime soon, either.

Three

"Hey! Come again?" Luke demanded, clobbering the porch steps with his work boots as he followed Josie inside. "What was that about Tallulah?"

Ignoring his question, Josie peered through the early morning sunlight at his house's front parlor. Her gaudy shoes made only a muted *clump, clump* as she meandered across the antique floorboards, past the tarp-covered furniture. She poked here and there, then lifted the lids of the authentic Craftsman-style benches built in the foyer. The tang of old cedar wafted out.

"You must know Tallulah," she said casually. "She's your boss, right?"

No. She's my meddling, bullheaded aunt, who's screwed up my life almost as much as — Hell. On the heels of that thought, Luke clamped his lips shut. Little Miss Rainbow Shoes wasn't getting to him that easily. Not until he knew who she was and what she wanted with Blue Moon.

He gave a noncommittal shrug. "How

do *you* know her?"

"Now *that* is a good story. Totally un-real."

Still in mid-inspection and with no ob-vious intentions of sharing that "good story," Josie waved her hand. Her gesture showed off five fingers tipped by bubble-gum pink nail polish. Nail polish like Barbie probably wore. If Barbie had finger-nails. Luke didn't know. Maybe she had little plastic fingernails? Jesus Christ. He was losing it.

"A good story?" he prompted. "I'm all ears."

She tossed him a mischievous look. "Looks like you're all muscle to me."

"Feeling is believing."

"I thought that was seeing." She rounded the room and paused beside him, appar-ently absorbed in examining the wooden ceiling beams. Her gaze met his. "*Seeing* is believing."

"You have your aphorisms. I have mine."

"Yours seem a little self-serving to me."

"No, ma'am." Luke gave in to the grin he'd been holding back. He might be losing it, but he was having fun. "I believe in full service all the way."

"Hmmm. Giving? Or receiving?"

"Either one. I hear it's the thought that counts."

"Too bad." Josie squeezed his biceps. Her eyebrows arched upward in apparent approval. "I'm more into *doing* than thinking."

Proving her point, she sashayed through the archway that led to the living room, leaving him with a choice view of her backside — and the feeling that he'd just stepped into the Twilight Zone. Luke stared stupidly at his arm. She'd touched him with no hesitation at all. With none of the game playing evident in the local women — most of whom wanted a husband, babies, and other unmentionables.

Out of nowhere, the realization struck him. He'd just encountered the rarest, most bachelor-threatening kind of woman.

The good-time girl.

Most men believed she was a myth. Watching Josie pass by the archway again, lips pursed in concentration as she absentmindedly fingered her tank top strap, Luke knew she was all too real. She was in his living room right now, letting her skimpy clothes slip seductively down her bare shoulder.

Frowning, he followed her. He needed more information.

Or maybe just a closer look.

"I knew the place came with furniture," Josie said as he entered the room, her voice echoing in the cavernous, twenty-foot-ceilinged space, "but I didn't expect this much of it."

Face alight, she perched on the tarp-covered sofa near the gigantic stone fireplace. Then on its mate directly opposite. Next she skipped to the wing chairs near the window and tested them, too. She looked like a kid in a candy store, like a road racer eyeballing a new Suzuki SV650 . . . like a woman who'd never owned anything as elaborate as a folding lawn chair, much less a twenty-room, thirteen-thousand-square-foot mansion.

Which was ridiculous. She owned things. A banana-colored wreck of a car, for one — he'd seen that himself. Also a lot of makeup, Chia Pet false eyelashes, and crazy shoes. What she *didn't* own was *his* house. But the ecstatic expression on her face right now . . .

Was none of his damned business. Unlike *her* business at Blue Moon, which Luke figured he had every right to know about.

"How long are you here for?" he asked.

"I dunno. Depends on how things go." *Bounce. Bounce.* "They told me this place was ready to move into, so I took the weekend off from work to check things out. There's another girl filling in for me. The way things are going, I might be here a loooong time." She popped upright and pointed to the left. "What's this way?"

"The east wing."

"Oooh! I have *wings?* No way!"

She flounced toward the library, leaving him admiring her backside again. It was a nice view. But it wasn't helping him get to the bottom of things. No pun intended.

Luke caught up with her as she left the book-filled, wood-paneled room. Her nose wrinkled in apparent disinterest.

"Not much of a reader?" he asked.

She gave an evasive sound, then glanced toward the next stop on her tour. "Not when I've got *this* to look at. Wow! You could park my whole trailer in here, awnings and all."

Josie hurried to the billiards room — all manly dark colors, carved wood, and mullioned windows. Big and comfortable, it was one of the few rooms Luke had actually bothered to open while working on the necessary repairs.

"Hey." He jerked his thumb sideways, offering his sternest look. "Get off the pool table."

"Isn't it fabulous?" She posed, pinup-style, from atop the green felt. She flicked a fingertip, sending the eight ball rolling toward the nearest pocket. She flung her head backward in obvious delight, shaking out her hair. "I feel as if I'm living in a movie! Or a game of 'Clue.' " Her eyes widened, and she bolted upright. "Hey. Do I have a conservatory?"

"No. About Tallulah. Whatever she told you —"

"That's okay." She gave a carefree wave. "To tell the truth, I'm not even sure what a conservatory *is*."

With an engaging grin, Josie hopped down from the pool table. She ooh-ed and aah-ed her way down the east wing hallway, investigating every room she came to. The servants' quarters. The study. The sitting room, the summer parlor, and each of the closets. Partway up the oak staircase to the second floor, she stopped.

"Hey. I don't even know your name." She fixed him with an interested look, one hand on the banister. "Give it up, mystery man. Who's the guy taking care of all this?"

"Luke Donovan."

Her mouth quirked. "You're kidding me. 'Donovan'? Like the town, Donovan's Corner?"

He tilted his head sideways — the most acknowledgment he dared to give.

"I guess you were fated to come here," she teased. "Mr. Luke Donovan of Donovan's Corner."

Fated to come here? He hoped not. This was temporary. With a noncommittal sound, Luke nudged her to keep going upstairs. He didn't like having her curiosity focused on him — or on his coincidental name. "I'm just here to fix up the place. Once that's done, I'm gone."

"You'll like it better that way, trust me." With a carefree bump and grind, Josie began climbing the stairs again. She craned her neck this way and that to see the fixtures, chandeliers, and carved wood moldings. "I was never happier than when I left this town in the dust."

Surprised, Luke glanced up. She didn't look like a local — or act like one. "You used to live in Donovan's Corner?"

She nodded. " 'Used to' being the operative words. Nothing short of *this*" — stopped at the landing halfway up the staircase, she flung out both arms to indicate Blue Moon — "could have brought me back, that's for sure. I had *no* idea what I was in for. Thank you, Tallulah!"

She grabbed the banister and looked

around, beaming. To her left, sunlight streamed through one of the house's antique Tiffany windows, brightening the dusty interior. To her right, Luke frowned, telling himself to just give it to her straight.

Tallulah made a mistake. You don't belong here.

Except he couldn't. He didn't want to. Not yet.

"Of course," Josie continued confidently, "the place is totally run down. The floors are wrecked. There are holes in the plaster. Things are falling down, literally *crumbling* away." She gave him a scolding look. "Don't think I didn't notice how few of the light switches actually work."

Stiffening, Luke scowled. He didn't know why he'd gone all candy-ass sensitive for a nitpicker like her.

"It's a good house."

"Are you kidding me? It's a freaking *mansion!* I've never seen anything like it. Not in person, at least. But let's face it — it needs work. A good scrubbing, too. The dust bunnies were definitely multiplying downstairs."

Luke scoffed. "Repairs come before cleaning."

"With an attitude like that, it's no wonder things look this bad. Come on. Show me the west wing."

She pranced upstairs like Queen of the Cleaning Products. Obviously she expected him to follow. Like an obedient puppy. Screw that. Luke might not want to disillusion her right away — say, before he'd gotten another cleavage shot — but that didn't mean he had to follow orders. Obstinately, he held his ground.

"Are you coming?"

"Look, Miss" — he cast about for the name of a cleaning product and came up with the only one he knew — "Armor All. You're new here, so I'll let this slide. Once. But I'm not here to give you the grand tour. I've got things to do."

Josie crossed her arms. The gesture nudged her cleavage one notch closer to centerfold status. It was just his luck. Curvy girls were his weakness. Even red-headed, bossy, pain-in-the-ass ones.

"Like?" she inquired.

"Like working on the porch roof."

"Those shingles?" She made a face, dismissing them with a wave. "They'll keep. Nobody ever sees the roof, anyway. If it rains you've got buckets for the porch, right? We should move on to more important things."

"Like?"

"Like uncovering all the furniture. Vacuuming. Making the place livable. Painting. That paneling is really dingy in the rec room. You know, where the pool table is? It could use something." Josie scrunched up her nose, mulling it over. "Like wallpaper. My friend wallpapered her bathroom and it turned out great."

Visions of flowered wallpaper danced through Luke's head. Five seconds later he realized that potpourri, pink-painted pool tables, and useless throw pillows were bound to follow. Holy shit. He had to hold his ground.

"Roof first."

"Don't be a party pooper. It'll be fab. But for now, how about the west wing?" She batted her eyelashes at him. "Wouldn't you rather show me around than get all grimy up on the roof?"

What he'd rather do was pretend she'd never sauntered up his driveway, all feminine curves and nonsense talk. But since that was impossible . . .

"Nope."

"Fine. I'll check out the west wing myself. In the meantime, would you mind carrying in my stuff from my car? I know technically you're here to take care of the house, but some of those boxes are really heavy, and —"

"Nope."

She looked perplexed. She regrouped quickly.

"Okay, then. I'll do that. I guess it *really* would've been too good to be true if my new mansion came with a hunky butler, too."

She raised her eyebrows meaningfully, letting an expectant flirtatiousness hang in the air. In response, a tingle shot all the way down Luke's spine. Damn, it had been a long time since he'd met a woman who got his blood pumping. Since before he'd been exiled to Donovan's Corner.

"Hunky, huh?" he repeated.

Josie let her gaze wander over him, starting at his work boots and ending at his eyebrows. "I call 'em like I see 'em."

"I'm still not hauling in your stuff."

"Fine." In a huff, she yanked up her wandering tank top strap again. She straightened to her full height. "But I do wish Tallulah had hired a more helpful handyman."

With her nose in the air, she headed farther upstairs. Hell. He'd gone and pissed her off. If she didn't watch where she was going, she'd break her neck. Especially with the —

"Aaaah!"

Thump.

61

The minute Luke heard Josie shriek, he knew what had happened. He galloped up the remaining stairs two at a time, stopping beside Josie near the top. She sat in a terry cloth–covered heap, blowing wisps of red hair from her eyes. A glance told him she was okay — just exasperated.

"That fourteenth step's a doozy," he said.

"*Now* you tell me." Groaning, she accepted his outstretched hand for support and got to her feet. Warily, she navigated around the hole he still hadn't fixed. "Okay. So 'ready to move into' might have been an exaggeration. I can accept that. Just give it to me straight. Is there *anything* in this place that isn't falling apart?"

"It's a good house," he repeated stubbornly.

Josie searched his eyes. Whatever she saw there apparently satisfied her.

"Good. Because if I'm getting in over my head, I want to know right now. *Before* I go to all the trouble of picking out a bedroom and moving in."

"Moving in? You just said 'ready to move into' was an exaggeration."

"I was exaggerating." She waved her hand. "I've rented worse. Besides, where else would I spend the weekend, except my

62

very own free mansion?"

Newly energized, she dodged the stairway hole in one surprisingly athletic leap. From the other side of it at the top of the stairs, she beamed at him, ponytail swinging. She pointed down the leftmost hallway. "West wing that way?"

In a flash, she was gone. Not waiting for Luke's reply, not waiting for the truth . . . not waiting for anything. If her plans for Blue Moon were as impulsive and off-the-wall as everything else about her, he was in for a world of hurt. Not to mention pink carpets, disco balls, and — God help him — ruffles.

Ugh. Grimacing at the havoc Josie might wreak on her own, Luke climbed the stairs and followed her.

What the hell. It was better than shingling.

By the time Josie had viewed all of the east wing (dusty), the attached greenhouse (moldy), and the great room (huge) dividing the house's two main halves, she felt seriously schizophrenic.

One minute, she couldn't believe her good luck. The next, she wondered if she was nuts to even consider accepting the reward Tallulah Carlyle had given her. Blue

Moon had clearly been magnificent once, but now it was an eyesore. Run-down, neglected, and critically lacking in several modern amenities.

She couldn't possibly live in it — at least not for much longer than this weekend. Discouraged, Josie realized that she hadn't quite thought this through. So far, she'd been lounging on pool tables and bopping from room to room, caught up in the fantasy of living in her very own mansion. The truth was, this was a time for decision-making, not fantasizing.

She thought about her new, improved circumstances. And realized that the idea of moving back to Donovan's Corner was trouble enough. Moving here without a job was unthinkable. Even if her rent — or mortgage, in this case — were covered, she wouldn't be able to support herself. Her savings were pretty good, but they'd only stretch so far.

Resigning herself to the fact that her unexpected reward was both more incredible and less usable than she'd hoped, Josie wandered through the rooms in the west wing. Every one of them bore signs of faded elegance. Inlaid parquet floors. Crystal chandeliers. Carefully protected furniture. But the floors were warped or scuffed, the chandeliers were missing their crystals or were simply nonfunctioning, and the furniture smelled of mildew and mouse droppings.

It must have been a very long time since Tallulah had seen this house. Either that, or Luke Donovan was a terrible handyman. In fact, to have let the place get this run down, he had to be the anti-handyman. Whoever eventually took over Blue Moon would have to keep a close eye on him — not that *that* would be tough to do — to make sure he was actually working. Instead of bench-pressing boxes of roof shingles, or whatever he'd done to become so buffed-up.

Sighing, Josie toed aside an empty mousetrap, then kept going. She'd wanted to believe this reward would be something special. A real second chance. The answer to all her restlessness and dissatisfaction. Undeniably, Tallulah's giving her Blue Moon had been a truly grand gesture. But Josie didn't see how she could possibly make something of it.

When she'd visited Tallulah's lawyer, Ambrose, after her initial phone call, she'd been understandably skeptical. As it turned out, he'd been expecting her. With — according to Tallulah's instructions —

papers drawn up and house keys waiting.

"According to Mrs. Carlyle, you didn't give her much to work with, as far as this reward business goes," Ambrose had said with a wink, thumping the stack of legal papers in front of Josie. "But that's never stopped Mrs. Carlyle in the past."

"She's done this kind of thing before?"

"Only on the rare occasion. Only when she felt a reward seemed particularly warranted," Ambrose had confided. "Not, of course, that you heard that tidbit from me."

"Of course." They shared a smile.

"In any case, Mrs. Carlyle has decided that you, Miss Day, deserve better than a shared double-wide trailer to live in. More to the point, she just happens to have the perfect solution to your housing dilemma . . . in your hometown. Quite the coincidence, hmmm?"

Coincidence. Yeah. Josie had wanted to bolt right then.

No *way* was she going back to that Aqua Net–soaked, small-minded gossip haven she'd been raised in. No way. But then the photographs of the house had come out, and the excitement of feeling like a lottery winner had taken over. By the time Ambrose had dangled the key over Josie's waiting palm, she'd been too filled with a sheer sense of impending adventure to resist.

Recklessness had always been her downfall.

Or maybe that was rebelliousness.

She shrugged. Either way, in the clear light of today's mid-April morning, second thoughts were setting in. Maybe she'd been too hasty in packing up all her things — not that there'd been that many of them. Her life's possessions had fit easily in her Chevy. Depressingly easily. She was twenty-seven years old. Was a trunkload — and backseat — full of clothes, shoes, and pink throw pillows all she had to show for her life?

The thought spurred her on. Continuing through the house with one ear cocked for sounds of Luke, she explored the upstairs bedrooms and the downstairs second living room. She tugged back musty velvet draperies to look at the weedy grounds. She closed her eyes and tried to sense if she belonged there.

Dispiritedly, Josie concluded that for her, Blue Moon was a pipe dream. She was a showgirl. Showgirls didn't belong in small-town northern Arizona, sweeping up pine needles. They belonged someplace where they could dance — where they could perform and come alive. Not to mention earn a living doing those things.

Deciding she had nothing to lose by finishing her tour anyway, she traversed a short hallway. She rounded a corner, opened a pair of double doors and stepped between them . . . and everything changed.

Wow. The room before her spanned at least a gymnasium's length and width, but it held none of a gymnasium's sweaty practicality. To Josie's surprise, this room held magic.

Painted in pale pink, floored in blond wood with arched windows along one whole wall, it was easily the most breathtaking in the entire house. Unlike the rest of Blue Moon, it contained no tarp-covered furniture, no old landscape paintings, no tumbleweed-size dust bunnies. Only beauty.

And possibility.

"Ahh," came Luke's voice from someplace behind her. "I see you found the ballroom."

Ballroom. Of course. Josie breathed in deeply.

"It's not a ballroom." She said the words slowly. Reverently. A few more steps carried her farther inside.

68

"Not anymore. But once upon a time —"

"No, it's a dance studio. A dance school." Trailing her fingers along the wall, testing her lightest dance steps on the dust-muted floor, Josie twirled in place. Yes. This could work. "*My* dance school."

Luke boggled at her. "Dance school."

"Yes. I've just decided it." This place was a lot like *she'd* been once. Before she'd headed to Las Vegas to become a showgirl. Full of potential, but in dire need of polishing. The realization filled her with a weird sense of affection for Blue Moon — and for this room in particular. "I'm going to open my own dance school."

He frowned. "Here?"

To her dismay, he even looked gorgeous while raining on her parade. He also looked as though he thought she'd gone completely bonkers. Defiantly, Josie lifted her chin.

"It'll be a huge success. I'll teach little girls to perform perfect pirouettes and little boys to samba like pros. I've got the training, the ambition — and now, the location." Picturing the place already, she swooshed her fingers through the air, pretending to unfurl a gigantic banner. "I can see it now. 'Dance lessons for all ages.'"

"No."

"Hmmm. What'll I call it? I know! Josie's Dance World. Dance Time. Dancers 'R' Us."

"No way in hell."

"That's no good. It'll alienate my students' parents."

With a professional's eye, she examined the room again. A ballet barre could go along the left wall. A bank of mirrors, behind it. With the floor buffed and the windows cleaned, the new dance studio would sparkle. Plenty of room for choreography, for group rehearsals, for a sound system . . .

Josie's enthusiasm built. For the first time in weeks, she felt excited about her future. Energized by it. This would be perfect! It was the answer to all her dissatisfaction. How had Tallulah known this was what she needed?

"It's a fantastic idea," she announced.

"It's a stupid idea. You can't do it."

Now he'd done it. Josie narrowed her eyes, fixing him with her most determined gaze. If he'd known her better, he'd have known that look didn't bode well for him.

"*Nobody* tells me I can't do something."

"I just did."

In emphasis, Luke folded his arms. His biceps bulged, making his cryptic black

70

tattoos flex. His T-shirt flattened against his perfectly taut abs. He really had a spectacular body. Too bad he was such a buzzkill.

"No," he added. "No, no, no."

That clinched it. If she hadn't been invested in the idea before, now she was. "Yes," she said blithely. "Yes, yes, yes. I'm doing it. And nothing you say can stop me."

"Oh, yeah?" He stepped nearer, disrupting her cha-cha-cha across the intoxicatingly wide span of dance space. "Try this one on for size. You show me your proof you own this place, and we'll take it from there."

Four

Josie hadn't had proof. Only promises.

But those — slapped together with her unstoppable zeal *and* her determination not to leave Blue Moon — were enough to change Luke's mind about her. Obviously, he should never have allowed her to gallivant onto his property in the first place. But now it was too late. Josie was fully invested in her va-va-voom lady of the manor impression. And he was fully screwed.

It was possible she was crazy. Seriously. Anybody who could look at his house's dilapidated old ballroom and see a dance studio had a shaky grip on reality. Hell, anybody who thought one living soul in Donovan's Corner wanted to *samba* had a shaky grip on reality.

He'd started out humoring her. Not wanting to burst her bubble, for whatever idiotic reason. Now he was stuck. Stuck with a loony redhead in his house and a problem he didn't have time to mess around with. Not if his plans were going to go forward.

"Damn it, Ambrose. Pick *up,* you old codger," he muttered, pacing the short length of the phone alcove at Frank's Diner. He didn't have phone service at Blue Moon. And he'd hurled his cell phone into the pine trees during his first week in town, sick of hearing it ring with calls from Donovan & Sons. So now he was stuck using the phone at the prime eatery in Donovan's Corner. "I want answers."

He'd gotten nowhere phoning Winkler, Young, and Dodge, Ambrose's law firm. The bubbleheaded secretary had informed him that "Mr. Dodge is out of the office indefinitely. I'm sorry, sir." Then she'd accidentally connected him to a conference call full of Japanese businessmen, leaving Luke more aggravated than he'd started out.

"Dodge residence. Barbara speaking."

Finally. The voice of reason.

"Barb, it's Luke." He took a few minutes to trade small talk with Ambrose's personal assistant. Then, "Listen, is Ambrose around? I need to —"

"Oh, sorry, Luke," Barb interrupted. "He's officially incommunicado. Headed out on a cruise with Tallulah. They left a couple of days ago. Something about investing in a new line of luxury ocean liners?"

It figured. Tallulah was always stirring up trouble somewhere. Cradling the phone between his chin and shoulder, Luke listened to Barb describe his aunt's latest venture.

As Barb nattered on about fleet-wide capacities, cruising speeds, stateroom specifications, and exotic ports of call, he motioned for the waitress to heat up his coffee. Through the diner's plate glass windows, Main Street hunkered down, as different from the world Barb was describing as his was from his father's.

A mishmash of dive bars, the hardware store, a beauty shop, and a couple of fancy-schmancy southwestern art galleries all crowded into sight. The street was a perfect slice of Donovan's Corner. Half small town, half tourist trap. His Harley, parked at the curb, was the only sign the twenty-first century had meandered to this part of the state at all.

"Fine. Thanks, Barb." He'd heard all he needed to. "Did Ambrose take his cell phone? Because I've been calling his cell number, and —"

"Nope," she chirped. "It's right here on his home office credenza. I reminded him, but . . . you know Ambrose."

Yeah, Luke knew Ambrose. He knew Ambrose only ever did what Tallulah told him to do — like bequeath the family's oldest and most overlooked estate in Arizona to every Tom, Dick, and Josie who crossed Tallulah's path.

Already his aunt had given Blue Moon to two other charity cases this year — one, a concierge who'd tracked down Tallulah's missing shih tzu, Crackers, at the Four Seasons Chicago; the other, an Atlanta psychic who'd supposedly put Tallulah in touch with her husband Ernest's spirit for two "glorious" minutes. Both the concierge and the psychic had required legal wrangling and an eye-opening tour of the house and grounds before they'd given up their claims.

There was a reason, after all, Luke had left the estate on the edge of falling apart for the past three months.

Not that Josie had been discouraged that easily.

"All right. I'll try Tallulah." After a few minutes' conversation, Luke had the rest of the information he needed — including the name of the cruise line and the particular ship his aunt and Ambrose had taken. "Thanks, Barb."

75

Luke said his good-byes, then hung up. He needed to talk to Tallulah next. To make a shore-to-ship phone call, to send her a telegram — whatever a person did to contact someone who was at sea. But for one long minute, he left his hand on the receiver, in no hurry to embroil himself in another battle with his forgetful aunt.

The truth was, he worried about her. Her forgetfulness, her grouchiness, her recklessness . . . They'd all gotten worse since Ernest had died last year. Blue Moon was only a case in point. Tallulah kept forgetting the place wasn't one of Ernest's dozens of properties, hers to fritter away. It was a family legacy — *Luke's legacy.* He had to make his aunt understand that she couldn't keep giving it away to strangers. No matter how damn much she liked them.

On the other hand, it wasn't as though Luke couldn't handle one pesky, long-legged redhead on his own.

If he knew women — and, let's face it, he did — Josie would bolt the minute she heard the second floor mice scratching their way through tonight's midnight snack attack. If she did gut it out until morning, a girlie-girl like her would never survive Donovan's Corner.

76

His certainty growing, Luke glanced outside. What he saw there confirmed his suspicions. The dearth of neon, the proliferation of pickup trucks, the stick-in-the-mud residents . . . No doubt about it. She'd bail out before the weekend was through.

He'd seen the Enchanté boxes Josie's stuff was packed in. And the Nevada plates on her heap of a car. He was dealing with Las Vegas Barbie here. There was no way she was going to embrace small town life — no matter how staunchly she insisted that she couldn't wait for Ambrose to FedEx the finished paperwork and the deed, which was supposed to happen any day now. None of that would matter in the end. Blue Moon belonged to Luke.

His decision made, Luke loosened his grasp on the phone. Wrangling with his aunt could come later. For now, he'd deal with Josie on his own. It was only a matter of time before she gave up on Blue Moon and accepted Tallulah's inevitable consolation prize — a different estate. All he had to do was wait Josie out.

That was going to be no problem. Hell, he figured as he returned to his coffee and ordered a celebratory slice of cherry pie, it was going to be easy.

Nothing in this town was ever easy. Josie had forgotten that about Donovan's Corner. The stoplights were all timed funny, because no one was ever in a hurry to get anywhere. The residents were hard to deal with, because at least ten percent of them hadn't bothered to turn on their hearing aids. And if you wanted something done, you had to make nice with the one person who could do it for you. Because unlike in the big city, there was usually only one source for everything.

Except beer, bait, and cigarettes, of course.

That point was driven painfully home to Josie as she stood at the counter of Copies 2 Go ("We Sell Lottery Tickets!"), trying to get permission to use one of the ancient photocopiers.

"It's just a flyer, see?" She waved the 8½ by 11 sheet she'd written, trying to make the permed-haired female clerk behind the counter understand. "I need about fifty of them."

"I don't care how many you need. Unless you have a local address, you can't use the copy machines."

"I do have a local address. I just don't remember what it is. It's that big house about a half mile outside of town. You know, the old one with the chimneys and the stonework and the gigantic yard?"

"Have you got a utility bill?"

"No. I'm still moving in. But —"

"Next." Permed Lady gestured for the customer in line behind Josie to step forward. "How're you doing today, Trudy?"

"Pretty good. Is that old Xerox in the corner free?"

"Sure, it is. Just go on and —"

"I'm sorry," Josie murmured to the customer. "But I wasn't finished yet." She elbowed her way forward and held out her flyer, which advertised her new dance school. If living in Vegas had taught her anything, it was that demand could never start being generated too soon. "How about twenty-five copies? That's all. Just a measly twenty-five. Please?"

"Look." The clerk frowned. "You out-of-towners come up here, putting up your posters and your new subdivision signs and whatnot all over the place, and then the city council gets all pissy with *me* because of the litter! I've had it. No copies." She glanced sideways. "Sure, Trudy. Go right ahead and use that Xerox."

Josie watched, frustrated, as the other customer trundled off to the beat-up copier.

"Is there another copy shop in town?"

"No." The clerk seemed to try to hide it, but a smug smile spread across her face anyway. "Looks like you're out of luck. Maybe you'd better go on back to Las Vegas."

Confused, Josie angled her head. "But I never told you I was from —"

"Oh, I remember you, Josie Day," Permed Lady interrupted. "We *all* do. We know what you've been up to, too." She leaned sideways and waved another customer forward. "Next!"

Two more customers pushed to the counter, crowding Josie out of the way. Flummoxed, she edged sideways. She wasn't sure what to do. If she didn't get her copies, she couldn't advertise, but . . .

Several more smirks followed her. Two elderly women whispered and pointed. Suddenly, Josie didn't care quite so much about generating dance school demand. Not today.

Clutching her flyer, she bolted for the door. If she'd ever needed a jazzy showgirl walk to help her hold her head high, it was now. But she couldn't quite manage it. Not when her so-called triumphant homecoming was turning out to be so much harder than she'd expected.

★ ★ ★

It got worse.

Strolling down the cracked sidewalk bordering Main Street, Josie wrinkled her nose at the exhaust billowing from the pickup trucks putt-putting past. She took stock of Donovan's Corner.

She noticed which shops were new, which were renovated, and which were the same old fabric store, convenience mart, and single-plex movie theater she'd grown up with. She breezed past the Chamber of Commerce. She dodged retirees out for their daily dose of fresh air. She pinpointed several good locations for putting up her (future) dance-school flyers, since — as Josie told herself firmly — there was no way that woman at Copies 2 Go was going to keep her down for long.

Then disaster struck.

"Josie? Is that you?"

Spinning, she confronted the owner of that voice.

Her sister.

"I *thought* that was you!" Jenna said, eyes wide with surprise. Holding a toddler in one arm and a bulging purse in the other, she looked exactly like what she was — a small-town wife and mother of two. "What are you doing in town?"

Awkwardly, Josie hugged her. "Just . . . a visit."

Jenna gave a disbelieving sound. "You haven't visited Donovan's Corner since you hotfooted it for Vegas. Come on. What's *really* going on?"

Well, I inherited a mansion. Sort of.

No. Josie couldn't tell her that. Not yet. Telling Jenna the truth would lead to the showgirl discussion, the saving-Tallulah discussion, and the April Fool's Day gullibility discussion. Then, as sisters, they'd be forced to segue into the dance-school impossibility lecture, the copy-shop scandal disclosure, and the general "why don't you grow up?" analysis.

Josie wasn't up for all that. Not when her elder sister — who'd always done *everything* right — was standing there in her nonscandalous blue jeans and oversize polo shirt, with her angelic little girl and (probably) a sensible purse full of sensible grocery coupons and a sensible shopping list. Full of healthy vegetables and prune juice.

Nobody was telling Jenna she couldn't use the Xerox machines. Nobody was whispering and pointing and frowning at her. Josie would be willing to bet nobody ever had.

So what was *really* going on?

Diversion. That's what was going on.

"Hey! Is this really little Emily? I don't believe how big she's gotten!" Smiling, Josie leaned toward the strawberry blond toddler. She honestly was adorable, dressed in pint-size overalls and a tiny flower-print T-shirt. "The last time I saw you," she cooed, "you were just a baby. And your big sister was about your size." She looked around. "Where's Hannah, anyway?"

Silence.

Uh-oh. Josie glanced up, temporarily abandoning her quest to capture her niece's flailing, chubby little hand in hers. It was just as she'd feared. Jenna stared at her as though she could see right inside her head — and knew perfectly well this whole conversation was a detour from the deadly "visiting Donovan's Corner" discussion.

But then she hitched Emily higher on her hip and, to Josie's relief, answered.

"Hannah's in kindergarten now. I just dropped her off at school."

"*Kindergarten?* Wow! I can't believe it." Kindergarten was one thing Josie had fond memories of. In kindergarten, no one had expected her to settle down, stay in her seat, or pay too much attention to things like good behavior. "Time really flies. That means Hannah must be, what, five now?"

Another silence.

Josie could feel something building between them. Something expectant. Something she wanted to avoid.

"Cute shoes," she blurted. Another bid for diversion.

Jenna wasn't buying it. She didn't so much as glance at her scuffed sneakers.

"Are you going to go see Mom and Dad?" she asked.

Yup, that was it. The thing Josie wanted to avoid.

So much for diversion.

"Well, I just got here. I mean, literally. This morning. I haven't had a chance to do much." *Besides go ga-ga over my gorgeous handyman, lug half a dozen boxes into my new tumbledown mansion, and launch a dance school scheme.* "So far."

"Mmmm-hmmm." With practiced ease, Jenna tugged a grubby stuffed monkey from the depths of her purse. One-handed, she offered it to fussy Emily. Then she gave Josie her patented *I'm older, listen to me* look. "Mark my words. You might as well just get it over with. By the time the five o'clock news airs tonight, the whole town

84

will know you're back anyway."

"I seriously doubt I'll make the news."

"You know that's not what I mean."

Josie wished she didn't. Adopting her most persuasive tone, she tried again. "You know, it would keep me *out* of the news if you didn't mention that you saw me."

Jenna rolled her eyes. Right. Josie had been crazy to expect any kind of deviant behavior from her saintly sister. Even for solidarity's sake.

With a sigh that suggested longstanding tolerance, Jenna held her ground. "You're going to have to see them sometime."

"Okay, fine." Josie looked away, pretending to be absorbed in the snail's-pace traffic down Main Street. "I'll stop by Mom's office."

"And Dad?"

"Dad? He's doing pretty well with that whole 'I've only got one daughter' thing." Josie shrugged, offering up a feeble grin. "I'd hate to break his winning streak."

"Josie —"

"No, don't worry about it. I'm fine." Feeling anything but, she looked around for an excuse to get away. "Anyway, I've got to run. I was just on my way . . . here." She pointed.

Jenna arched an unplucked eyebrow.

"Donovan's Corner Utilities?"

Josie nodded. "Yup. But it was great seeing you! Say 'hi!' to David for me, okay?" Jenna's husband, a plumber, was as flawless as Jenna was. "Bye! Bye, Emily!"

The little girl squeezed her fist in an awkward learner's version of a wave. The gesture pricked Josie right where it hurt most — her heart. She wished she'd seen Emily and Hannah more over the past few years. But with things so complicated . . .

"Later," she said, then ducked into the refuge of the town's combined electric, gas, water, and phone company. As long as she was hiding out, she figured she'd might as well get something useful accomplished — like having the utilities at Blue Moon transferred to her own name.

Not that going all sensible was a reaction to seeing Jenna or anything, Josie assured herself as she approached the customer service counter. Her perfect sister didn't have a thing to do with it. She just wanted to make sure she'd have hot water later. For a shower. Or a bubble bath. Or a Cup O' Noodles for dinner. That was all.

Waiting in line, Josie stared at the utility company's public service advertising. A poster about cost per kilowatt hours hung to her left. Another explaining low-flow showerheads was tacked up beside it. She tried to lose herself in the dancing water drop mascot pictured on the poster, but it was no use. The same old question kept poking at her.

Are you going to go see Mom and Dad?

The truth was, Josie didn't know. If she was going to live in the same town with them, maybe she might as well . . . No. For now, the answer was no. If her parents found out she was here in Donovan's Corner, they could track her down themselves. If they didn't . . .

Well, if they didn't, at least then Josie would know where she stood. Once and for all.

The old-timers were the first to notice.

In retrospect, Luke should have expected that. But he hadn't. He'd been too busy forking up his last bite of Frank's famous cherry pie when the hubbub started. By the time it spread to his rear-corner booth, it was a full-on scandal — and all the retirees at Frank's had front row seats.

"You ever seen hair like that?" one of them asked.

"No, sireee. 'Cept in a movie."

"Me, neither."

"Desiree probably did it down at the

salon," Byron Hill, Desiree's husband, volunteered. "She's always cooking up something crazy for them gals. Says it's 'hair art.' "

Skeptical chortles followed. Then nodding and murmuring took over. Whatever they were looking at, it had them transfixed. Swallowing his last bite, Luke gave in to idle curiosity. He squinted toward the diner's big plate glass window. He couldn't see a thing past the clump of gray-haired male retirees congregated in their usual booths.

"That hair *can't* be real," one of them said, pointing outside. "Not with a color like that."

Luke only knew one woman with unbelievable hair color. A weird prickling sensation whooshed through him. He told himself it was probably just a surge of impatience to be done with waiting for that one particular woman to give up on Blue Moon. He motioned for his check.

"Whoo-whee! Is that one of those belly button shirts? I've seen 'em on the Jerry Springer show, but —"

"Not lookin' like that, you haven't."

A moment of silence. Then more murmuring.

"Damn," old man McKee said, mopping

his brow with a napkin.

Luke consulted his scrawled-out guest check, then dropped a five dollar bill on the table. Enough with the mystery. Nothing ever happened in Donovan's Corner. If he knew the locals, they'd probably spotted Marianne Wilson on her recumbent bike. Any deviation from the norm passed for scandal around here. He slurped the rest of his coffee in a single gulp.

"Well, belly button shirt or not, it can't beat those shoes." One of the retirees chuckled. "Those are the damndest things I've ever seen. How do you think she stays upright?"

"Ballast," another retiree said knowledgably. "Plenty of ballast."

A hushed appreciation of feminine "ballast" followed.

Luke, being male, deigned another look outside. He was as big a fan of "ballast" as the next guy. And he had a sneaking suspicion . . .

"Will ya look at the way she walks?" Byron sounded awed. "Just like Marilyn Monroe."

"Yeah," breathed another retiree. "Or Jayne Mansfield."

"Quit yer gawking, you old coot."

Luanne, the waitress, whapped Byron upside the head. "You've got a wife at home. Or did you forget?"

"No. Sheesh." Byron rubbed the back of his head.

The rest of the men looked away for a minute, wearing sheepish expressions. Then McKee pointed outside.

"Hey, she's comin' this way!" he yelled. "Duck!"

Eight men scrambled for the closest booths. Two grabbed menus and buried their noses in them. Another waved his coffee cup at Luanne for a decoy refill.

The waitress gave him a withering look.

Luke grinned. If you wanted good service at Frank's Diner, it was a bad idea to ogle anybody but Luanne.

"Holy smokes!" one of the retirees said, staring outside again. "I know her. That's little Josie Day. Warren and Nancy's girl."

"Jenna?"

"No. The *other* one."

A shocked silence fell over the retirees.

Then, "The one who ran off to Las Vegas."

At that, even the local women in the nearby booths perked up their ears. Several bouffant-haired heads swiveled toward the diner's front door. Luke felt a strange en-

90

ergy in the air, an almost palpable curiosity. This was exactly what he'd meant about people in Donovan's Corner. It didn't take much to stir them up.

The bell over the diner's front door jangled. Josie stepped inside.

Her pink outfit and rainbow shoes were the same ones from this morning. Both looked twice as colorful as anything in the diner. In them, she reminded Luke of a Technicolor starlet in a black and white movie. The whole place sort of . . . faded to gray around her. She was all he could see.

"Hi, Luanne. Hi, Frank!" Not noticing Luke yet, Josie waved to the diner's employees, standing on tiptoes to see past the counter into the kitchen beyond. She surveyed the restaurant, then headed for an empty booth, her trademark sashay firmly in place. "Hey, Mr. McKee."

McKee's ruddy face turned ten times pinker. Luke would've sworn the man blushed. His reaction was contagious, too. Every last retiree surrounding him wore a similar rosy hue and aw-shucks expression.

"Hi, Mrs. Webster. Hi, Debra-Ann."

The women seated opposite the retirees stuck their noses in the air. The pair behind them snapped their ketchup-splattered menus upward to hide their faces.

Noticing them, Josie looked troubled. She continued gamely down the aisle between booths, all the same. Summoning up another smile, she nodded to two more customers. Then she greeted another pair, a husband and wife Luke recognized.

"How's it going, you two?" Her tone sounded warm. Friendly. "Still hanging out at Frank's, I see."

"Hmmph." The wife stood with such force that her hair curlers wobbled beneath their head-scarf moorings. She grabbed her husband's arm without another look at Josie. "Come on, Henry. I changed my mind about that pie."

"But you love the pie here, Linda."

"Not" — she shot an indignant look at Josie — *"anymore."*

The two bustled out of the diner. Openmouthed, Josie watched them. Then she seemed to realize she was still standing in the middle of the restaurant. She spotted an empty booth and slid onto the worn red vinyl, all her attention fixed on the menu propped behind the napkin dispenser. She pulled it out.

Aside from a trembling in her fingers, she seemed all right to Luke. Composed, straight-backed, and with a neutral expression on her face — although he sort of missed the beaming smile she'd entered the diner with. Bothered by what had just happened, he dragged his gaze away from her. What he saw when he looked around didn't improve his mood.

To a customer, every last person was either gawking at Josie or studiously *not* noticing her. He didn't get it. Donovan's Corner wasn't exactly a hotbed of friendliness to newcomers, but this was ridiculous.

Then he remembered. Josie *wasn't* a newcomer.

Another minute passed. He wanted to say something, but he didn't know what. Despite the fact that she'd just moved into his house, he barely knew her. Was she one of those talk-talk-talk women? Or one of those distract-me-with-gifts women?

These days, Luke didn't have much to offer in the gift department.

Josie kept her face firmly behind her menu. Only her Barbie-painted fingernails showed — and he didn't think they endeared her to the rest of the plainly outfitted people in the diner. She was a flamingo among pigeons, a customized flame-painted Kawasaki V-Star racer among stock motorcycles. She stood out, whether she wanted to or not.

Right now, she did not.

The hell with it. These yokels needed a lesson in how to treat a lady, Luke decided.

Before he could do anything, though, Josie surprised him.

"Luanne, when you get a minute, could I have the cheeseburger plate, please?" she asked suddenly, her voice carrying. "And a Diet Coke to go with it?"

The waitress, clear across the diner and with no obvious intention of serving her newest customer, didn't so much as glance up. "We're all out."

"Out of cheeseburgers?" Josie shot a significant glance at the tabletops surrounding her. Several of them sported thick white plates full of the day's special — cheeseburgers and fries. "You're out of cheeseburgers?"

"Yep." Luanne studied her pad of guest checks, then shoved her pen behind one ear. She put both hands on her hips. Her next glance took in Frank's rapt clientele. "I expect we'll be out of cheeseburgers all week long."

All week long hung in the air, as blatantly false as Josie's hair color.

Josie gave Luanne a steady look. "Fine."

She slid her menu behind the napkin

94

holder again. She rose, taking a few seconds to smooth out her track pants and tug down her tank top — motions that held the retirees mesmerized. Then, chin held high, she headed for the door.

Something about the way Josie walked there caught Luke's eye. He would have sworn she was sort of going *sideways,* with a swoosh and a bump that looked weirdly sexy. He'd seen something like those movements before, but he couldn't place where. They were theatrical. Dramatic. And goofy as all get out, if the truth were told.

Hell, he thought, getting up to follow her. She really *was* crazy.

Five

By the time Josie made it to her convertible and peeled rubber back to Blue Moon, she was boiling mad. She clutched her cell phone as she stomped across the circular drive, barely hearing Parker's commiseration on the other end of the line.

"I wound up doing a *showgirl walk* to get out of there," Josie said. "A showgirl walk! Just to try to hold my head up. I must be losing my mind."

"Nah. I did one into a Fantasy Tan booth last week," Parker confided. "The attendant probably thought I was nuts."

"But gorgeously tanned." Everyone in Vegas was familiar with Parker's perma-tan habit.

"Of course," Parker agreed, a smile in her voice. "Anyway, after a while the showgirl walk is second nature. We both know it. Jacqueline is a showgirl-walk Nazi."

Not comforted, Josie fumed. "I'm telling you, it's a nightmare here. The house

96

Tallulah gave me is a wreck, the people are mean —"

"So come home. You don't need that crap."

"— the stupid lock on the front door won't work." Cradling the cell phone with difficulty between her chin and shoulder, Josie jiggled the Blue Moon doorknob the way she had this morning. Nothing happened. "I was crazy to leave Las Vegas. I don't belong here, Parker. I don't. I never did."

Parker murmured sympathetically.

"I tried to get the utilities hooked up at my new house," Josie went on, "and the people at the utility company practically slapped me in cuffs."

"Oooh, kinky."

Josie rolled her eyes. "Apparently, I left some overdue bill unpaid when I left here. By now, with penalties and fees tacked on, it's a zillion dollars or something."

"So come home. Jacqueline is holding your spot for you, you know."

"I know. Thank God, too. It looks as if I'm going to need it." Josie glowered at the uncooperative door. She kicked it. "Even my house doesn't like me."

"It's not the same without you here. There's nobody to tell me cheesy jokes."

"Oh, Parker." At the loyalty in her

97

friend's voice, Josie felt a wave of home-sickness wash over her. Great. Less than twenty-four hours into her great adventure and already she was buckling under. "I don't know what I'm doing here."

"Hey, at least you're not trout fishing."

Josie mustered a weak smile. Giving up on opening the door for now, she sat on the porch steps. They were made of smooth stone, as cold and unwelcoming as the rest of the place.

"The thing is, I had this great idea to open a dance school here." At the admission, tears welled in her eyes. She blinked. The view of the overgrown estate grounds came into focus, reminding her — unfortunately — of exactly how big a mess this really was. "You know, like I used to talk about doing? There's this ballroom here that would be perfect for a studio. . . . Oh, who am I kidding? This whole idea was crazy to begin with."

"You could make it work."

That was Parker. Always encouraging.

"Or you could wind up one of those nutty old ladies who live in abandoned mansions. You could wear only black and peek out the windows at the neighborhood kids. They'd be so scared, they'd pee their pants."

"Nice vision of my future. Crazy Lady Wets-a-Lot."

"I'll keep you company. I do a great bloodcurdling shriek. Must be in the genes."

At that, Josie perked up. That sounded like a clue to Parker's mysterious past. "In the genes? What genes?"

"Umm, my skinny jeans. There's nothing like wriggling a size eight ass into a pair of size six jeans to make a girl scream bloody murder."

Josie was sure Parker was hiding something.

But before she could question her further, a distraction appeared. Luke. And he seemed to be bearing gifts.

"Parker?" Interested in spite of herself, Josie let her gaze roam up Luke's blue jean–clad legs, skim past his hips, and settle on the paper sack in his hands. "I've gotta run. Welcome Wagon's calling."

"Call me if you change your mind about that scary old lady routine," Parker said. "I'm there in a heartbeat."

"If I decide to terrify little kids semi-professionally, you'll be the first to know."

She snapped her phone closed, then confronted Luke.

"The stupid lock is broken again."

"I'll fix it."

"Don't bother. I'm leaving."

He angled his head philosophically. "Leaving?"

She nodded. "Yeah, tonight. As soon as I can get my stuff out of the house."

"Hmmm. You might as well have this first."

Unconcerned, Luke pulled something from the paper sack and held it toward her. A Styrofoam take-out box, balanced in his big manly hand. His big, stupid, didn't-fix-the-lock hand. Unreasonably, looking at him made Josie mad all over again.

"I don't want it."

"Spoiling for a fight, huh? Move over."

Before she could protest, Luke hunkered down and nudged her sideways. He settled his studly backside on the steps beside her, then balanced the take-out box on his thighs. Josie couldn't seem to tug her gaze away from the sight of his hands. They might be incapable of fixing the damned lock, but they did look tanned and gentle against the pearly Styrofoam.

Pearly Styrofoam? Geez, she was losing it. She had to get out before she started rhapsodizing about *supple cardboard* or something.

"Do you always sneak up on people like

this?" she groused.

"I came up past the carriage house." He nodded toward the pine trees, where the gravel drive meandered once it passed Blue Moon's front door. "You haven't seen any of the outbuildings yet."

"That's probably a good thing. If they look anything like the rest of the place, I'd probably have to fire you if I saw them."

"Geez. You get crabby when you don't eat." He patiently unfolded the arms she'd flopped, crisscross-style, over her lap. He set the Styrofoam container in their place. "Hurry up. Riding here on the back of my bike probably didn't improve that much."

Josie let it sit there. She had a perfectly good sulk happening and Luke was ruining it. It occurred to her that now that she was leaving, she didn't have to maintain an employer-handyman relationship with him. She could flirt all she wanted.

"Bike, huh? I love cyclists. No wonder you have such great muscular thighs."

His lips quirked. "Must be all that pedaling."

"What's so funny?"

"I ride a Harley."

"Oh." Her image of him changed. She pictured Luke on a rumbling bad-ass motorcycle, the wind in his hair and the sun glinting from his sunglasses. In her imagination, he looked good. Really good. Apparently she was as susceptible as the next girl to the allure of the stock bad boy.

Her bad boy reached over and popped the top of the Styrofoam container, unperturbed by its close proximity to her lap. Josie wished she could say the same thing. The smooth slide of Luke's fingers against her thigh as he steadied the Styrofoam left her rattled. She possessed none of his physical easiness — and, all at once, every ounce of the awkwardness that dance had been meant to train out of her.

Greasy, salty aromas wafted from the take-out box. Luke pinched three French fries in his fingers and, companionably, offered them to her. Josie shook her head.

Wow, he looked good. Even while eating filched French fries. His face fascinated her. The angle of his cheekbones, the deep color of his eyes, the shape of his mouth. This close, she could see whisker shadow darkening his jaw — could almost feel its scratchy texture. It made Luke look rough and ready. Sexy. Dangerous.

Catnip to a lifelong rebel like her.

"Ever been on one?" he asked.

"A motorcycle?" Abruptly switching her

focus to the pile of French fries in her lap, Josie grabbed one. She munched it while she considered motorcycle riding. "Not yet."

"Hmmm." His assessing expression settled on her. "Most people just say no. Or they look horrified. Like somebody asked them to lick pavement."

"So?" Hmmm. Was that a cheeseburger in there?

"So *you* said, 'Not yet.' " Seeming interested in that, Luke chewed a few more fries. He splayed his hands on the porch and studied her. "I might have finally found my dream girl."

His half-teasing, half-cynical delivery wasn't lost on her.

"Sorry. I could never live happily ever after with a man who bogarts the French fries." She burrowed deeper into the crispy pile, realizing exactly how hungry she really was. "Hey, there *is* a cheeseburger in here!"

Happy, Josie maneuvered the sloppy burger out of the container with both hands. It smelled divine. She took a bite.

"Mmmm." Suddenly, she couldn't get enough. "Yum."

Bemused, Luke watched her. "You looked like an 'everything on it' kind of girl to me. I got ketchup, mustard, relish, lettuce, tomato, mayonnaise, pickles —"

"*Lots* of pickles. Perfect!"

She munched her way through half the cheeseburger. It could have been hotter or less greasier, but to Josie it was the tastiest thing she'd eaten all day. She didn't know how Luke had known she was craving this, but she was glad he had.

"You're not one of those girls who orders salad on a date, then," he observed, reaching in the paper sack for a napkin to give her. "You eat real food. I like that."

"Are you kidding me? I hate salad. It's so . . . healthy." She shuddered. "Seriously. If salad were actually *good*, would people have to put all that stuff on it? Dressing and croutons and bacon bits? No, they wouldn't. I say, skip the salad and go straight to the bacon bits."

"Interesting theory."

"I've got a million of 'em." Happily, Josie took another cheeseburger bite. This was nice, actually. Friendly. With Luke she felt comfortable, even while swabbing up a ketchup drip. "Mmm-mmm."

"Good?"

"Delicious."

"Good." Luke paused. "Luanne says you're a stripper."

"Gaaack." Josie put a hand to her throat, sure she must have choked on that blunt statement. She swiveled to face Luke, heedless that she was still mid-bite. "A *stripper?*"

He shrugged. "That's what everyone in town is —"

"Hang on." She narrowed her eyes. "How do you know Luanne?"

"I go to Frank's sometimes. It's no big deal."

Josie's bite of cheeseburger suddenly seemed way too big to handle. It tasted exactly like the Styrofoam it had come in, too. Chewing mightily, she forced it down. She dropped the rest of the burger into the take-out container, then daintily wiped her pickle-juice-smeared fingers on a napkin and dropped it inside, too. She snapped the lid closed. Shoved the whole thing back to Luke.

"You can keep your pity burger. I don't need it."

" 'Pity burger'? What the — ?"

But Josie was already on her feet. Already heading for the front door. *He'd been there.* Luke had been there at Frank's Diner when half the town had given her the cold shoulder. The feeling of humiliation that had swamped her then was

105

nothing compared with the embarrassment she felt now. She didn't know why his opinion of her mattered — only that she didn't want it to.

This was *way* more than the "reward" she'd signed up for. It was past time to get her stuff and clear out. Josie jammed her key in the lock and rattled it, trying to remember the secret method Luke had shared with her during her tour of Blue Moon. Was it turn-jiggle-turn? Or jiggle-turn-jiggle? Damn. He was headed right for her. But she was ready for him.

Josie whirled. If there was any feminine justice in the world, there'd be sparks shooting from her eyeballs. Just to scare him.

He didn't even look alarmed.

"Hey." Luke held up both hands in surrender. He even had the gall to grin, his eyes crinkling at the corners. "Don't be mad at me. I *like* strippers."

"I'm *not* a stripper!"

His gaze zipped to her hips, then back again. "You sure about that? Because you've got all the right equipment."

"So do you. I'll alert Chippendales."

"Thanks. But I like my job here." He leaned his shoulder against the porch post, as aggravatingly relaxed as ever. Clearly,

106

feminine justice was busy elsewhere. "I guess you prefer to be called 'exotic dancers' these days, right?"

"Unless you're stocked up on fivers for my G-string." Josie pantomimed tucking money in her imaginary stripper regalia, then offered up an over-the-top hip swivel. "Then you can call me whatever you want." She batted her eyelashes.

He frowned over her sarcasm. "I like . . . Josie."

"Awww. Even though you think I take my clothes off for money, you *still* see me as a real person. That's sweet." Josie rolled her eyes. "Nice try, Lothario. Save it for the local girls. I moved out of Completely Gullible a long time ago."

Feeling battered, she shook the doorknob again. Nada.

Fine. She'd overcome difficult odds before. She could do it again. Josie wrenched out her keys, lifted her chin, and marched to the parlor window overlooking the porch. There was more than one way into this dump, and she was about to prove it.

"What's got me stumped," Luke mused from behind her, "is how you met my — Tallulah. She's not much into girlie shows."

"It wasn't a 'girlie show,' you Neanderthal. It wasn't even topless. I don't 'do' topless."

God, she couldn't *wait* to get out of here. Gritting her teeth, Josie raised the window sash. She threw her keys on the parlor floorboards inside, then hoisted herself on the windowsill in a straddle position. With dignity, she pushed her chin a notch higher. "It," she informed him, "was a revue."

As a snappy comeback, it was short-lived. Because the minute Josie toed the floorboards and stepped into the house, her ankle went *pop.* It gave way beneath her.

With a yelp, Josie fell.

Luke sprawled on one of the beat-up waiting room chairs at Donovan's Corner General, a six-month-old issue of *Sports Illustrated* on his lap. Not surprisingly, articles about last season's NFC playoffs weren't exactly riveting. He stared at them anyway, trying to take his mind off Josie.

No good. Tossing the magazine on a side table, he looked around. Unless you counted one grubby rug rat with a runny nose, the kid's harried-looking mom, and two construction workers — one with his thumb wrapped in a makeshift tube sock bandage — the place didn't offer much in the way of distraction.

He drummed his fingers on the chair arm. Propped one booted ankle on his bent knee. Switched legs. Stood, stretched, and paced the cramped length of the emergency room waiting area.

That weird hospital smell lingered in the air, some unavoidable combination of antiseptic cleaners and cafeteria food. The overhead intercom crackled with calls for doctors to come to various departments, and the receptionist tapped on her computer keyboard. Somewhere down the long mustard-colored corridor to his left, an alarm buzzed. In the curtained-off room to his right, Josie was being examined.

The glass double doors at the entrance swooshed open, admitting a jingly middle-aged brunette. She made a beeline for the reception desk. Her movements — brisk, no-nonsense, and vaguely tottering due to her high heels — made sunlight glint from her gold jewelry. She was covered in the stuff. Two thick necklaces, big dangly earrings, a pair of bracelets on one wrist and a shiny watch on the other, a lapel pin. In a town other than Donovan's Corner, that might not have been unusual. But around here, women didn't get gussied up much. She stood out.

"I'm Nancy Day," she told the receptionist, hitching her purse on her shoulder. "Here to see my daughter, Josie."

Luke's ears perked up. Josie's mother? No wonder she'd stood out. It ran in the family.

"Your daughter's being examined." The receptionist shot a curious glance at Luke — no doubt wondering why Josie's two visitors didn't seem to know each other. "She should be out in a few minutes, if you'd like to wait, ma'am."

With a hushed thank-you, Nancy Day teetered to the waiting area. Her bright clothes were as dressed-up as her jewelry was — several heads turned as she examined the available chairs. Seeing her hesitate, one of the construction workers rose partway. He cleared away a newspaper from a nearby chair, then motioned chivalrously for Nancy to take the seat.

Special treatment. Luke didn't doubt that Josie's mother received it all the time. She definitely seemed to accept it as her due — a lot like Josie probably would have. She smiled, then offered a gracious murmured comment to the construction worker. He grinned in a bashful, secretly pleased way — just like all the retirees at Frank's Diner had when Josie had greeted them. Nancy sat and crossed her legs, staring intently toward the examining area.

As though she'd willed him to do so, a doctor emerged.

Luke glanced from the familiar doctor to Nancy. He looked back again, impressed. Handy trick. If he could do that with his refrigerator and an endless supply of Budweisers, he'd be the most popular man in town.

"We're all set here," the doctor told Luke, obviously recognizing him as the man who'd all but carried the patient over the emergency room threshold. "You can see Josie now."

The doctor held back the curtain, indicating that Luke should follow him inside. Was that a frown on his face? Was the news bad? Luke bolted for the examining area.

He arrived there only moments before Nancy did. Despite that she was a head shorter and about sixty pounds lighter, she paused and raised an eyebrow at him. Clearly she expected him to make way for her to see her daughter.

"He was talking to me," they said in unison.

Nancy blinked in surprise. Then, evidently deciding Luke was delusional, she turned to the doctor.

"Is it bad? How is she?"

The doctor hesitated, looking confused.

"Oh, God," groaned a voice from inside the examining room. "Mom, is that you?"

"No need to sound so petulant, young lady." With a victorious glance at Luke and the doctor, Nancy swept past the curtain. Her high heels clip-clopped against the tile. "Of course it's me. I came as soon as I heard. Left in the middle of showing a new listing, in fact."

Luke followed. Josie sat on a padded green examining table in the middle of the tight-squeezed room, her leg extended and her pink track pants rolled up to the knee. Her ankle was wrapped in what looked like a stretchy Ace bandage. She seemed uncomfortable — although whether that was due to pain or her mother's arrival, Luke couldn't tell.

At the sight of her vulnerable bare leg and cantaloupe-size ankle, the lump of guilt in his gut got worse. He should have fixed the floorboards. Or warned Josie not to go gallivanting over the windowsill like that. But she'd looked so damned cute, all cocksure and full of determination. He hadn't thought twice about the potential

112

condition of the flooring, so he hadn't tried to stop her.

Self-importantly, Nancy stepped forward. "Did Josie give you any trouble" — she squinted at the doctor's name badge — "Doctor Villanova? I'm afraid my daughter has never been the most cooperative of patients."

"Mom." Josie crossed her arms. She rolled her eyes.

The doctor looked nonplussed. "She was fine. Now, about —"

"Oh, that's *so* kind of you to say so." Nancy winked, as though sharing a private joke with everyone. "I have to tell you, some people just don't quite understand my Josie."

Sensing his opportunity, Luke jumped in. "Especially people who think she's a *stripper*." With a knowledgeable shake of his head, he moved to stand closer to Josie. "They don't understand her at all."

Josie, Nancy, and the doctor all gaped at him.

"She doesn't even 'do' the topless stuff," he added. *That* was going to score points, big time. It might even make up for the crumbling floorboard Josie's foot had plowed through. He glanced at her injured ankle. It looked swollen to the size of the moose head on the billiard room wall. "Or girlie shows. She's in a revue."

Silence.

"Tell me, Luke." Josie cocked her head toward him, looking as though she was stifling a wiseass smile. "Exactly what *is* a revue?"

Crap. Didn't she know he was trying to help her out, here?

"It's a . . ." Remembering her plans for Blue Moon's abandoned ballroom, he decided to take a shot in the dark. He was good at improvising. "Dance . . . thing."

He didn't know if it was his delivery or his stance or just dumb luck, but Josie bought it. So did Nancy and the doctor, judging by their awed expressions. He felt as though he'd just rebuilt a vintage Indian Scout 741. Blindfolded.

Josie got over it quickly. She straightened atop the examining table with practiced — and, Luke would have sworn, exotic dancer–style — elegance. She addressed the doctor.

"So, what's the story?"

"Yes, is it serious?" Nancy cast a dramatic, concerned glance at her daughter's wrapped ankle. "Will she ever dance again?"

All that was missing was the violin music.

"It's just a sprain," Luke assured Nancy. "She'll tough it out."

Josie's mother looked at him as though he'd just pulled down his pants and flashed her.

"Er, who are you, again?"

"Luke Donovan. I'm Josie's —"

"Friend," Josie interrupted hurriedly. "He's my friend."

Not handyman, her fierce gaze telegraphed to him.

Whatever. Luke extended his arm to shake Nancy's decked out hand. He'd forgotten to account for the two rings on her right hand and the three on the left. Jesus. The woman was a walking QVC special.

Her smile enveloped him. It was like being walloped with a charm stick.

"Nancy Day. Sunshine Realty." Somehow she palmed over her business card in one deft move. "If you're ever in the market for a new home, please keep me in mind. I cover the entire county, including condos, vacation homes, and rentals."

Damn. For an older broad, she was dazzling. Also a little scary in her intensity. Luke would have gone back to roof shingling before admitting it.

"Mom, save the sales pitch. I promise you, Luke isn't interested in a new house."

Josie looked at the ever-patient Doctor Villanova. "I'm okay to leave now, right?"

"Yes." He consulted his chart. "You have a mild sprain. I ordered some precautionary X-rays, but no bones are broken. Your ankle is wrapped up now, but you should stay off your feet as much as possible for the next twenty-four to forty-eight hours." He explained procedures for icing and elevating the injury. "You can take an over the counter pain reliever as needed for any discomfort."

"Fine, I will. I know the drill. Thanks, Doc." Josie offered him a handshake, then watched him leave. The moment he disappeared through the curtain, she slid to the edge of the table, clearly intending to get down and — what? Hop to the exit?

"Hey." Luke lunged forward. "Stop right there. Are you trying to mangle the other ankle, too?"

He held out his arms. Josie regarded him mulishly.

"You're *not* carrying me out of here."

"Until you get a pair of crutches, I am."

"Wow, Josie. What a perfect gentleman. I think this one's a keeper!" Nancy beamed. She leaned conspiratorially toward him. "Let me ask you something, Luke. Do you rent or own? Have you ever considered lakefront property? It never fails to appreciate in value, you know."

"Mom!" Poised on the edge of the examining table, Josie speared her mother with an aggravated look. "What are you doing here, anyway? You weren't even supposed to know I was in town."

Nancy lifted her chin. Luke recognized the stubborn gesture. It had to be genetic.

"One of my clients heard you were back in town while she was IM-ing the members of her son's after-school playgroup," Nancy said with dignity. "Apparently, little Andrew Toureno's mother was in the waiting room when you came in."

Josie raised her eyebrows.

"Donovan's Corner is not the back of beyond, dear. We have the Internet now. Haven't you seen my Realtor Web page?"

Josie shrugged. "I'm not an Internet person, Mom. You know I don't like computers."

"Hmmm. Yes, that's right. Brainpower never was your strong suit. Well. We can't all be good at everything, can we?" Brightly, Nancy patted her daughter on the knee. "I'll just have to show you my Web site when we get home, then."

"Uhhh —"

"Of *course* you'll be staying with your father and me until you're recovered. I positively insist."

Josie's panicked gaze slid to Luke. She must have viewed him as the lesser of two evils, because her decision was immediate.

"Steady, there, Incredible Hulk. I'm coming your way."

She all but leaped into Luke's arms. He caught her with a grunt, then waited while she grabbed her purse, her abandoned rainbow sandal, and a sheaf of doctor's instructions. He liked holding her. She didn't squeal or pretend she might be crushing him or catch him in a stranglehold. She just held on, trusting he would carry her safely.

"We're out of here," she announced. "Mush, Hulk."

Great. He was getting sappy. She was getting bossy.

But he couldn't leave her to fend for herself. Especially not when her accident had been partly his fault. Luke headed for the door.

"Good idea," Nancy said, nodding from beside it. "You carrying her, I mean. Josie *definitely* shouldn't walk until we get a pair of crutches at the drugstore." With evident approval, she led the way out of the examining room. "My car is parked on the left side of the parking lot, Luke. It's a special zone for Chamber of Commerce members only." She spared him a proud over-the-shoulder glance as she tottered in the lead, showing how pleased she was to be among Donovan's Corner's finest businesses. "Follow me. I'll show you the way."

They stopped beside a shiny white Cadillac, a few years old but obviously well cared for. The driver's-side door sported a huge magnetized Sunshine Realty advertisement. From its center, Nancy Day's cheerful, makeup-spackled face beamed back at them.

"Well, here we are!"

"I see you're still driving the pimpmobile," Josie said.

"My clients are all terribly impressed with this car. They *love* riding in it when I show houses."

"That's because they're hoping to get lucky in the back seat. It's as big as my bedroom in Vegas."

Nancy pursed her lips. She gave Luke one of those *Kids. What can you do?* looks.

"Luke, I'll just get in and roll down the backseat window. You can shove Josie in that way. All right?"

He chuckled. Josie whapped him.

"Very funny, Mom. Tell you what. We've

got my car. I'll just meet you at your house, okay?"

Nancy looked skeptical. Josie plowed onward anyway.

"My convertible's parked right over there. Luke was nice enough to drive me here. I'll give him directions."

After a few more minutes' persuasion, Nancy got in her car. Wearing an uncertain look, she leaned out the window. She frowned at Josie. "Twenty minutes. Not an instant more. After that, I'm sending out a search party."

Unconcerned, Josie waved. "See ya! Love you!"

Nancy pulled out. Luke watched as she zoomed out of the special parking zone, then maneuvered her way into the light traffic. Five minutes later he was behind the wheel of Josie's crappy Chevy, ready to do the same.

He glanced at Josie. She sat awkwardly in the passenger seat, frowning at her ankle.

"So, which way to your Mom's house?"

"That way." She pointed.

He looked. "That's the freeway on-ramp. She didn't go that way."

"I know. I'm going back to Blue Moon to get my stuff, then I'm going home to

120

Las Vegas. There's nothing wrong with my right foot, and this isn't a stick shift. I can drive."

"But —" Confused, he gestured in the direction her mother had gone. "Your mom thinks you're going to her house."

"No." Josie waved off the idea as though she'd never suggested it. "It's easier this way. Trust me."

He couldn't believe it. "You're going to ditch your own mother?"

"It's . . . not like that." Biting her lip, she seemed to consider telling him something. Then, "It's complicated. You wouldn't understand."

Luke studied her. "I see why some people aren't thrilled you're back in town."

"What's *that* supposed to mean?"

"Nothing. Just that you never seem to do what you say you're going to do."

"Like . . . ?"

"Go to your mom's. Ice your ankle. Put up flyers." He paused, examining her stony profile. "Start a dance school."

She crossed her arms. "You don't even know me."

"I know you shouldn't drive with an ankle the size of a prizewinning heifer."

"Awww." She batted her eyelashes. "You country boys and your sweet talk."

If she only knew. Doggedly, he added, "I know you shouldn't go so long between tune-ups." He jutted his chin toward the Chevy's front end. "That's why your engine sounds like that."

"Like what?"

"Like it's begging for mercy."

"Oh, so now you're a handyman *and* a mechanic?"

"Yes." He ignored her surprised look. He was used to it. Staring her down, he prepared for his big finish. "I know you shouldn't let those busybodies run you out of town like this."

Her defiant gaze met his. "Nobody's running me out of town. *I* decided to leave."

"Okay. If you say so." Luke drummed his fingertips on the steering wheel. He shrugged. "But this looks a lot like running away to me. That must be what happened the last time you lived in Donovan's Corner, too."

The temperature in the car dropped at least twenty degrees.

"Look. Either drive me to Blue Moon or get out of the car so I can do it myself."

He glanced at her. Despite Josie's expression of bravado and her air of rebelliousness, she looked like hell. Or at least as close to it as a va-va-voom redheaded showgirl could get — pale-faced, shook up, and definitely in no condition to drive. He'd wanted her to leave, but not like this.

"Twenty-four to forty-eight hours," he said.

"What?"

"That's how long the doctor said you're supposed to recuperate. That's how long you're staying. At Blue Moon."

"Oh, puhleeze. Make me."

"If that's how you want it." Luke put the car in drive, then backed out. He was done arguing with her. "Consider yourself officially kidnapped."

Six

Being officially kidnapped wasn't that bad.

Not that Josie would've admitted it. Luke's simplified small-town "wisdom" had added insult to injury ("running her out of town" . . . ha!), and his know-it-all approach to how she should handle her sprained ankle had irritated her to no end.

Who did he think he was, anyway? The guru of Donovan's Corner? He was a hunk, sure. But when it came to her, he was way off base. Way, *way* off base. Josie was sure of it.

As a dancer, she'd had injuries before. She knew how to handle them — with rest and then retraining. As a former Donovan's Corner resident, she'd had her share of run-ins with the town's stuffier citizens. She knew how to handle them, too — by getting the heck out of Dodge. No dance school dream was worth being judged at every turn.

But apparently her humiliating so-called

homecoming had worn her down. Because when it came to the whole "kidnapping" scheme, Josie didn't quite protest as much as she wanted to.

Luke confiscated her car keys. He refused to move her boxes of stuff back to her convertible. He insisted on taking care of her for at least twenty-four hours. And Josie? She decided she really didn't have that much choice. After all, she'd been officially kidnapped.

There were probably worse things than being held in the grip of an idiotically appealing, macho handyman-mechanic, she told herself. Especially one who seemed stubbornly intent on pampering her until she recovered.

He was probably afraid Tallulah would fire him if Josie reported the terrible condition of the place. Or maybe his conscience was butting in because of the unrepaired-floor fiasco — something Josie couldn't quite hold a grudge about, given how nice he'd been about helping her.

She sighed, then turned her face toward the enormous stone fireplace. Savoring the warmth of the blaze Luke had kindled for her, she decided it didn't make much difference either way. When she *really* wanted to leave, she'd find a way to do just that.

Tomorrow. Or maybe the next day. For sure.

Honestly. It wasn't as if she wanted to stick around to indulge some kind of schoolgirl crush on him, or anything.

"Hey," Luke said by way of greeting as he entered the living room at Blue Moon — aka, Josie's detention center. "You haven't crawled out the back door and hitchhiked back to Las Vegas. I'm stunned."

"I stuck around for the view." She admired his arms, sinewy and perfectly tanned. Then his broad, T-shirted shoulders. Shoulders like those belonged on one of those Greek statues in a museum — or in the bed of a nice woman who'd appreciate them. "It's a nice view."

"Yeah. Flattery will get you everywhere. At least with me." He shot her a dazzling grin. "But I'm still not giving back your car keys. You're in no condition to drive yet."

"So you've said. Once or twenty times." She waved away the idea. "I'm just saying, you're not exactly what I expected in a handyman. *Especially* a Donovan's Corner handyman."

"What do you mean?"

She examined him. *Let me count the ways.*

"Well, for one thing, you've got all your teeth."

126

His grin widened, proving her right.

"For another, you're reasonably open-minded. Unlike *some* people in this town, you don't jump to conclusions. Much."

As though considering that, he frowned at the items he'd brought — a two-liter bottle of 7 Up, a package of Ding Dongs, and a deck of playing cards. He set them on the coffee table, then sucked in a deep breath.

"Wait, are you about to jump to a conclusion?" she asked, pretending to be horrified. "Don't do it!"

Luke wasn't deterred by her joke. "That's the second — or twentieth — time you've said something like that about this place." In the middle of opening the Ding Dongs, he regarded her curiously. "If you hate it here so much, why did you come back?"

"I dunno. Maybe I've got something to prove." Josie blinked, surprised. Where had *that* come from? "Or maybe I just wanted a cheeseburger at Frank's. Nobody makes them like that anymore."

Luke gave her a skeptical look.

"Come on. I'm *kidding*. What could I possibly have to prove to these old busy-bodies? Who cares what they think?"

He still looked unconvinced. Damn it.

"Besides, it's not every day a girl inherits a mansion of her very own. I got itchy. I *had* to check it out. Haven't you ever wanted to do that? Just chuck everything and take off to do something completely unlikely?"

A strange expression crossed his face. Josie guessed he had — or he'd wanted to. She wondered which.

"If you mean learn to samba," Luke said, "then, no."

Disappointed, Josie made a face. "No, I don't mean 'learn to samba.' " She felt sure Luke had been about to reveal something — something important. Something that had nothing to do with sambaing, and everything to do with *him.*

The truth was, despite her resolve to bail out on Blue Moon, she couldn't deny a certain attraction to the place. And to its caretaker. Luke was interesting, if a little too laid-back in the repairing-the-mansion department. He was gorgeous, if a little too mysterious. He was often funny, occasionally puzzling, and always gallant. Really, Luke had more going for him than the last four men she'd dated in Las Vegas had.

Besides, let's face it. She was as susceptible to that devilish grin of his as the next girl was. Maybe even more, since "devilish" generally promised "break-the-rules bad boy" — her favorite kind of guy.

Hmmm. Josie watched as Luke poked at the fire, sending sparks up the chimney. Now that she no longer planned to keep Blue Moon, there might be sparks happening of an entirely different kind. Luke wasn't off-limits anymore. She wasn't going to be his boss, and he wasn't going to be her handyman. That meant things were looking up. And here she was, with twenty-one and a half hours to kill. Doctor's orders.

"I meant something *really* unlikely," she prompted. "Like taking up skydiving or driving cross-country with nothing but a guitar and a Chihuahua."

"Is that the voice of experience talking?"

"Maybe." Josie smiled. This guy was a mind-reader. "Or maybe I'm just trying to jog your memory, Mystery Man. How about working as an extra on a movie set? Building homes for the homeless? Flying on a trapeze?"

Luke replaced the fireplace poker, then came toward her. "How about having my house taken over by a down-on-her-luck showgirl? That's new. And unlikely."

"Hey." Offended, she lifted her chin. "I'm not down on my luck." True, she'd been a little . . . *squashed* . . . by the events of her big homecoming. But she felt herself beginning to bounce back. Bolstered by a few hours' relaxation, the half pity-burger she'd wolfed down, and the solid comfort of Blue Moon, Josie felt better equipped to deal with everything. "But I do think it's cute how you love this place so much, you call it your own."

"Yeah. Cute." Wearing that frown again, Luke strode across the spacious living room. "You've got one thing right. This place is important to me."

"See? That's how I know I can trust you. You're dedicated to your work. That's not something you see every day."

He shot her a look. "You spent the whole day telling me how crappy my handyman work was."

"Well, you can't hold that against me. It's been a pretty tough day." Josie yawned. "Which means that now I deserve to cut loose a little. What with being kidnapped, and all."

"Come on. It hasn't been so bad." Luke hunkered down beside the coffee table, adjusting the pair of pillows beneath her propped-up ankle. "You got your choice of ground-floor servants' bedrooms. And you got to keep your cell phone."

"True. That's another reason I know I can trust you. A homicidal maniac ax murderer would *never* have let me keep my trusty Nokia." Josie patted the customized pink-sparkle-plated phone on the sofa cushion beside her. She'd called Parker with an update not two hours ago. "I figure you must be okay."

Actually, she figured he was more than okay. Strange as it seemed, Josie trusted him, which was more than she could say for most of the people she met. Unlike the high rollers, playboy gamblers, and entitlement-obsessed CEOs who came to Vegas with the idea that everything there was for sale — even the showgirls — he hadn't patronized her. Or lied to her.

Also unlike them, Luke hadn't tried to grab her ass.

She frowned, suddenly off-kilter by the realization. *Why* hadn't Luke tried to grab her ass? Was she the only one feeling a buzz between them?

Wondering, Josie tilted her head. Luke still crouched beside the coffee table, now exchanging her limp bag of frozen corn for a package of frozen peas. He patted it gently in place — the "icing" portion of her sprained-ankle treatment. He glanced at his watch.

"What's the matter? Got a hot date?" she teased.

He hesitated. Josie's heart stuttered.

Get a grip, she commanded herself. *You just met him. He doesn't even want to grab your ass.*

But that didn't seem to matter. As aggravating as Luke sometimes was — especially when arguing against her dance school idea — Josie had to face facts. His was one of the few friendly faces she'd encountered since setting out on her big adventure. Unlike another of those friendly faces — her mother's — *his* didn't belong to someone who'd once scraped Gerber mashed sweet potatoes out of her nose. That was a plus right there.

Besides, being with him just made her feel better.

"I'm timing the ice packs for your ankle," he said.

Great. She was getting sappy. He was getting practical.

What were the odds?

"Oh. Right. The ice packs."

"But if you want me to leave, I will."

Josie didn't want him to leave. But she didn't want to say so. After all, the man had (kind of) kidnapped her. She was still officially opposed to that.

132

Biting her lip, she glanced around the living room. Among all the tarp-shrouded furniture, Luke had only uncovered the sofa. The fire was great, but the shadows it cast in the corners and the whole *Scooby-Doo* atmosphere of Blue Moon at night was starting to spook her.

"I've got some things to do in the carriage house," Luke said. "I'll check on you in twenty minutes."

"Wait! You don't have to rush off."

He glanced over his shoulder, one eyebrow lifted.

"Umm, what's all that for?" She pointed to the things he'd brought. Yes, it was a lame distraction. It was all she could muster on short notice. Being kidnapped had damaged her flirting abilities.

Cooperatively, Luke lifted the soda. "Refreshment. Seven-Up is the only thing to drink when you're under the weather. At least according to Marta."

Finally. A personal detail. "Marta?"

"My . . . babysitter. When I was a kid."

"Ah."

Next, Luke lifted a Ding Dong. "Sustenance." He lifted the deck of cards. "And entertainment. But I'm having second thoughts about these. Playing cards might make this whole kidnapping thing

133

too much fun for you. You'll never leave."

"Only if you're lucky." Josie smiled. "Come on. I need some distraction and you're all that's available. You owe me."

He hesitated, then ran a hand through his hair. Was it her imagination, or was he reluctant to leave?

"What do you have in mind?"

"Seven-card stud." Her favorite card game. "Aces high, no limit, minimum bet . . . one Ding Dong."

With her good toe, she pushed a cellophane-wrapped chocolate cake into the kitty. Then she looked at Luke.

He put his hands on his hips. He arched his eyebrow. "Poker? With a Las Vegas showgirl? I'd have to be crazy."

"Showgirl?" That was the second time he'd mentioned that tonight. "I never told you that."

"You didn't have to." Hunkering down again, he picked up the cards and plucked them from the box. He executed a perfect two-handed riffle shuffle. "After getting all the gossip in town and listening to your mom jabber about you, I figured it out. Just because I work with my hands doesn't mean I'm stoopid."

He dragged over an ottoman and sat on

it, settling in. Josie watched his hands as he shuffled.

"I like that you work with your hands." To her, doing the kind of work he did suggested trustworthiness. Plus, it positively demonstrated studliness.

"I like that you work with your body." He waggled his eyebrows teasingly.

"Yeah. Most men do. But just for the record, that makes me a dancer, *not* a stripper." Reminded again of the day's events, Josie frowned. "I wish people in this town would get that through their thick heads."

"They might if you stuck around to show them." Luke dealt the cards. "But you're leaving once you're healed, right?"

"Damned straight, I am. Of course. Sure."

He gazed at her, a thoughtful expression on his face. "Add in a 'definitely' and I might believe you."

She snorted. "Shows what you know. I'm not staying here. I've already been through all that. For a minute, Tallulah's offer made me forget. But Donovan's Corner doesn't like me and I don't like it. End of story."

"You must come back here pretty often," he said. "To visit your folks."

Josie squinted at her cards. She gestured for another one, then wagered a second Ding Dong. Maybe if she pretended he wasn't going all *Barbara Walters Special* on her, he'd quit it.

Luke didn't even glance at his hand. "Or do they come to see you in Vegas instead?"

"Look, are you going to play cards or not?"

"Do they think you're a stripper, too?"

Exasperated, Josie met his gaze. "You're awfully inquisitive. For a guy, I mean. Most men would rather gnaw off their own toenails than have a conversation. Especially on purpose."

He wagered a Ding Dong, unbothered by her dig at his manhood. "Most women never shut up."

She pursed her lips demonstratively.

"Women are the ones who invented talking to plants."

She rolled her eyes.

"You must have something to hide."

"Fine." Josie raised her chin. She rattled off the facts. "I haven't seen my dad for a few years. He's happier that way. My mom sneaks off to Las Vegas every six months or so for a visit. She sees a few shows, throws a few quarters in the slots, and commandeers my bed for a few days while I sleep on the couch. Then she goes back to her life and I go back to mine. Sometimes my sister comes with her."

"What's she like?"

"My sister? Three years older than me and twice as perfect. So that's it in a nutshell. My life, from Donovan's Corner until today. Happy now?"

Luke examined the kitty, then spread out his cards. "Yeah. I'm happy. Full house, king high."

Josie gawked. It was going to be a very long night.

Usually she excelled at poker — a perk of spending so much time in casinos and of having accidentally dated a compulsive gambler when she'd first arrived in Vegas. But pitted against Luke, Josie found her game was off.

She tried to concentrate on the cards, and noticed Luke's incredible blue eyes instead. She tried to focus on winning, and got distracted by his husky laugh, his easy way with victory, his tattoos. She attempted to play her most cutthroat game of seven-card stud ever, and only succeeded in wishing Luke would scoot closer. Preferably to her side of the table.

Oblivious to her wishes, he sat opposite her on the ottoman with perfect casualness, legs cocked at the knee. Only a man could sit that way and still look so good. Drawn by his pose, Josie gave up concentrating on cards. Instead, she concentrated on *him* — which, as it turned out, was a lot more enjoyable.

Although Luke was big, he possessed none of the awkwardness that sometimes came with size. He seemed completely at ease in his skin, his posture relaxed and his movements purposeful. He also seemed strangely competent — as though he could fix something, carry something, or cradle something with equal ease.

She didn't know what it was about him that intrigued her so much. Was it the hard angle of his jaw, suggesting stubborn machismo? The rumpled darkness of his hair, suggesting uninhibited bed head? The sheer dazzle of his smile, suggesting he enjoyed himself . . . no matter what?

Probably it was all those things. And more.

Hours of manual labor at Blue Moon had definitely done Luke good, Josie observed. His whole body looked taut — his arms, his belly, his thighs. He rested his elbows on them and then pondered his cards, his face a study in shadows and light.

There was something about him. Something about a man who seemed to know what he wanted and how to get it . . . something Josie wanted to get closer to. Especially now that she was free to get to know her former handyman a little better.

"If you're trying to distract me by staring like that," he said without lifting his gaze from his cards, "it won't work. I have awesome powers of concentration."

Whoops. Caught. "Is that right?"

He nodded. "I'm undistractible."

That sounded like a challenge. "Wow. Impressive."

"Yeah." Luke added a Ding Dong to the kitty. "So whatever kind of showgirl hypnosis you're working on over there, you can just knock it off."

" 'Showgirl hypnosis.' " She smiled. "Well, now, there's one tiny problem with that. It only works if you actually look at me."

Pointedly, he frowned at his cards.

Experimentally, Josie nudged her shoulder. Her tank top strap slipped a few inches.

His poker-player's grasp tightened.

Josie's smile widened. "Peripheral vision counts."

Obviously realizing he was caught, too, he looked up. Somehow, the impact of his full attention took her breath away. Her whole body tensed expectantly. This was it. He was going to do . . . *something*.

"You need another bag of frozen corn." Luke headed for the house's distant kitchen.

Arrgh. Josie grabbed the Seven-Up and took a swig straight from the gigantic two-liter bottle. He *had* to be doing this deliberately. The accidental-on-purpose tank top strap maneuver was one of her best. It wasn't possible Luke was immune.

When he returned bearing a mushy refrozen bag of niblets, she tested her theory.

"If this were a real date," she said, watching him replace her makeshift sprained-ankle ice pack, "I'd have decided to let you kiss me good night by now."

Almost imperceptibly, his fingers fumbled.

She went on. "I'd start leaning in to give you an opportunity. I'd probably look at your mouth a lot to give you a hint. Like this."

Josie leaned nearer, her gaze fixed on his lips.

He squinted. "If you did that, most guys

would think we had something stuck in our teeth."

He was the most obtuse man on the planet. In the universe. Josie persisted. " 'Most guys,' " she said seductively, "don't get this treatment."

"You're bluffing."

"No, I'm not." She put down her cards, wishing she could get a little closer to him. Stupid ankle. It prevented her from just climbing over the coffee table and sitting on his lap. Then he'd be sure to get the message. "Really, I'm not."

"Yes, you are." Luke nodded toward their poker game. He snapped his cards on the table with a flourish. "My straight beats your royal flush. I knew you didn't have the hand to back up that bet."

Oh. He was talking about the game. Giving up all hope of ever winning at poker again, Josie sighed. She settled back on the sofa, watching him scoop up the rest of his Ding Dong jackpot. It figured. In this — just like in the rest of her life — she'd overplayed her hand.

Luke had never believed a simple game of seven-card stud could be fatal. But after four hands, three swigs of Seven-Up, and countless trips to the kitchen for vegetable ice pack replacements, he realized the truth. He was never going to survive this night.

He was never going to survive Josie Day.

She flirted, she smiled, she leaned over and treated him to a luscious view of her skimpily covered breasts. She joked, she sighed, she let her clothes fall *right off her body* without doing a damned thing about it. Okay, so it was only her tank top strap falling off, but Luke had as much imagination as the next guy. In his mind's eye, it was her whole top.

He tried to do the right thing. He concentrated on his cards, but her sexy laugh lured him away. He focused on the game, but her bare skin appealed to him more. He iced her sprained ankle until either it — or his hands — was going to freeze off. Still he felt himself weakening.

Josie was funny and vivacious and sexy. She said exactly what she wanted to say, when she wanted to say it. Despite the massive inconvenience of her presence in his house, Luke wasn't exactly sorry she was there. As the night wore on, the fact that he managed to hold on to his cards — much less *see* them — was a testament to the force of his will.

Either that, or he didn't want to take advantage of a woman who'd all but immobilized herself by spraining her ankle on a hole in his floor.

Go figure. It looked as though he possessed scruples.

There was no other explanation for it. Despite his genes, despite his upbringing, despite everything, Luke apparently possessed the kind of moral fortitude no Donovan before him ever had. His father would have been appalled.

But there it was. Scruples, a conscience, whatever you wanted to call it. Luke was a prisoner of his own stupid principles. They were keeping him from enjoying the night to its fullest.

"Damned scruples," he groused.

"What's that?" Josie asked from her perch on the couch.

"I said, here's that TV I promised."

Having finished off as much poker as he could stand — along with most of the Ding Dongs — Luke put down the set he'd carried from the billiards room, an ancient fifteen-inch color unit with a missing power button and fuzzy reception.

He plugged it in. "There's no cable in the house itself, but the local channels ought to come in okay."

"Super." She made a face. She nodded

toward the abandoned deck of cards. "Sure you won't go another round?"

"I'm sure. I'll put your crutches right here, so they're within reach." Luke propped them against the nearest arm of the sofa. He held out the TV remote, noticed its furry coating of dust, and rubbed it against his jeans to clean it. He handed it to her. "If you need anything, just shout. I left the windows open so I'll hear you."

"Where are you going?"

"Carriage house. I've got work to do. It's getting late."

"It's only nine-thirty!"

"Don't worry. The local programming will knock you out in no time."

She frowned. Somehow, even while frowning, she looked kind of cute. God help him. Another few minutes of this and he'd cave for sure.

"But I'm a night owl," she said. "Usually I work until past midnight."

Midnight. The time when fantasies ramped up and . . . No. Luke refused to weaken.

"I'll be back to check on you in the morning."

There. No harm, no foul. He was a decent guy who didn't take advantage of women with sprained ankles. He ought to

144

be proud of himself.

"Hey, Luke," Josie piped up. "Knock, knock."

"What?"

"It's a joke. A knock-knock joke. They're kind of my thing," she explained. "Come on. Knock, knock."

"Oookay." It wouldn't hurt to play along. Pausing beside the sofa, Luke glanced down at her. "Who's there?"

"Leena."

"Leena who?"

"Leena little closer. I want that good night kiss we talked about."

Surprised, Luke couldn't help but grin. The joke was corny, but the thought behind it wasn't. Neither was the expectant, suddenly vulnerable look on Josie's face. She clutched the TV remote against her chest and stared up at him, every ounce of bravado gone.

Yes, his mind prodded, but his body was already one step ahead. Luke knelt with one knee on the sofa cushion, feeling himself dip toward her. He was tired of resisting this, tired of saying no. One little good night kiss wouldn't hurt.

Hell, yes, his mind urged again, but his body had already voted to put one hand over Josie's and brace the other on the

145

back of the sofa. All the better to be nearer . . . nearer.

Luke rubbed his thumb over the back of her hand, enjoying the first real sensual contact they'd made. Josie felt good. Soft, warm, feminine. He smiled at her, and decided right then that he'd been an idiot not to touch her sooner. He couldn't remember what he'd been waiting for.

"If this were a real date," he said, letting his gaze drop to her mouth, "I'd already have done this."

"If this were a real date," she replied, sounding breathless, "we'd be way behind. You'd better hurry up."

"Uh-uh. I like to take it slow."

Demonstrating, he lowered his lips to hers. He kissed her . . . once. It was all he could trust himself to do.

When he raised his head, Josie opened her eyes. She lay back against the sofa cushions, looking dazzled. And irresistible.

"The hell with slow," he announced, and kissed her again.

This time, Luke brought his mouth to hers and felt the whole room spin. This kiss was small, the barest brush of his lips against hers, but it was enough to make him realize that kissing Josie was probably an even bigger gamble than playing poker with a showgirl.

For one thing, he was twice as likely to lose his shorts.

"Luke," Josie breathed. "Luke."

He pulled back slightly. Josie put her hand on his chest, spreading her palm over the front of his T-shirt. He felt the warmth of her touch and instantly wanted more. Their gazes met. There was something about the look in her eyes . . . something as intoxicating as the softness of her skin.

"I can't believe I didn't even know you until this morning," she said.

"I can't believe I waited so long to kiss you."

"Me, either." She smiled. "So how come I'm still waiting for a repeat performance?"

As far as invitations went, they didn't get any clearer than that. More than willing to oblige, Luke cupped her cheek in his hand. He leaned nearer. Another kiss, this one —

A blaring horn sounded outside.

Josie jerked. "What's that?"

It sounded again. Luke glanced up just as a sweep of headlights lit the room, then vanished. Gravel crunched outside as a vehicle rounded the drive.

Oh, shit. With a jolt, Luke remembered

where he was supposed to be tonight.

"Gotta run," he said.

With a hasty final kiss, he left for the carriage house.

Seven

Happily ensconced on the pool deck of the cruise ship S.S. *Extravaganza*, Tallulah reclined on her favorite blue-and-white-striped deck chair. For the past two days, she'd been up to her eyeballs in cocktails, exotic buffets, and mischief. As far as she was concerned, that meant everything was perfect.

"How's that mai tai, Ambrose?"

"It's eleven o'clock in the morning," her attorney said, turning his head on his matching deck chair. He squinted against the sunlight bouncing from the azure pool. "I'm not drinking a mai tai. I'm drinking orange juice."

"You always were an old fuddy-duddy."

"You always were a busybody."

"Damned straight." Tallulah adjusted her rhinestone cat's-eye sunglasses. "How else would I know what's right for you?"

Ambrose smiled faintly. "Me and everyone else."

"Exactly. Speaking of which, what did

you find out about our friend, the concierge? You followed up last week as I
asked you to, didn't you?"

"Yes. She's very satisfactorily settled in
at your lodge property in Aspen. And before you ask, your psychic advisor is doing
well, also." Ambrose adjusted his wide-
brimmed sun hat and crossed his linen-
pants-covered legs. He grimaced, probably
at the tropical heat. "Allowing her to turn
Ernest's mail order home siding business
into a psychic hotline was an excellent
idea."

"Yes. I knew it would be."

"Of that, I have no doubt at all. You are
never less than one thousand percent
pleased with yourself."

He was correct, of course. Satisfied with
the status of her latest protégés, Tallulah
beckoned a cabana boy. She ordered a
second mai tai, a plate of scrambled eggs
with bacon, and a massage reservation at
the *Extravaganza*'s spa. She wanted to be
completely relaxed by the time they
reached Barbados — and, after that,
Martinique.

"Oh, and young man?" she added,
calling him back. "Tack on a massage for
yourself, too. My treat. You look as if you
could use one."

150

His face brightened. "I will, ma'am. Thank you, ma'am!"

"You can thank me by not calling me ma'am. I am not a thousand years old." She made her expression as stern as possible. "Now, scoot."

Tallulah shooed the boy away, wanting him gone before she accidentally broke into a smile. She dreaded the thought of becoming one of those cutesy little old ladies — the ones who knit booties and wore pastels and dyed their hair blue. She did everything she could to prevent it.

However, she did believe in rewarding people who deserved rewarding. People like the cabana boy. Ambrose. Her friends, the former concierge and the psychic. And that redheaded showgirl, the one who'd reminded Tallulah of herself.

"What was that hotsy totsy's name?" she asked Ambrose, gazing critically at her scarlet pedicure as she tried to remember. "The one who Heimliched me at Ernest's casino?"

"Josie." Looking pained, Ambrose held up his copy of *USA Today* so it shielded him from the sunlight. "Josie Day."

"That's right. The trailer park girl. She claimed her reward for saving me, didn't she?"

"Yes. Eventually."

"Stubborn bit of baggage." Secretly proud of the girl for not being grabby, Tallulah paused. She thought about it. Damn it. Her memory just wasn't what it used to be. "What was her reward again?"

"Blue Moon."

"Blue Moon? That sounds like a golden oldie from the fifties." She scoffed, extending her arm to admire the clink of her vintage Lucite bangle bracelets. Once upon a time, she'd been quite the fashion plate. Still was, if you asked her. "You're making that up."

"Your family estate," Ambrose reminded patiently. "In Donovan's Corner. Arizona."

"Ahhh. The Grand Canyon state. We must visit there again sometime."

Ambrose remained tactfully silent. He didn't like to travel, the old codger. He'd rather stay home with his newspaper and his *Wheel of Fortune* and his dreary dietician-approved meals and never have any adventure at all.

Recognizing a hopeless case when he was lounging right next to her, Tallulah let the conversation lapse. She passed the time while waiting for her next mai tai by watching several men swim laps across the pool. They were wonderfully distracting,

152

every one of them bronzed and fit and athletic.

In their wake, a lone woman in a swim cap breast-stroked slowly. Her wrinkled face glistened with water each time she bobbed upward. Her arms were crepey, her skin freckled, her suit a practical black. She completed seven laps, each one wobbly but effective . . . each one solitary.

Go faster, Tallulah urged her silently. *Catch up.* But before long it was too late. All the men finished their laps. They climbed out of the pool and stood laughing on its tiled deck while they toweled off. None of them noticed the woman. Alone in the pool, she went on swimming. One, two. One, two.

Tallulah looked away.

"Ambrose, you've had too much sun," she announced, grabbing the newspaper from her startled attorney. "You look like a lobster. Let's head over to the sing-along piano bar and see what's shaking."

Despite what Luke had told Josie about the house being important to him, most of his time at Blue Moon was not spent there. Most of his time was spent in the carriage house, the big square building about two hundred yards south of the mansion at the

153

edge of the weedy lawn. It wasn't perfect. Hell, when he'd arrived there the place had been barely standing. But Luke had commandeered it anyway, and had never looked back.

The top half — formerly an apartment for the family's driver — became his living space, stripped down to its basics and filled with a few pieces of furniture he'd salvaged from the main house. The bottom half — formerly parking for the family's long-gone buggies and Buicks — became a garage, outfitted with as many tools and as much mechanical and diagnostic equipment as he'd been able to shoehorn in . . . and afford.

Some of the items were castoffs liberated from Donovan & Sons' tax-deductible donations pile, like the drill press and the hydraulic motorcycle lift. Others were contributions from friends, like the gas welder. Some of the tools he'd owned for years; a few were straightforward junkyard refugees. Luke didn't care. The important thing was that the whole setup belonged to him. It was the key to his future.

"Ha! Your dad would freak out if he could see you now."

At the sound of that familiar voice, Luke glanced up. Just as he'd expected, his buddy TJ Hardison stood at the bottom of the carriage house stairs. His gelled-up hair looked as though it had seen the wrong side of a blender. His eyebrow ring glinted in the light shining through the open carriage house doors. His Spiderman logo T-shirt was about as mature as the wiseass grin on his face.

He shook his head. "How the mighty have fallen."

"Bite me, Hardison," Luke said cheerfully. "The only thing that's 'fallen' around here is your IQ."

"Ouch." Chuckling, TJ meandered past a pair of half-rebuilt Indian Scouts and a prime '77 Harley-Davidson XLCR. He gave both motorcycles admiring looks. "You, my friend, are a grumpy asshole in the morning."

"Beats being a dickhead all day."

They both grinned. With their usual greeting out of the way, Luke squinted at the front shock he'd been disassembling. It belonged to a BMW cycle TJ had delivered last night. He'd towed it here from L.A. on the brand-new trailer hitched to the back of his brand-new pickup. Luke should have been expecting him, but he'd been otherwise occupied.

That was probably obvious, given the

way he'd bolted out of the main house to meet TJ last night. He hadn't wanted his handyman cover blown. But aside from a curious glance at the lights on in the mansion, TJ hadn't asked for details, and Luke hadn't volunteered any.

That was what women didn't understand, Luke thought as he jimmied the bottom of the shock casing and removed it. Well, that and the crucial importance of NBA playoffs. Not everything needed to be talked to death. Take TJ. He stood munching a corn dog he must have found upstairs, occasionally dipping it in the gallon jar of mustard he'd football-carried in with him. But did Luke ask him why? Hell, no. He didn't care.

Blinking against the tang of mustard filling his nostrils, Luke examined the shock. He nodded toward the tool bench. "Hand me that 9mm wrench. Whoever owns this bike beat it all to hell and back again."

"I know," TJ mumbled around a mouthful. "It belongs to one of those motorcycle club weenies in the corporate office. More money than smarts. He's practically wrecked the thing — that's why I brought it to you. I know you like a challenge." Using the corn dog as a pointer, he indicated

156

the BMW cycle. "If you can't fix that bike, nobody can."

"Enough with the pep talk, Lombardi. Hand over the —" Luke stopped, suddenly realizing what TJ had said. He gave him a sharp look. "You told him you were bringing it to me?"

"What do you think I am, stupid?"

"We've already covered that."

TJ flipped him the finger.

"Fine." Luke held out his oil-smeared palm. "Wrench?"

"Get it yourself." TJ swabbed at a mustard drip on Spidey's screen-printed leg. He gave up with a shrug. "I'm not your freaking assistant."

"I know. You're my dad's freaking assistant."

"Freaking *spy*," TJ specified, his wiseass grin in place again. "I'm Daddy Donovan's eyes and ears, reporting in on his former pride and joy. Remember?"

"I remember." Luke frowned. He didn't want to think about what TJ was *supposed* to be doing here in Donovan's Corner — keeping tabs on Luke, then reporting everything he discovered back to Robert Donovan. "But I don't think *you* do. The wrench is that long silver thing over there. See?"

Helpfully, he pointed.

"All *right,* you damned nag. Being around you is like having a wife or something."

TJ stuck his corn dog in the mustard like a candle on a birthday cake, then slouched to the tool bench. He wiped his hands on his baggy jeans — every inch the trained mechanic who'd learned not to sully the tools. He retrieved the wrench.

"Thanks."

TJ plucked out his corn dog, saluted with it, then went on munching.

Luke raised his eyebrows.

"I know. I should've brought you one," TJ said, waggling the dog. "But I didn't think you'd eat it."

Luke waited, knowing there was more to come. He hadn't spent the past five or six years around TJ without figuring out a few things about him.

He didn't disappoint.

"Dude, you're slipping." TJ shook his head sorrowfully. "I saw a box of Wheaties in your kitchen. Wheaties!"

"Hey. It's the breakfast of champions."

"It's the breakfast of kids. Or old geezers with their pants pulled up to their armpits. Don't tell me you've gone soft out here in the country."

"I'm about as soft as this casing." Luke thumped on the solid metal shock, preparing to pry off the top piece so he could test the hydraulic unit. "Besides, what are you, the bachelor police?"

"If I was, you'd be *so* busted."

"Like hell, I would. I've got a sink full of dirty dishes and my socks don't match. I think." He frowned, considering it. "Who knows? Anyway, I've got a gallon of ketchup to go with that mustard. So you can just back off."

TJ nodded. "Excellent."

They were back on even footing. All bachelors understood Luke's theory of grocery shopping. If a little was good, a lot was better. Buying massive quantities of everything ensured you only had to schlep a shopping cart once every few months. Hence, two gallons of condiments and a fridge full of economy size corn dogs. He'd grabbed both on a search-and-destroy mission through the warehouse zone of the local Shop 'N Save.

"You've got to watch yourself, though." TJ peered at the half-built carburetor on the nearby worktable, then at the rejiggered set of Earles forks by the window. "You get to liking it out here, you'll never come back to L.A."

Luke shook his head. "This is strictly temporary. Once I've sold Blue Moon and converted this place into cash, all this stuff is moving into a real shop." He scanned the carriage house, seeing past its hundred-year-old makeshift space to the modern mechanic's shop he planned to buy when he left Donovan's Corner. "It's only a matter of time."

"Yeah? You're that close?" Looking interested, TJ chomped the last bite of his corn dog. He started in on the spare he'd tucked in the back pocket of his jeans, first dipping it in the tub o' mustard. "Is that why you were working inside the house last night? Getting it ready to show to buyers?"

The last thing Luke wanted to do was discuss what he'd been doing last night. He grimaced, twisting the shock cover. "This is stuck. I'm going to need the blowtorch to heat it up."

"Come on," TJ prompted, not buying it for an instant. "You looked like *something* was going on."

With a sigh, Luke glanced up. He'd dodged this conversation last night, thanks to a few beers and the Suns game he and TJ had watched on TV after unloading the bike. He wouldn't be so lucky twice.

"You reporting this to my father?"

160

"Hell, no. He's still chewing on that piece of info I gave him last time." TJ grinned.

"What, that I'm spending all my time building a tree house out of empty Budweiser bottles?"

TJ chuckled, obviously pleased. "Yeah. That was a good one. I made you a drunk *and* a loony, both at the same time."

"Right. Really good." Luke rolled his eyes, then got to his feet. Giving up on the BMW's shock for now, he grabbed a rag to wipe his hands with. "You're very efficient."

Given the outlandish stories TJ had been reporting, Luke almost felt sorry for his dad. Thanks to TJ's flair for the dramatic, he'd been suckered into buying into some pretty bizarre things. But Robert Donovan had always been prepared to believe the worst about Luke. A long line of former headmasters, college deans, and European friends of the family had proven that.

He remembered why his father thought it was necessary to send TJ to spy on him in the first place, and all warmhearted feelings evaporated.

"Hell, yeah, I'm efficient," TJ agreed, not noticing Luke's frown. "Efficient enough to snag myself a new truck *and* a new trailer to go with it. I've gotta say, the

161

bribes are a nice perk of the corporate family spy business. Who knew?"

Cheerfully unbothered that he was both pretending to be spying *and* lying about what he'd learned to the man who'd hired him to do so, TJ put down his mustard. He wiped his mouth with the hem of his Spidey shirt, then glanced outside.

"I dunno. I'd be tempted to keep this place," he said. "It's not bad. Sort of like the Playboy Mansion, only without the bunnies. You could fix it up and keep it for weekends."

"I can't. It's either this or my mechanic's shop."

Luke wanted that mechanic's shop. Aside from disappointing his family, fixing things was his major talent. At the age of four, he'd recalibrated his Big Wheel for more torque. At fourteen, he'd spent shop class building his first street racer. He loved taking apart an engine and rebuilding it again. When he was fixing something, he could forget everything else.

"Dude, the last time I checked, your family owned one of the biggest freight trucking empires in the country," TJ pointed out. "Not to mention a whole bunch of other stuff. I hate to break it to you, but you're practically a freaking tycoon. You're rich. Wealthy. Loaded. Well-to-do. *Rolling* in dough."

"Not anymore."

TJ scoffed. "That's only temporary. You go to your dad, you apologize, everything's cool again."

"No. Screw that." Luke crossed his arms, glancing down at the tattoos that set him apart from his father's upper-crust, cocktails-and-country-club life. He'd never been able to satisfy Robert Donovan. He was finished trying. This might be the latest in a long line of standoffs, but this one had an important difference. It was permanent.

"Whatever. It's your stupid inheritance that's on the line, not mine." TJ sat on a '76 Yamaha TT500 flat tracker. He pretended to steer, making revving sounds like the oversize kid he was. "The longer you hold out in this feud, the longer my payola lasts."

"Glad I can keep your cash cow mooing."

"Hey. You're just lucky I'm an *honest* spy."

Luke had to admit TJ was right. He'd met TJ during one of his corporate stints at Donovan & Sons, and they'd hit it off right away. When TJ had first come to visit

163

him after Luke's exile to Blue Moon, Luke hadn't suspected a thing . . . until TJ had explained that his father had asked him to check up on his wayward son and report back. Nothing like a little corporate espionage — with a family feud twist.

"You suck as a spy," Luke had told TJ then, hardly able to believe the lengths to which his father would go to keep tabs on him. "You're not supposed to tell me what you're up to."

But TJ had laughed off the idea. "Why not? It's more fun this way. I'm a freakin' double agent. Besides, it serves your dad right for checking up on you at all."

Luke couldn't help but agree. Especially with his father's last words ringing in his ears.

If you want to live like a blue-collar grease monkey, you go right ahead. But don't expect me to respect you for it.

It sounded harsh. It sure as hell had felt that way. But Luke should have expected it. After all, Robert Donovan wasn't the kind of man who allowed his wishes to be ignored — and that was exactly what Luke had done.

He'd been stuck in the corporate offices of Donovan & Sons, fielding mounds of paperwork in an attempt to fulfill the optimistic "& Sons" portion of the company letterhead. He'd been trying to turn his attention from carburetors to spreadsheets, from disassembling big rigs to managing the men who drove them. But it was no use. Luke didn't want to be upstairs having some candy-ass meeting with the rest of the company vice presidents. He wanted to be downstairs taking apart diesel engines with the company mechanics.

That afternoon, Robert Donovan had discovered his only son in the shop — suit jacket and tie thrown to the side, both hands full of engine parts, rolled-up shirtsleeves blackened with motor oil. He threatened to disinherit Luke on the spot if he didn't quit tinkering with the freight company's trucks and start managing the freight company's paperwork.

Luke had refused.

Apparently, given Luke's past, that had been the last straw. To everyone's surprise but Luke's, his father made good on his threat. Overnight, Luke found himself stripped of his trust fund, his various residences, his cars, and most of his resources. All he'd had left was Blue Moon — an estate his father couldn't touch because Luke's grandfather had bequeathed it to him directly.

Luke figured that part pissed off his father to no end. He didn't know for sure. They hadn't spoken since that day.

To hear TJ tell it, Luke's dad had gotten softhearted afterward. He'd felt sorry for the way he'd treated his only son, and had sent TJ to make sure Luke was "handling things okay." Luke didn't buy it for a second. As far as he could tell, the only thing Robert Donovan cared about — had ever cared about — was his freight trucking empire.

The only thing Luke cared about, he told himself now, was proving that he could succeed on his own terms — proving that success *could* be found outside a corporate executive office. So he'd been cut off from the family fortune. Big deal. Luke didn't care about passing up bucketsful of cash and country club memberships. What he cared about was being publicly splintered from the family tree. That hurt.

And he had too much pride to let it continue.

If it was the last thing he did, Luke intended to make his mark . . . *his* way. Blue Moon would provide the seed money, and his mechanic's shop would provide the means. He'd force his father to respect him — and, in the process, turn the famous

Donovan determination in a whole new direction.

"What you need in this place," TJ said thoughtfully, "is a girlie calendar. You know. One of those freebies from a hubcap company or something. You don't have a single picture of a hot babe in a bikini lounging on the hood of a Mustang."

"Does it have to be a Mustang?" Luke grinned. "Because I'm a motorcycle mechanic."

"Seriously. You call yourself a professional, but — *hang on*. Who's *that?*"

TJ pointed outside. His mouth hung open. A flush rose on his face, making his cheeks match Spidey's superhero outfit.

Hell. Those signs could only mean one thing. TJ had just spotted Josie.

To make sure, Luke went to the window. Through its smeared glass, he saw his showgirl stowaway. She was decked out in some kind of miniskirt-plus-tank-top combo, crutches, and a determined expression that could not bode well for anyone in her path. Another minute and she'd make her way across the weeds to the carriage house.

"I take it back," TJ said, sounding awed. "You don't need a girlie calendar. You just need to look out your window once in a

167

while. *Damn.* No wonder you didn't tell me what you were doing last night. You were doing *her.*"

"Shut up, Hardison." Luke shoved his hand through his hair, acutely aware, all of a sudden, that he hadn't showered yet. He'd gotten up, brushed his teeth, and started disassembling the shock on the BMW bike. He'd planned to shower afterward. "You don't know what you're talking about."

Hastily, Luke wiped his hands on the shop rag again. Then he pulled down his T-shirt and checked his reflection in the shiny chrome of a Kawasaki's side mirror. He was in the midst of cupping his hand over his mouth to check his breath when TJ turned around.

And caught him.

TJ's eyes widened. "You're . . . what's it called? *Primping!* Jesus, Donovan. What the hell's the matter with —"

He broke off. Comprehension dawned.

Frowning, Luke jerked his hands down. It didn't help. His breath was fine. But he felt a nearly overwhelming urge to go upstairs and shower. Maybe even to shave. All in the thirty seconds before Josie got there.

"What's the matter?" TJ asked, grinning

wider than ever before. "Trying to figure out whether or not your socks and shirt match?"

Luke glanced down. God help him.

"Holy shit." TJ strode closer. He peered at Luke like a bratty kid gawking at the monkeys in the zoo. "I honestly don't believe it. You've got it baaaad for this girl."

"I do not." Damn it. If TJ would move his big fat head, Luke would be able to see how far Josie had made it toward the carriage house. "What do you know?"

"I know *plenty*." Looking irritatingly self-satisfied, TJ crossed his arms over his chest. Casually, he scraped his thumbnail over the dried mustard on his T-shirt. "I know you're probably hoping there's still time to slap on some Aqua Velva and *really* wow her."

Luke crossed his arms, ignoring him.

"I know I'm dying to find out who this mystery woman is."

Luke scoffed.

"I know," TJ said, "that you're probably praying I don't go outside right now and introduce myself to her."

Luke's insides froze. "You wouldn't dare."

"Oh, yeah?" TJ glanced outside. "Watch me."

Grinning, he bolted for the open carriage house doors.

Luke scrambled after him, one arm extended. He caught a whiff of mustard, a fleeting fistful of T-shirt, and then . . . nada. TJ twisted like a championship running back breaking a tackle, laughed like a hyena, and bounded into the Arizona sunshine.

Eight

For the fourth time since Josie had left the main house, one of her crutches sank in the grass and got stuck. Expertly shifting her weight to the opposite side, she steadied herself. She pulled. The crutch popped free, its rubber tip coated with mud and a few strands of Bermuda. It was a good thing she'd had a little practice with these things in the past. Maneuvering in them was no problem for her.

She raised her head and got her bearings. Behind her lay the house. Turning to view it from here, Josie could almost imagine the grandeur it must have possessed once, in its golden age. She sighed, savoring the thought.

Well, okay — she could picture it if she squinted. But it was still there someplace. She was sure. Which was part of the reason she was still here and not trying to drag her stuff back to her convertible.

She looked around some more. To the sides, weedy lawn greeted her, bordered

171

with pine trees and the occasional scrub oak. To the front, the squared-off carriage house stood — her destination. She set off again.

Male laughter burst into the stillness.

Huh? That didn't sound like Luke. She hadn't expected him to be here working so early, either. Frowning, Josie paused.

An instant later, someone ran from the carriage house. He came across the weeds straight toward her. She had just enough time to register a man in a cartoon T-shirt, baggy jeans, and wild hair. She didn't recognize him. But she did recognize Luke in hot pursuit.

He had to be chasing the intruder for a reason. It didn't look as though he was going to catch up, either.

Josie steadied herself. This morning, she'd decided to stay at Blue Moon — which made this her new home. She was finished being pushed around. Whoever this guy was, she was ready for him. She stuck out her crutch.

Too late, the man saw it. His eyes widened. "Whoa!"

He landed with a thud.

Josie raised her crutch, getting ready for a second burst of action. After all, there was no telling how fast a runner Luke re-

172

ally was. He might not get here in time. Tensed, she waited. At her feet, the man rolled over on the grass.

He'd only tripped. She was going to have to whack him.

"Wait!" Luke yelled.

Good. She didn't really want to whack him.

Luke grabbed the man by the shirt. Yelling something, he hauled him up. They tussled. Uh-oh. Judging by the look in Luke's eyes, he'd tangled with this guy before. Judging by the goggle-eyed look on the man's face, he knew what was coming to him. It probably *wasn't* a nice cozy hug.

Josie crutched herself backward, staring. She wished she'd brought her cell phone. But she'd only been setting out on a tour of those outbuildings Luke had mentioned yesterday. She hadn't expected to need to dial 911 on the way.

On the other hand, Luke looked kind of crazy. He was babbling something about Aqua Velva.

"Hang on. Don't hit him!" Warily, she held up both hands, wanting to stop the impending fight but knowing better than to actually insert herself in the middle of it. "I'll go inside and call 911. You stay here and hold him."

Yeah, that was it. She was a woman with a plan. Feeling proud of herself for helping apprehend the intruder — and helping prevent a violent, action-movie-style fist-fight — Josie turned around. She adjusted her crutches, preparing for action.

"Hit me?" the man asked, scoffing.

"Hit him?" Luke asked, cheering up.

Clearly, the idea of hitting hadn't occurred to either of them.

Confused, Josie turned again. Something was going on here. She glanced at Luke. "You weren't going to hit him?"

"Nah. I'd say you did a pretty good job of that already." He glanced approvingly at her crutch. "Nice work. When in doubt about the crazy guy headed your way, just whack him."

"I didn't whack him. I tripped him. There's a difference."

"Yeah. Semantics."

"It's not 'semantics.'" Affronted, Josie raised her chin. "It's a whole different thing. You're making me out to be some kind of bully, and I'm not."

"I'll bet TJ here would disagree. Right, TJ?"

"I landed on something vital," the man muttered, one hand on his forehead. "I think I have a concussion."

174

"Vital?" Luke asked. "You landed on your ass."

They argued for a minute — in remarkably good spirits, given the situation. Josie couldn't listen.

"TJ?" she repeated. Uh-oh. "TJ? You *know* him?"

They both looked at her.

Luke nodded. "Yeah."

TJ nodded. "Yeah."

They went back to bickering — in that idiotic way men had of relating to each other by slinging insults, swearing, and grinning like goons.

Sheesh. There was no help for it. Somebody was going to have to act like an adult here. Josie put her thumb and forefinger in her mouth and issued her standard whistle.

They both gawked at her, looking puzzled.

"Update, please," she said.

"Right." Luke released his grip on TJ. "Josie, this is TJ. Championship crybaby —"

"Arrogant prick," TJ muttered, his dark look aimed squarely at Luke.

"— and a friend of mine from L.A. TJ, Josie."

"Charmed, I'm sure," TJ said, smoothing a fist-sized wrinkle from the shoulder of his T-shirt. He summoned up a grin. "Next time, let's watch out for the knees, okay?"

Despite his smile, Josie was filled with remorse. She levered herself closer on her crutches. Now that TJ wasn't running like a lunatic, he looked like a pretty ordinary guy. Or more accurately, like a pierced, gelled, and cartoonified twenty-five-year-old man-child.

"I'm sorry," she said. "Really. I thought you were one of the teenagers Luke told me about." She glanced at Luke to validate her story. He offered a brief nod. "The ones who come here to vandalize the place."

Awkwardly, she patted TJ on the shoulder. He felt nearly as solid as Luke — which explained the *thud* he'd made when he went down. The realization made her feel twice as bad.

"I guess my self-defense instincts took over." She indicated her crutch. "I took a class last year. I hope you're okay."

TJ grunted. He rubbed his shin. "Remind me not to meet you in a dark alley."

"Yeah," Luke agreed. "I'm pretty sure she could take you."

Josie whirled on him. "I thought he was stealing something from the carriage house! I swear I did."

"That's what I'm here for. I would have caught him."

She didn't buy it. "Says you. He was miles ahead of you."

"Miles? Try two feet."

"Dude, she's right. It was *miles*." TJ grinned.

Luke shot him an aggravated look.

"I like you." Josie patted TJ's shoulder again, then looked him up and down to assess his injuries. Her tour of the outbuildings could wait, she decided. "I'm really sorry about tripping you. Come on. Let's go inside and get you an ice pack. We've got *tons* of frozen peas."

They started toward the house.

"Tons?" Luke trailed them, sounding aggrieved. "Try four bags."

"Dude." At her side, TJ tossed back a wise guy's grin. "The lady's always right."

"We're going to get along great, TJ," Josie said. "I can tell already."

Josie made her way to the refrigerator in Blue Moon's decrepit kitchen. She felt keenly aware that she was technically entertaining a guest — TJ — and the place was a wreck. In the light of day, the room looked even worse than she remembered. Sure, the kitchen had all the basic ameni-

177

ties — electricity, plumbing, and backup Ding Dongs — but it lacked a certain charm. It also lacked countertops that weren't cracked, cabinets that possessed doors, and a floor that didn't look like a fugitive from the grime police.

Oh, well. It wouldn't be this for long. Not if Josie had anything to say about it. Forcing herself to look on the bright side, she tucked a bag of frozen peas beneath her arm. She nudged the freezer door shut with her shoulder, then turned.

Luke was there.

If possible, he looked even better than he had yesterday — despite his whisker stubble, carefree wrinkled T-shirt, and old jeans. Frankly, those things only added to his bad-boy appeal. And they were all temporary. Changeable. The essentials were inherent — six-feet-whatever of capable muscles, masculine intensity, and unbridled sex appeal.

She stifled a sigh — of, she had to admit, unbridled lust.

"We need to talk," he said.

That put a damper on her baser instincts. "Don't you think it's too soon in our relationship for a 'talk'?"

"I'm serious." He took the peas.

"Hey! I need those to give to TJ." She

gestured toward him. He sat in one of the mismatched chairs at the scrubbed pine butler's table, examining his knee.

"Okay." Luke raised his arm like a quarterback. The bag of peas sailed through the air.

"Thanks, dude!"

"There. It's taken care of."

Josie cast a worried glance at TJ. He seemed happy.

"All right," she said. "What's on your mind?"

In answer, Luke put his hand on her arm. He helped her to the hallway where they could have some privacy, taking time for her crutch-using progress. Judging by his expression, this was serious. Once they were out of sight of the kitchen, he backed her against the wainscoting.

Josie glanced up at him curiously.

"Comfortable?"

"Ummm." She adjusted her crutches, wondering what was up. "I guess so."

"Then here's what's on my mind," Luke said, and lowered his mouth to hers.

Josie gave a little yelp of surprise. This wasn't smart, it wasn't polite, it wasn't . . . it wasn't going to stop anytime soon. At the realization, she melted. She just couldn't help it. The thrill of kissing Luke

179

overrode every other consideration — even the wainscoting gouging her butt.

Somehow, Luke's kiss drove every practical thought out of her head. All she could think about were his talented hands, gliding from her hips to her rib cage. All she could sense was the hard-bodied length of him. All she could want was . . . *this*. This, for a really long time.

Just as it had last night, Luke's kiss started out slow. It built to a seductive middle, ended on a passionate note, and promised lots more to come. Caught up in it, Josie curled her fingers in his T-shirt and just held on. His hand cupped the back of her head, his hip pressed her against the wall, his warmth and strength surrounded her. She loved that he was big enough to stand up to her height (which was tall), tough enough to silence her protests (which were few), and gentle enough to make her yearn for even more . . . more, more, more.

With an inner shrug, Josie surrendered completely. She'd always been impulsive. Sometimes that quality had its advantages. Hanging on to Luke for leverage, she threw herself into kissing him. The more the merrier. The more the better? She couldn't remember that saying right now and she didn't much care.

"I've wanted to do that since last night," Luke said, coming up for air.

Feeling equally breathless, Josie sucked in a gulp of oxygen. "Me, t—"

But then he was kissing her again, cutting off her words as though he simply couldn't resist her, and Josie couldn't help but go along for the ride. She was rewarded with an even deeper kiss, an even more inventive, more sensual, more amazing kiss than before. Enthusiastically, she kissed him back.

She and Luke fit together perfectly, with none of the awkward head-turning or nose-bumping that sometimes doomed otherwise good kisses. They were meant to do this. Obviously. Josie wasn't a woman who believed in fighting fate. She decided it that instant. She also decided she wanted more.

Unfortunately, Luke seemed wedded to his "take it slow" philosophy. He ended the kiss, then leaned back just enough that their foreheads touched. His smile felt endearing, sexy . . . intimate.

"Wow," she breathed. "Who says men don't know how to communicate?"

"I'm available for a good conversation anytime. Day or night. Discussion, chitchat, idle gossip . . . you name it."

"I don't usually talk this much with men I've just met."

"I'm the exception to the rule." His grin widened in a spectacularly macho way. "Why fight it?"

Josie didn't want to. She'd never felt this way about any man, especially not this quickly. Something about Luke just seemed to . . . *fit* with her. She was glad she hadn't left town yesterday. Fighting her impulsive instincts — every one of which had been screaming for her to bail out of Donovan's Corner — hadn't come naturally. But she'd done it.

Well, she'd done it with a little "kidnapping" help from Luke. But she deserved some of the credit, too. No one who knew her would have believed she'd give a second thought to anything. Maybe there was something to be said for not making snap decisions after all.

"Nice skirt," Luke said, drawing her attention.

He lowered his hand to the hem of her pink terry cloth mini. A look of unadulterated masculine appreciation lit his face. Her skirt might as well have been transparent — he couldn't possibly have looked any happier to see her in it.

"It's not as immodest as it seems. The panties match."

Okay, she was wrong. He *could* look happier to see her in it.

"I mean they're the kind that are designed to be seen. Pink boy-cut shorts."

Luke groaned. "You're killing me." He slid his finger along her hemline, tracing it to the back of her skirt. "I'll bet you don't look anything like a boy in this, no matter what kind of shorts you're wearing."

She definitely *felt* all woman. Especially with his heavy-lidded gaze traveling up and down her body like that, making her feel all tingly and zingy and wonderful. But then Josie remembered what had been bugging her about seeing Luke this morning, and that good feeling faded a little.

"Hey. Where'd you run off to last night?"

"It's not important." *Whoosh* went his fingertip along her skirt hem. "It's over now."

"I want to know."

Luke gazed down, looking absorbed. "There can't be more than twelve inches of fabric in this skirt."

"I'm five-nine. There's plenty of fabric in it." She grabbed his hand. "Look, if you have a girlfriend —"

That broke the spell. "No. It was TJ. Last night."

"TJ, with the horn-blowing?" Relief swamped her. It was stupid, but there it was. She was glad Luke didn't have a girl-friend — especially given the kinds of thoughts she'd been entertaining about him. "TJ, with the truck and the trailer at-tached to it? That was TJ last night?"

Luke's gaze swept up. His eyes sparkled. "You peeked."

Duh. Of course she'd peeked. "I did not!"

"You peeked out the window after I left. Admit it."

"I'll do no such thing." Damn those tissue-thin Blue Moon curtains. He must have seen her.

"If you didn't peek, how did you know it was a truck last night? With a trailer? You couldn't have seen all that from where you were sitting."

With dignity, Josie straightened. "I might have gotten a *glimpse* of it when I passed by the window. But I was only looking for the TV remote."

"The TV remote I put in your hand be-fore I left?"

He was such a know-it-all. "It slipped."

"Mmm-hmm."

184

Was it just her, or did he look pleased that she'd made a goofball of herself by spying on him? Josie decided she didn't care.

"I have to go take care of TJ," she announced, lifting her chin. She turned on her crutches. "I'm the one who whacked him. I mean, *tripped* him. Accidentally. He's my responsibility."

"Careful with those frozen peas," Luke called after her. "I hear those bags are *slippery.*"

The next few hours with Luke were the nicest — and longest — second date Josie had ever had. They sat in the kitchen mainlining a breakfast of coffee and Ding Dongs (which Luke *had* to have bought in bulk), laughing and talking, and she couldn't remember ever feeling so relaxed on a date.

Okay, so a hard-liner probably would have said it wasn't technically a date. First, because TJ was there — and everyone knew that if the guy brought a wingman, the date didn't count. Second, because it hadn't been preceded by an agonizing will-he-or-won't-he wait by the phone. Third, because the good night kiss had come first.

But Josie didn't care. After the string of

185

dates from hell she'd endured lately, being with Luke felt fantastic. She just wanted to enjoy it.

Of course it all fell apart right away. Exactly the way it usually did between men and women . . . the moment she got serious.

"So, I decided you were right, Luke," she said, putting down her coffee as a sense of excitement filled her. "I can't let the busybodies in this town push me around. I'm going to stay at Blue Moon."

"What?"

"You heard me. I'm staying. I woke up this morning and I thought about going back home to Las Vegas, and I just couldn't do it. I couldn't let those bastards get me down."

"Good for you!" TJ raised his Ding Dong in salute.

Luke shot him an aggravated glance. "Shut up, TJ. You don't even know what she's talking about." He looked at Josie. "Are you serious? I thought you were giving up."

She gave a dismissive sound. "That was just the exhaustion talking. I didn't sleep at all before I came here, you know. I just finished my last show for the night and zip" — she made a zooming noise, gesturing sideways — "headed straight here."

"Straight here from Las Vegas?" TJ asked.

She nodded. "I'm a showgirl at Enchanté."

"Sweet." TJ nodded approvingly.

"Or at least I used to be."

Josie gave TJ the capsule version of how she'd inherited Blue Moon from the casino's owner. As she explained, TJ aimed curious glances at Luke. Then he leaned back in his chair.

"So technically, Luke is working for you now," he said when she'd finished. "As a handyman."

"Right," she agreed. Why did TJ look so gleeful about that?

"And you're going to open a dance school here. To train up all the hot new showgirls."

Ah, that explained it. "Not exactly." She smiled at his crestfallen expression. "But once I find some students, I'll be teaching all kinds of dance."

"Cool." Satisfied, TJ went back to his coffee.

"Hey, aren't you happy for me?" Josie asked Luke. She nudged him, confused by his silence. She wanted a reaction. "I realize this means a lot of work for both of us. But you were already going to be painting and shingling and repairing stuff, right? And I can do the cleaning myself. That'll be my specialty, since I don't know squat about fixing up old houses."

She laughed, feeling her usual assurance return. "Then there's the dance studio, of course. We'll need to get mirrors and a ballet barre, and we'll have to polish the floor and put in a sound system. The usual. But after that, it'll be great!"

"Hey, I'll help you!" TJ volunteered, looking just as swept up in the excitement of it all as Josie was. "What the hell, I'm here anyway. I might as well keep busy."

She was touched by his generosity. "Aww, that's so nice of you. But you barely know me, TJ. And I practically maimed you as an introduction."

He waved off her concern.

She *did* need all the help she could get. If TJ was serious . . . "Are you sure?"

"You bet. I'll just —"

"He can't," Luke interrupted, his expression stony. "He's just visiting."

"I'll stay longer." TJ shrugged. "No prob. There's plenty of room."

"You're right about that," Josie agreed. "And don't worry, TJ, I'll pay you. Tallulah's lawyer gave me a small allowance. I guess Tallulah thought I'd want to redecorate or something."

"Tallulah? Luke's aunt, Tallulah?"

"Aunt?" Surprised, she glanced at Luke. He sat with his arms crossed, tattoos practically pulsing with resistance to her plan. "You never said Tallulah was your aunt, Luke."

"It never came up."

"Yes, it did. I'm pretty sure —"

At that moment, Josie realized the truth. Poor Luke. He was stuck doing menial labor at his wealthy aunt's overlooked estate, probably for a pathetic salary. No wonder he hadn't talked about it. He was probably embarrassed.

She vowed right then and there not to mention Tallulah again. She didn't want to make Luke feel any more like the family black sheep — something Josie had lots of experience with — than he already did.

"Anyway," she said brightly, changing the subject, "that doesn't really matter. I'm going to stay and TJ's going to help." She gave him a smile. "You can be Luke's handyman assistant."

"Luke's handyman assistant." TJ chuckled. "Believe me, I can hardly wait."

"See?" Beaming, Josie patted him on the

shoulder. "That's exactly the kind of attitude I'm looking for."

Luke grunted. The spoilsport.

"I don't get it," she said, squaring off with him. "Last night you gave me such a hard time for quitting. Now I'm staying and suddenly you're Grouchy McGrouch. I thought you'd be happy. So what gives?"

"Grouchy McGrouch?" His lips quirked in a small smile.

"That's better. You look slightly less constipated."

His smile vanishing, Luke got up to refresh his coffee. He glanced at the clock. "You'd better get started. In another hour or two, it'll be time to change your mind again."

Josie gaped at him. That was a low blow.

She didn't understand it. She'd expected Luke to be supportive . . . at least now that he'd gotten to know her — and her miniskirt — so much better.

But nobody pushed her around.

"Oh, yeah?" She scraped her chair back and grabbed her crutches, finished with trying to convince him. Actions spoke louder than words anyway. "Well, in another half hour or so, you'll be too busy nailing down roof shingles to care about the state of my mind. So there."

She turned, ready for a good huff out of the kitchen.

Her crutches tripped her up. Rats. They'd make storming out a little tricky. But Josie wasn't one to be held down by circumstances. She raised her chin and levered herself out anyway, with as much attitude as she could muster. It would have been a grand exit — except for feeling Luke's gaze pinned to her backside the whole way.

Stupid miniskirt. Nobody was going to take her seriously as long as she looked like a showgirl, Josie realized. That was another thing that had to change around here. And she knew exactly the way to do it.

The minute the *whap, whap* of Josie's crutches faded from earshot, TJ turned to Luke with a mile-wide grin on his face.

"Great girl. I can see why you're so crazy about her."

"I'm not crazy about her," Luke muttered. "She's a pain in the ass."

"Yeah. But what an ass."

"She can't make up her mind for more than two minutes at a time," Luke complained, staring into his coffee cup. "She's bossy and pushy and ass-high in delusions about what it'll take to fix up this place."

191

"Yeah. But what an ass."

"When she got here, I let it slide," Luke said, feeling his shoulders tense. He didn't know what was the matter with him, but he didn't like it. "I thought, what could it hurt? So she thinks she owns the place. Big deal. She doesn't. She won't hang around long. No harm, no foul."

"Yeah. But what an —"

"Watch it," Luke warned. "Not another word about her ass."

"I *knew* it! You're smitten." TJ grinned like a goon. "You're in loooove. Wait till old man Donovan gets an earful of this."

Luke gave him an evil look. "Don't you have somewhere else to be?"

"Not a chance, dude. Nobody's getting me out of here now. I'm a free agent, re-member? I've got permission from Señor Donovan to hang around Arizona for as long as I need to. Now that I know you'll be taking orders from Josie, I *need* to hang around for a long, long, loooong time."

"Bite me."

"Luke the Handyman. Handyman Luke. Hmmm." TJ gazed at a crack in the ceiling plaster, looking thoughtful. "Sounds like a kids' TV show. You're the new *Teletubbies*."

"The hell I am." Whatever that was. It didn't sound good.

"You're in love with the boss lady. You're in love with the boss lady." TJ got up and grooved around the kitchen, punctuating his chant with several grotesque hip thrusts and a shit-eating grin. "You're in love with the boss lady."

"Knock it off," Luke said. "I am not."

"Crap." TJ froze in mid-gyration. "I think I just dislocated something."

"Probably a few brain cells."

"Come on, Grouchy." TJ limped back to his chair. "Play it straight with me. You can put on that game face all you want, but I know the truth. You fell for this girl the minute you saw her."

"Bullshit." At the skepticism in TJ's face, Luke reconsidered. "Maybe I felt sorry for her. But that's it."

"Right. Sorry enough to drag her into the hallway for a make-out session."

At the memory of that, Luke reconsidered some more. He remembered the feel of Josie in his arms, the sound of her husky moan as he'd kissed her, the softness of her long, barely dressed body pushed against his. They'd fit together.

"Yeah, that happens to me *all* the time," TJ continued, his smart-alecky tone firmly in place. "I meet a girl, realize how pathetically sorry I am for her, and then make out like crazy."

"It was just a kiss." But it had felt like more . . .

"What I don't get," TJ mused, "is why you don't just tell her who you are. I mean, women go for the rich tycoon type."

"I'm not the rich tycoon type. Not anymore."

"You could be, if you apologized to your dad."

Luke frowned. "No woman's worth that."

"Whatever. All I know is, you keep a secret, women find out. They've got lie detectors built into their tits or something. Sooner or later, Josie's going to know the truth."

"If you don't shut up, she'll know right now."

"When she finds out you lied to her about who really owns Blue Moon, she's going to be pissed."

"There's no point telling her something that'll only cause trouble for us both. Besides, it doesn't matter. She'll never last that long." Luke thought of the reception Josie had received in Donovan's Corner and felt sorry for her all over again. "She'll give up and go back to Vegas."

"And leave you heartbroken?" TJ leaned

forward, both hands on his Spidey shirt in a gesture of puppy-dog misery. He mimed blinking back big tears. "No way. You'll never let her go."

Luke ignored him. He'd been caught off guard by Josie's announcement, that was all. But now he realized — he could afford to be nice to her. He could even afford to help fix up Blue Moon for her.

After all, it wasn't as though Josie was going to wind up with Blue Moon in the end. The estate would always be his. Tallulah would make it up to Josie with a different, better property. Josie could start her dance school somewhere else. In the meantime, she needed someplace to stay, right?

Right. Besides, he'd been planning on making those repairs anyway. He needed to, in order to sell the place for top dollar. What difference did it make if Josie thought he was fixing up Blue Moon for her and her doomed dance school?

Luke stood. "Come on. We've got shingling to do."

"Huh?" TJ looked up, comfortably sprawled with his feet on a neighboring chair. "Shingling?"

"That's right, *assistant*. Shingling. And I hear the boss lady is tough. So get your ass out of that chair and start assisting."

Nine

For the next two weeks, Luke worked harder than ever before. He reshingled the porch and parts of the main house. He fixed the rotting staircase, forced the heating system up to code, and started laying new antique-style floorboards in the parlor. He hammered and sawed, hauled and plumbed and caulked. Most of the repairs were basic — necessary because of neglect and the house's long vacancy — but there were a lot of them.

Anybody who saw him would have sworn he was working for Josie. Luke knew there was more to it than that. With every crack in the wall he replastered, he imagined Blue Moon's asking price going up. With every rain gutter he cleared and every broken pipe he soldered, he imagined taking the cash he'd make from the estate and converting it into the motorcycle repair shop he'd dreamed of.

Most often, he pictured the look on his father's face — the look Robert Donovan would wear when he realized that Luke had as much vision and determination as any other Donovan . . . and that he'd created the means to satisfy that vision with his own two hands — *not* his former trust fund.

The whole time TJ stayed at Blue Moon, munching corn dogs and asking Josie about showgirls. Sometimes he worked. Occasionally he mowed the weeds, started water fights with the garden hose, or followed Josie around to make sure she wasn't overdoing it while her sprained ankle healed. The rest of the time he concentrated on being his usual smart-mouthed self — and on getting in the way, preventing Luke from getting to know Josie in the way he'd have preferred to get to know her.

Intimately. Physically. Carnally.

Instead, Luke was pushed into a crash course on Getting to Know Josie — the "G"-rated version. With TJ constantly underfoot, Luke and Josie talked over coffee in the mornings. They talked over bologna sandwiches — the extent of their combined cooking expertise — in the afternoons. They talked, talked, talked over take-out pizza and beer in the evenings. Then the whole cycle started again the next day, punctuated by hammering and sawing and the smells of Lysol and Windex.

The weird thing was, despite his initial pissed-off objections to TJ's presence and the hands-off getting-to-know-Josie routine that had been forced on him, as time went by Luke found himself kind of enjoying it. He liked getting to know Josie in a different way . . . a way he didn't typically get to know women until much later. She was funny, he discovered. A little raunchy. And smarter than she looked.

Not that there was anything wrong with the way she looked. Hell, no. To Luke's eye, she looked terrific — even while wearing something as non-showgirlie as cutoff denim shorts, a tank top, and a pair of elbow-length, yellow vinyl cleaning gloves.

"I think I'm developing a kink for cleaning ladies," he told her, seeing her headed his way one afternoon with a bucket in one hand and a definite sway in her sneakered stride. "The minute you snap on those gloves, I get hot all over."

"That's the thought of me making you pick up a mop," Josie replied with a grin. "It's Cleanaphobia." She kept on going.

At that moment, seeing her smile and

her sassy little march in the opposite direction, Luke would have sworn he felt something special for her. He might even have paused to consider it — if not for TJ's irritating "you're in love with the boss lady" jig from the other side of the room.

Despite Luke's expectations, when it came to the cleaning she'd promised to do, Josie acted less like a spoiled showgirl and more like an ordinary woman. An ordinary woman who got excited over Swiffer dusters and wet-'n'-dry shop vacs, sure. But definitely a regular woman.

"I can't believe you're so cheerful about *cleaning*," he told her one day as she scrubbed the banisters. With vigor. "Most people hate it."

" 'Most people' meaning you?" she'd asked knowingly. But then she'd only shrugged and gazed at the results of her work with a smile. "I don't mind. I've never owned anything before. Now that I do, I want to take care of it."

She did, too. Every day Josie cranked up her boom box and carried it from room to room as she worked, often — once her ankle healed — dancing along with the music.

Luke didn't think she realized she was

doing it. He guessed dancing was so much a part of her, Josie couldn't hear any rhythm without moving. She two-stepped while vacuuming, wiggled her ass like J.Lo while washing windows, swiveled her hips in a sexy cha-cha-cha while carrying out the trash.

Once Luke even caught her tapping her toe to the beat of his hammering floorboards. He paused, deliberately changed his rhythm and started again. Josie's toe-tapping changed, too — and she added a head bob while she mopped. He didn't admit it to TJ, but he thought it was cute as hell.

Less endearing was her habit of ducking anyone who came to Blue Moon. The mail carrier, the meter reader, the newspaper boy — it didn't matter who. Josie didn't want to be seen. Luke couldn't blame her, especially after the way Luanne and the people in Donovan's Corner had treated her . . . and continued to treat her, whenever she ventured into town. But after a while, it got to be a problem. The doorbell rang and Josie bolted, leaving a trail of HandiWipes and Lemon Pledge behind her — and leaving Luke to pick up the pieces.

At first he didn't mind. Most of the time,

whoever was at the door — the mail carrier, the meter reader, the newspaper boy — was there to see him. Plus, answering the doorbell himself gave Luke a chance to keep his "handyman" cover story intact. But then everything changed.

Josie's family tracked her down.

"Tell her I'm not here!" Josie yelled, scurrying upstairs the first time Nancy Day appeared on the front steps in her megawatt jewelry and fancy Realtor's suit. "Tell her I went back to Vegas!"

Luke cracked open the door. He gave Nancy a bland look. "Josie says she's not here. She went back to Vegas."

Nancy Day smiled patiently. "I'll come back another time, then. Poor Josie never was very good at confrontation."

Luke doubted it.

"She's always been terribly stubborn, too. I'm afraid it's a bit of a family failing." Nancy sighed. Her gaze flitted over his shoulder. "By the way, did I hear the estate will be on the market soon?"

He eyed the anticipatory way she examined the foyer, as though measuring it for a real estate brochure. "You didn't hear it from me."

"Oh. Well. My mistake, then. This place would fetch a pretty penny, though. Do keep me in mind if the owners decide to list it!"

She pressed another business card in his hand, then tromped down the porch steps in her high heels. In the driveway, she shaded her eyes and gazed unerringly to the second floor window where Josie must have been peeking out. Nancy frowned, so briefly Luke thought he might have imagined it. Then she turned, waved gaily to a pine-needle-raking TJ, got in her Caddy, and drove away.

"She wants the listing," Josie said from behind him. She raised on tiptoes and gazed over his shoulder as her mother left. "The real estate listing for Blue Moon. That's all she comes out here for, you know."

Luke wasn't so sure. "Maybe she comes out here to see you."

"Hmmph. Not when I haven't got free show tickets and comped passes to Celine Dion at Caesar's Palace to give her, she doesn't. My mom *loved* it when I worked in Vegas."

"She might love having you in Donovan's Corner, if you give her a chance."

"No way. First I give her a chance. Then the next thing I know, I've got my whole family out here visiting." Josie shuddered. "No, thanks."

"Why not? How bad can they be?"

"Let's put it this way. There's a reason I moved two hundred miles away."

"You didn't move two *thousand* miles away," he pointed out. "You had to go to Vegas to become a showgirl."

"The distance involved was a definite perk, believe me." Deliberately, Josie dragged her gaze away from the empty driveway. She cocked one hip. "You don't believe me? How about this. You know those gross, chest-bursting creatures from the *Alien* movies?"

"Yeah."

"Compared with my family, they're pussycats."

Luke couldn't help but grin. "Isn't that a little harsh?"

"Oh, please. It's not." She crossed her arms over her chest. "I mean, come on. Do you get along perfectly with your mom?"

"My mom died when I was seven."

"Oh. Oh, Luke." Eyes widening, Josie reached for him. She patted him tentatively on the biceps. Then, as though suddenly making a decision, she hugged him. "Mmmmph. Mmmmph."

He couldn't understand a word. Putting his hand over her hair, he turned her head so she wasn't being smothered in his

T-shirt. When Josie decided to hug you, she really decided to hug you. She went all out.

"What?" he asked.

"I said I'm *so* sorry. That must have been awful for you. Oh, my God. I'm a complete idiot to have said something so thoughtless."

"It's all right."

"No, it's not!"

"My dad bought me a pony right afterward." He shrugged. "I think that was supposed to make up for it. That, and the riding lessons with my nanny."

Josie leaned back, gawking at him with a stricken look. Her pretty green eyes shimmered with tears. Whoops. He knew better than to tell that damned pony story — especially with the nanny chaser. He'd learned that a long time ago. What was the matter with him?

And what was the matter with Josie? She seriously looked about to cry. Given her usual bravado, he was surprised.

"Wow, are *you* a soft touch," he said.

Her mouth opened. Then her nose crinkled. *Aha,* that nose crinkle said. *I'm in on the joke, buster.*

"You're so full of it!" She sniffled. "Your nanny. As if. And a pony. Hah!" She gave him a feeble smack on the arm. "I can't believe you'd kid about something like that."

"It was a long —"

— *time ago,* he started to say, but she lunged at him again before he could finish. Her next hug knocked the wind out of him. She squeezed so hard, he thought his balls might pop.

"And just to make me feel better about saying something so terrible, too, I'll bet," she mumbled into the shoulder of his T-shirt. "You big softie."

"Hey. Watch it. That's not a nickname guys appreciate. Although the 'big' part is okay. Under the right circumstances."

"Whatever you say, Mr. Big."

"That's better."

"Just remember," Josie said, suddenly serious, "I'm here if you want to talk about it. You don't have to be tough with me."

"Okay." He patted her back.

Just as he started enjoying having her in his arms, Josie pulled away. And as she released him, even as she gave him one last "chin up" gesture of solidarity, Luke knew she was wrong.

He did have to be tough with her. He had to be tough with everyone. It was the only way to survive.

"Damn it! I should have known she'd double-cross me."

With a sinking feeling, Josie stared at the shiny SUV pulling into the driveway at Blue Moon. In the passenger seat, she recognized her sister — aka, the parent-pleasing traitor. Behind the wheel, she spotted Jenna's husband, David. And in the big white pimpmobile behind them, she glimpsed her mom and dad.

Damn it. She'd told Jenna to come alone.

"This is all your fault." She aimed a frustrated look at Luke, then glanced back at her family. "I give out one teensy-weensy little chance, and look what happens."

He glanced toward the driveway. "What?"

If he was too clueless to realize it, Josie wasn't enlightening him. "I'm going inside. Tell them I'm not here."

"Hold on." Luke grabbed her arm when she would have run from the porch. "I need you here. Don't let go."

He nodded toward the porch crossbeam, which she'd been holding over her head while Luke hammered it in place. Josie sighed. Because of its length and diagonal position, he couldn't hold it and hammer it simultaneously.

"You don't understand. I'm not ready for all of them at one time. I called my sister, but only because —"

"Yoo-hoo!" Jenna waved from beside her SUV's open rear door. She reached inside, unbuckled Emily from her car seat, and pulled her on her hip. On the opposite side, Hannah scrambled out. "The gang's all here!"

Josie felt a rising sense of panic. "Only because," she hissed to Luke, "I thought I'd, you know, give her a chance."

"Like I said to do."

"No, *not* like you said to do." Of *course* like he'd said to do. What did he think, she was made of stone? Knowing that Luke had lost his mother had really gotten to her. It had made her look twice at her own family . . . and the way she and her dad had been semi-estranged for years. "I was planning to do this anyway."

He only looked at her, his gaze filled with understanding. "If you say so."

She raised her chin. "I do."

"Okay." Luke flipped his hammer, then caught it in a fancy move that seemed effortless. He set it on the porch railing, looking cheery. "I can't wait to meet the rest of your family."

Josie frowned, still holding up the two-by-four. "What about needing to hold this?"

"Drop it. It'll keep." He crossed the porch, his gaze fixed on her family making their way toward the house. His work boots thumped the floorboards with authority — almost as though he owned the place. "We've got company."

He'd tricked her. Damn it. He'd kept her there just long enough that everyone in her family must have seen her standing on the porch. Josie was more than willing to run away — but not when anybody could see her doing it. She did have her pride.

"I don't want company," she said.

"Don't be a baby. Come on."

Well, that clinched it. Nobody called her names and got away with it. Deliberately, Josie dropped the lumber, leaving it to hang crookedly by its one hammered-in nail. It would serve Luke right if it fell off.

She wiped her sweaty palms on her Sunday-best cropped white denim pants. She straightened the knot she'd tied at the waist of her pink gingham shirt. She tossed back her ponytail. There. Primped, poised, and posture-perfect, thanks to her showgirl training.

All she needed was a feathered fan and a sequined headdress, and she'd have been able to tackle anything. In lieu of her usual accessories, Josie slipped her feet in the rainbow wedgies she'd left by the welcome mat and plastered on a smile.

Time to face her family.

That was easier said than done. Crossing the porch in Luke's wake felt more terrifying than crossing a Las Vegas stage ever had. The sounds of conversation, of gravel crunching beneath her family's feet, of her niece making chattering noises with her Barbie doll, seemed weirdly surreal.

She stopped at the top of the porch steps beside Luke, watching her family troop up to greet her. It had been years since she'd confronted them all together . . . not since she'd been crowned Miss Saguaro at the age of eighteen and had skedaddled for Las Vegas to try her luck as a dancer shortly afterward.

"There she is!" her mother sang out gaily, ascending the steps in front of the group with her usual self-confidence. She glanced over her shoulder, as though making sure everyone noticed she was in the lead. "Hello, pumpkin."

"Mom."

They shared an awkward hug. Her mother's perfume — Tabu, her longtime favorite — tickled her nose, more strongly than when they'd seen each other in the hospital emergency room. She must have applied it freshly for the occasion.

"I told you I'd track you down! Shame on you, for ducking your mother all this time."

"I've been busy." Josie gestured vaguely toward Blue Moon.

"You're never too busy for your family. Isn't that right, Warren?"

Nancy Day dragged her husband forward. She looped her arm through his, clearly intending to keep him there by force if necessary. Given their past, it just might be necessary.

Her father stood there stiffly. At the sight of him, Josie felt tears well up. *No, no, no.* Rapidly, she blinked them back. So what if it had been years since she'd last seen him? It wasn't *her* fault he'd refused to visit her in Las Vegas. And she'd been way too busy to come back to Donovan's Corner.

He cleared his throat. He nodded.

Josie waited. Her stupid hands trembled. She took a step forward, hoping to dispel some nervous energy. Her stomach tightened, then somersaulted. The tension was killing her.

Would he apologize? Make excuses? Pretend nothing had happened between them?

She wasn't sure if she should hug him, or maybe shake his hand, or nod, like he had. Was that what fathers did after their daughters grew up? Nodded?

She'd bet he didn't nod at Jenna, the perfect daughter.

Time slowed, leaving Josie plenty of opportunities to notice the new gray in her father's formerly dark hair, the new laugh lines around the corners of his eyes, the slight potbelly he'd developed. He'd aged, just in the few years she'd been gone. Seeing him was like watching a time-lapse film — one she'd never expected to find on the marquee.

"Josie," he said, nodding again.

Breathlessly, Josie waited. His voice sounded gruff. Clearly, he was having trouble expressing himself. But that was okay. Sometimes men were like that — especially men of her father's generation. Words didn't come easily to them. Thinking she'd be mature and try to make things easier, she took a step forward to hug him.

At the same moment, Warren Day turned to Luke. He extended his hand. Introductions were made all around. Josie was left standing there, off balance in more ways than one.

She lowered her arms. Had her father

actually *ducked* her hug? Or had he not realized what she'd been about to do? She couldn't tell. She chewed her lip, feeling confused.

Maybe that had been the problem all along. *Her* choices were completely obvious, while her dad's . . . her dad's had a way of hurting like hell.

She moved to the side while her family chattered and laughed. They all shook hands with Luke. He ruffled Hannah's hair and cooed over Emily's chubby little cheeks, looking unbelievably handsome and lovable and charming. Everyone gradually progressed up the porch steps until they stood in the shade of Blue Moon's newly repaired porch roof.

"Nice place," David said. They all moved inside.

Nobody noticed Josie wasn't with them. Alone on the porch, she listened as the hubbub faded. Footsteps clattered away from her. A weird mixture of relief and disappointment roiled around her insides. She clenched the porch railing and turned away, letting her gaze fall on her convertible.

Just a few hours' drive and she could be gone . . .

New footsteps sounded, coming closer.

They dragged her — unwillingly — away from her fantasy of hitting the open road.

"I told them you're putting away the hammer," Luke said.

He met her gaze seriously, silent understanding in his expression. Josie didn't know how Luke could possibly understand what she was going through. Her own family had waltzed right past her without noticing she hadn't come with them.

She tossed her head. "They'll never believe it. You should have chosen an alibi that *didn't* involve me being responsible."

He looked puzzled.

"Did you notice?" she asked, nodding toward the driveway. "They all parked behind my car. They fenced me in."

He didn't even glance at her convertible. "Come inside." Luke touched her arm, making her realize how tightly she'd been gripping the porch railing. "I'll be your buddy."

For a minute, she was flummoxed. Then, "Like in third grade? 'Everybody find a buddy'?"

"Right." He held out his hand. "Grab my hand, buddy."

"Hmmm. I'd have pegged you as the kid shooting spitballs from the school roof while everybody else obediently filed off for the field trip. You know, the loner type."

"No psychoanalyzing your buddy. And quit screwing around. Tiffany Koenig would've given up her whole Rainbow Brite collection to be in your shoes right now."

"Her whole collection? In that case. . . ."

Nervously, Josie put her hand in Luke's. His fingers intertwined with hers, leaving her feeling safe and protected and *almost* willing to face the firing squad inside.

"See? That wasn't so tough," he said. "Come on."

Grudgingly, she took a step forward. But even as she did, even as she enjoyed the simple togetherness of her hand in Luke's, Josie knew he was wrong.

It *was* going to be tough and she *would* be alone. When it came right down to it, she always was. It looked as though she always would be. Accepting that was the only way to keep going.

At least it had worked so far.

"Hey, Luke. Knock, knock."

By now, he'd learned the routine. "Who's there?"

"Freddie."

"Freddie who?"

"Freddie or not, here I come."

When Josie entered the shadowy house, she found everyone clustered in the kitchen around the butler's table — her mother and Jenna sitting side by side, David holding Emily in another chair, Hannah plopped on the floor, and her father standing nearby pretending to be engrossed in the latest wardrobe change for his granddaughter's Barbie.

TJ had arrived from somewhere — probably another of his experiments to see if he really could make Pop-Tarts burst into flames in the toaster he'd plugged outside. He'd propped one hip on the table edge, amiably chatting with everyone.

Luke leaned against the nearest counter. Josie moved with him, sticking by her safety zone. As though sensing her unease, he rubbed his thumb over the heel of her palm. The gesture felt reassuring. And ticklish.

Jenna glanced up. Her gaze skittered to Josie and Luke's linked hands. Her usual cheerleader-style smile faded a little.

"Nice place, Josie," she said. Her attention darted to Josie and Luke's hands again. "Your friend TJ was just telling us how the owner of Enchanté actually *gave* it to you?"

Josie nodded.

"*Gave* it to you? But I thought Luke was the —" Her mother broke off, glancing at him with a slight frown. After another few seconds, she shrugged, then scoped the room as though mentally auctioning off the fixtures and moldings. "Why in the world would he give you something so valuable?"

"*He* is a *she*, Mom. Tallulah Carlyle. It's kind of a long story, but —"

"Maybe Josie's the best stripper in the joint," her father said. "And this place is one gigantic tip."

"Warren!"

Jenna and David gaped. Even Hannah, apparently sensing the instant tension in the room, looked up from her Barbie.

"If I *was* a stripper," Josie informed her father, "you can bet your ass I'd be the best."

"Don't say 'ass,' dear."

She rounded on her mother. "It's okay for Dad to call me a stripper, but I can't say 'ass'?"

The tension notched higher.

"There *are* children in the room," Jenna pointed out, leaning over to clap both hands over Emily's ears. "You might consider that."

David frowned his best offended-

216

plumber's frown. "I knew this would happen. Something always does when Josie is —" He cleared his throat. "Why don't I take Emily and Hannah for a walk outside?"

He stood with the toddler in his arms, then held out a hand for Hannah to grab. They hot-footed it out of the kitchen.

"This has got to be some kind of record," Josie said, shaking her head. She let go of Luke's hand and strode across the floor, deftly avoiding the cracked slate they still hadn't replaced. "Two minutes, and already you're ganging up on me."

"We're not ganging up on you."

"Don't be so sensitive."

"It's not as though 'stripper' is an insult."

Of course it was. "The way Dad says it, it is!"

Her father stood. "I'll get the donuts."

"What?" Josie stared at his departing back.

"We just came from church," Jenna explained as their father made his way to the foyer. "We noticed you weren't there, so we decided to bring the coffee and donuts to you."

Another wave of disapproval washed over Josie. She felt it as keenly as she did the tension in her shoulders.

"Strippers don't go to church," she shot back.

Silence. Then her mother looked up. "*You* used to."

With a pang, Josie remembered. She remembered getting dressed up in a Sunday's best outfit that didn't involve a belly-baring gingham shirt and sexy white denim. She remembered sitting beside her family in a pew, singing hymns — and happily swaying to the organ music, even then. She remembered filing down to the church basement after mass to share coffee and donuts with the other parishioners.

She remembered feeling as though she'd belonged.

"I was six years old. I didn't know any better," she lied.

Her mother and Jenna exchanged a look. Ignoring it, Josie crossed her arms and went on pacing. If she just kept moving, maybe things would feel okay.

TJ glanced up with his usual obliviousness. "Hey, no problem. There's always next Sunday, right?"

Oh, no. Josie shot him a *shut up* look, but the damage had already been done.

"Yes!" Jenna cried, her face shining. "You can come with us next Sunday, Josie.

Seriously, the kids would love it. They hardly get to see you."

"It would make your father very happy. He's getting on in years, you know."

"Mom. You're both the same age."

"Still." Her mother waved off the notion, obviously seeing her technically advancing years as immaterial when compared with her husband's. "He won't be around much longer, you know. Would it kill you to sing one harmless hymn with him next Sunday?"

It just might. Josie looked to Luke to save her.

Blithely, he examined his fingernails. "You'd probably find lots of potential dance school students at church. Good networking."

Wham. No help from that corner. She frowned at him.

At the table, her mother and Jenna gasped. They both turned to Josie wearing excited expressions.

"Dance school? You're *finally* going to open your dance school? Here?"

"Oh, pumpkin! That's wonderful!"

See what you've done? she mouthed to Luke, but it was too late. Her mother and sister were already off and running, chattering about lessons, students, and — she

219

could *not* be hearing this correctly — family discounts.

Josie kept pacing. Why had she ever confided her dreams in them? During their last shopping-and-shows visit to Vegas, she and her mother and Jenna and Parker had all had one too many margaritas at her favorite Mexican food place. Josie had found herself describing, with tequila-fueled earnestness, her ambitions to open a dance school of her very own.

It's what I've always wanted, she remembered herself saying. Solemnly. Wistfully.

Stupidly.

"There's no way you can do this alone," Jenna announced firmly. "We'll help you."

"No! I don't —"

"Absolutely," her mother agreed. "No arguments."

And that was how, in the midst of running away from a family-mandated church appearance, Josie found herself with a "date" for next Sunday — and two unlikely allies in her quest to take over Donovan's Corner.

Ten

"I don't need those," Josie said, shaking her head at her sister. "Thanks, but I changed my mind. I've got it covered."

"Don't be silly. You don't have it 'covered,' " Jenna insisted. "Here."

She shoved the bundle she'd been carrying at Josie, nearly burying her in a pile of sturdy cotton, sweet prints, and sensible shoes. Clothes. For Josie to borrow. She'd thought her sister had forgotten all about what she'd originally called her out to Blue Moon for. Apparently not.

"On the phone, you told me you wanted to borrow a few things," Jenna said.

"On the phone, I told you to come alone." Pointedly, Josie glanced toward the doorway of her upstairs bedroom, which they'd slipped away to following her father's return with the donuts. From here, the sounds of family joviality — and TJ's carefree laughter — could barely be heard. "A-l-o-n-e."

Jenna scoffed. "You didn't mean that."

"Yes, I did!" Josie glanced at Luke, who'd followed them upstairs. " 'Come alone.' It's pretty uninterpretable."

Stubbornly, Jenna remained silent.

Just as stubbornly, Josie stared her down.

Luke stepped between them — probably to make sure Josie didn't karate-chop her sister. Or, more temptingly, give her an impromptu Mohawk. Anything to ease up Jenna's insufferable Goody Two-shoes image.

"I'll leave you two to your girlie stuff." He set down the cardboard boxes he'd carried from Jenna's SUV to Josie's bedroom. "When your dad was getting the donuts, he spotted one of the Harleys I'm working on. He wants to check it out."

Josie rolled her eyes. "Oh, God. Don't tell me you and my father are going to *bond,* or something."

Luke gave her a wink, just as though that *weren't* a horrifying notion. He made his escape.

"One of your *Harleys?*" Jenna raced to the doorway. "Wait! Don't show David!" she shouted after him. "Motorcycles are the terror of the highway!"

When she turned around, Josie was ready.

"I like motorcycles," she announced.

"You would."

Jenna moved farther into the bedroom Josie had adopted and refurbished earlier that week. She ran her hand over the antique bureau, the old-fashioned chenille bedspread, the oak cheval mirror. She frowned at Josie's treasured stack of glossy celebrity gossip magazines on the nightstand. Josie didn't care about fashion magazines, but she did like to keep up with current events.

"You like everything dangerous," Jenna went on, following up on her motorcycle discussion. "Including . . ."

Wearing a knowing expression, she angled her head to the doorway. *Including him.*

"What, Luke?"

"Yes, Luke! He's exactly the type you'd fall for." Jenna glanced at Josie's hand, as though remembering how Luke had clasped it in his downstairs — or expecting a diamond engagement ring to materialize on it. "In fact, you probably already *have* fallen for him." She pursed her lips. "You've got that look."

"What 'look'?"

"*The* look. The 'take me to bed, you big stud,' look."

Josie almost laughed. Said in her sister's prim tone, that lusty command sounded like a request to burn the Tupperware. "You say that as if it would be a bad thing."

"Guys like him are trouble," Jenna persisted. "Didn't you see those muscles? That attitude? Those tattoos?"

Josie couldn't stand it. "I licked those tattoos."

Her sister turned goggle-eyed. "You did not!"

She was right. She hadn't. But it was still fun to get Jenna's goat.

"No, you're right. He licked *my* tattoos."

Her sister's jaw dropped. She scanned Josie's figure, scandalized . . . but intrigued.

"Where are they?" she whispered.

"In your imagination. Sheesh! I don't have tattoos. They'd look bad on stage." Josie dropped the bundle of clothes on the bed. She frowned at them. "Did you borrow some of these from Mom?"

"No." Huffily, Jenna crossed the room. "They're mine. From my days as a working woman."

"Working woman? You sold wall-to-wall shag at the DC Carpet Emporium."

"We can't all have glamorous careers." Jenna raised her chin. "Anyway, those days are behind me now. David took me away from all that."

Josie knew the story. David had come in the Emporium looking for carpet to replace some he'd accidentally soaked while replumbing a customer's bathroom. Jenna had shown him a perfect match for the sample in his hand. Their fingers had touched while combing the pile. It had been love at first shag.

"And speaking of Mom," Jenna went on doggedly, "for your information, I *couldn't* come out here alone like you asked. Despite what you think, I didn't bring everyone along just to aggravate you."

Josie didn't believe her. She remained silent, trying to contemplate actually wearing some of this stuff. Culottes? Knit shirts with cartoon ducks on them? Gabardine suits with calf-length skirts? The dowdiness alone would suffocate her.

Obviously, she wasn't cut out for Goody Two-shoes duty.

"I was already meeting Mom and Dad at church," Jenna explained in a super-patient tone she probably used while telling Hannah to wash behind her ears. "And Sunday is family day for me and David and the girls. What was I supposed to do, pull a Josie and ditch everyone?"

225

Ouch. Stung, Josie stared at the plaid camp shirt in her hand.

"I'm sorry," her sister said quietly. "Force of habit. Usually you're not around to hear it."

Terrific. Josie had become a family slur. *Pull a Josie.* Sheesh. She could picture it now. Her mother: "Mow the lawn, Warren." Her father: "Nah. I'm going to pull a Josie today."

Double ouch. Trying not to think about it, Josie concentrated on folding the camp shirt. Fold. Crease. Fold.

Jenna moved a little closer. "It's just . . . you know," she said, sounding contrite, "you hurt Mom and Dad's feelings by coming home and then not visiting them."

Josie nudged aside an Army green square-heeled pump. "Yeah, Dad looked really broken up about it."

"You didn't exactly help matters. Did you seriously have to swear in front of him?"

"Damned straight, I did."

Jenna issued a long-suffering sigh. "You never change. Still chafing at the rules. Still refusing to be pinned down. Still going your own way, no matter what."

At that reminder of the family lore, Josie gave a rueful shake of her head. According

226

to their mother, as a child Jenna had been happy to play placidly in her infant seat or stay obediently in the yard. But nothing had been able to contain little Josie. She'd kicked down baby gates. Squirmed out of her stroller. Dashed away, whooping with laughter, whenever her mother had tried to confine her to a shopping cart's child seat.

"Playing it safe is overrated," she said.

"Well, that might be true in your world. But you'll need to do a little playing it safe if you want to succeed with your dance school in *this* world," Jenna lectured, obviously having realized her contribution to the plan. She glanced at Josie's outfit, her lips pursed in disapproval. "So long as you keep going around town like a sexed-up Mary Ann from *Gilligan's Island* —"

"Hey! If I'm anybody, I'm Ginger. The movie star."

"— nobody's going to take you seriously."

Glumly, Josie kicked her rainbow wedgie at the bedpost. She knew Jenna was right. Sort of. Why else would she have asked to borrow part of her sister's so-called wardrobe? But faced with the reality of tidy prints, button-up shirts, and actual tweed, she was having second thoughts.

Maybe she didn't need them. Maybe she

could make a good impression — and launch her dance school — without them.

"I'm pretty sure I'm allergic to 'sensible,' " she said. "Turtlenecks give me a rash."

Jenna snickered. "They do not."

"I like my clothes!" Josie protested. "What I wear has nothing to do with how well I dance. Or how well I can teach other people to dance. I've had a lot of training."

"You've had a lot of pole dancing."

"What?"

"That's what Dad's friend, Howie, told him," Jenna explained matter-of-factly, folding more clothes. "He said he and his buddies saw you in Vegas doing some sleazy all-nude revue."

"What? All-nude?"

Jenna nodded. "Dad was devastated. He hated the thought that his friends and neighbors had seen 'his little girl' naked."

"They never!"

With a shrug that said the truth was irrelevant when contradicted by juicy gossip, Jenna went on. "Word got around town pretty quickly. You know Donovan's Corner. By nightfall, people were saying you gave Howie a lap dance."

Josie was speechless. The thought of dancing within twenty feet of Howie Maynard's sweaty beer gut — for the dubious prize of twenty bucks tucked in a G-string — snapped her out of it pretty quickly.

"I've *never* given a lap dance in my life!" she sputtered. "I'm a *dancer*. A trained, professional lead dancer in a respectable show."

Jenna held up a pair of hideous tapered-leg baggy pants with a tapestry print. She nodded in approval, oblivious that that print would make even the cutest tush look like a lumpy frat house sofa.

"I know that," she said blithely. "But no one else does. When you didn't come back, people kind of assumed the stripper story was true. They all thought you were ashamed to show your face in town."

Astonished, Josie gaped at her. She couldn't believe what she was hearing. It left her feeling heartsick. Queasy. And really, really mad. No wonder people here had given her the cold shoulder!

Luanne, the people at Frank's Diner, the utility company employees, Miss Copies 2 Go, everyone she'd run into since coming back to Donovan's Corner — they all believed she was some kind of sleazy refugee from a made-for-TV movie: *When She Was Bad.* Everyone except Luke and TJ, both newcomers to town.

Why hadn't anyone told her this before? A stripper. No, a pole dancer! Sheesh. No wonder her own father had . . . No. *He* should have known her better. He should have given her the benefit of the doubt. She was his daughter.

"Dad should have trusted me." Remembering his snide "stripper" comment downstairs, Josie snatched blindly at the pile of accessories. "He should have asked me for the truth."

"You know Dad's not a talker."

"No." Bitterly, Josie crushed a bundle of enormous black vinyl purses to her chest. She could've stashed a Thanksgiving turkey in one of those puppies. "Just a listener."

"Either way, it's water under the bridge now," Jenna said. Busily, she sorted the clothes in two stacks — categorizing them, as near as Josie could tell, into the ugly stack and the dreary stack. "If you want to make your dance school succeed, you've got a lot of lost ground to make up for. A lot of people to convince you've changed."

"I haven't changed," Josie protested. "I don't want to change and I don't need to. Because I was *never* the person they thought I was."

"That's irrelevant. You've got to deal

with people's perceptions and then change them. Period."

"Oh, yeah?" Jenna's wholesomer-than-thou attitude was really starting to irk her. "Did they teach you that in carpet sales-person school? Or was it on *Sesame Street* last week? Tell me, Jenna. Because I've been too busy lap dancing to keep up on current theories."

"Don't take this out on me. And don't shoot the messenger. Somebody had to tell you."

" 'Somebody'? *Somebody?* Come on, Jenna. That 'somebody' was you — and you thought it was a good idea to wait *years* to share this little tidbit? Why didn't you tell me this before?"

"You never came home before."

Josie snorted. "So now it's my fault?"

Her sister sighed. "Believe it or not, Josie, you're not the only one who has problems." She fussed with the flower-pat-terned suit in her hands, then added it to one of the piles. Wearily, she glanced up. The light caught the dark circles under her eyes. "Can we just get on with the clothes, please?"

Taken aback, Josie stared. What was Jenna talking about? Problems? She'd never known her sister to have problems — or to

231

be anything less than sweet, grounded, and annoyingly in sync with their parents. The fact that she seemed less and less those things as the moments ticked past was unnerving.

"What's the matter?" Josie asked.

"Nothing. Here." Jenna plucked the flowered suit from the bed and handed it over. "Try this on."

"I'm serious. Tell me what's wrong."

"Nothing. Go on. I'll turn my back so you can change."

"Jenna —" Frustrated, Josie tossed down the suit her sister had given her. She stared at Jenna's ramrod-straight back. "I'm really sorry. I didn't know you were having problems."

"Clothes," Jenna sang out.

Grrr. Josie hated it when her sister goaded her in melody. "I already have a suit."

"Let's see it, then. Put it on." Keeping her back to Josie — probably to guard their combined virtues — Jenna gazed out the window overlooking Blue Moon's front lawn and driveway. She hugged herself. "Tell me when you're ready, and I'll look."

Josie didn't have much choice. She grabbed the one thing closest to a suit she'd packed and wriggled into it. She was fiddling with the waist closure on the skirt when Jenna spoke again.

"The problem is . . . Oh, it's hard to explain. And I know this is going to sound selfish." She waved her arm as though warding off the very idea. "But it's just that . . . when Mom and Dad are busy worrying about you, talking about you, wondering about you . . . where does that leave me?"

Josie didn't know. "In the clear? Enshrined as the perfect daughter?"

"Nowhere, that's where!" Jenna's voice cracked. "No matter what I do, it's never enough. No matter how much I do *right*, all that matters is what *you* do *wrong*. Now that you're back, I don't stand a chance."

"Of course you do." God, she was serious. Josie couldn't believe it. "You've got the trump card, remember? Grandkids!"

Jenna snorted.

Okay. Joking wasn't working. Honestly perplexed, Josie moved closer. "What do you mean, 'never enough'? It's *always* enough when it comes to you, and you know it. You're Mom and Dad's favorite. We've both known that for a long time. We just . . . don't talk about it."

Jenna remained silent.

"Come on, Jenna. Don't clam up now."

Josie fastened her skirt and smoothed out the hem. She glanced up, waiting for her sister's inevitable agreement . . . but somehow the world shifted. Jenna only stood there, determinedly watching a blue jay nest in a nearby pine tree. She gave no sign of feeling anything but as overlooked as Josie often did.

Could it be true? Could Jenna really feel as though she was never enough?

"If Mom and Dad don't see how fantastic you are, that's their loss," Josie said. "Honestly. Forget about it."

Jenna sniffed. "Wow. Things are really simple in your world, aren't they? Must be nice to —" She turned, stopped, took in Josie's outfit. Her eyes narrowed.

A twirl. "What do you think?"

Josie waited as her skirt settled just above her knees, as her prim suit jacket fluttered closed at the waist. The suit belonged to one of her roommates, Sheila, who danced at Bally's. Josie had thought it was one of her own outfits when she'd packed it.

It was coming in handy now, though. If she wasn't mistaken, Jenna approved. Her sister tapped her finger against her lips, walking closer. She bent her head and examined the fit, the fabric, the length of the skirt.

"That won't work," she announced.

"Why not? The skirt is modest, the jacket covers me, the top underneath isn't see-through or shiny or —"

Jenna grabbed a handful of fabric at the waist. She tugged. The whole suit fell away, baring a bodysuit underneath.

"It's a breakaway suit!" she cried, tossing it on the bed in disgust. "Do you think I was born yesterday?"

Actually, yes. Or at least the day before yesterday.

Josie hadn't thought Jenna even knew such a thing as a breakaway suit existed. In Donovan's Corner, even the bachelorette-party entertainment stripped down to a pair of gym shorts and tube socks. And a party hat.

With dignity, Josie examined the suit. "At least it's not tweed. I still think it would work."

"Sure. Barring a strong wind."

"I don't seriously expect anybody to yank off my clothes."

Jenna aimed a meaningful look toward the window — where the sounds of Luke's Harley being revved could be heard. She folded her arms over her chest. "*I* do."

Josie grinned. "And that would be bad . . . why, again?"

"Laugh all you want, but I'm serious," Jenna said. "If you think you can stay here in this house with him, *sleep* with him" — this last was said in a scandalized whisper — "and not fall in love with him, you're delusional."

"Luke lives in the carriage house, not here." *And I only wish we'd slept together.* "I'm not 'in love' with him."

"Not yet, maybe. But I know you. You form attachments. You like to pretend you don't, but you do." Jenna glanced at the crumpled breakaway suit on the bed. "Being immune to zippers doesn't make you immune to falling for someone special."

Luke *was* special. He was also talented and fun and he made her laugh. He was trustworthy. He believed in her. And okay, so sometimes Josie found herself gazing dreamily at him, imagining the two of them settling down at Blue Moon together with a pantry full of Ding Dongs and hundreds of long Sunday mornings they'd spend cuddling in bed.

But that was silly. Luke wouldn't cuddle. He'd throw her down and ravish her senseless.

Hugging herself at the thought, Josie grinned. Then she gave herself a mental kick. Luke was temporary. That was it.

"Har, har," she said, snapping herself out of it. "Enough with the stripper jokes, okay?"

"You and Luke together is a bad idea," Jenna insisted. "What do you really know about this guy?"

"Hmmm." Josie pulled an elaborately thoughtful face. "Let's see. I know he doesn't hound me about 'relationships' with a capital don't-go-there. Who are you, Dr. Phil?"

Jenna rolled her eyes.

"I know about Luke, okay?" Josie said. "I know all I need to know. He's hot, he's friendly, and he's good with his hands."

"He's Mr. Goodwrench, then."

"Actually, yeah. Kind of. He's a motor-cycle mechanic in his spare time." Josie spied the impatient look on her sister's face and relented. "I've got it under control."

"Mmmm-hmmm."

"Do you think that skeptical streak is hereditary? You might have passed it on to Emily and Hannah."

"Just be careful, okay?"

With another look at her sister's serious face, Josie nodded. Reluctantly. "Okay."

"Good. Now, about these clothes . . ."

Groaning, Josie gave up. Her sister nattered on, flinging polyester pantsuits and tied-at-the-collar blouses her way. The ugly pile and the dreary pile awaited her — but beyond them, so did her dance school dream. No matter what it took, she promised herself, she was going to get there.

All she had to do was reinvent herself, hang on long enough to dispel those stripper rumors, and find some students. Once everyone saw what a wonderful teacher she was, her new life would be on its way.

In the meantime, surely she could survive a wardrobe swap with her sister.

"Hey," Jenna said, an eager look in her eye. "Do you think I can borrow those rainbow wedgies?"

"Why not?" Josie slipped them off and handed them over with a sigh of resignation. "I won't need them. Not in Sensible City."

Eleven

"Dude. I think your dad's weakening," TJ said. "I think he's about to give in."

Upstairs in his carriage house apartment, Luke frowned. "I don't want to talk about my dad."

"But you could win back your inheritance. And your trust fund! Your dad was totally sucked in by the latest report I sent him." TJ waved his most recently acquired spyathon swag — the state-of-the-art PDA Robert Donovan had equipped him with. "*Totally* sucked in."

Luke told himself he didn't care. Not caring, he went on working on the Suzuki engine parts he'd carried upstairs to clean. Not caring, he squinted at the ESPN Classic basketball game on TV. Not caring — okay, maybe just a little bit — he stifled the instant, idiotic spark of hope TJ's words had caused.

He'd never been on the outs with his dad for this long. Sure, they'd had some hairy moments. Like the time Luke had been booted from his fifth boarding school (in a row) for staging indoor go-kart races. Or the time his dad had sent him to Europe during summer break to stay with some "cultured, civilized" friends of the family. Luke had returned with nothing but fond memories of a hickey-loving French girl and an increased mastery of metric-sized socket wrenches. Not exactly what his dad had had in mind.

"Hey!" TJ bounced on the sofa like a six-foot toddler on a sugar high. "Don't you want to know what I told him? Huh? Don't you?"

"No."

"I told him you've been spending your nights with a telescope, looking for aliens!" TJ chortled. "Dude! You're an alien-watching whack job."

"They're out there," Luke deadpanned, wiping motor oil from a piston. He replaced it on the newspaper he'd spread on the floor. "I've seen 'em."

"See? I knew you'd be into it." Enthusiastically, TJ went on. "Last week, I told him you were doing motorcycle stunts like Evel Knievel. Next week, you're going to start eating paste and gibbering."

Luke shook his head. "Why don't you just say I'm living in the local loony bin and be done with it?"

"Good idea. Note to self." TJ poked at his PDA with the stylus. He frowned. "Does nuthouse have one 't' or two?"

"Three."

"Oh. Cool." He paused. "Hey. Is your aunt Tallulah as gullible as your dad? Because if she is, you could probably convince her she meant to give Josie a different estate all along, dude."

"I'm working on it."

Luke had e-mailed Ambrose last week, using one of the patron-accessible computers at the Donovan's Corner public library, asking him to look into another property for Tallulah to give Josie. He hadn't heard from the attorney yet, but he was optimistic. Barb swore her boss checked his e-mail religiously. Still, it might be time for another tactic. A telegram? A shore-to-ship phone call?

A thumping on the stairs made Luke glance toward the doorway. Josie appeared there an instant later, scowling at her shoes — a pair of clodhoppers unlike anything he'd ever seen on her. Her outfit met the same criteria. Her dress was like something a modesty-crazed nun would wear on laundry day.

She propped her hands on her hips. Or

in the general vicinity. Given those clothes, Luke couldn't tell — she possessed about as much shape as the Michelin Man.

"Luke, I have to go to town, and my car won't start."

"Maybe you scared it, Sister Mary Burlap Bag." He grinned, figuring this had to be a joke. "What the hell are you wearing?"

Josie tilted her chin. "For your information, this is my new going-to-town wardrobe. It's going to convince everyone that I'm responsible, respectable, and trustworthy."

"It's going to convince them you got dressed in a mud pit."

"Very funny."

Examining her from head to toe, Luke couldn't prevent a sinking feeling. "You can't be serious. You look like . . . one of them!" He gestured toward town.

"Let me get this straight," Josie began.

Uh-oh. She took a step forward, revealing her taut, slicked-back hair and her lack of false eyelashes. Damn it, he'd kind of grown to like them. They were so . . . *her*.

"You think I look like a stuffy, prudish, small-town busybody? Is that what you're saying?"

"Uhhh." This had to be a trap. Another, more insidious version of the "do I look fat?" question. But Luke had never pulled his punches with Josie — except for that "I'm just the handyman" thing, which had gotten admittedly out of hand. He wasn't going to start lying to her now. Anymore.

Cautiously, he nodded.

To his astonishment, she brightened. She also tried to bounce up with glee. Her clodhoppers held her down.

"Yay! It's working then."

"Working?"

"To make me look dependable and reliable. Etcetera."

Luke wrinkled his brow doubtfully. "What was wrong with the way you looked before?"

"According to my sister, everything. Plus she said I looked like Mary Ann, when I *know* I'm more Ginger than that."

Confused, Luke angled his head. Hmmm. From here it looked possible that she'd skipped shaving her legs, too. He couldn't be certain. There were only a few inches of leg visible from mid-calf down.

"I think you look very nice," TJ offered.

"Awww. Thanks, TJ. That's sweet."

"Just like my fourth grade teacher, Mrs. Kurzweiler." TJ shook his head with a smile, obviously remembering. "She never let her hairy upper lip break her spirit."

"Ummm, that's . . . good." Brightly, Josie slung her suitcase-size purse over her shoulder. She glanced at the TV. "Hey! You've got cable in here." She gave Luke an accusing look. "In the main house, all I get are local access channels."

"Your dad hooked us up with five-tier cable last week," Luke told her. He'd been psyched to learn that Warren Day, hauler of donuts and admirer of motorcycles, was also an installer for Donovan's Corner SuperCable. "I thought he wired the main house, too."

"No. I didn't even know he was here."

Uh-oh.

"He's been stopping by a couple of times a week," TJ volunteered, looking up from his Chee-tos. "Hanging out, messing with the cable, checking out Luke's motorcycles. You know. Guy stuff."

Josie looked troubled. "He has?"

Luke sent TJ a *shut up* look. Josie had enough to worry about without wondering why her father was ditching her.

"Hey, don't worry about it." He touched her arm. "He probably meant to stop by to see you. He just ran out of time."

"Right." Josie blinked, then stepped

backward. She hated, he'd learned, being on the receiving end of sympathy. "So, about my car — can you fix it? It's going *klunk, klunk* whenever I try the ignition."

"Sounds like a problem with the starter." He wiped his hands on his shop rag, then got to his feet. "Tell you what. I'll take you to town myself."

"I don't know. I've got a lot to do today." Josie bit her lip. To Luke's disbelief, she pulled out a pocket calendar and riffled through the pages. "I'm going to help Jenna and the other PTSO moms serve snacks at Hannah's school. You'll be stuck waiting around for me."

"PTSO?" Luke cracked. "Tell me another one."

"Okay. After that, I'm applying for a business license and a Chamber of Commerce membership for my dance school. I figure it'll lend me some much-needed legitimacy."

She was serious. Luke was speechless.

But Josie wasn't. "I've got a full schedule all week, now that the heavy-duty cleanup around here is done," she continued matter-of-factly. "Tomorrow I'm going to network with local businesspeople at the library fund-raiser. Sunday I'm going to church with my family — you're both invited, of course. Next week I'm co-chairing a bake sale with Jenna's friends."

"Bake sale? You're the one who told me the 'on' light on the new oven meant it needed servicing."

Clearly undaunted, Josie nudged the toe of her clodhopper. She shrugged. "I'm telling you, Luke. By the end of the month, I'll have this whole town eating out of the palm of my hand. Once everyone gets a load of the new me, my fab dance school will be as good as launched."

He frowned, concerned for the first time. "You've been painting without opening a window again, haven't you? Getting giddy from the fumes?"

She laughed. "Have a little faith, will you? I can do it. Although we *do* still have to talk about ordering the ballet barre and the mirrors and the sound system for the dance studio. I swear you've been dodging me about that."

He had been. None of those things would belong in Blue Moon when he auctioned it off.

Luke shook off Josie's reminder. *I can do it,* she'd said. Hell. He wasn't worried she couldn't. He was worried what it might cost her when she did. Donovan's Corner had broken Josie's spirit once already. He didn't want to see that happen again.

"All right. But I'm driving you."

"Yes, sir." She saluted, picking up on his no-arguments demeanor. "Right away, sir."

Damn, she looked cute. That should have been impossible in her granny-goes-gallivanting getup, but somehow it wasn't.

You're in love with the boss lady! echoed in his head.

Steadfastly refusing to meet TJ's eyes, Luke headed for the bedroom closet. "I'll get you a spare helmet."

"Not one that'll crush my hair!" she called.

He glanced over his shoulder. As though primping, Josie put a hand to her hair — and encountered her drab ponytail. A glum expression crossed her face.

"Never mind," she said, sounding resigned. "Nothing less than an Aquanet shortage could wreck this 'do."

Her frown, paradoxically, gave Luke hope. So long as Josie felt discontent in her new clodhopper shoes, there was still a chance she'd return to her old rebellious self again — the self he couldn't seem to get enough of.

At Donovan's Corner Elementary, Josie wended her way through the maze of

247

desks, a box of cookies in one hand and a smile on her face. As far as she could tell, classrooms hadn't changed much. The walls and cubbies were still decorated with colorful pictures. The scents of dry-erase markers, Elmer's glue, and Crayolas still hung in the air. And somehow, it still felt as though adventure waited just around the corner.

Or maybe that was Luke waiting around the corner. He'd refused to just drop her off and come back later. Instead, he'd commandeered a tiny chair near the Lego center. With his arms folded across his chest and his tattoos out in full force, he looked like her tough-guy bodyguard — although what dangers he expected her to encounter in Hannah's kindergarten class, she didn't know.

"My name's Josie." She bent to place a bunny-shaped cookie on the next child's desk, trying to ignore the sweep of her hideous dress against the floor. "What's yours?"

"Jenascia."

"Jenascia? That's a very pretty name."

The girl giggled.

"So, how's kindergarten treating you, Jenascia? I used to like the pretend kitchen — I mean, *home economics* — area. Which is pretty ironic, since it's been twenty years now and I haven't quite learned how to cook yet. Unless you count Cup O'Noodles."

Another giggle. Josie's heart melted. These kids were cute! Even the grubby-fingered boys and the girl who wore glasses that made her eyeballs look like ET's. She smiled.

"Enjoy that cookie," she told Jenascia, then moved on.

At the next desk, she set down a cookie. "Knock, knock."

The little redheaded boy looked up. "Who's there?"

"Isabel."

"Isabel who?" he yelled, delighted.

"Isabel broken? 'Cause I had to knock."

It took him a second, but he got it. His nose crinkled. His mouth opened in a completely unself-conscious laugh, showing tiny Chiclet teeth. "Hey! That's a good one!"

They both chortled. One of the mothers hustled over.

"You're only supposed to hand out the cookies," she whispered, flustered. "Here. I'll do the rest of these."

"Ummm, okay."

Her smile fading, Josie let the woman

take the cookie box from her hand. She stepped backward to watch the other mother pass out the treats, feeling confused. Maybe she'd been too chatty? Too friendly? Too slow handing out the bunnies?

But kindergarten was a place where a girl didn't have to worry about settling down, staying in her seat, or paying too much attention to things like good behavior . . . wasn't it? She looked to Jenna for confirmation.

Her sister gave her a cheery thumbs-up sign.

Hmmm. That was weird. If super-picky Jenna thought she was doing okay, what was wrong with the other moms?

Josie glanced over the heads of the eighteen or so kindergartners. Most of the volunteer parents were busy pouring apple juice, wiping sticky fingers, or settling squabbles. It all looked pretty clear-cut.

Probably she just needed to make friends with the mothers. Invade their clique. Win them over, just as she had when she'd first joined the Glamorous Nights Revue. Regrouping with the intention of doing just that, Josie joined another parent volunteer near the reading station.

"Whew!" she said conversationally.

"These kindergartners have some amazing energy, don't they? If I had that much stamina, I could do the flamenco all day *and* all night."

The startled-looking mother gave her a sidelong glance. Her eyes widened. "Sorry. I just remembered I'm supposed to be . . . over there."

With a nervous-looking smile, she shelved the book she'd been holding. She skedaddled to the other side of the room as if Cujo were snapping at her sensible flats.

"It's a *dance*," Josie muttered. "The flamenco. Heard of it?"

Sheesh. Shunned in kindergarten. This sucked.

Refusing to be held down, Josie approached the teacher.

"Hi, I'm Josie. Jenna's sister. We met right after the bell rang." She offered her most dazzling *I'm responsible* look — the one that usually ensured a new contract at Enchanté when renewals came due. "The cookies are passed out now, so I thought maybe I could do something else to help. Take those worksheets off your hands and give them back to the kids, maybe?"

The teacher started. She clutched the papers to her chest, obscuring the Crayoned-in alphabet animals the students

251

had drawn on them. "Oh, no! That's all right. It's perfectly fine. No worries. I can do it. No. No, thank you."

Wow. Somebody needed to cut back on their caffeine.

"Okay. In that case, have you had a chance to look at the flyers I brought?"

Josie had packed along two dozen handwritten information sheets for her upcoming dance school, hoping to interest the kindergartners — or their parents — in taking lessons. Josie herself had started taking ballet at the age of four, followed by tap dancing and gymnastics at seven. Her mother had hoped all the activity would give her a "productive outlet" for her energy.

"Oh, yes, your flyers are all taken care of," the teacher told her, looking relieved. "Thomas's mom said she'd hand them out." She pointed to a group of mothers near the classroom sink. "She's the blonde in the yellow shirt, right over there."

"Thanks." Zeroing in on the blonde, Josie headed that way.

Although the parents were supposed to be helping with classroom tasks, as Jenna was doing near the motion discovery station, these mothers huddled with their heads together. The sound of their voices drifted toward her. Josie recognized that pose — and that low buzz. She'd experienced both backstage every day at Enchanté. They were the universal signs of juicy gossip.

No problem. She'd read some interesting stuff about Jennifer Aniston's birthday party for Brad Pitt just this morning in *US Weekly* magazine. She'd join in.

Before she could, one of the mothers waved a flyer. "If she thinks she's getting my Brianna in on this, she's crazy!"

"Yeah." The nearest mother nodded. "She's not teaching *my* child indecent stripper moves!"

Josie froze. They were talking about her.

"I can't believe she has the nerve to even *suggest* such a thing," Thomas's mom said. "These are kindergartners!"

"You're right. You should throw those flyers in the trash, Justine," another mother advised. "That woman is a bad influence. Our children don't need to learn 'dancing' " — she added spiteful "air quotes" to the word — "from someone like *her.*"

Josie was stunned. The nasty comments hit her right where it hurt . . . smack in the middle of her hopes for the future.

Well. If those prissy, two-faced, know-it-alls thought they were going to pass judgment on *her,* they had another think coming. Josie sucked in a breath. She barreled forward, her burlap-bag dress sailing behind her like a muddy flag.

"For your information," she began, "I'm —"

"Ouch!" bellowed a masculine voice from the corner. "I think I broke my toe!"

Luke. Hesitating for a nanosecond, Josie glanced backward.

He lay curled on the floor, incongruously huge compared with all the pint-size furniture. Gaping kindergartners surrounded him. Wincing, he grabbed his booted toe.

"Arrgh. Arrgh!"

Whatever he'd done, it must have been agonizing. There was no way a burly guy like Luke would practically bawl in front of a bunch of five-year-olds — not unless something drastic had happened.

The snooty mothers forgotten, she rushed over. Jenna and Hannah joined her halfway there, looking concerned.

"Luke, what happened?" Josie crouched beside him, checking for injuries. She touched his biceps, just above the tattoo that encircled it. "Are you okay?"

"I'm fine now." He scowled. "Must have been a cramp."

"A toe cramp?"

"Sure. Yeah." He nodded, looking vaguely defensive. His gaze shot to the mothers. They were gawking now, too. He bared his teeth, a menacing expression darkening his features.

What the . . . ? Startled, Josie blinked. But when she glanced at Luke's face again, he seemed his usual happy-go-lucky self. She guessed she'd imagined the whole thing.

"Come on," she said, hauling him up. "Why don't you try walking it off so that toe cramp doesn't come back?"

"Good idea." Purposefully, Luke strode toward the gossiping mothers.

They scattered like sunshine before a storm.

Hmmm. Weird. Josie turned to Jenna, only to find her sister watching Luke with a speculative expression.

"I was just thinking," she mused. "Maybe those tattoos don't tell the whole story after all."

Twelve

Luke watched Josie approach the customer service desk at the Donovan's Corner Chamber of Commerce office, a clipboard in her hand. Despite the grueling afternoon she'd been through, she smiled at the female employee sitting there.

"Excuse me. I'm not sure about filling out this form. Should I put my name here" — she tapped the clipboarded form with her ballpoint — "or the name of my business?"

"I wouldn't worry about it too much if I were you," the clerk said. "Most new businesses fail, you know. In a couple of months, it probably won't even matter."

Luke stared. Was it his imagination, or did the clerk seem just a *little* too gleeful about the prospect of Josie's dance school failing? His muscles tightened. Intervening on Josie's behalf was getting to be a habit.

She tilted her head — a pose Luke recognized as her version of patience. "Thanks for the advice. But I've been doing the unexpected my whole life. I figure that ought to work in my favor this time around."

The woman *hmmph*ed. Apparently, she was immune to Josie's amazing smile. "Yeah, that's what everybody thinks," she said sourly. "Don't count on it."

"I'm counting on talent. And maybe a little luck."

"Not to mention a G-string," the clerk muttered, "and a little baby oil . . ."

That was it. Luke rose. "She's a *dancer.* In a revue."

"Yeah?" The clerk rolled her eyes. "Have you ever seen her 'dance'? 'Cause I heard —"

She went on jabbering. But it was her "air quotes" on the word *dance* that had Luke seeing red. He stepped nearer.

Josie grabbed him. "Luke, don't. This is silly."

He didn't think it was silly. That clerk's attitude was the last thing Josie needed today — especially after the abuse those hoity-toity PTSO mothers had heaped on her. He shot the woman a warning look.

"Really," Josie insisted. "Stop. You might get another toe cramp."

Luke backed down. Reluctantly. He needed Josie to believe in his stupid toe cramp diversion. Otherwise, she might realize the truth — he'd invented the whole thing to keep her from goading those PTSO ninnies into snubbing her altogether. He only wished he'd caught on to what was happening before Josie had heard them trash talking. Protectively, he stayed where she'd stopped him.

Keeping one hand flattened against his chest, Josie pulled something from the depths of her purse. She slapped a business card on the counter — a handwritten discount voucher for a free dance lesson. She'd been sprinkling them around town all day. She'd even left several at Hannah's school for the teachers and staff. Right about now, Luke figured they were being used as cage lining for the school's mascot, Herbert the gerbil.

"If you want to find out what I really can do," she told the clerk evenly, "bring that card to my dance school's grand opening next month. Who knows? By then, I might actually have figured out how to fill out these forms."

Flashing another impossible smile, Josie held up the clipboard. The Chamber of Commerce paperwork fastened to it fluttered, partly covered with her loopy, curlicue handwriting. She wrapped her hand tighter around Luke's arm, then tugged him toward the seating area with her.

"Come on. I'll just wing it with this paperwork."

Frowning, Luke let himself be led — but not without another cautionary look at the clerk. He made a mental note to make sure Josie's application eventually got filed. If it were up to this employee, it might accidentally get "lost." He was just familiar enough with paper shuffling — thanks to his unwanted days at Donovan & Sons' corporate headquarters — to know those things happened sometimes.

Josie wiggled onto the seat next to him. She studied the clipboard. "Okay. This can't be that tough, right?"

But as she peered at the application, frown lines puckered her forehead. Her lips moved as she reread the instructions. Her shoulders hunched. Josie filled out a few more blanks, hesitated, then scribbled out her answers and wrote new ones. She chewed her pen, looking worried.

Finally she drew in a deep breath, closed her eyes, and banged her head against the wall behind them. *Thump.*

Luke couldn't stand it. "Want some help?"

"Sure." She groaned, rubbing her head. "Have you got a brain transplant handy?"

At her obvious frustration, tenderness filled him. He wanted to make things right, to crush everyone who'd disappointed her, to fix it so Josie was never unhappy again. Luckily, her eyes were still closed. She couldn't see any of those cornball feelings on his face.

"Let's see. Brain transplant . . . brain transplant." He patted his jeans pockets, then his dark blue T-shirt. He shrugged. "I must have left it in my other suit."

A fleeting smile passed over her features. That was better.

"It figures." She opened her eyes, treating him to a disarmingly vulnerable gaze. "Me plus paperwork? Ugh. You might have noticed, but brainpower isn't really my strong suit."

Luke remembered her mother trotting out the same tired theory. But he didn't believe it.

"Anybody who can figure out how to get TJ to dust all twelve of the chandeliers has plenty of smarts," he said. "And who's the genius who dreamed up those peanut butter and pineapple sandwiches last night?"

She waved her hand. "That doesn't count. We were out of bologna. I was only improvising."

He gave her a mock fierce look. "Who?" he demanded.

Another wavering smile. "Me."

"I told you so. They were good." He'd polished off two of those freakishly tasty sandwiches himself, and not just because the Ding Dongs were gone. "And who figured out how to work the power buffer to polish those miles of Blue Moon flooring?"

Josie had. "That was simple. It was a weight-counterweight question. Intuitive body mechanics. Anybody could have done it."

Luke disagreed. "*You* did it. You've got brainpower. It's just nontraditional. Like mine."

"Yours? Oh, yeah?" Raising her eyebrows, Josie leaned back in her chair, her clipboard across her knees. She gave him an interested look. "How's that?"

"Well, look at me. I'm educated, talented —"

"Modest." She grinned.

"— and ambitious. I was brought up in a good household, with every advantage. There wasn't anything I couldn't do or have or try." *Whoops.* At Josie's curious look, Luke scaled back on the *Silver Spoons* routine. "The way most people figure it, I ought to have a skinny-ass pencil-pusher

261

job someplace. Withering under fluorescent office lights. Punching out the guy in the next cubicle because he stole my stapler. Bulldozing my way up the corporate ladder. Right?"

"Well, I think a bulldozer would pretty much destroy the corporate ladder. But I get your point."

"But I wanted to work with my hands." Luke held them up, turning them over, spreading his fingers wide. They were callused. Scratched. Even scrubbed clean of motor oil, they bore all the signs of being workingman's hands. "Fixing things was what I was good at. What I've always been good at. Taking things apart, putting them back together again, tweaking whatever I can get a grip on. I was *made* to be a mechanic."

At the words, he felt it. Now more than ever. Why couldn't his damned father see that?

"But most people don't count that as a smart career move," he said. "Most people don't count that at all."

Josie took his hand. She enfolded it between her soft palms, then lay her cheek against their joined hands. Her gaze met his. Steadily. Knowingly.

"Most people don't know how brilliant

you are at it. Or how much you love it."

Luke scoffed. Feeling weird and raw, he withdrew his hand. He hadn't meant to give away so much. He frowned. " 'Love it' is pushing it."

"No, it's not." Her intent gaze never left his face. "You *do* love it. When you've got something scattered in pieces around you — the furnace at Blue Moon, a bunch of motorcycle thingamabobs, that lawn mower TJ accidentally broke —"

"He was racing it against the push mower." Luke knew, because he'd been driving the old-fashioned version. Damn it.

"— you get this look on your face," Josie insisted. She took his hand again and squeezed it. "I think . . . I think it's the same look I get when I'm dancing."

Struck by the comparison, he gazed back at her. In that moment, a connection grew between them — a connection born of understanding. Similarity. Acceptance.

And lies, his conscience niggled at him. *She thinks you're a handyman.*

Screw you, Luke told his damned conscience silently. He had more important things to think about right now. Like the admiration in Josie's face. The sparkle in her eyes. The warmth in her touch. He couldn't remember the last time anyone had touched him with so much affection . . . so much faith. Until now, he hadn't known how hungry he was for both.

"I haven't seen that look," he told her, giving her hand an answering squeeze. "I haven't seen you dance."

Josie's eyes widened. "No kidding? Now that my ankle's better, I practice every day in the studio — even *without* a ballet barre and mirrors and a sound system."

He made a face, trying to joke about the improvements he never intended to make. Still, her reminder stung.

"I've got to be ready for my students," she went on. "I really want to *give* something to them, you know? Something good. I think that was what was missing in my Las Vegas life. Giving." She tilted her head, studying him. "Come on. You mean you've never sneaked a peek at me?"

Luke shook his head. He'd heard the music coming from her boom box, had heard the muffled *shump-shump* of her feet as she'd moved across the former ballroom, had seen her emerge afterward all sweaty and glowing. But he'd never watched her.

The guilt had kept him away.

"I never wanted to watch," he said honestly.

Which, it turned out, was *exactly* the wrong thing to say.

Luke didn't know how or why, but all of a sudden Josie stiffened. Tension ratcheted up between them. Even the clerk sensed it. She scurried to some Chamber of Commerce back room, leaving him and Josie alone in the dingy reception area.

I never wanted to watch, he reviewed. Nah, that seemed harmless to him.

"You're afraid." With an expression of dawning revelation on her face, Josie let go of his hand. "You're afraid you'll see something you don't want to see. You're afraid they're right!"

"What? Who's right?"

"You're afraid everyone in this town is right. You don't want to see for yourself that I *am* a stripper!"

"Don't be ridiculous. You're not a stripper."

"Don't try weaseling out of it now. The truth is beside the point. It's *perceptions* that matter!"

"But you're a dancer," he protested. "In a Revue."

"Hmmph." Josie slung her purse over her shoulder. She picked up her clipboard with jerky motions. "So you *say.*"

Her emphasis on *say* wasn't lost on him.

His "get out of jail free" card had just gone belly-up.

"Josie." Confused, Luke watched as she ripped off her paperwork and stuffed it in her purse. "If you were a stripper," he asked reasonably, "don't you think that's something I'd *want* to see?"

"Hah!"

Hmmm. His enthusiasm to see her naked wasn't working in his favor. Go figure. Luke scratched his head.

"As *if* I'd let you see!" She stomped to the door.

He recognized his cue. "Wait. Hang on, damn it. I thought you were mad because I *hadn't* tried to sneak a peek at you. Now you're pissed because I said I want to?"

Josie opened her mouth. She seemed to think better of whatever argument she'd been about to make and shoved open the Chamber of Commerce door instead. A blast of mingled pine and exhaust scents — the ambiance of downtown — whooshed toward Luke.

Her clodhoppers clattered down the crumbled steps.

"Okay," Luke tried stubbornly, grabbing their motorcycle helmets so he could follow. "Never mind. I *don't* want to see you naked." It was almost true . . . when

266

she was wearing that burlap bag dress. Sort of. Okay, so it wasn't true at all. But he was in a corner here. "How's that?"

Josie's angry over-the-shoulder gaze shot to his foot. He forced himself to limp. Maintaining that toe cramp was going to be a pain in the ass.

"Are you trying to say I'm fat?" She jabbed her finger at his chest. "Because *you're* the one who got me hooked on Ding Dongs, buddy. I was a perfectly moderate Twinkie user until you came along. This last five pounds is your fault."

"You're not fat." He knew the correct answer to that question. Always. In the middle of the mostly empty sidewalk, he looked her up and down. "You're perfect just the way you are. Even," he added with flagrant generosity, "in that dress."

Not mollified, she crossed her arms. "You'd be *lucky* to see me naked."

"Fine. Next time, I *will* watch you dance," Luke said, fighting for patience. "I'll invite TJ. We'll make nachos. We'll tap a keg. It'll be a party."

"Let me guess. A skanky bachelor party, right? Hmmph."

"Huh? Who's getting married?"

Clearly exasperated — however nonsensically — Josie whirled. She stopped beside his motorcycle at the curb. He hoped she didn't kick it. Those shoes of hers could snap a strut.

"For the last time, I'm not a stripper!" she yelled, flinging her arms to the sides. "Hello, Donovan's Corner! I. Am. Not. A. Stripper!"

A dozen sparrows fluttered from the trees.

"Jesus, you're scaring the birds."

Josie glared. "You know what?" she announced. "I don't want to see *you* dance naked, either."

"Uhhh . . ." Bummer.

"And," she added, waving her arm with a crazy, triumphant gleam in her eye, "I *do!* So there."

"Which is it?"

"Both!"

Judging by her victorious smirk, Josie thought she had him. She thought she was winning. Feminine logic. It made about as much sense as sweaters on cocker spaniels.

There was only one way to settle this.

"Whatever you say." Luke set down the pair of helmets he'd been carrying, getting ready.

"Good." Josie tossed her head. She looked confused for an instant — probably missing the usual swoosh of her ponytailed red hair — then snatched her helmet from the sidewalk. "I'm glad we got that straight."

"Me, too." Luke pulled off his T-shirt. He dropped it beside his waiting helmet, then paused.

Josie headed for his Harley. "Let's go."

He waited until she glanced backward again, then put his hand on his hip. He rotated his pelvis, Elvis-style. He gave her a wink.

"Hey! What are you — where'd the — what the — where'd your shirt go?" Her gaze whisked up and down his naked torso. She goggled. "What are you *doing?*"

Improvising. Refusing to say so, Luke hooked his thumbs near the top button of his jeans. He gave Josie a smile as he went on gyrating. *And winning.*

"I'm dancing naked," he said. Shit, mountain towns were cold in May, even in Arizona. Was that snow in the air? "And *not* naked. Half-naked dancing. Just like you wanted."

Her eyes widened. "I . . . ."

"You . . . ?" He raised his brows.

"Uhhh. I forgot."

He had her. Leisurely, Luke moved his hand lower, as though preparing to drop trou right there on the Main Street sidewalk. Hell, there was a decent landscaped shrub cover. No one was around. He was wearing boxer shorts. So what if he showed a little skin? A little beefcake?

At least he'd win this damned nonsense argument.

Grinning, he swiveled his hips again.

At the same time, Josie lunged forward. "Stop it!"

Her hand clapped over his, right on his fly. Her shocked gaze traveled the same path. Just for an instant, her expression went from shock to . . . curiosity. Heat flared in his groin. Luke quit worrying about snow.

"What are you, crazy?" Her warm breath tickled his icy chest hair. She sounded scandalized. "You'll get arrested!"

"If you keep your hand there, we might both get arrested." He looked down. "That feels pretty good. Just a little to the left —"

Flustered, she whisked her hand away. Her cheeks turned pink.

I win, he thought. Triumph filled him. Luke took a minute to savor the sensation, then scooped up his T-shirt. He pulled it over his goose bump–covered flesh, feeling a grin tug at his lips.

"Want me all to yourself, huh? No sharing with downtown Donovan's Corner?"

He winked. "I knew you were bluffing. You *do* want to see me naked."

Josie rolled her eyes. He had to admit, she gave a good show of indifference. It almost beat his toe-cramp impression.

"It's not your nakedness I'm objecting to." She thrust his helmet at his midsection, making him release a gust of breath. "I *like* that. It's your dancing. You need lessons, pal. And I'm just the woman to give them to you. Come on."

Josie was officially in over her head.

Standing in the middle of Blue Moon's ballroom-turned-dance-studio, she reconsidered how she'd gotten to this point. Something about naked dancing . . . Luke performing a beefcake burlesque across the street from Crazy Harry's Used Car Lot . . . her copping a feel like a tipsy, lust-crazed bachelorette.

That had been an accident, of course. Her grabbing him had been completely unintentional. She'd been going for his, uh, motorcycle keys. His crotch had interfered. She'd only wanted — *altruistically,* she reminded herself — to stop Luke from dropping his pants on Main Street and making a fool of himself.

But somehow, the only fool was her. For

leaping before she looked — *again.* For acting on impulse — as usual. For not moving her hand away fast enough and for *almost,* kinda-sorta wondering about what kinds of intriguing personal details waited only a few inches beneath her palm.

At the memory of her hand on Luke's fly, Josie felt flustered all over again. She closed her eyes in mid dance turn, struggling for composure. He'd been right, of course. She *had* wanted to see him naked. Dancing or otherwise. Preferably in her arms. Now that she had an opportunity for both those things, though, she couldn't bring herself under control long enough to take advantage of it.

When she tried to mambo, her knees went weak. When she stepped in Luke's arms to waltz, her palms sweated. When she resorted to a less-affecting tango, her heart beat so hard every time he came near, she thought she was having a panic attack.

What was the matter with her? A person would think Josie had never flirted via dancing, had never seduced with a hip sway or bedazzled with a twirl. But with Luke nearby, she seemed to forget everything she'd ever learned about keeping things casual, about keeping things light, about not getting her heart — or her feet — too entangled.

She giggled like a goofball. She blushed and stammered and lost her rhythm. She felt her breath catch in her throat whenever Luke smiled . . . and felt her defenses fall straight away whenever he said her name in that husky, sexy, all-too-knowing voice of his.

It wasn't just a physical thing, either. That was what worried Josie the most. The weirdest qualities in Luke affected her. His endearing way of humming — not that he'd have admitted it — when he concentrated on the dance steps she'd been teaching him. His sweet way of letting her choose the music, the dances, the knock-knock jokes. His macho way of pretending his toe cramp didn't bother him in the least.

In fact, he was so convincing about that, it seemed the injury had never happened at all.

Fortunately for Josie, it had. And it was her only saving grace. Because of Luke's painful kindergarten cramp earlier, she was forced to be mindful. She couldn't push him too hard. Couldn't let him take all her weight in the dips. Couldn't shove him to the floor, straddle him, and kiss him senseless while stripping off his T-shirt and —

Whew. Mountain towns were hot in May, especially in Arizona. Was that a heat wave in the air?

"You're doing pretty well," she told Luke, lying through her teeth. He was doing *fabulously.* "That mambo was an improvement over our first attempt. Just loosen up a little more and you'll be there. Like this."

She demonstrated by rolling her shoulders. Luke followed the motion, his arresting blue eyes admiring every detail — just as though she'd staged a hot-to-trot burlesque show of her own.

Maybe, Josie realized belatedly, a body-centric activity like dancing wasn't the most brilliant idea. But it was too late for second thoughts now. And she'd always been an "if it feels good, do it," kind of girl. Besides, she'd already started. So she just let go and allowed the sinuous motion to work its way down her body.

After all, she was a professional. Right? This didn't have to mean a thing.

Halfway through, she dared to glance up at Luke. He looked as though he wanted to touch her. And boy, oh, boy, did Josie want him to do it. She wanted him to caress her shoulder, to trace the slope of her breast. To hold her hips in his hands, to absorb some of those practiced warm-up motions . . . to demonstrate a few warm-ups of his own.

"Most people are too stiff for dancing," she explained breathlessly, trying to keep up her lessons-only façade. "But this warm-up routine really helps, even if you've worked through a few songs already. See?"

Luke nodded. His Adam's apple bobbed, drawing her attention to his bristly jawline, his rugged masculine features, his thick dark brows. Wow, he was gorgeous. Even better, he was good at the whole rapt-attention routine, too. Most men didn't realize how crucial that was, but Luke's gaze never left her.

If Josie hadn't known better, she'd have sworn that he was affected by her warm-up routine. That he felt almost as revved-up by all this as she did. But since she was still wearing her god-awful lentil soup–colored dress — which faithfully obliterated all signs of feminine curves — she knew that wasn't the case. No man got turned on by two oranges in a potato sack.

"Now you try," she encouraged. "Go ahead. Give it a go."

Luke did. His version of the warm-up move should have looked like most men's did — like Frankenstein's monster getting

275

his groove on. Head bolts and all. But it didn't. It showed no self-consciousness and, because of that, looked sexy as hell.

"That's pretty good," she said, attempting to sound doubtful as she circled him. Shamelessly, she added, "But you'd better try it again."

He did. Oh, God. It was even better this time. Powerful, loose, and hot-hot-hot. Luke kept going, apparently getting into it. Then suddenly, he stopped.

She felt bereft. "What's wrong?"

"Warmed up enough yet?" he asked.

"Uhhh —"

He nudged her chin upward with his fingertips. The gesture effectively closed her gaping mouth.

"I thought so." He grinned. "That looks like a 'yes' to me."

Yes, yes, yes! echoed stupidly through her head, just like in those orgasmic shampoo commercials. Josie fanned herself.

This would never do. Not only was she out of control, Luke *knew* she was out of control. She'd practically drooled on the man. If they ever progressed to flamenco, she'd need a bib.

"Well. I think I've proved my point," she announced, striding barefoot toward the boom box. She jabbed the power switch, cutting off the Spanish instrumental music she'd chosen. The resulting silence resonated in the empty ballroom. "You *did* need dancing lessons and now you've had them."

"That's it? That's all you've got?"

"What do you mean?"

In answer, Luke spread his arms, showing off his wide shoulders and muscular chest. His biceps tattoo peeked from beneath one sleeve, its cryptic black symbolism reminding her of her first interpretation of it. *Think twice.*

"You've got me all warmed up with no place to go."

She lifted her gaze to the sexy-as-sin smile on his face. The *knowing* sexy-as-sin smile on his face. *All warmed up with no place to go.* Uh-huh. There was no *way* Josie was taking that bait.

"You know," she observed instead, "if I didn't know better, I'd swear you've had dance training before."

"Only those ballroom dancing lessons." He shrugged. "At that private school in Switzerland."

"Har, har. Did your pony cha-cha with you?"

He ignored that, looking thoughtful. "But I'm not sure the lessons took. My tango's a little rusty."

Rusty. Yeah. So "rusty" it made her forget her own name. Feeling vaguely disgruntled and completely vulnerable — neither of which were welcome emotions — Josie stepped around the pair of lace-up oxfords she'd borrowed from Jenna and had since discarded for the dance lessons. She stood in the patch of sunlight streaming through the mullioned window, her back to Luke. Somehow, it felt safer that way.

"That's enough lessons for today."

He murmured noncommittally.

"I know I told you I needed to experiment with a dance routine for Jenna to perform for David," Josie went on. "In addition to teaching you a few things, of course. But I think I've got that nailed now."

"Mmmm."

"I mean, I know Jenna told me she'd been feeling kind of 'housewifey' lately —"

"So you said."

"— kind of out of sorts ever since Emily was born. But like I told her — and you — I really think a night on the town, dancing, will do the trick. If that samba doesn't put some zing in their yabba-dabba-do, nothing will."

"Mmmm-hmmm. Yabba-dabba-do."

"You can help me demonstrate it for her when she comes out here to whip up practice cupcakes for the bake sale next week," Josie rambled on, wondering if he was even listening. All those "mmms" and "hmmms" didn't sound very convincing. "You can be David in the dance demonstration, and I'll be, ummm . . ."

"Jenna."

"Right. Jenna. My sister." Geez, even her cover story was falling apart. One little touch from Luke, one minor accidental crotch grope, one harmless warm-up move, and suddenly she couldn't think straight. "So. Good night, then."

Determinedly, Josie headed for the ballroom's double doors. She needed to get rid of this horrific, scratchy dress. To finish filling out the dreaded Chamber of Commerce paperwork. To figure out why Luke could scramble her best intentions while she . . . just couldn't seem to resist him.

"Josie."

She stopped. "What?"

"It's only four o'clock in the afternoon. 'Good night' might be a little premature."

She glanced at the traitorous sunlit window. Damn it. "I'm planning ahead. It's my new motto. 'Always plan ahead.'"

"Hmmm. Good motto."

Not looking as if he believed her — and justifiably so, to be honest, because come on . . . Josie was the least planned-ahead person on the planet — Luke stepped nearer.

"Want to hear mine?"

She wasn't sure. Judging by the look on his face, it might be dangerous somehow.

Her stupid impulsive side — which apparently lived for danger — had other ideas. It was already nodding her head.

"What's your motto?"

"Don't waste a minute," Luke told her, his gaze dropping to her mouth. "Don't waste a minute, because you never know when your time's running out."

"Mmmm." She pondered that, trying not to stare at his lips in return. "That's kind of a depressing motto, don't you think so? I mean, my motto's got years' worth of Girl Scout troops behind it — or maybe that's Boy Scout troops. Who says 'be prepared,' anyway?" He had nice lips, she noticed. Sensual, perfectly shaped . . . *ahem*. She regrouped. "But then 'be prepared' isn't quite the same as 'always plan ahead,' is it? So I guess what I'm saying is —"

But by then he was already pulling her in his arms, and next he was kissing her, and Josie forgot her entire argument altogether.

She forgot her argument, her name, her birthday, her reasons for coming to Blue Moon. She forgot what Twinkies tasted like, how heavy a feathered headdress was, how many principal dancers were in Enchanté's afternoon matinee. All she could remember was Luke, and how wonderful it felt to be in his arms.

His strength surrounded her. He cradled her face in his palms, and Josie felt the warmth of his touch all the way to her toes. He kissed her until she'd swear her eyes crossed from the sheer pleasure of feeling their mouths and hearts and needs combine, and she felt . . . just as though she'd never get enough.

"Don't stop," she whispered.

"Never," Luke answered and lifted her higher against him.

She felt her toes leave the floor, felt her breasts crush against his chest, felt his hands brazenly cup her backside as he held her against him. The sensation left her dizzy. For a tall girl like Josie, being held like this — being held as though she were weightless, as though her man needed her closer, *closer* — was a rare treat. Only the showboys at Enchanté had ever lifted her before — and that was strictly professional. This . . . was strictly pleasurable. Strictly an occasion to wrap her legs around Luke for leverage and just hang on.

He twirled them both, and she screamed with laughter. He kissed her again, and she clutched at him with raw need, kissing him back. She touched him everywhere she could reach. His shoulders bunched beneath her hands; the lean muscles in his back fascinated her. He felt more solid than any man she'd ever known, any man she'd ever imagined. He felt solid enough to withstand anything — even the shakiest of futures.

Josie buried her fingers in his clean-scented hair, raked her nails over his T-shirt-covered skin, inhaled the essence of a man who wanted her so much that he'd braved the Frankenstein's monster warm-up routine before making his move.

Blissfully, she kissed him again. When he lowered her to her feet, she explored the muscular terrain of his chest. From this vantage point, he smelled like soap and fresh laundry — two things she'd never expected to find so incredibly arousing. Now, with Luke, she did. She buried her face in his shirt and sucked in a big lungful of air.

All of a sudden, it hit her.

"Bounce Mountain Spring scent!" Josie blurted, identifying that intoxicating fragrance. She wanted a whole box of it to remind her of Luke. A whole case. Economy size.

"Tide with Bleach!" he yelled back.

"Huh?"

"Spray 'N Wash. Soft Scrub Lemon. Windex."

Wrinkling her nose in confusion, Josie interrupted him before he could recite the contents of aisle three at Safeway. "What are you talking about?"

"Just helping you out with your cleaning products fetish." His smile dazzled her. "I can be a pretty cooperative guy. If that's what makes you happy."

Oh, God. Bounce Mountain Spring.

A flood of embarrassment rushed through her. Josie grabbed two fistfuls of Luke's T-shirt and hid her face in the fabric, waiting for her cheeks to quit burning. She couldn't bear to look at him. He had to think she was some kind of kook.

"Hey." His gruff voice intruded. He stroked her hair, trying to encourage her to quit snuffling his T-shirt. "Cut it out. I never knew about any of that stuff before you came along. This is a first for me, too." He hesitated. In a low, seductive voice, he added, "Mop 'N Glo."

Awww. If anybody could make aisle

three sound drop-dead sexy, it was Luke. Josie melted.

"You're willing to sweet talk me with cleaning supplies? Even though it's completely crazy? Even though it's not even what I meant?"

With a serious, macho expression, he nodded.

"Oh, Luke." Her hands trembled as she raised them to his cheeks, feeling the faint scratch of his beard shadow beneath her palms. Even though his five-o'clock shadow was a four-o'clock overachiever, he'd never looked better to her than he did at this moment. "No man's ever done anything that nice for me before."

He smiled at her. That was when Josie knew. She *was* in over her head — and not just from the dancing lessons, either. From being with Luke. She couldn't imagine a future without him in it, couldn't remember a past when she hadn't wanted him. She cared about him. Needed him.

Loved him. It was as simple as that.

Suddenly her sister's words popped into her head. *You form attachments. You like to pretend you don't, but you do.*

Jenna was right. She was attached to Luke!

For an instant, Josie panicked. She didn't

know what this meant, what this might lead to, what she was going to do. But then, somehow, all her worries whooshed away.

So what? So what if she was in love with Luke? Maybe things would work out. Maybe they could have something special together. Something unique and lasting and real. After all, Josie planned to stay in Donovan's Corner. She was committed now, having appeared in public dressed in burlap and ugly shoes. As far as she knew, Luke planned to stay here, too.

She was the woman who loved him. Even if he didn't realize it yet. She needed to know for sure what the future held.

"So . . ." Force of habit made her strive for casualness as she raised her face to his. "I've been wondering . . . What are your plans for the future?"

He looked as if she'd asked him to try on a tutu.

"The future?"

"Yes, the future. You know, what are your plans for next week? What will you be doing next month? What are your plans for after Blue Moon's finished? That sort of thing."

She waited expectantly.

Nada. Maybe more explanation was

needed. After all, Luke might not be attached to her yet. She'd only just realized their connection herself.

"Pretty soon my dance school will be up and running. There won't be as much work to be done around here." It occurred to Josie that this conversation was veering dangerously into lady of the manor versus handyman territory. She gentled her voice. "I know we haven't talked about it. But you must have plans for the future, right? Hopes? Dreams? Fantasies?"

She gave him an encouraging nudge. Just as she'd hoped, her mention of *fantasies* made a fraction of the tutu-terror leave Luke's eyes. Feeling more sure of things, Josie snuggled up to him. She looped her arm around his taut middle, enjoying the warmth and chiseled feel of his body. This was one of those moments, she realized — one of those "couple" moments when two people really bonded while discussing their future.

"I want to know," she coaxed. "It's important."

Luke cleared his throat.

"I don't talk about the future."

Then, obliterating all possibility of further discussion, he disentangled himself from her arms and walked away.

Thirteen

On-board the good ship S.S. *Extravaganza*, Tallulah straightened her vintage Pucci headscarf and gazed up at the sunshine. Being on vacation was good for her, she decided. Even a working vacation.

"About this cruise line." She transferred her attention to Ambrose, making sure he was listening. "I've decided to invest. So get that deal cooking, because I'm ready to sign."

Her attorney blinked at her from the shade of his ever-present sun umbrella. He gave no sign of what he thought of her decision. He had his laptop computer open in front of him, a bottle of disgustingly healthy V8 vegetable juice beside him, and a stack of *Wall Street Journal* issues at his elbow.

"Don't sit there gawking at me like a pig in deep mud!" she groused. "Get cracking with the paperwork, why don't you?"

Ambrose raised his dignified hand to his aristocratic face. He thumbed his nose at her, fingers waggling.

Tallulah laughed. There was a reason she and the old geezer got along. Unlike most people — her beloved, departed Ernest being the other exception — Ambrose wasn't afraid of her. He was persnickety, tightfisted, and as ticklish as a trout, but he wasn't afraid of her.

"If you'd quit blabbing, I would," he said with asperity. "A person can't work with you motor-mouthing over there."

"You can't work anyway. You went senile ages ago."

"I'm surprised you realize it. You did, too."

With another laugh, Tallulah reclined on her deck chair. Maybe they were both a little less than razor sharp. But today she didn't care. Today she felt almost like her old self again.

At the realization, a helpless sigh of near-contentment overcame her. Shocked, Tallulah glanced quickly at Ambrose to make sure he hadn't noticed.

Predictably, he had. But he'd misinterpreted it.

"Try some of my Mylanta. It'll fix you right up."

She smiled, her secret safe. The source of that sigh was true enough, though. She wouldn't be able to hide it forever. This trip had been good for her, however much Tallulah hadn't expected it to be. The cruise ship was a cocoon of sameness, a reassuring regimen of blue skies, blue ocean waves, and blue cocktails. After all the changes she'd endured since poor Ernest's passing, its constancy had felt like a blessing.

Bobbing around on the S.S. *Extravaganza* had taught Tallulah a valuable lesson. Things could never really stay the same.

Even if a person wanted them to, they couldn't. Human beings required change, or they'd go stark raving mad. How else to explain the insane dining options offered here? They ranged from early breakfasts to full breakfasts, mid-morning snacks, light lunches, full lunches, brunches, afternoon noshes, Grand Victorian teas, multicourse dinners, late-night munchies, and gala midnight buffets — all in the course of twenty-four hours. There had to be a master plan involved.

Fortified by the thought, Tallulah ordered another cocktail. A virgin one. Yes, without *any* kick. She made the cabana boy lean very, very close so she could order the alcohol-free version without alerting Ambrose. He didn't need to know that this constant proximity to his tediously wholesome habits was beginning to rub off on her.

All the while, her attorney tapped industriously on his computer. Tallulah found the familiar click-click of the keys ridiculously reassuring. Things were moving forward now. *Life* was moving forward, and she was moving right along with it.

"There. Initial contacts made," Ambrose announced. He lay one patrician hand atop his notebook's hinged screen, surveying her with a strange expression. "This ought to augment your portfolio nicely."

"Good. I'd suggest you quit looking at me that way, then. You resemble a lovesick moose. Frankly, it's not appealing. I don't know how the former Mrs. Ambrose put up with it."

He went on giving her that peculiar look. "This is a big step. The last acquisition your husband was working on before . . ." Ambrose cleared his throat. "Before everything."

Tallulah frowned. She didn't want to think about *before*. Or, quite honestly, *afterward*. Or *everything*. Not yet. The damned sunshine wasn't *that* potent.

She grumbled.

"I mean it, Tallulah." Ambrose's voice softened. "Ernest would be proud of you. For all you've done, for all your strength, for all your courage. Very proud."

A lump rose in her throat. Coughing, Tallulah tried to clear it away. The ridiculous thing was as stubborn as her attorney. It wouldn't leave her alone, either.

"I'm proud of you, too," Ambrose said.

She *hmmph*ed. "Sentimental mush does not entitle you to a larger retainer," she pointed out. "Drink your V-8 juice before its damned healthfulness starts affecting *my* thinking, too."

Ambrose only smiled.

"Tonight," he declared, "we're celebrating. I'm ordering a bottle of champagne and a private dinner, and you're putting on one of those fancy designer dresses from your stateroom, and we're celebrating."

Considering it, Tallulah glanced at her attorney . . . her friend. They'd worked together for a long time. Years. Eons. But he'd never invited her to put on one of her cherished Chanel gowns just for him. She wasn't sure what to make of it.

"Are you sure you're up to it?" she asked. "You missed your two o'clock application of SPF one billion. You might need to go lie down instead."

To her consternation, Ambrose only waited — with the damnable patience of a man who cheerfully read six newspapers every morning before breakfast. He shook his head, smiling slightly.

"We're celebrating."

"Fine. I insist on wearing my pearls."

"You'll look ravishing in them."

Tallulah gave him a narrow-eyed look. "During your morning jog around the promenade deck, did you bump your head?"

"No."

She didn't believe him. "I knew all that fresh air and exercise was dangerous."

"Be quiet." He appeared to be attempting a stern look. A smile kept intruding, and it was very unusual. "I have work to do. Memos to write. E-mails to read. Look, here's one from —"

"I don't care who it's from." Flummoxed by this bizarre change in his behavior, Tallulah frowned. Ambrose seemed positively lighthearted. That wasn't like him at all. "We were in the middle of discussing our celebration plans."

"That's not strictly true. You agreed to our plans — indirectly, I'll admit, but I'm accustomed to that — by saying you planned to wear your pearls. In reply, I stated the obvious — that you would look ravishing in them. After which you attempted to divert my attention by insulting my fitness routine. You never could accept a compliment."

Tallulah stared. What was happening between them? It was true that sealing the cruise line deal was a breakthrough of sorts for her. She hadn't been able to face the thought of finalizing Ernest's unresolved interests until now.

But this, with Ambrose . . .

Unable to cope with all the changes at once, she resorted to the time-tested tactic of women everywhere — picking an argument. It was childish, but she didn't care. "None of this matters. I can see you'd rather work than talk with me."

Ambrose — dear, crotchety Ambrose — gave her an uncommonly astute look. "You don't believe that."

Tallulah swept her gaze to his humming laptop computer.

"I see." He snapped it shut, lifted it in his arms, and carried it to the *Extravaganza*'s railing. He hurled it overboard.

"There." He dusted off his palms. "Now about our celebration —"

Oh, Ambrose. He really meant it.

"Our celebration's already begun." Giving up her first real smile of the past year, Tallulah eased sideways and patted her deck chair. "Come into the sunshine, you old fart. We've got plans to make."

Oh, no. No way. Nobody ditched Josie like that and got away with it.

I don't talk about the future.

Ha. As if *that* was going to hold water. No woman alive would have accepted such a lame excuse for dodging a conversation. Determined to get a straight answer — now that she'd recovered from her initial shock — Josie bolted after Luke. They had a connection, damn it. He wasn't avoiding it with some cheesy exit line.

I don't talk about the future.

"You do now, buddy."

Head held high, Josie veered for the front door. Luke owed her an answer — one that made sense.

Outside, her bare feet struck the front porch floorboards. At the same time a loud, familiar rumble hit the air, reverberating through her body. Luke's Harley. After riding on it with her arms clasped tight around him, Josie recognized that dangerous rumble — and what it meant. She hurried down the steps.

Too late. Luke roared past, grim-faced and headed in the other direction.

She stared, disbelieving. It couldn't be true, but it was. Luke. Leaving. *Really* leaving. His T-shirt fluttered against his broad back, buffeted by the wind. His shoulders tensed, his thighs gripped the motorcycle's seat, his whole body leaned toward escape. Without looking her way, he revved the engine, then raced around the curve of the drive.

I don't talk about the future.

He couldn't be gone, just like that. Like a bad boy out of a movie, like a heartbreaker on a Harley. Gripping the porch post, Josie waited. She listened to the motorcycle engine, poised to meet Luke halfway if he decided to turn around.

Gradually that rumble faded.

Next it disappeared altogether . . . just like Luke.

Gawking at the empty drive, Josie realized the truth. Luke wasn't coming back. Not now, and maybe not for some time. She might be attached to him, but if he felt the same way about her — and she'd have bet her last sequined showgirl's halter top he did — he wasn't giving in.

But why? What in the world was in his future that could send him roaring away

295

like that? Stymied, Josie drummed her nails on the porch post. She'd known men who couldn't commit. Men who refused to share, who wouldn't open up, who hid things such as a wife and twin daughters in Topeka. But Luke wasn't like them. He'd told her lots of things about himself. They'd laughed, they'd talked . . . they'd started falling in love.

Or at least she had.

Now Josie felt like a fool. She'd bared her hopes to Luke, and for what? For a choking waft of exhaust and a prime view of his motorcycle prowess in action, that's what. At the moment, she wasn't in the mood to admire his form, finesse, or expert cornering, either.

Frustrated, she smacked her palm against the porch post. The resulting sting restored a little of her clearheadedness — as did the sound of male laughter carrying across the lawn from the carriage house.

TJ. He'd know what the story was on Luke.

Josie grabbed the wrought iron pull on the carriage house's old-fashioned entrance. She slid open the heavy door with superhuman strength, powered by indignation and determination. Inside, a pungent whiff of motor oil, cold engine parts, and burned Pop-Tarts greeted her.

This was where Luke and TJ spent much of their time when not working on the rest of the estate. Josie didn't get the appeal of disassembled motorcycles, hydraulic lifts, and grimy engine parts. But she knew Luke loved it, so she didn't mind leaving things as they were for now.

Spotting TJ with a shop rag in hand, she headed toward him. She maneuvered past two motorcycles and a battered car being worked on — her trusty Chevy convertible, with its hood up and the engine exposed. The sight stopped her. She'd thought Luke had been repairing the starter, but now it looked as though TJ was . . . never mind. She had more important things to deal with.

"TJ, I need some answers," she announced.

TJ angled his head from beneath the hood, looking surprised but prototypically cheerful. "Hey, Josie! How's it going?"

"Not very well. Luke's gone. He peeled out on his Harley and drove toward the highway."

With a shrug, TJ wiped his face with the shop rag. "Don't worry about it. Luke does that all the time. It just means he's thinking."

Thinking. Hmmm. "Good thinking or bad thinking?"

"Just thinking." TJ scratched his head, then shot a glance toward the staircase leading to the upstairs apartment portion of the carriage house. "He's always done that."

"You've known Luke a long time, then?"

"I guess so. Five or six years, maybe. Since we started working together for the first time."

Excellent. That meant TJ was the perfect informant. Settling in, determined to get some answers about Luke's mysterious future, Josie leaned one hip on her car's driver's-side door. She watched TJ as he examined the engine.

"So, can I ask you something?"

"Shoot." He pointed one greasy finger toward the workbench. "But first hand me that socket wrench, would you?"

She did.

He stared at the tool in his hand. "You actually did it. How'd you know which one was the socket wrench?"

"I helped my dad fix stuff sometimes when I was a kid. It was kind of fun, actually." She missed those days. Glancing up, she caught his skeptical look. "What's the matter? Did you think all showgirls were born wearing a G-string and a headdress?"

"Nah. But I kinda hoped they sprouted that stuff when they turned nineteen and never wiggled out of it."

She couldn't help but grin. "*You* try having a permanent wedgie. You'd 'wiggle out of it' sometimes, too."

"I guess so." TJ tightened something with the wrench, then leaned back to examine the engine. He glanced sideways at something Josie couldn't see. He frowned.

"So, about Luke," she began.

"Right. What do you want to know?"

"We were talking about the future a little while ago, and —"

A clatter near the stairs stopped her in mid-sentence. Surprised, she looked up to see a man galumph from the upstairs apartment carrying two cans of Pepsi. He stopped cold at the sight of Josie.

"Dad! What are you doing here?"

Obviously caught off guard, Warren Day only stared at her. Then he started to smile. Josie's spirits rose. An instant later, an uncertain look flashed across his weathered face, then a mulish one. She plummeted back to earth again.

"Did you come out here to fix the cable? Luke and TJ said you installed it," she said, striving to sound normal — to sound as though her heart *hadn't* suddenly started pounding like crazy. "I guess the SuperCable wiring always was a little touchy, right?"

She gave an awkward titter — all the laughter she could manage to lighten the situation. Her father hesitated.

Josie held her breath. This felt completely ridiculous. She was treating her own father as though he were a shy wildebeest at the local zoo. But maybe that was what he needed, she reasoned. That and a nice bribe of his favorite episodes of *M*A*S*H* on DVD.

He cleared his throat, then glanced at TJ. "I didn't know you had company, TJ. I'll just take off, then. We can always watch that game some other time. See you later."

Josie hadn't heard so many words from him all strung together since she'd come back to town. But, she couldn't help but notice, none of those words had been directed at her.

Hurt, she watched her father turn away. He seemed at a loss as to what to do with the sodas in his hands. He settled on clunking them on the workbench, then grabbed his jacket.

At the sight of it, a familiar melancholy gripped her. That was the same banded-collar red windbreaker her dad had always worn in the springtime, whether the weather demanded it or not.

"Don't want to get caught in the rain," he'd always told her and Jenna, cheerfully shoving his arms in the ratty thing. "Better to be ready."

"Yeah. Ready for the nerd parade," she or her sister would say. And everyone in the family would laugh. It wasn't for nothing Josie had cultivated her love of knock-knock jokes.

Now, though, her father avoided her gaze.

"Josie," he mumbled tersely, then turned to leave.

Another hello-good-bye.

That was it. On the heels of Luke's defection and days' worth of being beaten down by skeptical, snooty townspeople, Josie had finally had enough. She wanted her father back.

"That's *it!*" she cried. "I've had *enough* of men who won't talk to me — men who bolt at the sight of me!" She stepped in front of her startled father, blocking his exit. "We're going to talk, and we're going to do it right now."

He frowned. "I've got nothing to say."

"Fine. I've got *plenty* to say."

Her father seemed wary — justifiably so, Josie figured. She wanted answers, and she was finished worrying about offending him while getting them. After all, how could things possibly get worse?

Her dad barely spoke to her. He looked vaguely queasy at the sight of her. He'd tried to *shake her hand* as a greeting a couple of weeks ago. If she was going to stay in Donovan's Corner — and she was — this couldn't go on.

She moved forward, hands on hips. "Let's just lay things out on the table, okay? Jenna tells me you think I'm a stripper."

"Uh, I've got to, um, go do . . . something," TJ blurted.

He scurried upstairs, setting a land speed record for Hasty Retreats from Family Squabbles.

"I still want to talk to you about Luke!" she yelled.

"Uh-huh. Okay. Later."

As his footsteps faded, Josie turned back to her dad.

"Jenna tells me you've believed I'm a stripper for years —"

"Your sister ought to mind her own business."

"— ever since," Josie persisted, "Howie Maynard told you I'd given him a lap dance. A lap dance!" The very mention of it irritated her all over again. "I don't know what planet Howie's been living on. But here on earth, I don't give lap dances to anybody. Much less to Tiffany Maynard's dad!"

Her father stubbornly stared at a can of Pennzoil, just as though the notion of Josie erotically entertaining the father of a girl she'd been on her high school prom planning committee with *weren't* unthinkable. Apparently his complaint about Jenna was as far as he was willing to go.

"Dad, how *could* you?" She stared at him, hands fisted, willing him to answer her. "You swallowed that whole stupid story — hook, line, and sinker."

The Pennzoil remained as riveting as before.

Josie wasn't having it. "You didn't even ask me about it," she said, determined to get to the bottom of things. "Does Howie's word mean more to you than mine does? *Somebody* raised me to be honest, you know."

At that mention of her childhood, her father compressed his lips. He seemed determined not to weaken. "Howie Maynard and I go way back. You wouldn't understand."

"Try me."

Silence.

"Fine. Why don't I float my own explanation, then?" Josie gazed at the motorcycle banners hung on the walls, trying to summon some patience. "Okay. Let's say Howie went to Vegas. Let's say he went to a topless show. It happens."

Grudgingly, her father darted a look at her. Hmmm. Maybe she was getting somewhere.

"Let's say that when he came home, *Mrs.* Maynard found out about that topless show," Josie continued, warming to her hypothetical scenario, "as wives often do. What's she going to say next? 'That's nice, dear. See any good boobies?' "

Her father chuckled.

Looking shocked, he immediately sobered.

"No! She'd be mad," Josie cried, flinging her arms up in exasperation. "Furious, even. She'd demand an explanation."

"Women," her father admitted wryly, "usually do."

"So what if Howie, remembering his good buddy Warren's daughter — *me* — who'd recently gone to Vegas, grabbed at the closest straw? What if he said, 'Gee, honey. I just wanted to see if that story was true about Josie Day working in a strip club. That's all. I didn't even *look* at the boobies.' "

Her father shifted. He stuck his hands in his jacket pockets, looking uncomfortable — possibly at her repeated use of that juvenile description.

"Dad." Earnestly, Josie moved closer. She wanted to shake him, to hug him, to make him see reason. "Isn't it possible," she asked very, very quietly, "that Howie lied to you?"

Her father puffed out his cheeks in his classic thinking pose. He refused to look at her.

"Isn't it possible," she asked further, "that Howie just made a mistake? That he got befuddled by the sight of so many —"

"Don't say it!"

"— *topless women* that he only *thought* he saw me?"

Her father frowned. He scrubbed his hand over his jaw. Then, reluctantly, "Howie did admit later that he'd overheard Tiffany telling some of her friends she thought you'd gone to Vegas to become a stripper. That's what gave him the idea."

She'd guessed right. Stunned, Josie gawked at him.

"You *knew* Howie made it up?"

"No!" Her father drew himself up to his full six-foot-three, reminding her exactly where her showgirl height had come from.

"He didn't make it up. He got the idea to go see you . . . *there*" — the *there* seemed to pain him — "because of what Tiffany said. At least that's what he told me later."

Josie shook her head. "You can*not* be the same man who told me Jimmy Stone was lying about the 'money tree' his family supposedly planted beside their jungle gym."

He frowned at the Pennzoil. He gave no sign he remembered that conversation when Josie had been a gullible fourth grader. Or that he intended to back down now.

"Howie never saw me, Dad! I'm not a stripper!" She thought of another tactic. "Didn't Mom and Jenna tell you that? They came to Vegas enough times to know."

"Yes, they covered up for you. But —"

" 'Covered up' for me?" Astonished, Josie felt her mouth drop open. "What? Why? Even if that were true — which it's not — why in the world would they do that?"

"To keep seeing shows. And to keep going shopping." Her father gave her a defensive glare. "Your mother loves that Fashion Show Mall on the Strip. She tells me so every time. It's 'Nordstrom this' and 'Neiman Marcus that' for days whenever she comes back home. There's nothing like that mall around here. Half her jewelry collection came from that place."

Looking beleaguered, he hunched his shoulders.

"Oh, Dad." Josie sighed, feeling sad. Her father had been two conversations away from the truth for years, but he'd never realized it. "Mom does love to shop, but that's not the only reason she and Jenna came to Las Vegas."

"Yeah. There were shows, too. That Lance Burton guy."

And me. The so-called "stripper."

Biting back a frustrated retort, Josie strived for patience. "Howie was wrong, and Mom and Jenna aren't covering for me. They never were. I'm telling you the truth. I'm a *dancer,* nothing more."

She waited, but he remained silent.

Josie couldn't do the same. "If you'd ever come to see me, you'd have found that out for yourself."

And that was the crux of the matter. All these years, she'd been hurt by her father's refusal to watch her perform at Enchanté. She'd waited for him to show up. She'd sent free tickets, show schedules, brochures and promotional photos. But it had all been a waste of time.

307

"I lost jobs because I refused to dance topless," she said. This might be a lost cause, but she needed to tell him the whole story anyway. "I lost *good* jobs, jobs I needed. Because I knew that if I was wearing nothing but two pasties, a G-string, and a smile, *you* wouldn't come to see me."

Refusing to see her even now, her father looked away. The setting sun's light slanted through the carriage house's window, casting an orange glow on his aged features. How had so many years gone by?

"I never quit hoping you'd come to watch me dance." Her eyes filled with tears. It was hard to force the rest of her explanation through her suddenly tight throat. Her next words came out wobbly. "All I ever wanted was for you to be proud of me."

Her dad's chin quivered. He darted a glance at her — and that glance held. His eyes, as green as her own, turned red-rimmed and misty. Still he held himself stiffly apart.

"Jenna had no right to tell you any of this."

"Why not?" Josie sniffled, gesturing wildly. "Half the town's talking about your 'scandalous stripper daughter.' The other half's already beaten the subject to death down at Frank's Diner."

"It's none of Jenna's business." Her father looked grim. "Ever since she married David, she's been nosy and —"

"Oh, no. Don't you dare take this out on Jenna! She's happy with David, and that's good enough for me." No matter that her brother-in-law had perpetual plumber's butt and was so uptight even his nostrils were pinched. "Don't you dare upset Jenna any more, because I won't let you. And one more thing!" Reminded of something else, Josie straightened, gathering all her strength. "Jenna's sensitive. She needs you. So don't you dare wreck things with her, too."

A suspicious frown. "What's that supposed to mean?"

"It means . . ." She remembered her talk with her sister and decided to just go for it. For Jenna's sake. "It means I'm not the only daughter who's disappointed you."

He scoffed. "Jenna doesn't disappoint me."

You're the only one who does that, was the silent rejoinder.

"Well. Fine. Next time you see her, you might try telling her that. She could use hearing it." Impending tears squeezed Josie's voice again, making it hard to go on.

"While you're at it, tell Jenna you love her. She needs to hear that, too."

Her father looked skeptical. "She already knows that."

"Really?" Blinking back tears, Josie gave him one last, long look. "Like I do?"

He didn't say anything.

A minute later, he left.

Fourteen

Sitting at Frank's Diner with a slice of pie at his elbow and a cup of coffee in his hand, Luke waited for the pay phone to be free. Since he'd arrived, an out-of-towner had been monopolizing the thing, complaining to his cell phone company about the lack of transformer stations "out here in the boonies." Not even Luanne's repeated glares had been enough to scare the guy away from the phone alcove.

Nearby, all the usual suspects filled the diner's red vinyl booths. Retirees chatted, couples shared an early dinner, a few teenagers forked up Frank's famous pie. Putting down his coffee, Luke stared at his own slice of apple à la mode. He didn't know why he'd ordered it. Force of habit, he guessed. He sure as hell didn't have any appetite today. Not after what had happened with Josie.

I don't talk about the future.

Damn. That was the mother of all lame excuses. But he'd been backed into a corner. He didn't want to lie to Josie anymore — especially given the way he felt about her. But he couldn't tell her the truth yet, either. Not until he got things settled with Tallulah and Blue Moon.

Which explained what he was doing here at Frank's.

Casting an impatient look at the pay phone hog, Luke pushed aside his pie. He signaled Luanne for the check. There were other pay phones in town. He'd find one, he'd call Ambrose, and he'd sort out this whole mess. Pronto. Because until he did, his secret was only going to get bigger.

I don't talk about the future.

How could he? How could he tell Josie he planned to sell Blue Moon, use the profits to open his own mechanic's shop back in L.A., and put Donovan & Sons behind him for good? How could he tell her how much all that meant to him?

He couldn't.

Pursuing his future would crush hers. At the least it would put her dance school dreams in limbo. Luke refused to do that to her. Until he had Tallulah's assurance that she'd give Josie another property, he intended to keep his ownership of Blue Moon a deep, dark secret. Especially from the woman who thought the place was hers.

312

Swearing under his breath, he signaled Luanne again.

He'd never thought it would come to this. He'd been sure he'd hear from Ambrose by now. Especially after the two follow-up e-mails he'd sent. But he hadn't. And Luke wasn't sure where to go from here. If he refused to lie to Josie and he couldn't tell her the truth, what else was there?

Damn. He frowned, impatiently fiddling with his paper-napkin-wrapped fork. Things never should have gone this far. He'd expected Josie to give up — or himself to get bored. But neither of those things had happened.

Instead, he'd gotten sucked deeper and deeper into a relationship he'd never planned for . . . with a woman he'd never expected. A woman who looked good to him in burlap, who induced him to cha-cha, who turned misty-eyed over detergent names. A woman who worked wholeheartedly, and who hugged him with exactly the same intensity.

Even if he couldn't stick around to see her succeed, he wanted to make sure she did. Josie deserved it.

With a nod for Luanne, Luke tossed down a five and headed for another pay phone. It was time to take serious action.

"Come on, TJ. Come down here. I won't bite."

Peering upstairs toward the carriage house apartment, Josie waited. After all the hullabaloo with her father, TJ had made himself scarce. She didn't blame him. Family arguments were no fun for anybody — least of all Josie, the family black sheep. But despite her puffy eyes and tear-smudged cheeks, she still wanted answers. There was no time like the present to get them.

Mustering up an encouraging singsong, she tried again. "Yoo-hoo! TJ! I've got Pop-Tarts."

Gently, she shook the box. At the familiar rustle of the wrapped pastries, TJ's shaggy-haired head popped into view.

"Pop-Tarts? Why didn't you say so?"

He rambled down the stairs, pausing at the bottom to look around. Seeing nothing but Josie's Chevy, motorcycle parts, and the usual mechanic's accoutrements, he shrugged. He accepted the Wild Berry frosted pastry she held out.

Josie had snared her informant. "So, tell me. What's Luke got planned for the future?"

"Wow. You don't waste time."

"Not today, I don't." Heck, she'd already annihilated her relationship with her father *and* outed her sister's familial insecurities. Although she'd meant well in both instances, she figured she had nothing to lose by jumping in with both feet now. "Well?"

"I'm not supposed to tell you." TJ took a bite of Pop-Tart. His expression turned from cautious to blissful. "Luke doesn't want anybody to know until it's a done deal."

"Until what's a done deal?"

TJ remained mum. He shook his head.

So Luke *was* hiding something. "Why the secrecy?"

A shrug. "If it was anybody else, I'd say he didn't want people to know what he was up to in case he screwed up." TJ poked at his Pop-Tart, pushing in some of the jam-like filling. He licked his thumb. "But Luke never screws up. Not when it counts. With him . . . I think he just wants to be left alone."

"Alone? Why?"

"I dunno. Because he's a solitary kind of guy?"

"Seriously, TJ. Be straight with me."

He gave her a contemplative look. Then he sighed. "When Luke left L.A., he was pretty pissed. He'd had it. A lot had happened, and . . ." TJ stopped. "Nah, I shouldn't talk about it."

But it was just starting to get good! Perkily, Josie lifted the snack box. "I've got more Pop-Tarts," she coaxed.

He looked hurt. "I can be bribed, but I can't be bought."

"Sorry."

"It's cool."

"It's just that I care about Luke, okay? I do. I didn't want to, but it happened, and now it's too late. So I want a little information. I want to know about him."

To her dismay, tears filled her eyes. Damn it. Angrily, Josie swiped them away. After all she'd been through today, something as innocuous as TJ's reluctance to talk couldn't possibly be the one thing that pushed her over the edge.

"I just" — she sucked in a gulp of air, determined to continue — "want" — another gulp — "to know" — gulp — "if we have a future together."

TJ looked concerned. Awkwardly, he patted her shoulder.

"Because — Luke said — he doesn't talk" — huge gulp — "about the future. Ever."

Ever emerged in one long wail, despite her best efforts.

"Oh, come on, now. Don't do that," TJ pleaded. "Don't cry. I didn't mean . . . you know. I'm not trying to be an asshole about this. It's Luke's no-talk rule, not mine."

"I know." She sniffed. Blinked up at him. "It's not your fault. It's just so frustrating!"

He nodded.

"It's worse than wearing these clothes!"

He looked surprised.

"Worse than running out of Ding Dongs!"

He looked impressed. Reluctantly, he patted her again.

"Maybe I can tell you a little bit. Luke doesn't have to know you heard it from me, right?"

She brightened. "Right! I won't tell him, I swear."

Josie crossed her heart. The gesture seemed to convince TJ of her sincerity, because he finally dished.

"He wants to open a motorcycle mechanic's shop. Kind of like this one." TJ swept his arm sideways, indicating the renovated carriage house. "Only bigger and mondo-successful. So he can show his dad."

That made sense. Luke *did* love working on motorcycles.

317

"Does his dad like motorcycles, too?" she asked.

"Nah, he pretty much thinks they're the scum of the open road. To Luke's dad, nothing beats a big rig loaded up to hit the highway."

He must be a truck driver, Josie decided. Tough, no-nonsense, all-American. But woefully misguided when it came to his son. How else to explain his resistance to Luke's idea?

"Hey, motorcycles aren't so bad." She felt indignant on Luke's behalf. And protective of his dream, now that she knew he had one. "They're fun. They're easy to park. And you can personalize them with custom paint jobs, just like a manicure."

TJ nodded, giving her a *what can you do?* face. "You can't tell that to Bob Donovan, that's for sure."

They shared a moment, linked in their disapproval of a father who looked down on his own son's dream.

"I know about stubborn fathers, believe me," Josie said. "But I still don't get why Luke's plan is supposed to be such a big secret. People open mechanic's shops all the time."

TJ pretended not to hear her. Very deliberately, he grabbed another Pop-Tart. He tore into it like a man belting down one last tequila shot for courage.

"Why are Luke's plans such a big secret, TJ? What am I missing here?"

Nada. She kept going.

"And why does Luke need to be super-successful to show up his dad? What's the deal with that? Do they have some kind of rivalry going on?"

"Rivalry?" He scoffed.

"You're right. Men probably outgrow that kind of stuff."

"No, I'd say 'rivalry' is putting it lightly. Those two totally butt heads all the time."

Just like her and her dad. Josie's empathy for Luke grew.

"Luke doesn't fit in with his family. He never has," TJ said. "His relationship with his dad makes yours with *your* dad look like a walk in the park."

"Geez, do they fire bazookas at each other, or something?"

"Just about." He dropped Wild Berry crumbs on his T-shirt. Noticing, he gave a halfhearted sweep. "It gets pretty bad. I've been there for a couple of the arguments, including the last one." He whistled. "It was a biggie."

"What was it about?"

"Can't say."

"Who was right?"

He seemed taken aback by the question. "You know, a month or two ago, I'd have said Luke was. But by now I'm not so sure. Luke kinda shoots *himself* in the foot with a bazooka sometimes, if you know what I mean."

Josie did. In the past, the same had been said about her.

"No wonder Luke got all bent out of shape when I started talking about his job at Blue Moon being almost over with." She frowned, remembering their conversation. "He probably hasn't saved up enough money for his mechanic's shop yet. So he doesn't *want* his job to be over with."

"He definitely needs cashola," TJ agreed.

"And there I was, practically rubbing his face in the fact that he's running out of time." It was so obvious. Josie couldn't believe she hadn't realized it before. "No wonder he didn't want to talk about it."

TJ gave a noncommittal sound.

His lack of enthusiasm for her theory didn't bother Josie. Things were finally clicking together. Luke. Blue Moon. His hopes for the future, which were endangered by her being there — endangered by her dance school.

It was a mess, all right.

"I'm surprised Tallulah didn't make some kind of accommodations for Luke to keep working here indefinitely. I mean, he *is* the handyman. It's not his fault Tallulah decided to give the place away."

"Yeah. Anyway, I should probably get back to fixing your Chevy. That starter's a little tricky."

"Do you think he'd take a job from me? I probably can't match Tallulah's salary, but I do have some money saved up —"

"No! *Don't* offer Luke a job." TJ looked uncomfortable, probably at having revealed any part of his friend's secret. He shot a longing look toward her ailing car. "Men have, you know, pride. Luke won't want pity."

"It's not pity, it's practicality. He needs money. Before you know it, my dance school will be bringing in plenty."

"Yeah. Right. Still . . . Don't say anything to Luke, okay? He's, uh, sensitive about the situation with his dad. And he wouldn't want you to know about his motorcycle mechanic's shop plans. I shouldn't have said anything."

"Don't worry. I'll tell him I charmed it out of you."

"No! Don't tell him anything!"

"I'm kidding." She gave TJ a teasing arm punch, feeling warmhearted toward him. In his own uncouth way, he'd tried to cheer her up — tried to help her. She appreciated that. "I won't say anything. Luke's secret is safe with me."

Especially now that Josie knew the rest of the story — knew that pursuing her future had accidentally endangered his. She felt bad about that. It wasn't something she'd seen coming, but now she could start fixing things. By contacting Tallulah, for instance, and finding out if she had another estate for Luke to work on. Or networking in town to see if the Donovan's Corner Garage had any openings for mechanics. It could work.

Sure. It *had* to work. Because there was no way Josie could be happy if achieving her own dreams torpedoed Luke's.

She glanced at TJ. He'd edged closer to her Chevy's ailing engine, socket wrench in hand, looking as if he regretted their whole conversation. Thanks to him, though, Luke's reluctance to confide his future plans felt entirely different to her now.

"You know, it's kind of sweet, actually," she mused. "You guys all think you have to be so tough for us, like Luke with his secret mechanic's shop plans. When really, women don't mind a little vulnerability. A little trust. A little faith."

TJ shook his head. "Sure. You say that now. But it never turns out that way."

"Of course it does."

"Uh-uh," TJ disagreed. "Women *say* they want all that crap. But then if we guys let our guard down for a minute — wham! You're bailing out on us for a thick-necked jerk named Spike who bench-presses Buicks and smashes beer cans on his forehead."

Josie laughed. "I think my friend Parker dated that guy."

TJ looked vindicated. "See? Proves my point."

"But she figured he was a fixer-upper. By the time Parker finished with him, Spike was picking out Chardonnay and wearing turtlenecks."

"Whoa. That's uncool."

"Come on. Spike *likes* getting his eyebrows waxed now."

"Hey." He shot her a warning look. "Don't make me regret telling you about Luke. I only did it because I thought you'd be *good* for him."

"I will be," Josie said seriously. "I promise."

Then she gave TJ a hug and headed out the carriage house doors, ready to make her future and Luke's merge — in the best way possible.

Fifteen

Over the next several days, Luke found himself busier than ever. First, with motorcycles. Second, with Ambrose. And third with Josie.

Word had gotten around about his carriage house "garage," especially his expertise with vintage motorcycles, so he had all the repair work he could handle. His efforts to contact his aunt's attorney continued, but his phone calls and e-mails went unanswered. And on top of everything else, he found every excuse to drive Josie to town on his Harley.

Doing so was an extra effort — and not strictly necessary, since TJ had already fixed the starter on her heap of a convertible — but it was worth it. Worth it for the feel of her plastered against him, hugging him from behind as they took the mountain curves. Worth it for her squeals of delight as he revved the engine. Worth it for the trust she gave him every time she climbed on his motorcycle.

Trust wasn't something Luke took lightly. Not after what had happened with his father.

Josie's mission to turn herself into Donovan's Corner's most respectable showgirl transplant wasn't something she took lightly, either. Every day she climbed off his motorcycle and handed him his spare helmet. Every day she slicked back her hair — usually in a prim bun — and adjusted her baggy, buttoned-up clothes. Every day she told Luke she'd be fine.

"You don't have to hang around. I can handle it."

But every day, Luke stayed by her side anyway.

He was always glad he did. Because no matter what reputable activity she had planned — a charity drive, a networking lunch, or ordinary grocery shopping — some numbskull in town always felt compelled to badmouth her. That meant Luke needed to run interference . . . so his list of "injuries" grew. It wasn't the best diversion, but it was all he had.

"I swear, Parker," he heard Josie saying on her cell phone to her showgirl friend from Las Vegas, "it's as if Luke's gone klutzy or something. First that toe cramp at Hannah's kindergarten, then a sprained thumb at the bank. And a pulled muscle after church, too. I don't know what's going on."

Luke grinned. If he was lucky, she never would. If he was *really* lucky, people in town would quit dissing Josie before he was forced to dislocate a shoulder.

Unfortunately, though, her campaign wasn't that successful yet. Her dance school's official debut loomed closer all the time, but the uptight residents of Donovan's Corner didn't seem ready to see Josie as anything but a scandal in the making.

Not that their die-hard skepticism stopped her. Undaunted, she outfitted herself in one dowdy getup after another. She carried a briefcase and baked cookies for the members of the Better Business Bureau — who seemed to grudgingly appreciate the gesture, if not the charbroiled results. She talked her heart out, tacked up flyers until her fingers ached, and tirelessly stumped for her dance school.

Her natural charm should have been enough. But if it wasn't, Luke figured she had good odds of wearing down the naysayers through sheer stubbornness alone.

Overall, life was good. Josie didn't ask him about the future again, and he didn't volunteer the information. Why look a gift horse in the mouth? Instead, they simply spent their days together. They worked, they talked, they kissed. They ate cheeseburgers at Frank's, raced along the pine forest back roads on his motorcycle, laughed over TJ's cheesy kung-fu movie picks from the local video store.

Luke, despite knowing he shouldn't, fell even harder for Josie. And the next time she danced, both he and TJ watched.

She was unbelievable. Lithe, limber, and dazzling in her precision. He'd never realized how much sheer athletic work went into dancing, but Josie made it look effortless. When she danced, she relaxed . . . and she came alive. As impossible as it seemed, Luke thought he'd never seen her look happier than while whirling in a series of complicated steps.

"Okay. That was my standard audition routine," she announced, flushed and eager, when the first song ended. "This next bit is something I made up just for fun."

While they watched, she performed again. She arched her back, she flung her arms in the air, she executed the trickiest moves with a smile. Somehow, even though Josie wore nothing but plain track pants and a tank top, she sparkled. Luke could almost see the spotlights and sequins and glitter. Or maybe that was just the natural glow all around her.

"Woo-hoo!" TJ yelled, applauding enthusiastically. He stuck his fingers in his mouth for a piercing wolf whistle. "Go, Josie! Go, Josie!"

"Cut it out." Luke gave him a shove. "I'm not doing 'the wave' with you."

"Buzzkill."

But Josie only smiled wider, her body radiant with hard-earned sweat. She twirled to the other end of the ballroom to show them another move. Despite his grumblings to TJ, Luke couldn't tear his gaze away. He thought she was magnificent.

Someone else did, too. Toward the end of that week, Josie earned her first student: her niece, Hannah.

Luke never would've credited Josie's starchy sister, Jenna, with enough gumption to enroll her daughter in the town's most notorious new dance school. Especially since doing so meant openly defying her posse of PTSO moms. But apparently rebel stubbornness genes ran in the family, because Jenna arrived at Blue Moon with baby Emily on one hip and Hannah's hand in hers. She announced that dance class was in session.

"Go ahead, honey." She nudged her daughter forward, then met Luke's open surprise with a defiant tilt of her chin. "Hey, *somebody's* got to start the stampede to this dance school."

"Damned straight," Luke agreed, approving.

Her loyalty touched him. It got to Josie, too, because she turned all weepy. Ten minutes of apology-filled hugging and blubbering passed ("No, *I'm* sorry!") before both women pulled themselves together enough to get on with things. In the meantime, Luke and TJ were left to deal with Jenna's befuddled offspring.

Luke wasn't happy with the arrangement. For one thing, it potentially involved diaper changing. But by the time Jenna scooped a babbling, drooling Emily from his arms again, Luke had decided babies weren't so bad after all. There was a lot to be said for a person who smiled that much. Especially when that person was toothless.

The lessons were on.

At five years old, Hannah was shy and a little pudgy. Her arms and legs flopped. Her brown bangs hung in her eyes. But even Luke — who didn't know squat about kids — had to admit the girl was adorable. She bumbled into the ballroom, gawking at moves culminating in a hip thrust at the end — and a pouty over-the-shoulder look. It was vintage pint-sized sexpot, complete with a hair toss.

Jenna stared, openmouthed. "Uhhh . . ."

"Good, right, Mom?" Hannah asked breathlessly. She couldn't have looked more thrilled with herself.

"It's terrific. You nailed it!" Josie enthused. She gouged her elbows in Luke's and TJ's ribs to either side of her. "Look, these guys are speechless! Wasn't it terrific, you two?"

"Awesome!" TJ said.

"Very dance-y," Luke added. Ouch.

"Thank you, thank you!" Hannah jumped up and down. She seemed oblivious to her mother's continued — stunned — silence. She twirled in place, her cheeks shining.

"Show your mom your other dance," Josie encouraged.

"Okay!"

Hannah spun off to the center of the room. She assumed some sort of ready position, held her arms in a pose over her head, then took several tiptoed steps. She twirled again.

"It's a movement from *Swan Lake*. Classical," Josie explained. She beamed at her

the crystal chandeliers overhead, we
shorts and a T-shirt and a pair of pa
knee socks.

"They're her soccer socks," he
Jenna explain in an aside to Josie. "Ha
wanted some padding between her an
floor in case she fell down." She le
nearer, out of her daughter's ea
"She's convinced she'll fall. I'm
soccer hasn't done much to improv
coordination."

"That's okay," Josie said, shimmyir
ward Hannah. She wrapped her
around the girl's shoulders and gave
sunny smile. "We'll have fun, won'
kiddo?"

They seemed to. Especially judgir
the expression on Hannah's face whe
emerged a half hour later, winded ar
sheveled — but ecstatic.

"Mom! Mom! I learned that new
move! You know, the one I saw on T

Jenna looked puzzled. "Which
move?"

"The one in Britney's video!" Ha
said. "Look!"

"One-two-three-four!" Josie said, c
her.

Hannah performed a wobbly but d
series of steps while Josie kept time

moves culminating in a hip thrust at the end — and a pouty over-the-shoulder look. It was vintage pint-sized sexpot, complete with a hair toss.

Jenna stared, openmouthed. "Uhhh . . ."

"Good, right, Mom?" Hannah asked breathlessly. She couldn't have looked more thrilled with herself.

"It's terrific. You nailed it!" Josie enthused. She gouged her elbows in Luke's and TJ's ribs to either side of her. "Look, these guys are speechless! Wasn't it terrific, you two?"

"Awesome!" TJ said.

"Very dance-y," Luke added. Ouch.

"Thank you, thank you!" Hannah jumped up and down. She seemed oblivious to her mother's continued — stunned — silence. She twirled in place, her cheeks shining.

"Show your mom your other dance," Josie encouraged.

"Okay!"

Hannah spun off to the center of the room. She assumed some sort of ready position, held her arms in a pose over her head, then took several tiptoed steps. She twirled again.

"It's a movement from *Swan Lake*. Classical," Josie explained. She beamed at her

332

the crystal chandeliers overhead, wearing shorts and a T-shirt and a pair of padded knee socks.

"They're her soccer socks," he heard Jenna explain in an aside to Josie. "Hannah wanted some padding between her and the floor in case she fell down." She leaned nearer, out of her daughter's earshot. "She's convinced she'll fall. I'm afraid soccer hasn't done much to improve her coordination."

"That's okay," Josie said, shimmying toward Hannah. She wrapped her arm around the girl's shoulders and gave her a sunny smile. "We'll have fun, won't we, kiddo?"

They seemed to. Especially judging by the expression on Hannah's face when she emerged a half hour later, winded and disheveled — but ecstatic.

"Mom! Mom! I learned that new dance move! You know, the one I saw on TV!"

Jenna looked puzzled. "Which dance move?"

"The one in Britney's video!" Hannah said. "Look!"

"One-two-three-four!" Josie said, cueing her.

Hannah performed a wobbly but decent series of steps while Josie kept time, the niece. "I like to start with something fun to catch a student's interest — in this case, the Britney move — then move on to something more traditional."

"Do it again! Do it again!" TJ yelled, enthralled.

They all gawked at him.

"Hey, I like ballet. Shoot me."

With more encouragement, Hannah repeated the dance. Her movements — as obviously beginner as they were — actually held some sort of grace. It was a miracle, Luke thought. Like the Jets winning a playoff.

"Bravo!" came a voice from behind them. "Excellent!"

They all turned. Applauding, Nancy Day strode toward them in a yellow suit, high heels clacking, sunlight glinting from her jewelry. She must have let herself in, a ballsy move that didn't surprise Luke. What did surprise him was the expression on her face. For the first time ever, she looked downright kind . . . and a little contrite.

"Grandma! Look! Look what I can do!" Hannah yelled.

Against all Luke's expectations, the girl didn't show off her Britney moves. Instead, she repeated the *Swan Lake* dance. He glanced at Josie, eyebrows raised, but she only shot him a pleased, knowing smile.

"Every girl has a little ballerina in her."

He guessed so. Because now Hannah pirouetted all through the ballroom, hands overhead in an approximation of every cartoon ballerina he'd ever seen. Unlike Tom & Jerry, she looked pretty adept, even with those soccer socks on. He was impressed.

"That's wonderful, Hannah," Nancy Day called. "Good job!"

She glanced at Josie. Then frowned. "Don't give me that look, Josie. I knew all along you'd make a fine dance teacher."

"Why, because I'm so bossy?"

"No." A smile played around Nancy's mouth. "Because you're so talented. Now let's see what you three have done to this place, shall we?"

She assumed the lead in a tour of the renovated mansion, covering the ground floor and then following the repaired staircase to the second floor. In every room, Nancy oooh-ed and aaah-ed over the changes Josie and Luke and TJ had made. She commented on the bathrooms' honeycomb tile, on the gleaming mullioned windows, on the refurbished floorboards and wallpaper and paint and every other detail under the sun.

"Structurally, this place looks like a million bucks," Nancy announced when they entered the kitchen. She leaned against the countertop beside Luke. "But aesthetically it's missing something. Some sense of . . . hominess, I guess."

"That's because I haven't put my personal stamp on it yet," Josie told her. "Having this much space — for the first time in my life — is pretty overwhelming to deal with."

"We decided to keep it neutral," Luke agreed. "That way it'll be easier to —"

Abruptly, he cut himself short.

Easier to sell the place later. It had been right on the tip of his tongue. Damn it. What was the matter with him? A person would think he *wanted* his secret out in the open. All this family togetherness — and all those Hallmark moments with Hannah and Emily — must have worn down his usual wariness.

"— easier to rent out some of the rooms in the east wing," Josie finished for him, not looking up as she fiddled with the microwave. "Right, Luke?"

She slapped a nuked hot dog on a fluffy bun and slid it across the table to Hannah. The girl chowed down.

"You want to rent some of the rooms?"

335

Nancy asked, seeming more interested by the minute.

"Yes," Josie said, still bustling around. She filled the coffeemaker's basket with Arabica beans, then added water and turned on the unit. "I mean, let's face it. This place is too big for me, and I'll probably need an income to tide me over until my dance school takes off." At that, she smiled gratefully at her sister. "My savings aren't going to last forever, and the renovation fund Tallulah gave me is just about tapped out."

She opened the refrigerator and withdrew a bottle of ketchup for Hannah. The conversation turned to talk of Jenna's upcoming salsa dancing night — a surprise she'd planned for David now that Josie's lessons with her were finished.

Luke still couldn't believe he'd participated in them as the requisite David stand-in. He'd felt as if he'd been drafted into a boy band — minus the gelled hair and animatronic moves — but Josie had insisted he'd done well. Her thank-you kiss had almost made him believe it.

Amid the murmurs, Nancy gave Luke an appraising look.

"Your 'neutral' decorating would make this place a cinch to pitch to buyers," she remarked in an undertone. "Sure you don't want to list it? I'll bet it would rake in a bundle."

"Save the sales talk." He frowned at her, irritated at having nearly blurted out his plans for Blue Moon — and, upon hearing Nancy's offer, feeling pissed off on Josie's behalf. It would only hurt her feelings to know her mother was shilling for sales. "I thought you were here to see Josie."

"I'm here to see what you three have done here. Professional Realtor's interest." She said the words loudly, surveying the room with a regal tilt to her chin. To Luke alone, she added, "Cut me some slack, you big galoot. A mother's got to have her excuses. If Josie thought I was visiting her on purpose she'd hide in a closet, and you know it."

He couldn't help but grin. In the past, Josie had done exactly that in an attempt to evade her family. Having met them, he understood why. But now, for some weird reason, he found himself warming up to Nancy. He was beginning to believe her flashy suits hid a tender heart.

He tuned back into the conversation.

"As soon as we get the mirrors and the ballet barre and the sound system," Josie was saying, "we'll be all set to launch the dance school."

Damn. That again. The enthusiasm in her voice was plain as she went on discussing her dance school plans. Charitably, no one mentioned that she still needed a lot more students, too.

"I can manage without some of the equipment for a while," she continued, waving her arm blithely, "but — wait, all that stuff is on back order, right, Luke?"

Pretending not to hear, he grabbed several mugs and headed to the gurgling coffeemaker. He felt like a jerk the whole time. Damn it. How had he gotten into this mess?

Josie shrugged, cheerfully overlooking his silence. "I'm not worried," she told the others. "It'll all come together somehow, I just know it. It's only a matter of time."

Luke hoped so.

"Well, the ballroom's well on its way, and the rest of the place looks completely ship-shape," Jenna volunteered, visibly impressed as she surveyed the changes. "It looks like you'll be ready for your opening day."

"Good thing, too," Nancy said. "That means all those dance school advertisements your dad cooked up through Donovan's Corner SuperCable won't go to waste. They've been airing for a solid week."

Everyone stilled. Josie's mouth dropped open.

"Of course, they're mostly on in the middle of the night," Nancy continued merrily, oblivious to the astonishment in the room, "when rates are cheaper. So you might wind up with a dance school full of insomniacs." She rubbed the countertop. "Oooh, is this granite? Granite has great resale value."

More staring.

Jenna recovered first. "Forget the countertops, Mom! Dad's been advertising Josie's dance school?"

Carelessly, Nancy nodded. "Yes, to recruit students. He's buddies with the guy who books ad space, so he called in a few favors. You mean none of you have seen the ads?"

"We put our TV in storage," Jenna said, shooting a pointed look at her hot-dog-munching daughter. "After *certain people* took it upon themselves to start watching MTV."

"Whoa. No TV? That's harsh," TJ said.

"No, it's not. It's sensible. Watching less TV is supposed to bring families together." Jenna jiggled Emily on her lap. "At least that's what *Parents* magazine says."

"Jenna's bible," Josie explained, smiling

affectionately at her sister. To her mother, she added, "I'd love to see Dad's ads, but I don't have cable out here."

Luke shrugged. "I mostly watch ESPN."

"Hmmph. All that effort gone to waste." Nancy shook her head. "I'd better not tell Warren."

A moment slipped past. Tentatively, Josie spoke up.

"What . . . what made Dad want to do that? The ads?"

The hopefulness in her eyes pained Luke to see. He frowned. Josie didn't deserve to be given the runaround this way. After everything TJ had told him about the argument she'd had with her father, he didn't have high expectations.

Remarkably, Josie still seemed to.

"Mom?" she prompted. "Was this your idea? Did you make Dad place those ads?"

Nancy scoffed. "I can't 'make' your father do anything."

Both sisters snorted.

"Yeah, *right*. Tell us another one," Jenna said.

"Fine." Tilting her chin, Nancy went on. "The truth is, your father just did it. He didn't ask me, he didn't tell me. I didn't even find out what he was up to until I saw one of the ads myself. Believe me, I *don't* enjoy being kept out of the loop."

Now it was Josie's and Jenna's turn to smile.

"When I asked him about it, he said something strange, too." Nancy hesitated, as though unsure whether or not to confide the rest. Then, prodded by her daughters' expectant faces, she relented.

"He said, 'Whatever you do, don't tell Josie. She'll yell at me about boobies again.' " Nancy looked puzzled. "Which doesn't even make sense. Discussing 'boobies' with me, his wife. Me! Hmmph. Your father must have been having a break with reality when he said that."

"I know what he meant." Josie's eyes shone. "He meant I got through to him."

"Got through to him? About what?"

"About me. At least a little bit. It's not everything, but it's definitely a first step."

Skipping across the room, Josie hugged her startled mother. Next she hugged Jenna and Hannah and Emily in turn. She hugged Luke, squeezing him with what he'd swear was special enthusiasm. She stepped sideways to hug TJ, but he warded her off with both hands.

"Hang on. I don't even understand what's going on here."

"You don't have to," she blurted happily. "C'mere!"

"Uhhh —"

But Josie crushed his lanky body in her arms anyway, shaking him from side to side with enthusiasm. Any minute now, she'd just plain pop with happiness, Luke was sure. He'd have been thrilled to see it — if he trusted it. But he didn't. As far as he was concerned, fathers couldn't be depended on.

Josie stopped, then surveyed them all with a wide grin. She paused in the kitchen's arched doorway, her face joyful.

"You know what this means, don't you?"

Mutely, Luke shook his head. Given the energy radiating from her, he was almost afraid to wonder. So was everyone else, apparently. They remained mum.

"It means I'm going to visit my dad, for one thing! And it means that from here on out, I'm trying harder than *ever* to start my dance school!"

Then she chortled with glee and pounded upstairs, ready for her next assault on Donovan's Corner.

Sixteen

Treading across the grassy expanse of Donovan's Corner City Park, Josie carefully balanced a tray of a dozen cupcakes. They were part of her contribution to the annual Founder's Day festivities — an afternoon's worth of picnicking, parades, vendor booths, a 10K run, covered wagon rides, and more. Most of the town usually attended the event, making it an ideal opportunity to drum up business for her dance school.

Feeling proud of herself for wrangling an invitation to participate *and* for actually producing the cupcakes she'd promised for the bake sale fund-raiser, Josie strode through the park with Luke at her side. Her prim outfit for the day consisted of Jenna's castoff green gingham dress, combined with a matching headband and white Keds.

She sure hoped this getup was making the right impression. She couldn't be certain, since the headband cut off airflow to her brain. But at least the shoes weren't orthopedic look-alikes, and although the dowdy dress hung all the way to her ankles, it did allow freedom of movement. Josie had to keep reminding herself not to wiggle too much when she walked. Or, God forbid, to accidentally lapse into a showgirl strut. Her nervousness made that a distinct possibility.

All this is necessary, she reminded herself. *It's necessary to convince these people you're serious.*

Now that she was getting closer to her goals — thanks partly to her dad's advertising help and partly to Jenna and her friend Sophie, who'd enrolled her twin daughters in dance classes two days ago — Josie felt more determined than ever. But determination alone wasn't enough to erase the memory of Luke's disheartening reaction to her ensemble when she'd descended the stairs this morning.

He'd folded his arms over his chest and looked her up and down, an expression of disappointment on his face. Then, "I don't think that's really you."

"What's not really me?"

"This whole thing." The sweep of his muscular arm indicated the prim outfit she'd shoehorned herself into. "It's crazy. It's not you. Where are your false eye-

344

lashes? Your ponytail hair extension, 'Frank'?" He squinted. "Where are your *breasts?*"

Affronted, Josie clapped her hands over her chest. She guessed her new "mini-mizer" bra was working. "This is my new, serious look, remember? This *is* me."

Although she did, she admitted silently, miss Frank. They'd been through a lot to-gether. And, she admitted further, she still thought her false eyelashes were fun. Plus, this stupid new bra squashed her like an overly enthusiastic date.

She frowned.

"It's not you," Luke insisted, his voice gentling. "I know you're determined to tackle Donovan's Corner. Hell, I admire that! But I don't think changing yourself into someone else is the way to go."

There was only one answer to that.

"The old me wasn't working," she said tartly, then flounced toward the kitchen to pack up the cupcakes.

Looking at them now, Josie smiled to herself, despite her morning's rocky start. It had taken her six hours to bake those chocolate-frosted goodies yesterday. Six long, floury, batter-spackled hours, during which she'd used up all the swear words she knew and then invented new ones.

In her frustration, she'd forbidden Luke and TJ to enter the kitchen, for fear she'd hurl a spatula — or a cake mix box — at their heads. Somehow understanding, they'd complied. Hanging on through singed fingertips and a serious icing-licking high, Josie had finally emerged triumphant. Now she had four dozen chocolate treats, of which she carried a dozen herself. Luke chivalrously handled the additional three trays.

Josie figured she was on her way.

The baking problems hadn't really been her fault, she reasoned as she nodded to some townspeople, then passed beside a fluttery-leafed stand of Aspens. She was pretty sure her new oven was possessed. It burned things willy-nilly, spewed smoke at the oddest moments, and had a major grudge against actually baking anything that contained butter. Or sugar. Or, pretty much, edible molecules of any kind.

After Jenna's painstaking lessons and the whole "baking cookies for the Better Business Bureau" fiasco, she'd thought she'd gained valuable experience. It turned out she hadn't. But that didn't matter. Multicolored icing and sprinkles could hide a multitude of sins, if applied creatively enough.

Showgirls *definitely* knew about creative embellishments.

Also, Josie knew she had other things to offer besides culinary skills — things like dancing expertise, a good heart, and a full assortment of jokes. Speaking of which . . .

"Hey, Luke. Knock, knock."

"Who's there?"

"Twain."

"Twain who?"

"Twains are what wabbits take twips on."

A grin spread over his face. He chuckled. Of all her joke recipients, Luke and Parker were the only ones who never let her down.

Josie laughed, too. There. That was better. Now she could face the inevitable barrage of judgmental Donovan's Corner residents with a positive attitude.

Dodging face-painted kids and tail-wagging entrants in the Founder's Day Costumed Dog Show, they dropped off the cupcakes at the appropriate booth. Luke manhandled his three trays onto a prominent corner. Josie set down hers with utmost care, sliding it between a plastic-wrapped platter of brownies and a towering pile of oatmeal cookies. Her cupcakes, with their swirls of icing and generous sprinkles, definitely looked the fanciest. She was pleased.

"I know this sounds silly," she said as her fingers skimmed the tray, "but I wish I didn't have to leave them."

Luke took one look at her downcast face and pulled out his wallet. He glanced at the booth's elderly attendant. "How much for the cupcakes?"

"Fifty cents each, young man."

"I mean for all of them. How much?"

"All of them? All four dozen?"

He nodded.

"Well, you get a discount if you buy more than one." She put on the eyeglasses strung on a chain around her neck and squinted at the handwritten price sheet. "Says here they're supposed to be four-fifty a dozen, so that makes . . ."

Josie realized what he was up to and made a grab for his open wallet. She missed.

"No, Luke." She tried again. "I was only kidding!"

"You want to keep them," he said, setting his jaw. He went on counting bills, holding his wallet too high for her to reach. "I'm making sure you can."

That was sweet of him. The big lummox.

But she couldn't let Luke spend his hard-earned money on her. Especially while he was still saving up for his secret motorcycle mechanic's garage. When a person needed cash, every penny counted. Josie knew that.

"Don't you want to . . . save your money?" she asked.

A crooked grin. "I can afford twenty bucks."

"Eighteen. And maybe you can't afford it."

"I'm not destitute. Don't worry about it." He faced the attendant. "I'll take all four dozen, please."

"No, you won't!"

Josie wiggled her way between Luke and the woman in the booth, intercepting the money before it changed hands. She was a showgirl, not a fiscal genius. But if growing up in a trailer park on the wrong side of Donovan's Corner had taught her anything, it had taught her the value of a dollar. She knew what needing money could do to a person's future.

"Stop it. I refuse to contribute to your financial downfall."

"Financial downfall? Be serious."

"I am. Please don't spend your money on me."

"Josie." He rubbed his hand over his jaw, looking confused. "I'm buying the damned cupcakes!"

She couldn't believe it. He was even more stubborn than she was. Gazing into his determined, handsome face, Josie decided there was only one thing to do.

Make something up.

"Okay, fine. I didn't want to tell you this, but . . ." Putting on her most reluctant expression, she bit her lip. She batted her eyelashes — a less effective move without her falsies, she had to admit. "But the truth is, I worked really hard on those cupcakes. All that baking, all those sprinkles. I want other people to see them, too."

He looked puzzled. "You do?"

"Yes."

"*And* you want to keep them."

Helplessly, she nodded.

Luke's expression turned savvy. "This is one of those 'I want to see you dance naked and I *don't* want to see you dance naked' things, isn't it? Girl logic. Right?"

Sure. Why not? Whatever preserved Luke's cash flow. And his pride.

"Right. So I don't *really* need you to buy all those for me, as nice at that would be. I'd only want to leave them here for people to admire anyway."

"You're crazy," Luke said. "Absolutely crazy."

But in his warm, husky voice, *you're crazy* sounded a lot like *that's okay*. And paired with the warm, loving look in his eyes, *absolutely crazy* somehow sounded very much like *I care about you, no matter how nuts you might be.*

Amazed, Josie smiled at him. In that moment, the whole world narrowed to just her and Luke. He smiled back, and her heart turned over. She didn't know how she'd set out to help him and wound up being treated to all these good feelings herself. But she did know that when Luke put away his wallet, the coast was clear.

Happy in her crazy-love haze, she turned again to admire her cupcakes. "They do look nice, don't you think so?"

Luke nodded. Funnily enough, his attention stayed fixed on her instead of her cupcakes. Josie gave a dreamy sigh.

"Those cupcakes look gaudy," the attendant volunteered, clearly growing impatient with them. "Showy. Too many sprinkles, that's what I say. *Way* too many sprinkles."

The good mood between Josie and Luke fizzled.

"That doesn't mean they won't taste good," she said.

She ought to know. She'd nearly made herself queasy sampling the leftover cupcakes that had gotten welded to the pans yesterday. Putting her money where her mouth was, Josie dug in her purse for fifty cents and slapped it on the counter. Then she chose the flashiest, most chocolaty, most sprinkle-bedazzled cupcake of the lot. She set it in front of the attendant, meeting the woman's accusing glare with a tinfoil-bright smile.

"Here you go! My treat. Try it. You might like it."

Skeptically, the attendant examined the cupcake. She looked as if she expected it to grow legs and do a rumba.

"Just one nibble," Josie coaxed. "You can't judge a cupcake by its sprinkles, you know."

If anything, the woman's look of sprinkle mistrust grew. But she did pick up the cupcake and sniff it. Gingerly, she took a bite. She chewed.

Her face brightened. "It's good!"

"See?" *Whew.* "It's pretty *and* it's delicious."

"Just like you," Luke whispered in her ear.

Feeling herself flush, Josie grinned. *Score one for the showgirl.* People in Donovan's

Corner might not have welcomed her back with open arms, but that was all starting to change. Once everyone got used to the new Josie Day, they'd change their minds about her *and* her so-called scandalous dance school. Just like the bake sale lady had changed her mind about the cupcake she was finishing.

"It's really, really good," the woman said. "Even with the sprinkles."

"I'm glad you like it."

"Mmmm!"

"I hope you'll tell everyone to buy one."

The attendant nodded, her mouth full. She licked chocolate icing from her fingers, looking a little stunned. Either she *really* liked that cupcake or Josie had overdone it with the double layer of icing she'd applied.

Nah. There was no such thing as too much embellishment. Josie reminded herself of that fact as she said good-bye and pulled Luke toward the rest of the festival events. No such thing as too many sprinkles. Fanciness and fantasy were good for people sometimes — just like Luke was good for her. She couldn't remember why she'd ever hesitated to get involved with him.

"That was an impressive job you did

with the bake sale lady," he said, squeezing her hand. "I think you made a convert."

"I ought to be good at it by now. Making converts, I mean. I've been practicing for weeks." She'd had the occasional positive result to show for it, but for the most part success still felt frustratingly elusive. "Weeks and weeks and —"

"Don't worry," Luke told her, stopping her with a smile. "You'll get there. One cupcake at a time."

With those simple words, Josie knew she would. She'd conquer the world . . . one cupcake at a time.

All around them, the park overflowed with families and teenagers and retirees out for a carefree afternoon. The sun shone down, the pine trees perfumed the air, the whoops of children laughing filled the park. Josie felt happy to be a part of it. For the first time ever, it seemed as though coming home to Donovan's Corner might turn out okay.

Hand in hand, she and Luke walked past the apple-bobbing booth and a stand selling Indian fry bread. They smiled at the costumed "frontiersmen" who meandered by, spurs jangling. They cheered on the people lining up for the Frontier Days 10K — including Nancy and Warren Day. They stopped to chat with some friends of Luke's in Harley-Davidson T-shirts and bandanas.

It was plain to Josie how impressed they were with Luke's knowledge of motorcycles.

"He's got a knack for 'em," one of the men said. "Plain and simple. If Luke had himself a bigger shop, or another mechanic to work for him, he'd have all the work he could handle. There'd be bikers from clear across the state stopping in, especially with the highway so close."

"Maybe someday he will," Josie said, hugging Luke closer. She tilted her face up, giving him a proud look. "Maybe someday he'll open his own mechanic's shop. Maybe it'll be right here in Donovan's Corner!"

Luke remained silent — a tactic that would have worried her more if she hadn't already known, via TJ, about his secret. As it was, it only made sense that Luke didn't want to talk about his plans until they were official. Until then, the least she could do was encourage him. So she did.

"I'm convinced Luke can do anything he wants to do," she said, and everyone agreed.

It should have been a perfect afternoon.

And it would have been . . . if not for the whispers dogging Josie's every step. For every old friend she reconnected with, another, *less* friendly Donovan's Corner resident stood nearby, staring and pointing at her. For every local vendor she successfully networked with, another huddled in the next booth, whispering.

"Just look at them," she told Luke, shaking her head. "I've been here *weeks* now, and still I'm the scandal du jour — only without the scandal! It doesn't matter what I do." She crossed her arms. "This is a major case of two steps forward and one step back."

"Isn't that 'one step forward and two steps back'?"

"Hey, you have your truisms and I have mine. I'm trying to be optimistic."

It was tough, though. No matter how she tried to ignore it, the finger-pointing and gossiping still got to her.

Frustrated, Josie tried to counter it by handing out free dance lesson cards. She talked with more people. She met many, many more of Luke's motorcycle-repair customers. But no matter what she did, the people she really needed to reach remained tooth grindingly elusive. The upper crust of Donovan's Corner — and the parents who could afford dance lessons — ignored her.

Josie didn't know what else they expected from her. She'd tried to prove her trustworthiness and respectability. She'd applied for a business license, completed all the paperwork for her Chamber of Commerce membership, and lunched with the ladies' auxiliary. She'd abandoned her cute clothes and learned to bake. She'd even resisted having a torrid, scandal-producing affair with her handyman. If those weren't serious sacrifices, Josie didn't know what was.

What did they think she was going to do? Strip down to a red feathered costume and start doing Rockette kicks?

Seeing the expression on her face, Luke slipped his arm around her waist. Gently, he tugged her in the opposite direction.

"I hear they're giving tours of some of the old Victorian houses at the edge of the park. Let's go check one out."

"Sure," Josie agreed, raising her chin.

She refused to let a few setbacks — and a little gossip — get her down. If nothing else, maybe she'd get a few good decorating ideas today. Her mother's comments about how "neutral" Blue Moon was hadn't been lost on Josie. In Momspeak, that meant "boring." In Realtor, it meant "saleable." Neither one was exactly the effect she'd been going for.

To start, they chose the Kincaid House, an 1880s timber-framed manor with several gables and an elaborate wraparound porch. The line for Founder's Day admission snaked along the house's wrought iron fence. After Josie and Luke stepped in place, the line grew even longer behind them.

"Wow, this is even more popular than the — ouch!"

Somebody *pinched* her! She whirled around, looking for the culprit. The four men behind her raised their gazes innocently to the sky, but Josie wasn't fooled. This was hardly the first covert butt pinch she'd received since returning to town. She knew all the signs. She glared at them.

"Go figure," Luke said, not noticing as he watched the line inch forward. "Here I thought the line for deep-fried Twinkies was long."

"Only when you go through it three times, Hungry Man."

He grinned. Thirty seconds later . . . another pinch.

This time, Luke felt her flinch. "What's the matter?"

"Nothing. I'm just excited to get inside, that's all."

Hopping forward in faux enthusiasm, Josie managed to put just enough distance between her derrière and the happy-fingers guy. She was home clear until the ticket attendant stopped her at the house's front door. He kept his hand on the velvet rope cordoning off each tour group.

"Hey! You're that showgirl, aren't you?"

She nodded. Warily at first, then with a smile. The ticket attendant hadn't called her a stripper. He'd call her — correctly — a showgirl. He'd even looked interested in her job. Maybe she really was making progress in Donovan's Corner . . . changing her image for good.

"Yes, I'm Josie Day. I don't think we've met."

"Heck, no! I'd have remembered meeting you. You're practically a celebrity around here." The man leaned closer. "Tell you what. *Your* admission's free."

"Thank you! That's so nice of you."

"Free for an autograph, that is." He thrust a printed tour brochure her way. "Or maybe something a little more *personal*. Like a private dance?" He leered. "How 'bout it? I've never had a 'private dance' from a showgirl before."

He chuckled, looking eager.

"You're not having one today, either, pal." Luke stepped forward, looking menacing.

Josie waved him back. She'd been wrong. *Now* she knew what she was dealing with. A showgirl groper. Never mind that they were two hundred miles away from Las Vegas. She recognized the type. She knew how to deal with it, too.

Unfortunately, kneeing this guy in the *cojones* probably wouldn't help her win friends and influence dance students.

"Sorry, I don't do private lessons," she said, pretending to misunderstand. She handed him her card. "But if you're interested in a group session, you might be in luck."

"A group session?"

She nodded. "Mmmm-hmmm. I'm planning to do five a week."

The pinchers gawked. Two of them shoved forward.

"Hey, I'll take one of those cards!"

"Me, too!"

Sweetly, Josie passed them out — even to the jerk with the wandering fingers. Who knew? Maybe he had a sister who wanted to learn how to fox-trot. "Tell a friend," she reminded them. "The first time is free."

Clutching his card and grinning, the attendant waved them through for the next group tour. Feeling as though she'd handled that awkward situation pretty well, Josie traipsed into the cool, dim interior of the Kincaid House. She paused in the foyer to breathe in the familiar, calming smells of lemon oil, wallpaper paste, and antique upholstered furniture.

"Oooh, look at the banister." Raising her face to the intricately carved and polished wood, she followed it to the second story landing. "It's so pretty."

"Let's get a closer look." Luke pulled her toward it.

"Wait!" She pointed to the floor. "We're supposed to stay on the red carpet track."

"Since when do you follow the rules?"

He kept going, wearing an inscrutable expression as he pulled Josie in his wake. She glanced over her shoulder in dismay. The crimson runner laid along the tour's velvet-roped path fell farther and farther away as they headed in the other direction.

"Stop," she protested. This was exactly the opposite of the sensible behavior she'd been trying so hard to stick to. "Everybody else is heading toward the parlor. We're missing the tour."

"We'll make our own tour. Come on."

Their group vanished from sight through the next passageway. But Luke only held up the velvet rope blocking off the stairs and gestured for Josie to duck beneath it. Goaded by his I-dare-you demeanor, she did.

They wound up strictly off-tour, in an upstairs bedroom furnished in shades of red and beige, with tasteful tasseled accents and lots of mahogany furniture. The view took Josie's breath away. *This* was what a historical house was supposed to look like. It was really impressive. Cozy, too, after Luke shut the door behind them.

"Wow, will you look at the light fixtures? And the bureau? And the *bed*. Fantastic!" Josie wandered through, skimming her fingers over it all. "I wonder why they made it so high? I thought people in the olden days were supposed to be munchkins compared with us."

She bent at the waist, trying to peer under the enormous four-poster.

"They'd have needed a stepstool to get into this thing," she mused, raising the hem of the fancy spread. Beneath it were two

362

more layers of lacy dust ruffles. "Maybe it's built in?"

"Forget the bed." Luke's big feet stepped into her field of vision. He loomed over her, powerful and determined. "Do you know what those guys thought you were promising them?"

"What guys? The guys in line?" She followed the edge of the bed, feeling for a built-in stepstool. She guessed Luke's silence was confirmation enough. "Who cares what they thought? All I'm offering are dance lessons, and you know it."

"If I do, I'm the *only* one who knows it."

"Hey. Whatever brings people through the door is okay by me. After that, I'll hook them with my skill and personal charm." Still bent by the bed, she angled her head sideways and grinned up at him. "I'm not exactly in a position to be choosy when it comes to potential dance school students. Besides, who knows? Maybe one of those guys is a tangoing savant. Or a closet Baryshnikov. At the least, they might turn out to be great dance school publicity — future stars in my dad's cable TV ads."

Luke stared her down. He was serious.

She wrinkled her brow. "Geez. From this angle, you really look mad."

"I *am* really mad. Jesus, Josie! What's

the matter with you?"

"Nothing! Nothing's the matter with *me*." She levered upward, the bed forgotten. She stuck her hands on her hips, all the frustrations of the day boiling over in a single instant. "And speaking of me, why are these things always my fault, anyway? Huh? How come it's never *their* fault? The pinchers and the whisperers and the stupid lechers?"

"All I'm talking about is —"

But she was on a roll. She wasn't stopping now. "Am I just supposed to sit back and take it? Huh? All the gossiping and the groping and the —"

"Somebody *groped* you?" Luke looked fit to spit nails.

She waved it off. "Happens all the time. The point is —"

"The point is, you're supposed to tell me this stuff."

He paced as he said it, crushing the delicate carpet beneath his work boots. Energy crackled from him — that, and a certain fierceness Josie didn't quite understand.

She frowned, her aggravation fading. "Why?"

"Why what?"

"Why in the world should I tell you this stuff? It's my problem, not yours."

His face darkened. "You should tell me so I can kick some ass in your defense."

She rolled her eyes, refusing to see his Neanderthal gesture as anything less than ridiculously protective. Okay, also a little sweet. But still ridiculous.

"Settle down, Cro-Magnon Man. I can take care of myself. I don't need defending."

His mouth straightened. "Sometimes you do."

Puzzled, Josie angled her head. "I'm fine. So there's a little pinching going on. So what? That doesn't mean you have to pick fights with half the town."

"Yes. Yes, it does." From across the bedroom, Luke sent her a beseeching look. "You don't get it. I can't give you Blue Moon. I can't buy you presents or fancy jewelry."

"Don't worry. My mom's got a lock on all the jewelry within a fifty-mile radius, anyway."

He didn't even crack a smile.

"Come on," she protested. "I'm kidding."

But Luke wasn't.

"Hell, I can't even buy you four dozen freaking cupcakes!" he said, spreading his hands in frustration. "All I can do is keep everybody out of your damned way until you get what you need for your dance school. That's it."

And it's not enough, his tense shoulders said. *Not nearly enough.*

"Oh, Luke. That's enough. It really is."

He stood rigidly apart from Josie, not looking at her.

"Nobody's ever wanted to stick up for me before. That's huge! Are you kidding me? I'm the trailer park tomboy who grew up to be a showgirl. That didn't exactly make people cheer for me."

"It should have," he said gruffly.

"Or love me."

He glanced her way. "I don't see why not."

"So the fact that you go against the crowd and stand on my side . . . well, either that means you're just as much a knee-jerk rebel as I am, or it means you actually think I'm okay."

He crossed the room. "I think you're okay."

"Then show me," she said, smoothing her hands over his broad chest. She glanced up into his face, wanting to erase the lines of tension there. "Show me we're okay together."

Relenting, Luke did. He lowered his

head and kissed her, tunneling his fingers through her hair in an expression of urgency Josie couldn't deny. Faced with it, she held on and kissed him back, a whole waterfall of feelings pouring through her. Gratitude. Pride. Love. She didn't know what touched her more — Luke's desire to help her or the unabashedly fierce way he'd *insisted* on doing it. Either way, she thought it was wonderful.

When their kiss ended, she fixed him with a no-nonsense look. "I just want to make one thing perfectly clear, though. Technically, I'm way too strong to need defending."

"Oh, yeah?" Luke raised a brow. "Well, technically, I'm way too smart to argue with you about that."

"That *is* smart of you."

"But I will say this. You deserve respect, Josie." He brought his hands to her cheeks and cradled them tenderly — the way he might have touched a delicate flower. "Until you get that respect, I won't stand by and let people hurt you."

She glanced down. "I'm okay. It's not a big deal."

"I don't believe that." He flexed his wrists, bringing her face to his again with gentle insistence. He searched her eyes.

"And if *you* do, we've got some talking to do."

Something in the way he said it finally got through to her. Luke believed in her. He honestly did. No matter what she did or didn't do, he believed in her. That meant the world to her.

Josie drew in a deep, shuddering breath.

"Why do they do it?" she heard herself ask. "Why do they all think the worst of me?"

Luke's gaze softened. To Josie's absolute dismay, she felt tears building in her eyes. A lump rose to her throat. Swallowing past it, she croaked out the question again.

"Why, Luke? Why do they all think the worst of me?"

For a long moment, he was silent. Then . . .

"Because they don't know you," he said simply. Surely. "No one who really knew you could ever think the worst of you."

"Ha." She sniffled, wanting desperately to take back the question. This would teach her to turn over rocks she didn't really want to look underneath. "My dad thought the worst of me."

"I can't talk about dads. I haven't had the greatest experience in that department. But I can talk about *you*. I know I'm right.

Someday, I swear, everybody will see the truth about you."

"Yikes. What a terrifying idea."

Her grin must have looked unconvincing, because Luke only went on gazing at her in that intent, deeply absorbed way he had. This must be, Josie thought inanely, what a disassembled motorcycle engine would experience if it could feel Luke examining it. If it could feel him preparing to make it whole again.

"It won't be terrifying," he said. "It'll be great."

"Easy for you to say. You won't be the one all in pieces."

He angled his head, looking confused. And gorgeous. And macho and strong and white-hot wonderful. She didn't know how she'd lucked into having him, but she felt giddy with joy about it, all the same.

"Never mind," she said. "If I ever get a chance to be me again" — she gestured toward her hated green granny-dress getup, so necessary for her dance school dream but so *not* her — "I promise you'll be the first person I call."

"That's right. You'll be calling to hear me say 'I told you so.' "

"Oh, yeah?" Josie teased. "You're that sure of yourself?"

"Nah." Luke lowered his hands to her waist. He spread his fingers over her hips, then tugged her against him, pelvis to pelvis, in one insistent movement. "I'm that sure of *you*."

His next kiss stole her breath. It wiped her thoughts clean of everything except the man in her grasp, the feel of their mouths coming together, the heat and urgency of the moment. Josie crowded against him on sneakered feet, raising on tiptoes to be closer . . . closer. She buried her fingers in his hair and kissed him back, and all the while she only needed one thing. Only wanted one thing.

More.

"I'm sure of you, too," she whispered. A smile burbled up from somewhere inside her. Josie couldn't fight it back. Didn't even want to. "So take me, Luke. Take me, because I'm yours."

Groaning, he agreed. They fell backward on the four-poster's rumpled coverlet, rolling until they fit together like two pieces of a forgotten puzzle. Hip against hip, belly against belly, chest against chest. Josie panted and arched against him, and when Luke's hand found her breast, when he caressed her through the DayGlo fabric of her dress, she bit her lip to keep from screaming aloud with pleasure.

How had she waited so long for this? Waited so long to feel Luke's strong hands holding her close, to feel the hard, hot length of him against her thigh? She didn't know. She didn't care. She only wanted more. More, more, more.

She ran her hands over his back, feeling the muscles flex. She grabbed his arms for balance, admired the tattoos she'd once thought looked so dangerous. Luke wasn't dangerous. Josie knew that now. Not so long as he was in her arms . . . in her heart.

"Yes," she murmured, "just like that."

She'd never felt so out of control, so eager and impatient and ready. It took ages for him to kiss her again, eons for her to strip him of his T-shirt. She didn't want to waste time with her dress, so she only covered Luke's hands with hers and helped him hike it up. The glide of his callused palms against her skin was everything she'd hoped for. Hot. Sensual. Expert.

"Wait," she gasped. "I want —"

To touch you, too, she'd been planning to say, but something else grabbed her attention. It came from far away, barely heard over their panting breaths.

It was . . . it was . . . Josie couldn't quite identify it as Luke's hands slid from her knees to her thighs. A riot of good sensations followed the movement. Oooh . . .

"Now that we've seen the first floor and basement," a distant voice intoned, "where the servants spent most of their time, we'll continue to the second floor. This part of the Kincaid House was meant for the family . . . a more private space."

Private space. Breathing hard, Josie stilled with her hand on Luke's fly. *The tour!*

She jerked upward. Beside her, Luke froze.

"The tour! I forgot about the tour!" she whispered harshly.

If they found her here, it would be the talk of the town. Panicked, Josie jumped from the bed. The mattress dipped as Luke did the same. Hastily she smoothed her dress, then her hair. With her ponytail and stupid June Cleaver headband secured again, she looked back at Luke. He was still semi-naked. Gee, he looked terrific.

Hang on. *Focus.*

"Your T-shirt! I threw it over here someplace . . ."

She grabbed it from the cheval mirror it had gotten snagged on and pitched it to him. With a pang of regret, she watched as he pulled it on. In seconds, he looked dispiritingly respectable again, his naked chest, gorgeous arms, and rippled abs all covered by plain black cotton.

"Your hair!" She hurried over to smooth a pillow-rumpled hank, then stepped back to examine the rest of him. Perfect. Maybe they could pull this off after all.

"It's fine. We look fine. They probably won't even come in here," Luke said, angling his head with a posture of readiness. "The door's closed."

Breathing hard, they stared at it. From beyond the paneled oak, voices and footsteps came closer. Old floorboards creaked.

"Just hold still," he warned. His smoldering glance zipped over her figure, looking for anything out of place.

Josie felt her knees weaken. If he kept looking at her that way, so hot and so knowing . . .

She couldn't possibly stand still. Anyone who came in the room would see her need for him at fifty paces. She turned to the window instead, pretending to look out at the view of the city park sprawled below. Pine trees, people walking in twos and threes, balloons and colorful tents.

Yes, that was better. A good six feet separated her and Luke. They couldn't possibly look more innocent.

"The bed!" he whispered.

She looked. The huge four-poster was completely wrecked, rumpled and rolled on. There was no doubt it had seen some hot and heavy action — and recently, too. No surprise there. Luke lunged toward it, grabbing the edge of the messy spread. Josie snatched the other edge. Together they fluffed it, then spread the coverlet. They each rearranged some pillows.

"Good, good," Josie murmured. "That looks perfect."

Footsteps came closer. They stopped.

"Oh! That's strange," said a voice from the hallway. "This door isn't supposed to be closed."

Heart pounding, Josie flew to her window. Luke stepped to the opposite window, pretending an urgent interest in nineteenth-century woodworking.

The door burst open. Someone gasped.

A prim-looking docent stood there, the entire tour group crowded behind her. She took one look at Luke and Josie, and her whole face turned red.

"You! I always *knew* you were up to no good!"

Josie faced her bravely, determined to stand her ground. As she did, she realized this was no ordinary docent. That buttoned-up, tour-giving, ex-Miss-Saguaro-runner-up was Tiffany Maynard — Howie the Loudmouth's daughter.

"You were wild growing up," she said, "you were wild when you went away to Las Vegas, and you're wild now!"

Luke gave her a bland look, not recognizing Tiffany as anyone but an ordinary docent. Then he turned to Josie. Where had he gotten the pocket tape measure in his hand?

"See? These windowsills are six inches wider than the ones at Blue Moon," he said. "That's the difference."

Home restoration! It was the perfect cover. She could have kissed him for thinking of it. Or honestly, for any reason at all.

"Six inches?" she confirmed, suppressing a naughty grin.

They both gave Tiffany identical wide-eyed looks.

"You don't fool me!" she cried, arms crossed. "You're up to something, Josie Day. You always were. And you — you, with the tattoos. Get away from that windowsill."

Obligingly, Luke stepped away. A scowl darkened his expression, though, and his jaw flexed.

"I'll have to ask you both to leave this instant."

Trembling, Josie raised her chin and moved toward the door. Halfway there, Luke caught her hand in his. They edged through the crowd of tour goers, all of whom had fallen silent and gaping.

Not for long, though.

The murmuring started up before they hit the stairs. By the time they reached the first landing, a full-fledged gossip tornado had kicked up behind them. Terrific. All her hard work, undone in an instant.

"I always *knew* that girl was up to no good," came a judgmental voice. "Never was, never will be."

Never will be, Josie thought. *Never will be.*

Maybe they were right. But if she couldn't shake her reputation, she decided in that moment, the least she could do was earn it.

Seventeen

The good news, Luke realized after they left the Kincaid House, was that Josie's sexy, hip-wiggling, take-no-prisoners shimmy was back in full force. The bad news was, she was using it to walk away from him. As mesmerizing as that sight happened to be, he didn't much like the implications.

"Hey, Josie. Wait."

She stopped in the parking lot beside his motorcycle, her expression unreadable. Luke frowned. Something about her had changed. She seemed to have added three inches to her already willowy height, and the angle of her chin made him nervous as hell.

Probably, he told himself, she was bugged by that tight-assed busybody who'd booted them out of the Kincaid House.

"That docent didn't have anything on you," he said, hooking his thumb toward the tour they'd just left. "She was guessing. Trying to stir up trouble. Don't let her get to you."

"I'm not. I'm just ready to leave, that's

all. I made plans to meet up with some old girlfriends later tonight, and I need time to get ready."

Luke examined her, his suspicions growing. He'd swear something was different. "You look fine to me already."

She scoffed. "Are you crazy? I can't go out for a girl's night looking like this." She held out her dress's gaudy green fabric, letting it billow a good foot in both directions. "I look like an Amish hooker. *Not* the impression I'm going for, trust me."

He did trust her. But he didn't trust her mood.

"I'm sorry," he said, intent on getting to the bottom of things. If he knew women — and he did — an apology was always a good place to start. "I got carried away in there. On the bed. You just felt so good, I —"

"It's over with. Don't worry about it, okay?" Josie grabbed the spare helmet and tugged it on. She hiked up her dress with both hands, then straddled his Harley. "Let's go. I've got lots to do."

Acres of bare, showgirl-perfect leg showed from beneath her still hiked-up dress. Temporarily befuddled by the sight, Luke just stood there. That outfit wasn't half bad when worn that way.

The sound of Josie snapping her fingers brought him to.

"Earth to Luke. I don't know how to drive this monstrosity, but I'm willing to give it a go. Toss me the keys."

The hell he would. "I'll drive."

All the way to Blue Moon, Josie hugged herself to him. Her curvy dancer's thighs gripped his hips; her breasts teased his back. Her dress fluttered behind her like a battle pennant, green and wild in his rear-view mirror.

What the hell was going on? The change in her had him bewildered. Luke couldn't pinpoint what it was, but he'd bet it had something to do with her absolutely steely sunniness — and her new willingness to flaunt her showgirl gams. *That* wasn't part of the respectability playbook she'd been using until now. Neither was the rebellious whoop she'd let loose as they'd peeled out of the parking lot.

Climbing off his Harley at the estate, Josie took off her helmet the way she always did. No metamorphosis there. She raised her hand to smooth her sensible ponytail.

Or so he thought. Instead, she wrenched something loose, threw away her headband, and let down her long hair for the first time in weeks. It tossed around her face in the breeze, impossibly red and inexplicably *her*. With a plink of her fingers, she pitched away her ponytail holder.

She ruffled up her hair. "Ahhh. That's better."

"I'll say." He took off his helmet. "I like your hair that way."

"Me, too. I'd forgotten how much."

Small talk. Between two people who'd all but hooked up a half hour ago. People who'd lived in each other's back pockets for weeks now. What was going on?

Perplexed, Luke turned over his helmet in his hands. Josie wouldn't talk about anything real. He couldn't read minds. That left them at an impasse.

He swore under his breath. One more try wouldn't kill him.

"Let's talk inside," he volunteered.

"Later." She whisked his helmet from his grasp and put it down on his bike. "I've got beautifying to do, remember?"

She smiled, but her attitude still felt weirdly distant. Distracted.

Luke realized what it must be. "Are you pissed because I said you look 'fine' earlier? Because what I meant was that you looked gorge—"

She shushed him with her finger on his lips. Wearing a bemused expression, Josie

380

lowered her hand. Her fragrance wafted toward him on the same breeze that tousled her hair.

"I'm not mad at you," she said.

More confused than ever, Luke stared at her. "You looked —"

Cutting him off, she rose to kiss him. The touch of her lips, although brief, felt soft and sweet.

"I'm not mad," she repeated.

Stupid relief filled him. "You *looked* mad."

"At you? Nah. You knew the truth all along." She gazed at him with her usual directness. "It just took me a while to catch on."

"Catch on to what?"

"To the truth. About me." Her cell phone rang. With an apologetic glance, she fished it out of her purse. "Hang on. Just let me get this. It looks like it's Parker."

He nodded his approval.

"Sure?" She paused, poised to flip open her phone.

"Yeah. I've got things to do in the carriage house anyway."

Josie's chattering voice faded as he crossed the lawn. Luke headed for his garage, feeling grateful for the getaway. That probably made him an asshole. But right now, escaping to a world he understood — a world where the problems were concrete and fixable — sounded pretty damned good.

That didn't mean he didn't care about Josie, though. Halfway to the carriage house, he stopped. Frowning, Luke glanced backward.

Engrossed in her conversation, Josie cradled the phone to her ear, her expression hidden by the tangles of hair in her face. Head down, she toed off her sneakers. She scooped them up and dangled them carelessly from her fingertips.

Ordinarily, she'd have worn them all the way into the house — another of her self-imposed "rules for respectability." Today, she wiggled her bare toes in the grass, then meandered toward the porch.

Hmmm. That was weird. He debated going back and pressing her for answers. But then his mind spun toward the latest of his growing list of jobs — the carburetor repair he'd promised to do on a friend's Harley — and Luke kept going. Whatever Josie's problem was, she'd tell him when she was ready. Until then, he might as well get some work done.

Making her way upstairs, Josie paused on Blue Moon's east wing landing. She held the phone to her ear, hardly able to believe what she'd just heard.

She'd been cut from her show at Enchanté.

"I'm really sorry, Josie," Parker was saying. "I wanted to come there and give you the news in person, but with the schedule the way it is . . . well, you know. Two shows a night, matinees — it's just impossible."

"I understand." Woodenly, she climbed the stairs again.

"This was the best I could do. Management's sending you a 'nonrenewal of contract' letter, the cold-hearted bastards. Can you believe that?"

Josie nodded. Then she realized her friend couldn't hear a nod. "I guess that's just the way it's done," she managed.

"Not when I'm around, it's not. The least you deserve is to hear about it from someone who loves you."

"Thanks." Her throat closed up, making it hard to speak.

"I'm sure it's only temporary," Parker rattled on, sounding concerned. Also, irritated on Josie's behalf. "You know how Jacqueline is. She gets in those choreographer snits of hers. One whisper from her and a dancer's cut. It could have happened to anyone, honestly."

"I know. You're right."

"If it's any consolation, Greg really fought for you."

"That was nice of him." Greg was the producer at Enchanté. They'd worked together on the Glamorous Nights Revue for six years now. "Tell him thanks for me, okay? Or maybe I'll just do that myself. Yeah. I'll call him."

"Josie . . ." Parker hesitated, worry in her voice. "Are you going to be okay? I know you've got your dance school in the works and everything, but it's not every day a girl gets cut. I know how much that hurts. You've been with the show a long time."

"I'll be fine." In her bedroom, Josie sank on the chenille-covered bed. She felt numb. "Not having the show to come back to feels kind of weird. It'll take a while to get used to the idea, that's all."

There was a momentary silence. Josie let herself fall backward, feeling the coverlet billow around her. She ran her hand over its softness, still holding the phone to her ear. She sighed. She really hadn't seen this coming.

"That's it. I'm coming down there," Parker announced. Something scraped in the background, then paper rattled. "I can borrow Thad's Jeep and be there in a couple of hours, tops."

At Parker's loyalty, tears prickled Josie's eyes. God, she was sick of crying. It wasn't like her at all.

"No! No," she insisted, forcing a note of assurance into her voice. "Getting yourself fired — right along with me — won't accomplish anything. You've got a show to do. I'll be fine. Really. Besides, you and Thad will be married soon, right? If you want to buy a house in one of those new subdivisions, you'll need *both* your incomes."

Parker hesitated. "You're my friend. You're more important than a cookie-cutter house in suburbia. Thad and I can stay in our apartment for a few more years. Heck, I'll throw in an extra fishing trip every six months. He won't notice a thing."

Sniffling, Josie grinned. "I know how much you love *eau de trout*."

"That's right. So don't try to change my mind."

"Seriously, Parker. Don't come here. I'm so busy putting everything together for my dance school. . . . We'd hardly have any time together," Josie fibbed. It wasn't strictly true, but she didn't think she could face her best friend's sympathetic company right now. She just might crumple. "I'll be fine. Hey! I feel better already."

"You do not. Five bucks says you're wrapped up in a blanket, shivering, right this minute."

Stunned, Josie stopped in the midst of covering herself with a double layer of chenille bedspread. Whenever she got truly upset, she always got the chills. She'd forgotten Parker had been there for some of those bundling-up episodes — such as the one she'd been through the first time her dad had been a no-show for one of her performances.

"Shows what you know," she said haughtily, trying to keep her teeth from chattering. "For your information, I'm sprawled out practically naked, like a drunk high-roller at the pool."

"Really?" Suspicion sounded plain in Parker's voice.

Josie glanced at the fluffy mounds of chenille. She ducked her head beneath one, cell phone and all. Ahhh. Blissful heat.

"Would I lie to you?"

Parker was too smart to fall for misdirection. "Why don't you want me to come?"

Leave it to Parker to ask the tough questions. The truth was, Josie didn't want her best friend to see her fail. Which was exactly what she was doing at the moment, thanks to Donovan's Corner's refusal to let bygones be bygones . . . and showgirls be dance teachers.

"I *do* want you to come. I miss you!" At least that part was truthful. "But really, I'm up to my eyeballs trying to get my dance school up and running."

"You already said that."

"Besides, you'd hate it here."

Parker scoffed. "I've been to the boonies before."

Helplessly, Josie smiled again. It was only a small smile, but it was a start. "Your calling it 'the boonies' is kind of a red flag. Just give me a couple more weeks, okay?"

By then, Josie figured either her dance school would be up and successful or she'd have been run out of town on a rail. If it was the latter, she planned to have earned every scandalous moment leading up to it. Starting tonight.

"Fine," Parker relented. "But call me to-morrow to check in. I mean it!"

Josie agreed. She said her good-byes and hung up.

It was finally time to cut loose.

"Hot damn!" TJ said, clattering down

the carriage house stairs. "I am looking *fine* tonight!"

Luke glanced up. His buddy strutted into the garage and posed beside a beat-up Kawasaki, his knobby elbows and lanky frame nearly upsetting the bike. His gelled hair defied gravity. His ensemble for the night defied common sense.

He couldn't have looked more pleased with himself.

"Look," Luke deadpanned. "It's Yahoo Serious, all decked out for the prom."

"Laugh all you want, monkey boy. When the hottie I met at the Founder's Day festival sees me looking like this, she'll be *all* over me."

"Either that or she'll be running away from you. Is that shirt as radioactive as it looks?"

"It's clean!" TJ sniffed his armpits. "Pretty much. And check out what's on the front."

With a game show hostess flourish, he indicated the lettering on his T-shirt. *I'm with stupid,* it said. The red arrow below the words pointed to his crotch.

"Classy," Luke said.

"Wait! You haven't seen the back yet."

Proudly, TJ pivoted. *So is she,* the back read. This time, the arrow pointed left.

He looked over his shoulder, grinning. "Funny, right? The only trick will be keeping Amber on this side of me." TJ pantomimed putting his arm around a girl. "So the shirt's accurate."

"Yeah. She'll love that."

"All the ladies like a man with a sense of humor."

Luke wiped his hands on a shop rag. "Where are you taking this laugh-a-minute girl? Provided she doesn't bolt the minute she sees you?"

"For your information," TJ said with dignity, "I'm a romantic guy. I'm letting *her* decide."

"Wow." Luke raised his brows. "I'm impressed."

"Between hanging out at Bubba's and going cow tipping."

He rubbed his hands together in anticipation. TJ, a native Los Angelino through and through, had obviously gotten all his ideas about small-town life from the movies.

"This isn't the Wild West," Luke informed him. "There aren't any cows around here."

"Hmmm." Momentarily crushed, TJ gazed at the ceiling. A small pucker marred his pierced brow. He brightened. "I guess it's Bubba's, then! I'm off to pick up Amber. I didn't get all decked out in my best clothes for nothing."

Palming his truck keys, he meandered to the carriage house exit. Luke grinned at the suspiciously shaped scorch mark on the back of his board shorts. Apparently, TJ's big-date prep had gone beyond putting on an almost-clean novelty T-shirt and sniffing his pits . . . all the way to actually ironing.

"Hey, your shorts are on fire."

"What? Where?" Slapping at his backside, TJ turned around like a dog chasing its tail. The minute Luke guffawed, he wised up. "Screw you, Donovan. Josie told me Amber would appreciate the freaking gesture."

Josie. That explained where he'd gotten hold of an iron. Luke sure as hell didn't have one.

"You must really like this girl," he mused. "Next thing you know, you'll be ironing *her* clothes."

Good-naturedly, TJ flipped him the finger.

"Or writing her love letters. Sending her flowers —"

"Flowers?" TJ swore, a strange expression flashing over his face. He hurried upstairs, only to return with a scraggly bouquet of carnations in his hand. "Good thing you reminded me. I don't want to leave these babies behind."

Luke plucked out the plastic *Get Well Soon* spike stuck in the midst of the blooms. "Quickie Mart?"

"Damned straight. And I got Amber these, too."

"Breath mints?"

"Just in case. Don't worry, I know how to be subtle."

Luke doubted it. Before he could make a wisecrack, though, TJ tossed a sealed envelope at his chest.

"Hey, I almost forgot. That came for you today."

Turning it over, Luke frowned. It looked like an invitation. The envelope was made of thick paper, and his name and address were written on the front in fancy calligraphy.

"I got a phone message for you, too," TJ added. "From the secretary at Donovan & Sons. Something about a property you were looking at for your mechanic's shop? The owners couldn't track you down on the cell phone number you gave them —"

Luke flashed on the cell phone he'd hurled into the woods. "— so they called the company looking for you."

TJ fished a crumpled Snickers wrapper from his pocket. He smoothed it against his chest, then handed it over.

"Here's the 411. Names, phone numbers, all that stuff. I guess the deal they were working on fell through, so the property's available again. If you work fast." TJ squinted at Luke. "Is that the place you told me about?"

"The one with six repair bays and most of the equipment intact," Luke said. "Yeah."

He knew the one. It was his dream property, the perfect place to locate his motorcycle mechanic's shop. He'd thought it was a lost cause when he'd left L.A. Evidently, it wasn't.

If you work fast.

"Dude, that's awesome!" TJ punched his shoulder, looking psyched. "Once you lock down that place, there's no *way* your dad can look down on you. Not if you have a sweet setup like that."

Silently, Luke turned over the wrapper. There was only one way he could *work fast* to snatch this opportunity. He'd have to finally list Blue Moon for auction. He'd have to finally sell the place . . . right out from under Josie.

"Jesus, Luke. You look like somebody just kicked a puppy. I thought this was what you wanted. To get out of here and go back to L.A."

"I do." Or at least he always had. Determinedly, Luke shook off his weird mood. This *was* good news. News he'd been waiting for. "It's perfect."

"Call 'em," TJ advised. He plucked out his beloved spyathon-swag PDA and tossed it to Luke. "Use that. It's got a phone built in. Seal the deal, then take Josie out to celebrate."

Luke doubted Josie would want to celebrate this news. Not when it meant she'd lose Blue Moon.

He frowned at the wrapper. The contact information there looked clear enough, even written with what must be a permanent marker in TJ's angled scrawl. No excuses there.

"Maybe we can double-date sometime before you leave," TJ blathered on, looking as happy-go-lucky as Luke *didn't* feel. "You and Josie and me and Amber. That would be sweet. Oh, and dude? Don't look for me to show up back here anytime soon. I might be out *all* night."

"Only if you're lucky," Luke said.

"Or Amber's lucky." With a chortle, TJ

headed out the doors, flowers in hand and spikes in hair, ready for a night of "romance."

Luke sank onto the nearest vintage Indian bike, the opened invitation in hand. He frowned, bugged not by the innocent invitation to his cousin Melissa's upcoming wedding but by the handwritten note she'd included. He looked at it again.

I know you and your dad aren't exactly getting along right now, Melissa had written, *and I'm sorry about that. But a wedding is a once-in-a-lifetime thing, Luke. I don't want a family feud in the middle of it. Maybe it would be better if you stayed away. Just . . . stay away and give your dad some time.*

Stung, Luke stared blankly at the nearest Kawasaki. He guessed his whole family knew about what had happened with his dad. Usually, they kept their perpetual disagreements to themselves. But not this time. This time, Robert Donovan meant business.

If you want to live like a blue-collar grease monkey, you go right ahead. But don't expect me to respect you for it.

The funny thing was, Luke had. Naïve as it seemed now. He *had* expected his dad to respect him for it. And the rest of the

394

family, too. After all, Robert Donovan hadn't been born a freight-trucking tycoon. He'd been born the son of a banker and the grandson of a man who'd amassed much of the family fortune in the five-and-dime business.

Every generation of Donovans had made their own way in life, starting with the nineteenth-century lumber mill owner who had — unbeknownst to Josie — built Blue Moon and founded Donovan's Corner. Even Tallulah had carved out a niche in business before marrying Ernest Carlyle. Donovans came with an entrepreneurial streak in the genes. Luke wasn't exempt.

"Settle down. Relax. Take advantage of *not* having to struggle for everything," his dad had said to him once.

But Luke didn't mind struggling. He didn't mind working hard and he didn't mind getting his hands dirty. Hell, he didn't see how he could live with himself if he *didn't* do those things.

There was more to him than a fat bank account. More to him than being the family black sheep or the name at the bottom of somebody's paycheck. If he'd never laid eyes on a motorcycle, if he'd never felt the urge to take something apart and put it back together again . . . things might have been different. But he had. There was no going back now — not if he wanted to feel like *himself.*

It wasn't the money he missed. Most of that had been tied up in accounts and trust funds and investments anyway. A few assets would have come in handy right now to buy Josie a replacement dance studio, but cash wasn't really the answer. No, what Luke missed most was trust. Trust and faith.

And open invitations to family events.

Not that he was panting to go to a stupid wedding. Far from it. But he'd grown up with Melissa, damn it. They'd shared summer vacations and Jolly Ranchers and Ping-Pong tournaments. They'd sneaked out to the movies to watch *Aliens* together when both their parents had declared it off-limits. He deserved to see her walk down the aisle in one of those froufrou dresses, to get shit-faced at the reception, eat wedding cake, and make a cheesy toast . . . to give her a hug as she started off on her new life.

Jesus, he was getting sentimental over this crap.

Frowning, Luke examined the invitation again, then the note. Melissa wouldn't have sent it if she wasn't worried — if she didn't believe there was a real chance Luke's feud with his dad would wreck her big day. He owed it to her to stay away.

He *had* to stay away.

Luke swore. Of all the screwed-up things in life, this definitely fell in the top ten. But telling Josie the truth about Blue Moon would be worse.

"Hey there, handsome," came a sexy voice from the carriage house entryway. "Can you give a girl a hand?"

He looked up. Just as though he'd conjured her there, Josie stood in the growing night. Framed in the light from his work lamps, she looked wild and free and a little bit loopy. Her hair tumbled loose. She held a sweating glass of something pink in her hand — something, judging by her crooked smile, that was just as intoxicating as the way she looked.

She turned her back to him, exposing a long column of shimmery bare skin. Her dress gaped at its zipper.

"Do me up, would you? I can't reach."

Over her shoulder, she batted her eyelashes at him. Her fakes were back, he realized. A ridiculous sense of relief filled him. *Josie was back.*

He put down Melissa's wedding invitation. Carefully. In a place where it wouldn't get soaked in motor oil or covered in screws. He wove his way between the disassembled motorcycles, stopping when he reached the place where Josie stood beneath a shop light.

No, he hadn't conjured her up. He never could have imagined anything as amazing as the way she looked tonight.

He examined her dress, hesitant to touch it with his big mechanic's hands. Pale, floaty, and plunging down to *there,* it somehow seemed innocent and provocative at the same time. Dressed like that, Josie looked every inch the seductive showgirl, accustomed to champagne and glitter and neon nights.

"Just do up the zipper," she said, lifting her hair out of the way. "I tried, but I couldn't quite reach."

Her next over-the-shoulder glance made a lie of her words. Luke would have bet anything — even that perfect L.A. property he wanted — that she hadn't tried to zip up her dress at all. That she'd shimmied into its whisper-light fabric, walked outside with it threatening to fall off at any moment, and found him here.

Found him speechless. Fumbling. Unable to take his gaze from the smooth expanse of naked skin that stretched from her shoulder blades to the luscious curve of her ass. Just looking at her made him sweat.

He exerted a superhuman effort to reach for her zipper.

"The only thing a dress like this is good for," he said as he pulled it up, "is making men wonder what you'd look like without it."

"Maybe." She smiled, then let her hair tumble over her shoulders. She turned. "But all I'm looking for tonight is a chance to cut loose. Not to make men wonder."

Luke doubted it. Even zipped, that dress looked indecent.

"It's been a tough couple of weeks." She sipped her drink, making a small sound of appreciation as she did. "I could use a night off. It's *exhausting* being respectable."

He shrugged. "I wouldn't know."

Josie scrutinized him, from the tops of his work boots to the top of his head. She lingered over his tattoos. She smiled.

"No, I guess you wouldn't. I like that about you." Brightening, she came closer. She trailed her fingertips over his chest. "I like *lots* of things about you."

She weaved, nearly toppling. Luke caught her.

"Whoa. Maybe you ought to ease up on the pink stuff."

"Are you kidding me? This is my own invention. A little pre-cocktail cocktail. Chambord plus vodka plus . . . something else I can't remember right now. Try it."

She pushed it toward him. Liquor fumes wafted upward.

"No, thanks." Making sure she was steady on her feet, he let her go. He didn't trust himself not to pick up where they'd left off at the Kincaid House. Given how much he wanted Josie, it wouldn't take much for him to loosen his stance on not seducing tipsy women. "I'm more of a beer guy."

She squinted. "Maybe. But something tells me you've got more than a nodding acquaintance with expensive whiskey, too. Maybe even champagne. After a few years in the casino, a girl learns to size up a fella's tastes. You've got high roller written *all* over you."

On the word *all*, she teetered sideways. Thank God she didn't know how close to the truth she really was.

"That's because you're drunk. I'm just a mechanic."

"Maybe so." Josie's expression zipped from thoughtful to purposeful in that exaggerated way sometimes caused by a few cocktails. She gave him a canny look. "But that doesn't explain your pony."

Her *aha!* tone made him smile.

"My pony doesn't like whiskey or champagne, either." He put his hand to the small of her back, inciting a serious urge to drag her upstairs and tell her girls' night to go screw itself. She'd look good on his apartment's lonesome bed — and even better on him. "How about some company on your big adventure tonight? You're going to Bubba's, right?"

Bubba's — also the site of TJ's big date with Amber — was one of Donovan's Corner's most popular watering holes. It featured foot-long margaritas, dollar Jell-O shots, and two kinds of beer — regular and lite. Plus pool tables, a regular live band playing covers, and a pack of shit-kicking locals.

Josie nodded vigorously. Several times. Luke grinned, resisting an urge to clap a hand on her scalp like a guy with an overactive bobblehead on his dashboard.

"Yes, Bubba's. Where the drinks are sloppy and so is the dancing. But men aren't invited. Sorry." She touched his arm, seemed to get distracted by the glide of her fingers over his bare biceps, and sighed. She snapped to. "In fact, the girls ought to be here any minute to pick me up."

She peered through the open carriage house doors, searching the night for her friends. Luke was relieved she wasn't driving herself, especially given the state she was in.

"You're getting a head start, then."

He inclined his head toward her drink. She seemed to interpret the gesture as a request for her to drain the whole thing in several impressive swallows. She plunked her empty glass on his workbench, exhaling in satisfaction like Barney on *The Simpsons* — after he'd quaffed a pint of Duff beer.

"You could say that. I figured I was justified in having a few pre-cocktail cocktails, what with Parker calling to tell me my job at Enchanté was kaput, and all."

Luke stilled. "Something happened to your showgirl job? I thought they were holding it for you in case you came back."

"They were. *Were* being the operative word."

"But you're the second-lead dancer."

"Not anymore. I got cut." Breezily, she waved off the news. "Whacked. Booted. Dumped. Whatever you want to call it.

The upshot is, my contract wasn't renewed. I won't be dancing in Vegas again anytime soon."

She shivered, suddenly looking vulnerable. Luke could have kicked himself. He should have known there was something more going on. In all the time he'd known Josie, she'd never guzzled anything stronger than an occasional beer.

He hauled her in his arms. "Damn, Josie. I'm sorry."

"It's okay." She wiggled against him, determined — it seemed — not to accept his sympathy. "I've still got Blue Moon, right? If I didn't have this place, I don't know what I'd do."

Luke froze. Her words settled in his gut like lead. She *wouldn't* still have Blue Moon. Not for long.

"You could always dance with another show," he said. "Another revue."

She didn't seem to notice he'd purposely avoided mentioning her dance school plans in Donovan's Corner.

"Probably not. The timing's bad." She rubbed the goose bumps on her arms. "I missed most of the auditions while I was here baking cupcakes and getting my butt pinched."

Concerned, Luke tilted her chin up. Her

403

chipper delivery seemed seriously at odds with her crestfallen expression. No sign of tears . . . but that didn't mean they weren't in there somewhere. Drowning in pink liquor.

"Don't tell me there's no butt pinching at auditions," he heard himself say with mock severity. "You could've been multitasking."

It was a lame thing to say. But it brought a smile to her face, all the same.

"Very funny, wise guy. You're just sorry *you're* not the one who did the pinching."

"Oh, yeah? It's not too late. Come here."

The instant his hand made contact with her derrière, she squirmed away, shrieking with laughter. She clattered across the carriage house floor, predictably agile in three-inch heels.

The realization only made him feel worse. Josie was made to strut her stuff — to dance like there was no tomorrow. Coming here had wrecked her past . . . and it wasn't doing her future any favors, either. Thanks to him.

"Hey." He grabbed her arm, gazing into her upturned, laughing face. "I've got to tell you something."

"Oooh. Something big, bad, and serious, I'll bet."

He nodded, needing his somber demeanor to wipe the goofy grin off her face. Christ, this was hard. Now that the moment had come, Luke wanted nothing better than to pretend none of this was happening. But he couldn't.

A man wasn't a man if he couldn't shoulder the hard times.

"Yes," he said. "It's serious."

"Save it." Oblivious to his struggle, Josie flung her arms to the side. She twirled in place, her dress glittering in the shop lights. "Tonight's for cutting loose!"

"I mean it, Josie." He was a jerk for telling her now, when she was least equipped to handle it. But given the circumstances, waiting any longer would be worse. "There's something you need to know."

"Don't be a buzzkill. I'm going to make another cocktail." Buoyant and graceful, she grabbed her glass. "You want one?"

"It's about Blue Moon," he persisted.

She frowned. At that moment, headlights swept the drive, illuminating the lower level of the carriage house with their glare. Luke held up his hand to shield his eyes, swearing beneath his breath. Her friends' timing couldn't have been worse.

A low-slung Jetta idled in the drive. Its

engine chugged as though it was all it could manage to ferry around that much laughter, lipstick, and perfume. Dance music poured from a sound system that probably cost half as much as the car.

"Yoo-hoo! Josie!"

"Get out here, girl!"

"Step away from the hunk," intoned a female voice.

Josie laughed. "Whoops, that's my ride! Gotta go."

Abandoning her cocktail glass, she skipped across the carriage house. She pressed her mouth to his. Her gaze met — and held — his with surprising coherence.

Fleetingly, Luke wondered about that. Had some of what he'd been trying to say sunk in?

"Thanks for being there for me. That means a lot," she said. "Especially tonight."

Before he could reply, Josie let out a crazy feminine whoop. She discoed her way to the car. Two breaths later, she jetted away in a flurry of laughter and gravel-spitting tires.

The only remaining sounds were crickets chirping. His fluorescent work light buzzing. And the harsh swearword Luke released next. It sounded a hell of a lot less peaceful than the first two sounds did.

Alone, he stepped to his worktable. He picked up Josie's forgotten glass and turned it over in his hand. It felt cool, faintly sticky. One edge still bore the imprint of her pink lipstick. He thought of her shining face, thought of her lips against his . . . thought of the screwed-up mess that awaited them both.

Swearing, Luke smashed the tumbler against the carriage house wall. Then he grabbed TJ's PDA-turned-cell-phone and headed upstairs.

Eighteen

Surrounded by a thumping beat, lots of barhopping bodies, and all her old friends, Josie did her best to let her hair down at Bubba's. She talked. She laughed. She drank margaritas and danced with her friends . . . danced the way she had before she'd ever heard of Enchanté or chorus lines or showgirls — with flailing arms and gyrating hips and moves copied straight from MTV videos, just as she had at seventeen.

Nothing had changed in this part of Donovan's Corner. Josie had been underage when she'd left town, officially too young to hang out in bars. But like every other teenager in the area, she'd spent her share of time at the place anyway, waiting for her parents to finish up a pair of post-work drinks or for her grandfather to wind up a game of darts.

It had been on Bubba's pool table that Josie had first learned the game; in Bubba's back room that she'd been dealt her virgin hand of poker. At the time, being admitted to Bubba's smoky, beer-soaked atmosphere had made her feel worldly. Adult. Slightly *bad*.

And tonight? Tonight it still did. Which was perfect, because those were exactly the feelings she'd been looking for — especially *bad*. Bubba's was the ideal launching pad for the rebellion she had in mind. After all, rebellion was what everyone expected of her anyway.

I always knew that girl was up to no good. Never was, never will be.

Beside her, her friend Brandi hoisted a Jack Daniels shot.

"To Josie!" she said.

"To Josie!" everyone echoed, raising their own drinks.

Josie drank, pounding her margarita glass on the table with gusto. She didn't know why she'd waited so long to reconnect with everyone. She guessed that until now, a part of her had felt that coming home to Donovan's Corner was only temporary. Now, despite her difficulties in starting up her dance school, she knew she was here for good.

On Monday, she'd renew her efforts to gain the town's support. Heck, she'd redouble them, she promised herself. But tonight . . . tonight she intended to forget all her troubles.

"Another round?" her friend Kim asked.

"Absolutely!" Josie replied.

The band kicked into a new song. All Josie's friends squealed in recognition. "Let's dance!"

She headed for Bubba's minuscule dance floor, her shoes peeling from the coating of sticky spilled beer she encountered with every step. Conscious of the gazes on her as she passed by, Josie smiled and chatted. She didn't care who thought her dancing was too wild or her dress was too skimpy. Tonight she just wanted to feel like herself again.

Waving her arms overhead, she danced with Brandi and Kim and the rest of her friends, all in a group. They didn't care who watched, didn't care how many men tried to horn in on the fun. They only laughed and shimmied until a slow song started, then decamped to their table for another round.

Josie sipped her margarita, listening to Brandi and Kim rank a crew of flannel-shirted construction workers from one to ten. She sighed. Was this as scandalous as it got? Girl-on-girl dancing, man-ogling, and tequila? This didn't do justice to *I al-*

ways knew that girl was up to no good.

Maybe for someone like Jenna this would constitute crazy bad-girl behavior. But for Josie? For Josie, it barely qualified. Especially given how scandalous she was supposed to be.

She remembered breaking the rules being a *lot* more fun than this. Remembered the thrill of dodging curfew, the excitement of staying out late, the slightly dangerous allure of knowing that *anything* could happen before sunrise.

Putting down her margarita, Josie scanned the bar. Now that the shock value of her risqué dress had worn off, her presence here wasn't even raising eyebrows. She didn't know why she'd struggled so hard to be respectable until now.

But there was no getting around it. Tonight she craved freedom. *Needed* it. Usually, this restless feeling sent her down the highway in her convertible, headed toward a new adventure. But now she was stuck. Stuck in Donovan's Corner.

Out of the corner of her eye, she spotted a familiar shaggy-haired man edge through the crowded bar, a blond woman at his side. TJ and his date, Amber. Smiling, Josie waved to them.

That was when it hit her.

She was wasting her time with a who-cares? rebellion like hanging out at Bubba's. She needed something bigger, badder, more outrageous. Something like . . . having a torrid fling with her tattooed, hard-bodied handyman.

Yeah. That was *perfect*. What was she waiting for?

Leaning toward her friend Tanya, the night's designated driver, Josie cupped her hand around her mouth. "Can you give me a ride back to my place, please? I'm going to call it a night."

There were murmurs of protest and plenty of good-bye hugs. But ten minutes later, Josie was on her way. Blue Moon awaited, and along with it . . . Luke.

He was awake when she got there — but just barely. Rumpled, shirtless, and barefoot, Luke answered her knock at his apartment door looking deliciously relaxed . . . and a little surprised to see her standing there. Josie dropped her purse and drew in a deep breath, eager to unleash a little pent-up rebellious energy with him. The sooner the better.

"What's up?" he asked. "Back already?"

In the background, the TV cast flickering light on his sofa. Luke must have muted the sound, because all Josie could hear were crickets chirping outside, far away . . . and the pounding of her heart. Now that she was here, she felt a little nervous.

But *nervous* was for non-rebellious, non-showgirl types. Not her. She was brave and bad and on the verge of seducing her very own handyman hunk.

"I got bored with my big night out," she said.

Coming here had been right. She knew it. She stepped inside, feeling assured by the masculinity and coziness all around her . . . and by the all-out scrumptiousness of the man before her.

Luke's jeans hung low on his hips, displaying lots of bare skin and the perfect amount of chest hair. He smelled of soap and shaving cream. Apparently, her rough-and-ready mechanic had showered and shaved while she'd been gone.

That was convenient. No razor burn to mar her rebellion, her taste of freedom, her little bit of cutting loose before going back to respectability. Josie could hardly wait.

"That's too bad." Seeming vaguely confused, he glanced behind her at the empty threshold. "You were looking forward to your girls' night."

"I figure there'll be compensations to cutting out early." With a secret smile, Josie dropped her sandals beside her purse. Then she edged the door shut with her hip. She turned the dead bolt. "For instance . . . this."

Luke was busy staring at the dead bolt in puzzlement when she grabbed him. Feeling wild and seductive and free, Josie pushed him against the closed door and kissed him. He tasted of toothpaste and freedom and everything she needed. This was even better than she'd imagined.

"And . . . this."

Breathlessly, she pressed herself against him, letting her body say everything she'd never dared to. Like *I want you. I need you. I'm crazy, crazy, crazy in love with you.* And Josie felt crazy, too. She felt wild with hunger and need and all the yearning she'd tried to deny for so long.

She'd wanted Luke for years . . . forever.

"And . . . *yes* . . . this."

She kissed him again, her tongue meeting his as she brought her hand to his fly. Luke jerked. He moaned into her mouth as she found the rigid length of him and stroked him through his jeans.

"Oh, God." He broke off their kiss, his mouth open as he pressed his cheek to

414

hers. "Josie . . . What are you doing?"

"Everything I should have done a long time ago." She leaned back and gazed into his eyes, wanting to show him exactly how much she meant it. "Everything I've wanted to do. *Everything.*"

Shaking his head, he caught her hands in his. He maneuvered them away from the door.

"You're still drunk. You don't know what you're doing."

But as he released her and crossed the room, he sounded hopeful — hopeful that she *did* know exactly what she was doing. Josie smiled. At the least, Luke deserved credit for not letting a tipsy woman ravish him . . . for not taking advantage.

On the other hand, if she was still drunk, that little buzz had given her the courage to do this. The courage to finally let loose everything in her heart. She couldn't be sorry.

"I don't?" She gave him a teasing arch of her brow, then followed him to the sofa. She wrapped one arm around his middle to hold him close, then used her other hand to stroke him again, more boldly this time. "I don't know what I'm doing?"

He closed his eyes, all his muscles taut. "Josie . . . stop."

It would have been a more effective warning if he hadn't sounded so raspy, so distracted . . . so sexy. She knew she was affecting him, and that knowledge was powerful stuff. Josie wanted more. More.

"But you feel *so* good," she murmured. After another caress, she pushed him on the sofa, then straddled him. Her shimmery dress puddled around her thighs. "Why don't I keep going for a while? You can decide if I know what I'm doing later, after you've had more experience to judge with."

"This isn't . . ." Luke swallowed, his throat working with the effort. His gaze, so intensely blue, lifted from her bare thighs to her face. Looking as though he were making a supreme sacrifice, he said, "We should talk first."

That was funny. He sounded as though he could barely speak.

"Okay." Dreamily, Josie trailed her hand up his broad chest, enjoying the rush of having so much pure masculine power at her fingertips. She stroked his tattoos. Kissed his neck. "Mmmm. You taste good, too. Why don't I just keep touching you for a while? You can talk, and I'll listen."

Smiling to herself, she rubbed against him, then went on kissing his neck. Luke's whole body went rigid. He moaned again, more loudly this time. It turned out that her big, tough handyman liked having his earlobes nibbled. Imagine that. Fortunately, Josie loved tasting every available inch of him. Every single delectable inch.

"You know, this dress is *so* thin," she remarked, trying to sound offhanded. Given the yearning building inside her with every second, she doubted she succeeded. "It feels almost as if I'm not wearing anything at all . . . doesn't it?"

To demonstrate, she pushed her breasts against him. Her nipples leaped to attention, sensitive and responsive. Enjoying the subtle drag of her breasts across his bare chest once more, she sucked in a breath. It was true. Her dress felt too whisper-thin to offer much resistance.

"Ahhh." He curled his fingers into the sofa cushion, strong and male and determined — apparently — not to touch her in return. "You're killing me."

"You know what they say." A kiss. "What a way to go."

Luke gave her a wary look. "Are you *sure* you're not still drunk?"

Considering that, she paused in the midst of nibbling his lower lip, then leaned back just far enough that she could test the fit of his jeans again. She encountered the hard, hot length of him. *Yes.* Her next caress came coupled with a look of wide-eyed innocence.

"Is that what you wanted to talk about before? Drinking?" she asked. "You did say you thought we should talk."

"Uhhh . . ." He pulsed beneath her stroking hand.

"It's all right. We can talk later." Fighting the temptation to undo his fly and *really* make him moan, Josie brought both hands to his face instead. She framed his rugged features in her palms, savoring the sight of the man she loved. "Right now, I have other ideas. Because you know . . . anything can happen before sunrise."

His eyes widened. Josie nearly laughed aloud with giddiness. This was more like it. This rebellion, this wickedness, this *love.* Victory was in her reach now. There was no turning back from here.

"For instance," she said, offering him another kiss in encouragement, "at some time before sunrise, you could find yourself touching me. Like this."

She caught Luke's big palm in hers and pressed a kiss to its center. Boldly, she brought his hand to her breast and curved his fingers around her.

"Mmmm," she moaned. "I've been waiting for you to touch me, Luke. *Wanting* you to touch me. Go ahead. *Please.*"

He gazed at his hand, seeming surprised to find himself cupping her. His attention wandered to her face for a minute, but whatever he saw there must have encouraged him. Slowly, with ever-increasing absorption, he gave a gentle squeeze.

Josie squirmed, hardly able to believe how good his touch felt. She wanted more. She told him so.

Goaded by her whispered words, he brought his other hand up to join the first. Now he cupped her fully, and Josie could hardly stand it. She stilled in his lap, waiting breathlessly. *Touch me,* she begged silently. *Give in.*

"I've been thinking of you all night," he said, his voice deep and shiveringly sexy. "Ever since you left."

"You . . . have?" Geez, it was hard to talk in this situation.

He nodded. Gave her another caress. "Thinking of you in this dress. Out of this dress. In my bed."

He glanced up, his features filled with concentration and a seductive sort of cockiness. Leisurely, Luke rubbed his thumbs over her nipples.

At that incredible sensation, Josie's knees weakened. She toppled lopsidedly on his lap, forced to clutch at him for balance. She was surprised to learn she couldn't find it. For the first time that night, balance eluded her . . . and not because she was tipsy. Because things had changed.

As though her reaction dissolved the last of his barriers, Luke took control. He looked into her face and stroked her once more, and it was all Josie could do to withstand the simple, sexy smile that spread across his face.

That smile didn't bode well for her. Not if she wanted to keep things on the path she'd intended. The path of pure rebellion.

"You're right," he said casually. "Anything *could* happen before sunrise. For instance, I could do this . . ." He unzipped her dress in a single movement, leaving it to flutter precariously from her shoulders. "And open up all sorts of possibilities."

Josie gasped, feeling an unexpected rush of cool air hit her skin. But not for long. Assuredly, Luke put one hand to the small of her back, and warmth permeated the whole area. Skin to skin, she felt branded with possessiveness, with desire, with purposefulness. As though knowing exactly how she felt, Luke trailed his fingers up her spine, awakening nerve endings she'd never been aware of before. How could something so ostensibly innocent feel so good?

Before she had a chance to puzzle it out, he spread his fingers at the nape of her neck and brought her down for a kiss, angling her head in exactly the way he liked it . . . exactly the way Josie liked it, too. He kissed her with a hunger that was undeniable, with an expertise that was thrilling, with a sense of abandonment that was irresistible. Swept along in its wake, she moaned and kissed him back, stretching her jaw wide to accommodate more, more, *more*.

He plied her with caresses, ran his hands over her body until Josie couldn't tell where her skin stopped and his began. He nudged her dress away and kissed her shoulder, his mouth skilled and inventive and seductive. Wanting more, she pulled down the pale pink fabric and offered herself naked to him, rewarded at last by the sweet feel of his mouth on her breasts.

"Yes," she whispered, and closed her eyes in bliss.

There, in the flickering glow of Luke's TV, in Luke's tiny carriage house apartment, in Luke's big, strong arms, Josie felt more herself than at any other time. She let herself go and simply *felt,* for the first time in forever. The more she opened herself to Luke, the more he gave her in return. More kisses. More sweet talk. More . . . just more.

She'd come here looking for rebellion. Instead, she'd found warmth, acceptance . . . love. To her immense surprise, it turned out those were all the things that really mattered. All the things that mattered between her and Luke.

"Pink panties." He growled the words in pure masculine appreciation as his hands slid up her thighs and encountered the slippery, skimpy nylon covering her. "I wondered about that. Wondered if you were wearing anything at all under this dress."

He cradled her derrière in his hands, kneading and caressing with an urgency Josie loved. Breathlessly, she pushed his hair from his face and kissed him once more.

"If I'm right, I won't be wearing them for long."

"Damned straight."

With a powerful movement of his arms and shoulders, Luke flipped her on her back. The sofa cushions caught her, pillowing the impact. He followed her down, paused to fling away the wayward TV remote, stripped off her dress.

"Mmmm. You look beautiful. All over."

"So do you." She smiled and held his mouth to hers for another kiss, arching against him in abandonment. It felt easy to trust Luke, easy to believe he'd make everything all right. "But you're wearing far too many clothes."

Josie wriggled her hands between them, a task made harder by the renewed attention he paid to her neck, her shoulder, her breasts. She found his fly and worked feverishly at it, finally creating an opening big enough to use as leverage. She pushed.

"Hang on," he panted. "Easy on the equipment."

"I'm eager, that's all."

"I love that." Luke propped himself on one elbow, strong and sure, his biceps bulging at the edge of her vision. "I'm eager, too. But first . . ."

He slid lower. Two seconds later, his fascination with her pink panties returned. He kissed her squarely at the center of them, then twined his fingers in the elastic and tugged them down, baring her fully. The look of awe on Luke's face then made her love him even more.

On the verge of telling him so, Josie felt his fingers gently part her. She felt his mouth on her belly, on her thigh, on her . . . *oh, God.* Clutching the sofa cushions, she let loose an uncontrollable moan. Her body stiffened, then bucked upward. She might have known Luke would have an incredible talent for this. After all, it involved making her want to scream.

Tenderly, he brought his hands to her hips. Held her steady. Went on loving her. Josie curled her toes and shook all over, knowing there was no way she could withstand this for long. Luke gave a wonderful rumble of enjoyment, a rumble that vibrated all through her, and if she hadn't been gripping the cushions so hard, she might have come apart right then.

"You feel amazing," he said, showing her with another kiss, another lick, another subtle brush of his lips against her exactly how much he meant it. "Warm and wet and . . . mmm."

Josie nodded, her hair tangling around her face as her breath came faster. Sensing her need, Luke proceeded with maddening slowness . . . perfect slowness. Everything narrowed to the glide of his mouth, the pulse of her body, the intimacy and beauty of the connection between them.

"Please, Luke . . . more," she gasped.

Somehow, he understood. With a gentle, anticipatory smile, he moved away. He levered upward, shucking his jeans in a hasty movement that still managed to take way too long.

"Hurry up," she said, sitting up to help. "Let me."

But by then his crumpled denims had hit the floor, and so had whatever he'd been wearing beneath them. Luke stood before her proud and hot and huge, and Josie felt her heart pound even faster as her fingers found the steely length of him, naked for the first time. She glided her hand over him, savoring the ragged indrawn breath he gave in response.

"No wonder your jeans looked so tight," she said. "No wonder you felt *so* good."

Then there was no more time for words. He reached for her and cupped her chin in his hand, then tilted her face up to meet his gaze. He looked at her evenly. In his expression, Josie glimpsed emotions she never thought she would. Caring. Wanting. Indescribable, indefinable tenderness.

This was more to Luke than a casual encounter, she realized then. More than a meeting of bodies, more than a few laughs in the night. More than the culmination of weeks of flirting. More, even, than mere re-bellion. This was sharing. Steamy, sexy, can't-get-enough sharing. And maybe, just possibly, it was love for him, too.

He smiled. "If you keep looking at me that way, I'll have to take you right here. Down and dirty. No holds barred."

"Promises, promises," she teased.

"You're asking for it now."

He laid her down and kissed her. Josie loved that even in this moment, they were in sync — that even now, while they were both completely naked, they still con-nected in that special way. With laughter and fun and openness. She'd never found another person who understood her the way Luke did. Who thought she was won-derful, exactly the way she was.

He trailed kisses over her body, leisurely and expertly enough that she forgot her name, forgot where they were, forgot ev-erything except the thrilling pressure of his lips on her skin . . . there, there, *there*. He caressed her, whispered lovely, wonderful things to her, told her in ways both sweet and raunchy exactly what he had in mind for her. And then, just when Josie thought she couldn't withstand another minute, somehow Luke made everything better.

He entered her in one molten, incredible

thrust. Moaning, she rose to meet him. After that, there was nothing but loving, nothing but sensation, nothing but the sounds of their breathing and the hot, sticky slide of skin against skin. With a guttural sound of pleasure, Luke entered her again. Again. The room blurred around them, losing all meaning as they grew closer . . . closer.

"Ahhh, Josie. *I love you. Love you.*"

The words tumbled over themselves, hoarse and needful, but Josie didn't care. Jubilantly, she wrapped her arms even tighter around Luke.

"I love you, too," she whispered.

Freed by her confession, she let go completely. There was no holding back the orgasm that swept over her next, blinding and amazing and absolutely soul-deep. Luke gazed into her eyes as she shook beneath him, loving every thrust, every touch, every moment. She put both hands on his backside to hold him to her, and that was all Luke needed. He came with a roar, a sofa-shaking crescendo that seemed to surprise even him.

Long moments later, he kissed her. Even more than everything they'd just shared, that kiss united them . . . made them one. In love.

"Wow," Josie breathed. "Wow, wow, wow."

"Yeah." With a sigh of contentment, Luke pulled her against him. He wrapped his arms around her from behind, then gave her shoulder a tender nip . . . a soft kiss. "You're amazing."

"And *you're* cuddling." As far as she was concerned, that made him her dream man for sure. Happily, she clasped his forearms and hugged him to her. She wiggled her derrière, settling herself more comfortably against him on the — thankfully — roomy sofa. "Go figure. Tough guy Luke Donovan. A cuddler."

He snorted. "So what? You're a screamer. I guess that makes us even."

She gasped. "I am not a 'screamer'!"

"Says you." Languidly, he freed one hand to comb her hair away from her face. His fingers, caring and sensitive, skimmed over her temples. "But I was pretty close to you. I know I heard a scream or two."

The machismo in his voice made her smile. She probably *had* screamed. A little. Being with him had felt more intense, in so many ways, than anything she'd ever experienced.

Smugly, she wiggled a little more. "I sure am loving all this cuddling."

428

A sigh. Then a husky admission. "Me, too."

Even though she couldn't see his face, the warmth in Luke's voice let her know his smile echoed hers. Feeling safe and satisfied and oh-so-beloved, Josie snuggled closer and just let go. Neither of them said anything about the *I love you*s they'd just exchanged. But Josie knew they didn't need to.

Now that her feelings were out in the open, she accepted them completely. She loved Luke, and she was staying at Blue Moon. Nothing else was necessary.

Not even a hint of rebellion.

Nineteen

I love you.

Afterward, while rummaging through Blue Moon's kitchen for a fortifying snack for himself and Josie, Luke guessed he should have resisted those words. But somehow, because of her, he hadn't wanted to. As he'd looked into her face, as he'd felt her so warm and wonderful beneath him, something had happened. It was almost as though his heart had just . . . opened. He'd felt it. He'd said it. End of story.

I love you.

And when Josie had said it back to him? There weren't any words to describe the way he'd felt then. Humbled? Awestruck? As ecstatic as a guy who'd just found a mint condition '68 Harley-Davidson KR lowboy flat tracker? Yeah, those all fit. And then some.

The truth was, Luke hadn't wanted to resist those words. Hadn't wanted to resist *Josie*. It wasn't part of the macho code, wasn't admissible in a room full of bachelors, but what he'd said was true. Including that bit about her screaming, damn it. Luke didn't care who knew it.

Inspired by the thought, he paused in his search through the cupboards. Man couldn't live on snack foods alone.

"Come here, you." He pulled Josie closer.

She came willingly, dressed in a short silky robe with her hair rumpled and her skin damp. They'd showered together — upstairs in the west wing's deluxe refurbished bathroom, where the enormous tiled shower left plenty of room to make the most of steamy water and slippery bodies. Now, he kissed her.

"This isn't getting us any closer to sustenance," she complained, sliding her hands down his back. She cupped his bare ass, pulled him into his favorite soft, snug spot between her hips, gave a low purr of approval. "Especially with you naked like this. If we're not careful, we'll have a repeat of the shower incident."

He grinned, remembering. "And that would be bad . . . why?"

"Because we need to pace ourselves."

"Screw pacing. Let's go for a record."

"And because I feel a little weak in the knees."

"That's because of all this good lovin', baby," he said, his voice purposefully deep.

She guffawed.

"Are you laughing at my sexual prowess?" Impossible. "You're trying to goad me now."

"So what if I am?"

"I'll have to abandon the search for snacks and teach you a lesson."

More laughter. "No way. I'm starving."

"Then don't poke the bear."

Putting on his sternest face — but feeling a little relieved, if the truth were told — Luke went back to opening cupboard doors. He had his studly moments, but damn. He wasn't a machine. Three times in three hours? That would be a world record.

Listening to Josie cheerfully humming behind him, he pushed aside two packages of hot dog buns and a canister of Kool-Aid. He spotted a box of Ding Dongs *way* in the back. If he could just reach past the granola Josie had bought in a doomed attempt to "healthy" them all up, he'd be in business.

"Hey, Luke. Knock, knock."

Almost had it. . . . "Who's there?"

"Turnaround."

"Turnaround who?"

"Turnaround and get a surprise."

Huh. She was slipping. That one wasn't even funny.

" 'Turnaround' isn't even a real name." He glanced over his shoulder. "It doesn't fit the knock-knock dynamic."

She dropped her robe.

His argument went right out the window. So did his quest for the Ding Dongs.

"Now you've done it." He examined her satiny skin, her luscious curves, her sassy, come-and-get-me smile. "Looks like it's world record time."

"Looks like it." Josie blew him a kiss. "*If* you can catch me, tough guy."

She bolted for the door, her cute derrière flashing him as she went. After a rueful shake of his head, Luke followed. Thirty seconds later, he caught her on the stairs. She shrieked and started laughing as he hauled her in his arms. He kept climbing, action hero style.

In her bedroom, he dropped her on her four-poster.

"That's for making me chase you," he growled.

"It was the least you deserved," she said breathlessly, "for dissing my knock-knock joke."

"Oh, yeah? Try it again."

"Okay. Knock, knock."

"Shut up and kiss me."

"Hey. That's not how it's —"

"I love you, and kiss me."

"Now *that's* more like . . . *mmmph.*"

Tired of waiting, Luke pressed his mouth to hers in an urgent kiss. Now that he was on the road to record breaking, he had half a mind to try out every room in the house. He felt pretty sure that Josie — given her moans of enjoyment and the sexy way she wiggled against him — would go along with his plan.

Since Blue Moon had about twenty rooms, that meant . . . *ahhh, never mind,* he decided as she flung her arms around his neck and pressed herself tighter against him. The bottom line was, that meant life was good.

Really good.

That night — okay, that *morning,* since they didn't make it to sleep until near sunrise — Luke dreamed of hammering. He dreamed of pounding, of clanking, of a persistent clattering just at the edge of his . . . hell. That wasn't a dream. That was real knocking. Someone was knocking at his front door.

Ignoring it, he rolled over, feeling his

muscles stretch. He sighed. He slung his arm over Josie's middle and pulled her closer to him. A warm, bone-deep sort of contentment washed over him, unlike anything he'd ever experienced before.

Maybe it was her bed. Her bed, with its flowery sheets and mounds of pillows, felt far cozier than his ever had. But Luke knew it was really her. Really Josie. Snuggling against him, she looked almost as beautiful asleep as she did awake.

Happily, he gazed at her. One of her false eyelashes was crooked. Her mouth hung open in a fly-catcher of a gaping maw. Ding Dong icing smudged in her hair.

He smiled. She looked great to him, even now. But when she was awake, there was love in her eyes. That made her more beautiful than anything else ever could.

Ahhh. Drowsily, Luke contemplated the coming day. After he'd given Josie sufficient time to recuperate, he'd fix her breakfast in bed. Froot Loops, toast, juice. The perfect balanced breakfast — even the box said so. Then he'd take her outside for a walk and show her his favorite place on the estate — a spot where the mountain runoff formed a stream, with a pretty little waterfall at the end of it. She'd like that.

Maybe he'd bring a blanket. They could

lie down together beneath the pine trees. He could kiss her beneath the open sky, and before they knew it they'd be —

Knock. Knock. Pound.

Jesus. Whoever was down there was damned persistent. Frowning, Luke edged across the mattress, trying not to wake Josie. The hearty door-knocker downstairs was probably a real estate agent, a door-to-door salesperson, a pain-in-the-ass neighbor. Obviously, he was going to have to get rid of them.

He couldn't remember where he'd left his jeans last night. Probably outside the west wing shower, along with some of his stamina and many of his misperceptions about how demure women were when it came to sex. Luke grabbed a blanket from the chest at the end of Josie's bed and wrapped it around his middle. There. That would have to be good enough for telling whoever kept knocking at his freaking door to go away.

He trundled downstairs, running a hand through his bed head hair. He squinted against the sunlight streaming in through the mullioned windows and felt his whiskery jawline. Whoever was at the door was going to get an eyeful, but Luke didn't care. He just wanted to make sure Josie didn't wake up before she was properly rested for that streamside picnic he had in mind.

"Yoo-hoo!" came a familiar voice from the front porch. "Josie, my dear! Do let us in. Ambrose is having a panic attack at the thought of being bitten by a mosquito."

"Mosquitoes carry malaria," came an also-familiar, but more evenhanded, voice. "Not to mention the West Nile virus. If you'd given me time to apply some insect repellent before we left our hotel —"

Oh, Christ. Filled with foreboding, Luke yanked open the door. His aunt Tallulah — and her attorney, the absentee Ambrose — stood cooling their heels on Blue Moon's threshold.

"Luke!" his aunt cried in surprise.

Ambrose tilted his head at an inquisitive angle. "Luke."

Luke, despite being well-identified by that point, unleashed a word far less mentionable.

"Watch your language," Tallulah snapped. "And get out of the way. We've been waiting here for *ages*."

"Fourteen minutes," Ambrose clarified.

His aunt stepped into the foyer. No, Luke amended, she *glided* into the foyer, like the *Queen Mary* coming to port. She kept her head at a regal angle. Her barrel-shaped body seemed to move without the benefit of bendable joints. He hadn't seen her in person for months, but her gray hair, steely expression, and indomitable spirit seemed unchanged.

Ambrose followed her, peering with interest at the mansion. His suit looked immaculate, his posture West Point worthy, his gaze, when he looked at Tallulah standing just in front of him . . . holy shit. His gaze looked soft and warm with affection.

With *love*.

Luke blinked. He had to be hallucinating. Nobody looked at Tallulah that way. The old battle-ax — much as he loved her himself — didn't exactly inspire sappy poetry and dedicated admirers. Ernest Carlyle had been just her speed, tough and no-nonsense and powerful. But Ambrose?

Ambrose was obviously an old softie at heart. Amazingly, his aunt didn't seem to mind that a bit. Luke was still gawking when she turned in search of her attorney and . . . no *way* . . . put her hand in his. Voluntarily. Even tenderly.

"What are you doing here?" he demanded.

"That's a fine way to treat your favorite

438

aunt. I might ask *you* the same thing."

Luke waited, arms crossed.

"I'm surprising *you*, apparently." Tallulah's gaze dropped to the blanket around his waist. Her lips pursed in evident disapproval. "You look like a squatter."

Leave it to her to go on the offensive immediately.

"I look like somebody just woke me up. If you don't like it, don't knock on people's doors at —"

"Ten-thirty-two," Ambrose specified. "Long past time for civilized people to be awake."

"I'm not civilized."

His aunt and her attorney both seemed to agree. After another censorious sweep of Luke's impromptu blanket cover-up, Tallulah raised her curious face to Ambrose's.

"Do we have the wrong estate? I thought this was the one I gave to that showgirl. You know, Josie Day."

"You did. You gave her Blue Moon. This is Blue Moon."

Tallulah looked bewildered. "If that's so, then what's Luke doing here? Especially naked?"

"I'm not naked. I'm wearing a blanket. You woke me up." Releasing an exasperated sigh, Luke clenched his blanket tighter to his waist. Clearly this was going to take longer than he'd expected. "I'll go change."

But even as he spoke, his aunt's expression changed. She spotted something over Luke's shoulder, and a broad smile spread over her face.

"There you are, Red!" she called. "Come on down here!"

Red. It had to be Josie. Josie, who still didn't know the truth about Luke's ownership of Blue Moon. And Tallulah and Ambrose, who definitely *did.* Once they started talking . . . hell. Why hadn't he seen this coming?

Gripped with dread, Luke turned.

Josie stood at the top of the stairs, her face pale and confused beneath a tumble of vivid hair. She'd shrugged into her shortie robe. Her legs looked long and lithe beneath it. But her expression . . . Her expression filled him with a sense of apprehension so strong it rooted him to the spot.

Slowly, she started down the stairs.

"I didn't want to wake you," he called, gesturing lamely at his aunt and Ambrose. "I heard somebody at the door, so I —"

"Save it." Tilting her chin, Josie reached

440

the bottom of the stairs. She didn't come any closer, and she didn't look any happier. She directed her gaze at Tallulah. "Are you here to take back Blue Moon? I know I don't have the deed yet, but it's supposed to be on its way. We had an agreement. A contract." She angled her head in a brusque greeting. "Ambrose."

He smiled gently. "A pleasure to see you again, Miss Day."

Josie only stood there, looking from Ambrose to Tallulah. The defensiveness in her stance confused Luke — until he remembered she still thought she owned Blue Moon. Clearly, she felt threatened by Tallulah's arrival and wanted to protect her rights to the place. This was a side of her Luke hadn't seen before. A side of her he respected.

He stepped toward her. "Josie, before this goes any further, I have to tell you —"

"No, I *can't* take the place away from you," Tallulah boomed, interrupting him. She hurried to Josie's spot beside the banister, looking — if Luke hadn't known better — almost embarrassed. "That's not why I'm here. Not exactly."

Ambrose cleared his throat meaningfully.

"Hold your horses. I'm getting there." Tallulah cast an over-the-shoulder glance

441

at her attorney. Then she leaned toward Josie in a girl-to-girl fashion. "Ever since we got married, he thinks he can boss me around. Hmmph. Does *he* have a few surprises in store."

"Married?" For an instant, Josie's face cleared. "Wow! That's wonderful! Congratulations."

"We did it at the *Extravaganza*'s onboard wedding chapel. Nice place. What a night!" Tallulah confided. "All those champagne toasts. I've never had so much fun! I wore my pearls. Ambrose likes them. He says —"

"Married?" Luke blurted.

"Yes, married," Tallulah said. "Happily married."

"Your aunt is a wonderful woman," Ambrose added stiffly.

"I *thought* I detected a spark between you two." Josie wagged her finger, smiling at them both. Probably she thought her claim on Blue Moon was secure. "I have to say, you've never looked better. You're absolutely glowing."

Tallulah preened. "Well, it never would've happened if not for that cruise. Ambrose positively swept me off my feet."

"I had to," Ambrose said, sparing her a fond glance. "That cruise was my golden opportunity. My last chance to declare myself. If I hadn't gotten my Tallulah alone on that ship, away from her usual duties and distractions, I simply don't believe we would be here together today."

He squeezed Tallulah's hand. Tallulah giggled. Was that a blush on his aunt's cheeks? Luke wondered. Surreal. Still, if this was the news they'd come to share, he'd have a chance to tell Josie the truth about Blue Moon himself. The way he should have last night, when he'd first tried to.

"I *have* been a little grouchy lately," Tallulah agreed.

"You had good reason. But that doesn't matter a whit. No longer, my love."

They leaned together and kissed. Luke couldn't believe his eyes.

"Get your paws off my aunt!"

An eye roll. "He's my husband now."

"I don't care. You two are giving me the heebie-jeebies."

"Yes. Well." Ambrose cleared his throat again. " 'Heebie-jeebies' aside, Luke is correct. My courtship rituals are not quite appropriate conversational fodder, especially given the circumstances. We should get back to the business at hand."

Not the least bit chastened, Tallulah

went on. "What he means is, I should quit blathering and get on with what we came here to tell you," she said to Josie. "See, the truth is, Red, I can't take Blue Moon away from you. Because it was never mine to give."

Luke caught Josie's puzzled glance. No, no, no . . . not like this.

She crossed her arms. "Never yours? What do you mean?"

"I know it sounds confusing," Tallulah said, reluctance dampening her voice. "For what it's worth, I didn't know about any of this until yesterday when Ambrose finally came clean about what he'd done."

Her attorney looked chagrined. "What Tallulah means to say, Miss Day, is that she made a mistake in giving you Blue Moon. It simply wasn't available for dispersal. The property already had — *has* — an owner."

"Although what he's doing squatting here," Tallulah said, shooting Luke a puzzled glance, "and not living the high life at one of his other estates, I can't imagine. It's not as though my nephew is lacking in resources."

That wasn't strictly true, Luke knew. But apparently his aunt was the only family member who *hadn't* yet heard of his feud with his father — and his subsequent cut-off from the family fortune.

"Your . . . nephew?" Josie repeated.

"Of course." Tallulah frowned at Luke. "You two look pretty cozy. He must have told you. *Luke.* Luke owns Blue Moon, along with several other —"

"Not anymore," he said through gritted teeth.

"— estates, an oceanfront condo, a place on the upper east side in New York, several motorcycles and cars — including a perfectly ostentatious Ferrari — a yacht . . ."

Josie's mouth dropped open. Tallulah rambled on, reciting all the things Luke had so recently lost. He couldn't listen. None of those things mattered as much to him as what stood at risk right now.

Josie.

"You mean he never told you?" Tallulah asked.

Looking numb, Josie shook her head. Her wintery gaze fell on Luke, leaving him cold inside.

"He never told me," she whispered.

"You're the exception, then," Tallulah said blithely. "You see, I really haven't been myself lately. I keep forgetting this place is a Donovan family holding, not a Carlyle property. The last two times I gave somebody Blue Moon by accident, Luke couldn't clear either of them out of here fast enough."

Josie arched her brow. She swallowed hard. "There've been others?"

"Only two, as I said." Tallulah waved a bejeweled hand. "My psychic advisor — she has her own hotline now. And a former concierge who helped find my poor shih tzu, Crackers. He's running a lodge in Aspen. They're both very happy. Happier than they would have been here, probably."

"Probably." Eyes narrowed, Josie nodded. Her voice sounded preternaturally calm. "Blue Moon is a Donovan family holding, you said? So Luke's not the only one who has all that stuff? The condos, the yacht, the Ferrari?"

"Heck, no." Tallulah chuckled. "We're all filthy rich." She shrugged. "We come by it naturally. Ever since Angus Donovan opened his lumber mill and founded this town, there's been one entrepreneur after another in the family."

"Hmmm." Josie nodded slowly, seeming to let that sink in. "Did all the Donovans specialize in lying, like Luke? Or is that his own particular area of expertise?"

"Err . . ." Tallulah looked at Ambrose.

Luke had to do something. Hurriedly, he

stepped toward Josie, reaching for her.

"I tried to tell you. I tried to straighten things out. The other night. Last night," he said urgently. "And before that, too. Hell, I must've contacted Ambrose a dozen times, but I couldn't reach him."

"Why?" Josie asked, her eyes wide. "Did you want to have *me* thrown out of this place, too?"

"At first, yes." Anguished, Luke thrust his hand through his hair. He couldn't lie to her anymore. Not after this. "But then everything changed —"

"Then you realized you could dupe me into staying," she interrupted, her voice wavering. "You must have really gotten a laugh out of me, huh? You and TJ. Pretending to be regular guys, with the Top Ramen and the beer and the 'handyman' jobs. I'm dying to know — is TJ a secret gazillionaire, too?"

"Josie —"

"You're right. It doesn't really matter." She waved off his next touch, talking much too quickly. "What matters is, I'm officially trespassing." She shivered, pulling her robe closer around her. "I guess I'd better get my stuff and clear out before the founding family of Donovan's Corner has me booted out."

"No, Red!" Tallulah protested. "We'd never do that."

But Josie only turned away, glancing upstairs as though gauging the long trek ahead of her. She drew in a breath.

This couldn't be happening. Luke reached for her.

"Wait. Let me explain."

"I've heard plenty." Ignoring him, Josie extended her hand stiffly to Tallulah. "I know you meant well. Thank you. This place will always have special memories for me." At that, her composure faltered. She managed to suck in another breath and continue. "I'm grateful for that. Just visiting here was more than a trailer-park refugee like me could ever have hoped for. Honestly."

She shook Ambrose's hand next. "You're a kind man. I know this wasn't really your fault, so please don't worry about it. I hope you and Tallulah will be very happy together."

Ambrose nodded, clasping her hand warmly. He murmured an apology. Softly, Tallulah did the same. Luke only stared.

Josie was leaving.

This *really* couldn't be happening. Not like this.

Helpless and pissed and confused, Luke

stood by with one fist clenched and the other holding up his stupid blanket. He felt Josie slipping away with every moment that passed, and he didn't have the damnedest idea how to stop it. She was turning into someone he didn't know, someone polite and distant and cool.

He shook his head, denying it all.

"She's not really leaving," he told his aunt and Ambrose, desperate to make that understood. His voice cracked, forcing him to clear his throat. "She's just mad right now. She knows she doesn't have to —"

"Good-bye, Luke."

The next thing he knew, he was staring at Josie's outstretched hand. The hand that had touched him so sweetly last night. The hand that had helped him repair the last piece of his legacy, the hand that had held his own during awkward mambos and romantic moments. The hand that had cradled his face as he'd heard her say "I love you" for the first time.

"Good-bye," she repeated.

Defiantly, Luke tightened his jaw. He wouldn't allow this to be over between them. He wouldn't accept it.

"Shake her hand," Tallulah commanded. "Don't be an ass."

"This is a rather awkward situation,"

Ambrose added, sympathy in his voice. "It really wouldn't be chivalrous to prolong things, Luke."

Screw that. He'd prolong things as much as he wanted, if it meant keeping Josie near. If it meant making things right between them again.

"No," he told her roughly. "I won't let you go."

"Well, now there's where you're mistaken." Josie swallowed hard, her eyelashes fluttering. She clenched her robe tighter, pulling at the silky fabric. "Because you don't get to decide. This might have all been some kind of game to you, Luke. But it wasn't to me. It never was to me."

"It wasn't to me, either." He kept his hand at his side. "I never wanted this to happen."

"Well." A ghost of a smile. "I don't doubt that. This isn't half as much fun as fooling me, is it?"

She withdrew her hand. Gave him a long, silent look.

"I don't have much to pack," she said. "I'll have my stuff out in half an hour."

Her chin wobbled. Yanking it higher, Josie hurried upstairs. A few moments later, her bedroom door closed behind her with a muted click. Luke stood frozen to the spot, wondering what the hell to do now.

Tallulah marched over. She whacked him on the shoulder.

"What did you do to that girl?" she demanded. "She looked heartbroken."

"Yes, Luke." Ambrose delivered a similarly steely glare. "Explain yourself. I'd say your aunt deserves elucidation."

"I want you both to leave," Luke said woodenly.

They peered at him. Both seemed taken aback.

"Now," he clarified.

They hesitated, glancing at each other and then at him.

"You understand why I couldn't answer your E-mails about this matter, don't you?" Ambrose asked. "If Tallulah had realized this business with Miss Day and Blue Moon was problematic, she would have wanted to come home. She would have booked a stateside flight from Curacao or St. Martin. I would have missed my opportunity to show her how I feel about —"

"Now!" Luke roared.

They jumped. Muttering indignantly under her breath, Tallulah strode to Ambrose's side. He caught her elbow in his hand and escorted her across the room. At

451

the threshold, they both glanced backward.

"You're making a mistake," his aunt said. "It's not us you're mad at. It's yourself."

"If you don't follow her, you'll regret it," Ambrose added.

The hell of it was, Luke already did.

"Leave me alone," he said. "Just . . . Leave me alone."

An instant later, they did. But Luke didn't feel any better. He gazed upstairs, deliberating. Then he hitched up his blanket and went to find his pants. Some things a man just shouldn't have to face without underwear.

Twenty

Josie was freezing. She dragged another sweater on top of the clothes she'd already shivered into, keeping one eye on the bedroom door the whole time.

Any minute now, she assured herself as her teeth clattered, Luke would come knocking. He'd explain everything. And his explanation — although she couldn't imagine what it might be — would make everything make sense. He'd pull her in his arms and kiss her. Everything would be okay, just like it had been before.

Before she'd known he'd lied to her from the start.

Hurting anew at the thought of it, Josie marched to her closet. Moving was better. Moving kept all those terrible thoughts at bay. Moving kept her from remembering the night she and Luke had just shared, the things they'd said, the closeness they'd found.

I love you.

Had Luke been lying about that, too?

Yanking clothes from their hangers, she threw everything on her rumpled bed. She refused to think about waking up with Luke gone, about hearing voices downstairs, about the instant she'd realized why Tallulah and Ambrose might have come — to take Blue Moon away from her.

If only she'd known. Blue Moon was gone, that was true. But Josie had lost something a lot more precious. She'd lost Luke. Or at least the Luke she'd thought she knew.

A bitter laugh escaped her, mingled with a sob. The hoarse sound scared her. If she didn't get out of here soon, she wouldn't be able to drive. She'd be crying too hard to see the road.

Blinking rapidly, she glanced at the door again. Nothing. It had been ten minutes now, long enough for her to shakily dress and start grabbing her things. Where was Luke?

Why did she even want to see him?

Angrily, Josie scraped the rest of her clothes across the rod. She grabbed an armload and dropped it on the bed, hangers and all. Luke had lied to her. He wasn't the person she'd thought he was. Neither was she, if she'd been gullible enough to buy his handyman routine. For all she knew, he owned Blue Moon and half of Donovan's Corner, too.

It was all so humiliating. So hurtful. So stupid.

In the midst of searching for a box to pack her things in, Josie paused. Her chest hurt. Her eyes burned. She needed another sweater. Or maybe some mittens. Wishing she had a pair for her icy fingers, she put her hands in her pockets and stared in the closet. Where were the cardboard boxes she'd used to move in?

Then she remembered. She'd flattened them all and given them to Luke and TJ to use while they painted the rooms at Blue Moon. She'd thought they'd make good cardboard drop cloths to protect the floors. By then, she'd decided to stay. She'd never expected to need those boxes again.

Hah. The joke was on her, wasn't it?

Resolutely, Josie grabbed her car keys. She opened the bedroom door and cautiously examined the hallway. Everything seemed quiet. Probably Luke was busy cooking up another alter ego. IRS agent. Longshoreman. Lounge singer. Before today, any one of those would have seemed about as likely as his turning out to be a secret multimillionaire.

Loaded down with clothes, she headed

downstairs. Some of the pants and shirts and sweaters were hers; some were things she'd borrowed from Jenna. They all had to go. Everything had to go. Including her.

At her convertible, Josie hurled everything in the back seat. Since the top was down, packing was going to be a breeze. Five trips later, she'd nearly crammed her old Chevy completely full. Shoes and pillows poked out of the pile at odd angles. A framed picture of her family rested in the passenger seat and her scented candles lined the floor in the back. Her celebrity gossip magazines wedged into the space behind the driver's seat.

Even out here in the sunshine, Josie felt cold. She hugged her arms to herself and glanced up at the Arizona sky, trying not to think about anything except packing, leaving, moving on.

Preferably before she buckled and started bawling.

All that remained were a few pairs of shoes and the box she kept Frank in. Striding inside, Josie thought about her ponytail hair extension. Now that she no longer had a job at Enchanté, she didn't really need it. She didn't see how she could ever dance again, given the way she felt right now. But she scooped Frank up from her former bureau anyway, then paused in her bedroom for one last look.

Her throat clogged with tears. Another cold front threatened to overtake her. Shivering, Josie closed her eyes against the misery that swamped her. Why couldn't Luke just love her? she wondered. Why, why, why?

Okay. This whole "last look" stuff wasn't working out so well. No wonder she'd always made it her policy to leave without looking back — to move on to the next adventure without mourning the last. It was better that way. Less painful.

Picking up the pace, Josie hurried downstairs. She passed the ballroom-turned-dance-studio, but didn't dare peek inside. That would only make her remember her dreams, her hopes . . . the laughter-filled afternoons she'd spent teaching Luke how to dance.

By the time she reached the porch, everything looked blurry. Juggling Frank's box and her rainbow wedgies, she stopped to swipe her hand across her eyes. When she'd pulled herself together enough to drag in a deep breath and move forward, what she saw waiting for her stopped her in her tracks.

Luke.

He leaned against her convertible, dressed in jeans and a black T-shirt, his arms crossed over his chest and his expression inscrutable. He looked as though he'd been there for days. Which was only fair. Because all at once, Josie felt as though she'd waited at least that long to see him again.

Idiotic hope sprang to life inside her. This was it! Luke was going to explain. He was going to make everything okay. He was going to morph back into the man she loved . . . the man who loved her. Gathering all her strength, Josie traversed the few steps separating them. She met his gaze squarely.

His jaw was a stony line, his eyes a bleak blue. In them, she thought she detected regret . . . even a heartache that matched her own. She was right. He was going to explain everything. She held her breath, waiting.

"Why are you wearing all that stuff?" he asked, looking bemused as he nodded toward her outfit. "Sweatpants, a scarf, a T-shirt. A sweatshirt *and* a sweater." His gaze meandered to her head. "A hat?"

Defensively, Josie adjusted her knit cap. "I was cold."

"It's seventy-five degrees out."

"So?" He didn't even know about her silk long johns, her wool socks, or the leggings beneath her sweatpants. Thank *God* he didn't know the real reason she needed all this. "Wearing it was easier than packing it. Get off my back."

They stared at each other for a minute. Josie felt pulled toward him, drawn to claim a little of the warmth they used to share. Resisting it, she waited. Luke *had* to have an explanation in him somewhere.

As though realizing he hadn't yet delivered it, he spoke.

"You can't leave," he said in a rough voice. "You have dance students to think about. Hannah. Sophie's twin daughters. That uncoordinated kid with the freckles. They're counting on you."

He said it proudly, as though he'd devised the perfect reason she should stay at Blue Moon. Unfortunately, it wasn't the reason Josie was waiting to hear.

"That's it?" she asked.

He spread his arms. "It's enough. You can't bail out on your obligations."

Completely disillusioned, she set her jaw. "Watch me."

Not looking at him, she tucked her shoes safely between the car door and her clothing pile. She added her hair extension

459

to the niche below the glove compartment. There. Everything was stowed. Everything except her.

"Your dance school is your dream," he insisted.

She turned, her temper suddenly flaring. "You might not have noticed, but my 'dream' is over with. I don't have a dance school. I don't have a *place* for a dance school. Which is fitting, since I also don't have a job or a place to live."

"Stay here."

Her mouth gaped. "As what? Your live-in joke generator? No, thanks. I know you must be bummed that the fun's over with, but you and TJ will just have to find some other stupid girl to laugh at."

"It wasn't like that. You know that."

"You're right. It was worse. Because I *believed* you." She sucked in a ragged breath, determined to go on. "I guess that's just how stupid I am. Apparently, stupid show-girl Josie Day can't tell the difference between love and a lie."

Luke frowned. If she hadn't known better, she'd almost have been persuaded by the grief in his eyes, by the defeated angle of his shoulders. As it was, Josie hardened herself against both. She was finished believing in him. Just as Luke was

460

finished believing in her.

That was what hurt the most. She'd really thought he *believed* in her — believed in her dreams and in her chances for achieving them. She'd thought he'd seen the real her and loved her. Instead, he'd only been pretending. Lying, all along.

"I'll buy you a new studio," he said, sounding exasperated and gruff. "I planned to all along. It'll be better than Blue Moon, better than that ballroom. There'll be mirrors and a ballet barre. A sound system. All that stuff you wanted."

Revelation widened her eyes. So *that* was why he'd dodged her about outfitting her studio. He'd known all along she would never have it — would never succeed.

"Don't do me any favors."

"I *want* to do you favors. Any favors you want."

But she couldn't believe him. Wouldn't.

"You made a fool of me, Luke! You let me run around town, fighting everyone." She gulped in a breath, feeling tears threaten again. "Fighting to make my dance school happen. All along, you *knew* I wouldn't succeed. You knew I *couldn't!* Not without Blue Moon. But you didn't care."

"It wasn't like that."

461

"Enlighten me, then." She crossed her arms.

He opened his mouth, stared into the distance, seemed unable to muster a reply.

"I see." Turning, she headed for her beat-up Chevy's driver's side door, gravel crunching beneath her feet.

"Jesus, Josie! Give me a minute, will you?"

Looking frustrated, Luke gazed at her. Beseechingly, he held out his arms. All she could see were the inky tattoos she should have heeded all along. *Think twice.*

"No. I gave you everything I had." Summoning all her strength, she palmed her keys. Opened her car door. "Obviously, it wasn't enough. Neither was I."

Her vision blurred, but she refused to cry.

"You were all I wanted," Luke said.

"Maybe." Her throat squeezed, making the words hard to get out. "Or maybe you wanted Blue Moon more."

He scowled . . . but he didn't deny it. That was when Josie knew it was time to leave.

"You said you don't have anyplace to go," he said, sounding aggravated, sounding disbelieving, sounding at the end of his rope — as though *she* were the one causing all this hurt between them. "Where do you think you're going to go?"

As if he really wanted to know.

"Anywhere but here," Josie said and finally drove away.

Luke was still standing there when TJ drove up in his truck, blaring the horn and grinning like an idiot. He parked in a flurry of dust, then ambled over with a breakfast of a strawberry shake and curly fries in hand. Smelling them reminded Luke he hadn't eaten. Not that he cared.

"Dude! Wassup? Besides my bad, crazy self, I mean. What a night . . . if you catch my drift." He waggled his eyebrows — an impressive feat, given the size of them. "Me and Amber totally hit it off."

"She seemed like a nice girl."

"Yeah. I'm almost tempted to stay in this Podunk town, instead of going back to L.A."

Back to L.A. Luke had been so wrapped up in Josie, he hadn't thought about his plans to go back home.

Grinning, TJ munched one of his fries. He offered a couple to Luke, who silently shook his head. With a shrug, TJ looked over his shoulder.

"Hey, I thought I just saw Josie driving

toward town. I guess that repair job on her Chevy's starter worked out okay, huh?"

Luke nodded. He put his hands in his pockets, feeling as if he'd just been kicked in the gut. He still couldn't believe Josie had gone. Watching her leave him had been worse than his fight with his dad. Worse than being estranged from his family. Worse than losing his former fortune. Worse than all of it.

He'd thought Josie saw the real him — the real, motor-oil-splattered self everyone else wanted to ignore. He'd thought she loved him. But no woman who could bail out on him this easily could ever have loved him, Luke decided in that moment.

TJ peered at him. "You look weird. Did you wake up to a Clay Aiken song on your clock radio this morning? Eat a bad burger? Lose a fight with your nose hair clippers?"

"Huh?" Snapping back to reality, Luke focused on the last thing TJ had said. "I *knew* you borrowed those clippers. Your Sasquatch schnoz is the reason they're dull, you asshole."

"Hey, it's not my fault. Blame those *Queer Eye* guys. I'm hyperaware of body hair now."

Luke shook his head. He was in sorry

shape. He couldn't even be bothered to give TJ hell about watching reality make-over TV. Next thing he knew, he'd lose his taste for Ding Dongs.

Damn. There it went.

Aching, he turned away. He didn't want TJ's super-spy vision detecting any other expressions of misery. Things were bad enough without having to *talk* about everything.

"I've got things to do," he said, keeping his voice curt as he scanned the roofline and upper story of Blue Moon. "More repairs to make. We've been slacking off. If I'm ever going to unload this place, it's got to be up to snuff."

"Be serious," TJ scoffed. "You're never unloading this place. Josie needs it for her dance school, and you've got plenty of work in your carriage house garage. I saw that Kawasaki you got in yesterday. Bent forks, right?"

"Josie's gone. So's her dance school." Jesus. He could barely force the words past his constricted throat. Swallowing against the ache, Luke examined the estate's grounds. Blue Moon was all he had now. "My 'garage' is strictly small-time. I want more."

TJ goggled. "Josie's gone? Gone where?"

Luke shrugged. "Doesn't matter."

Frowning, TJ stepped forward. "Why did she leave? What the fuck did you do to her?"

That did it. "I didn't do *anything* to her! She just left. She quit on her dance school and she . . . left."

Yeah, Luke thought. Josie quit on her dance school, just like she'd quit on him. It was her fault things had wound up this way. Hadn't he given her a chance to stay at Blue Moon? Hadn't he offered to buy her a new studio? A better studio?

Damned straight, he had. He'd been reasonable. She was the one who'd pushed, who'd misunderstood, who'd run away.

"I don't believe it." TJ's stance was rigid. "Josie's not a quitter."

"You keep telling yourself that," Luke said. "Maybe you'll start believing it."

"I *do* believe it, you asshole." Dumbfounded, TJ smacked him on the shoulder. "What did you do to make her go away?"

Pissed off and hurting, Luke stared him down. "Go on. Smack me again. Give me an excuse to kick your ass."

TJ shook his head sorrowfully. "Somebody ought to kick *yours*, that's for sure."

"Think you're tough enough? Huh?" Luke shoved TJ's chest. "Come on."

The contact enlivened him, made him feel purposeful for the first time all morning. Adopting a fighter's stance, he waved TJ forward. A knock-down, drag-out fight sounded pretty damned good right now. Maybe if he was busy pummeling TJ for being such a jerk, he'd forget the sight of Josie walking away.

But TJ only held up both hands in surrender. He gave Luke a look filled with pure disgust. "You're pathetic. And you know what? I'm glad Josie's not here to see it. If you were thinking straight, you would be, too."

He got in his truck, offered a final glare, then drove away. For the second time that day, Luke was left staring at the vacant drive, wondering how his life had gone from perfect to empty in the space of a single morning.

Force of habit made Josie hit the brakes as soon as she turned into Pine Acres and passed the familiar handmade sign (*children playing, please slow down*) posted on its weathered two-by-four stake. Keeping a close lookout through her misery-hiding sunglasses, she gripped the steering wheel and kept going at a fifteen-mile-per-hour pace.

The trailer park's curvy asphalt streets

were as mazelike as they'd been when she, a gawky sixteen-year-old, had learned to drive on them. They wound past every variety of mobile home, some with awnings and skirts, most with patio slabs in tidy backyards. A few trailers looked worse for the wear. They showed their age in sun-faded pastel siding and staked-out plastic flamingos that hadn't been pink in years.

Josie had thought coming here would be painful. Instead, she found it strangely comforting. Driving past the same chain-link fences, stubborn petunia beds, and broken-down cars up on blocks left her feeling that some things really did continue. That goodness and comfort really could survive in a world where your dreams got crushed and your job got lost and your dance school went bust and your mansion went kablooey and the man you loved turned out to be someone you didn't really know at all.

Gulping back a sob, she kept going. All she had to do was navigate another right turn, drive past the Pine Acres community rec center, and then . . . there.

Josie parked her car in her parents' drive, behind the pimpmobile and her father's old Toyota. She sat there for a minute, listening to the pings and sighs of her engine cooling. She drew a deep breath.

The Day family's double-wide trailer didn't look very different. It was still baby blue, still decorated with an awning and poured concrete porch steps, still showed off swag curtains at the living room windows. Josie remembered looking at those windows on her walk home from the school bus stop, thinking that they looked like fancy eyelashes on her house's face. Then, she'd believed theirs was the nicest trailer in the park.

She wasn't that naïve anymore.

It was probably just as well.

Straightening her sunglasses, Josie drew in another breath. She opened her creaky driver's side door and climbed out, sparing a glance for her piled-up things — they'd be fine here for now — and for the yard to her left. Marigolds grew in concentric circles at the base of the mailbox. They were probably her mother's handiwork. Nancy Day liked keeping up appearances.

She knocked on the door. It was Sunday, she recalled when there was no immediate answer. Maybe her parents were still at church. Or maybe they'd peeked out the swag-curtained windows and spotted her, and had decided to give her a taste of her own medicine. Gripped with misery and a strong sense of regret for having dodged them when she'd come to town, Josie knocked again.

The door opened, releasing the aroma of smoked bacon and eggs. Her father stood on the threshold, dressed in his Sunday best Haggar trousers and a short-sleeved checked shirt, his hair combed back. His expression looked unreadable.

"Josie," he said.

Oh, God. Not this. Not him. Not now. She knew she wasn't strong enough to withstand another battle with her dad. She should have gone to Jenna's, Josie thought in a panic. But with two kids, Jenna and David didn't have room for company.

Blinking behind her sunglasses, Josie distracted herself by adjusting her knit cap. It still wasn't very warm.

"Hi, Dad," she said awkwardly. "Is, um, Mom home? Because I need . . . well, I need . . ."

To her mortification, she couldn't force the words out. Her throat closed up around a fresh onslaught of tears. She felt her chin wobble, her face begin to crumple. No, no, no.

A harsh breath. "I need a place to stay for a while," she blurted.

Silence fell. The world looked too hazy

with unshed tears for Josie to gauge the expression on her father's face. All she knew was that he didn't say anything for what felt like eons. He was right, she told herself. Her parents didn't have to help her. She was a grown woman. It was stupid to come crawling home like this.

"Your mother's here," he said. "But I can handle this."

Oh, God. Oh, God. He sounded so . . . stern. So tough.

Had she ruined things between them forever by confronting him? Steadying herself for defeat, Josie fisted her hands.

"You stay as long as you want," she heard her father say.

He opened his arms and hauled her to him. Josie stumbled in her three-inch layer of wool socks, but she landed against his big, broad chest, and her dad caught her securely. He patted her on the back, his manner hearty and humbled and filled with compassion. His aftershave penetrated the haze of her disbelief — and everything else within wilting distance.

"It'll be all right, Josie," he said, his voice gruff. He held her apart from him, examined her face, tweaked her cheek the way he had when she was twelve. "Nancy, bring this girl a blanket. She's cold just like you.

471

I'm going to get all that rigmarole out of that car of hers. When was the last time you had the shocks looked at on that heap, anyway, Josie Marie? It could probably use a tune-up, the way it's dragging on the ground like that."

"That's just because it's loaded up with all my stuff, Dad. That's everything I own in the world."

"Since when do you own two tons of 'stuff'? Must be all those shoes, just like your mother. . . ."

Still muttering to himself, he tromped down the steps. Left behind, Josie looked through the doorway into the house.

Her mother stood there watching her, the Sunday paper strewn at her feet. Her coupon organizer lay on the coffee table. Her special coupons-only scissors rested beside it on top of a colorful circular, everything ordinary and bland and wonderful. She spread her arms. Josie saw that she was holding the crocheted afghan that had decorated the family sofa since the eighties.

"Whatever it is," her mother said, gesturing for her to come closer, "we're here for you, honey."

And that was when Josie knew . . . you really *could* come home again.

Twenty-One

The week after Josie's Chevy had rattled and coughed its way down the drive away from Luke was the worst he could remember. Determined to crush his heartache beneath hard work, he took it outdoors. There'd be no wussy wallowing around for him, goddamn it. Just work, work, work.

With that in mind, he lay belly-down on Blue Moon's front yard. The smell of dirt and torn-up grass filled his nostrils as he wrestled with a defective sprinkler head, trying to pry it loose. Every day that passed, he told himself grimly, was another chance to get the estate ready for auction.

The L.A. property waited for him, promising exactly the setup he'd always wanted. The setup that would impress his dad and finally put an end to their stupid argument. The setup that would prove, once and for all, that Luke Donovan could make his own damned way in life.

If he hurried, he figured he could make

things happen in time for Melissa's wedding. All he had to do was unload this place — getting the cash he needed in the process — then trade it all in for the mechanic's shop of his dreams.

Too bad he didn't give a damn about it anymore.

Still, this was all he had, Luke reminded himself. He scraped his fingers around the sprinkler head, digging a shallow trench for leverage. This — Blue Moon — and his self-respect. He'd gone a long way to preserve both. He sure as hell couldn't be expected to pick up all his marbles and quit now. Especially for a woman who'd leave him at the first sign of trouble.

A woman like Josie.

He had enough fickle people in his life already. TJ, for instance. He'd gone batshit when he'd heard about Josie leaving, and he still wasn't over it. Whenever he saw Luke coming, he got an ugly look on his face and headed the other direction. That was a fine way for a long-time friend to act.

"Asshole," Luke muttered, pulling on the frozen sprinkler.

TJ seemed to think *Josie* was the wronged party here, not Luke. Even though Luke had explained about volunteering to let Josie stay at the estate. Even though he'd explained about the substitute dance studio he'd offered to buy her.

"Yeah. As *if* Josie's going to believe *that*," TJ had scoffed, shaking his head. "You blew it, dude."

Even remembering that conversation pissed Luke off. What about loyalty? Solidarity between friends? *Right and wrong?* Christ. TJ acted as if Luke had personally packed up Josie's stuff and driven her away himself.

And Tallulah. Tallulah, Tallulah. Where to start? She'd been here every day, fresh from her hotel in Donovan's Corner, specifically to badger Luke — with her backup singer, Ambrose, on the coulda-woulda-shouldas.

"You're as stubborn as your idiot father," his aunt was saying now, her litany unchanged from yesterday. She loomed over him with a lemonade in one hand and a folding fan in the other, looking for all the world like a bitchy, over-the-hill southern belle. "You couldn't compromise your way out of a wet paper bag."

Luke went on digging.

"You've lost the ability to apologize. Worse, you don't even see a *need* to apologize! That's your problem. That and the fact that you view every last thing in black and white."

Luke brushed away some dirt. Yanked. No dice.

Tallulah edged nearer, blocking out the sun. "You couldn't find your own backside with both hands and a map," she announced. "I'm ashamed to be in the same family with you."

Luke pressed his lips together, struggling for patience. "You're standing on my sprinkler head."

"I should stand on your *head* head!"

Great. Tallulah wasn't budging. Neither was he. Now he'd never get this sprinkler head out.

Ambrose stepped forward, a sun umbrella in hand. "What my darling wife means is, she's frustrated you didn't tell her about your problems with your father earlier."

"Exactly," Tallulah said.

"And she's angry you won't even talk with Miss Day."

"That's right."

"And she wishes you'd pull your head out of your posterior and start acting like the man you're supposed to be instead of a sulky four-year-old."

Tallulah and Luke both gawked at Ambrose.

476

He raised a brow with dignity. "The street of marital influence runs both ways."

Exasperated, Luke wriggled his hand from where it had gotten wedged between the dirt, the sprinkler head, and Tallulah's orthopedic shoe. He rolled over in defeat. The grassy ground cradled him, flat and reliable beneath his back. A fly buzzed over him, then flitted away on the pine-tinged breeze.

He just wanted to close his eyes and forget everything.

"Don't you two know any knock-knock jokes?" he asked.

Silence. He didn't need to open his eyes to feel their confusion. It beamed down on him as strongly as the sunshine.

"Josie used to tell knock-knock jokes," he admitted.

The minute the words left his mouth, Luke wanted to stuff a dirt clod in his stupid yapper. Tallulah and Ambrose didn't need to know how he pined for one of Josie's lame jokes. How he yearned to hear her laughter. How he trudged through the mansion with his heart in his shoes, wishing she'd come dancing through one of the rooms with her boom box in hand.

"She liked to clean," he heard himself say. Shit. What was his problem? At least he hadn't confessed everything. Everything like, "The smell of Formula 409 still makes me think of her."

Oh, crap. Morosely, Luke flung his arm over his eyes to block out the sun — and Tallulah and Ambrose's undoubtedly befuddled gazes. If he were smart, he'd stick his arm over his mouth and shut the hell up. If he were smart . . . If he were smart he'd never have let Josie go.

Tallulah cleared her throat, obviously getting ready to say something. Probably something inspirational or sappy or otherwise Hallmark-card-worthy. Luke didn't think he could stand the sympathy right now. Wincing, he waited for the Schmalt-zapalooza.

"Maybe you can squirt some Formula 409 around your new mechanic's shop," his aunt suggested. "To keep you warm at night."

"Pigheaded pride won't tell you knock-knock jokes," Ambrose added.

Luke opened his eyes. His family — at least all its members who were currently on speaking terms with him — loomed over him. They looked irritatingly certain and impossibly self-righteous.

"Hit me when I'm down, why don't you?" He pinched the bridge of his nose, feeling a monster headache coming on. "You two are brutal."

"We're right, and you know it."

"Nope." Wearily, Luke got to his feet. "What I know is there's still a lot to be done around here if I'm going to get a decent offer on this place. See you around. I've got work to do."

"Stubborn fool," Tallulah muttered as he walked away.

"Jerk," Ambrose added.

Luke didn't care. He'd had enough weakening for one day. He'd lived without Josie once, and he could do it again. No matter how much it hurt.

"Josie, you've got company," Nancy Day called.

Reluctantly, Josie lifted her gaze from the TV screen. In the murkiness of the swag-curtained living room, she could barely identify the man who walked in . . . until he spoke.

"Whoa. It's a freaking *cave* in here. Hey, are those Funyuns? Pass the bag. Got any Pepsi?" He flopped on the sofa, amiably nudging aside her swaths of blankets. He rested his elbow on her dog-eared stack of *In Touch* magazines. "What are we watching? Anything good?"

Cheerfully, he helped himself to the Velveeta-smothered nachos on the coffee table. He munched one, glancing from the flickering TV screen to Josie. Expectantly.

Of everyone who'd been pestering her to "just snap out of it" for the past week, TJ was the one Josie found hardest to disappoint.

"E! Entertainment Television," she said without enthusiasm. She'd been mainlining it pretty hard lately, trying to think about something else besides missing Luke. "This is behind the scenes with *101 Hottest Heartthrobs.* Either that, or it's *Fashion Police:* Beyoncé. I can't remember for sure."

TJ nodded, surveying the snacks she'd laid out. After several days' practice, she was getting pretty good at selecting the best junk foods for drowning her sorrows with. Bugles. Strawberry Nestlé Nesquik. Pop Rocks. Between the Wonder Bread, the boxed mac 'n cheese, and the sugary goodness of Pixy Stix, Josie figured she hadn't eaten anything without the essential "artificial colors" food group since walking out of Blue Moon.

But in spite of that, and in spite of E!'s nonstop celebrity coverage, she still couldn't quit thinking about Luke.

"It's going to be tough to do those ballet moves of yours with a gut full of microwavable burritos," TJ observed, squinting at her paper plate. "You'll blow your students out of class with 'New Hungry-Moose Size!' farts."

Josie guffawed. She couldn't help it. "That's 'New Hungry-*Man* Size,'" she clarified, pointing to the wrapper.

"*You'll* be moose size if you keep shoveling it in like this." Looking concerned, TJ put down the Funyuns. He gazed into her eyes. Solemnly, he announced, "It's time to turn off E! TV."

"No!" Josie grabbed for the remote.

Too late. Her parents' nineteen-inch Zenith zapped off.

Moaning, she sank on her mound of blankets. She wasn't quite as cold these days, but she liked having their coziness around her. It made her feel better. Doing without E! TV definitely did *not*.

"You suck, TJ. Give me back that remote."

"Not until I tell you some stuff I should have told you a long time ago."

She cast him a suspicious look. "Is it about Luke? Because if it is, I don't want to hear it."

"It's not about Luke. It's about . . . Link.

481

Yeah. This guy named Link, who met this girl. Janie."

Proudly, TJ grinned. Josie rolled her eyes.

"Eeeeeh," she grunted, making her best "time's up" game-show-buzzer sound. "No, thanks. I've wasted enough time thinking about Luke Donovan and his megabucks."

"See, that's where you're wrong. He doesn't *have* —"

With a stubborn display of her palm, Josie stopped him. She felt way too miserable to argue today. A part of her had never quit hoping Luke would find her and apologize. The rest of her still felt too hurt by his lies to care.

All she had now was E! E! and Cap'n Crunch. Wearily, Josie grabbed the opened box from the coffee table. She plucked out a handful of Crunch Berries. She passed the box to TJ as a sort of peace offering, feeling relieved when he grudgingly accepted it. After all, *he* wasn't the one who'd stomped all over her heart.

The sound of crunching filled the living room. Josie ate her Crunch piece by piece, saving the sweet pink "berries" for last. TJ ate his by the palm full, cheerfully unbothered by the crumbs he dribbled on his Donovan's Corner Suds 'N Duds T-shirt.

She nodded toward it. "Did you get that from Amber?"

"Yeah. She's the Laundromat attendant."

"That's nice. Good for her. Glad you two are happy."

More crunching. Increasingly, Josie wondered if TJ had somehow figured out she wasn't *quite* over Luke yet. She was still vulnerable to thinking of him, dreaming of him . . . wanting him. Their breakup, coming hard on the heels of their incredible night together as it had, had really devastated her. She couldn't risk actually *talking* about him. Not yet.

"So," TJ said offhandedly. "About Link. He's got this real hard-ass of a dad, see? And this dad, he's always cracking down hard on him. He thinks he's a screw-up."

"La, la, la. Not listening!" Josie sang out.

"When Link was just a little kid, his mom died."

Oh, geez. "Come on, TJ —"

"And his dad, he just went to work after that. That was all he did. Work, work, work. Building his freight trucking empire. He went to work and shipped Link to boarding school." TJ shrugged. "Boarding school after boarding school. Link kept getting kicked out for taking things apart. And drag racing. And amping up the power on the parents' night billboard."

Josie had to know something. Determinedly, she kept her tone light. "Was there really a pony? And a nanny?"

"I think so." TJ frowned. "I met Link after all that. By then, he was busy trying to be a big boss at, um, Blowhard & Sons. Like his dad wanted. But it didn't work out too well."

I can't talk about dads, Josie remembered Luke saying. *I haven't had the greatest experience in that department.*

Sympathy filled her. Maybe some of the things he'd told her *had* been true, she thought reluctantly. Maybe some of the important things had been real — and so had his feelings for her. Maybe, maybe . . .

No. Luke had hurt her and he hadn't cared. She wouldn't care, either. She wouldn't. Wouldn't. Wouldn't.

"What happened?" she heard herself ask, hugging a throw pillow to her chest. "What happened at Blowhard & Sons?"

Arrgh. She could have drowned herself in Kool-Aid just for saying the words. What was the matter with her? Why give TJ more ammunition for his annoying

Luke defense theories?

But TJ wasn't the one who made Josie lean forward to catch every word he said next. And TJ wasn't the one who made her sit up straight in surprise, who made her catch her breath in commiseration, who made her tear up at the finale to "Link's" life story.

"He can't even go to Melissa's wedding?" Josie wailed when he'd finished. Reaching for a tissue, she accidentally dabbed her eyes with a dried-out marshmallow Peep instead. Stupid junk food. She accepted the tissue TJ handed her. "Luke's lost everything, *everything*, and nobody in his family will even take his side in this feud with his dad?"

Appalled, she stared at TJ.

He nodded. "That's pretty much it."

"Even though all Luke wants is to be a motorcycle mechanic instead of a freight company big shot?"

"Yeah. I guess I should've explained the whole story, back when I told you about Luke wanting to open his own shop. But I figured Luke would kick my butt if I did."

A sniffle. "Won't he kick your butt now?"

"He'd like to." Remarkably, TJ grinned. "But he's pretty dog-tired after working on

Blue Moon night and day."

Blue Moon. Instantly, bitterness washed over Josie. No matter how sorry she felt for "Link" now, it didn't feel good to lose the man you loved to a house.

"Hey, hey. Don't do that." TJ put down the Cap'n Crunch. He leaned forward, awkwardly patting her blankets in the vicinity of her shoulder. "It's not like that. Come on. You're the first person Luke cared about who didn't nag him to wash the motor oil off his hands. He needs you."

He couldn't possibly need her as much as she needed him. Defiantly, Josie stuffed a Twizzler in her mouth. She chewed furiously.

What was wrong with TJ? Why was he putting all this stuff in her head? She didn't want to empathize with Luke. She wanted . . . She wanted to *be* with him. Oh, criminy.

"Does *he* know that? Does *he* know he needs me?"

"He asked you to stay, didn't he? He offered you a new dance studio, didn't he?" TJ said. "In guy talk, wanting to do stuff for a woman means something."

"Yeah. It means he wants to buy me."

TJ rolled his eyes. Abruptly, Josie realized that Luke — stripped of his inheri-

486

tance, his trust fund, and all his properties, couldn't buy much more than *she* could. Which amounted to a gumball. Or maybe half a Twix bar.

Feeling overwhelmed and confused and, yes, strangely hopeful for the first time in days, she kept her voice small.

"Is Blue Moon really all he has left?"

TJ gave her a meaningful look.

"*Now* it is," he said. "Without you. Without you being with him, together. Like, forever. You know, true love style."

TJ had never been one for subtlety.

"I guess I could ask my mom to list Blue Moon for him," Josie mused. "She'd know how to get the best price for it. You know, in an auction or something."

"You don't care if Luke sells the place?"

"I wouldn't go *that* far." She sort of missed it. All that work, all that cleaning . . . Josie had formed an attachment to Blue Moon. But there were other considerations here.

"That's really awesome of you," TJ enthused, eyes wide.

"It's not that big a deal." His blatant approval made her feel twitchy. It wasn't as though Josie was *forgiving* Luke or anything. All she was doing was giving him a leg up on the competition. A helping hand toward settling things with his dad, the way she had with hers.

"Besides," she said with forced breeziness, "if I can't have Blue Moon, some moneybags mansion-owning wanna-be might as well pay through the nose for the privilege, right?"

"Hell, yeah." TJ laughed and grabbed another nacho.

"But you'd better not tell Luke," she warned him. "He doesn't need to know I'm involved in this."

"Scout's honor." He held up a nacho, swearing-in style.

"As if *you* were ever a Boy Scout." Filled with a weird sense of energy, Josie flung off her blanket. For the first time in days, she actually felt good about something. "I'll go talk to my mom right now."

It wasn't everything, she decided. But it was a start.

Tallulah slouched in a booth at Frank's Diner, a Garbo-style scarf on her head. A pair of Jackie O sunglasses hid most of her face. Turning up the collar of her trench coat, she scanned the restaurant. Her contact wasn't here yet.

"Mmmm." Across the table Ambrose paused in mid-bite, an expression of bliss on his distinguished features. "This apple pie is beyond compare. Especially with this — what did you call it? Reddi Wip? — on top. Delicious."

"Shhh. Pull down your fedora and be quiet. You don't want to be recognized, do you?"

He smiled at her. "You're enjoying this."

"Don't be ridiculous. It's meddling."

"Which is why you're enjoying it."

"Hmmph. I'm only doing what's necessary."

"You're in love." Smiling, Ambrose pointed his fork at her. "You want everyone else to be in love, too."

She was saved from answering that sentimental — if accurate — twaddle by the arrival of her partner in crime. Tallulah waved him over, thrilled by their clandestine meeting.

TJ slid in the booth. "Hey, how's it going?"

"Where's your disguise?" Tallulah demanded. She waved at his Laundromat T-shirt and baggy surf shorts. "Do you want us to get caught?"

"Chill out." He signaled for Luanne, the waitress, by pantomiming a cup of coffee in his hand. When she nodded, he looked back at Tallulah. "We won't get caught.

They're both on the hook now."

She leaned forward. "Josie's come around?"

"Almost. How about Luke?"

"Almost," Tallulah and Ambrose said in unison.

The three of them smiled.

"Family meddling sure beats corporate spying," TJ said. "But Luke would kill us if he knew about this. Josie, too."

"It's for their own good. They'll thank us in the end." Confidently, Tallulah snitched a bite of her husband's piecrust. "My, that is tasty. Oh, Luanne . . . ?"

Two days after the sprinkler head incident, Luke still hadn't gotten Tallulah's irritating comments out of his head. Ambrose's, either.

Pigheaded pride won't tell you knock-knock jokes.

Damn it. That one had really gotten under his skin.

Was it possible he was being too stubborn? Had *always* been too stubborn? Even with his dad . . . and Josie?

Luke considered it, picking up his paintbrush to apply another coat to the repaired beams on the house's porch. He slapped on some Colonial Blue. All around him, the estate lay quiet. Too quiet. TJ had started spending more and more time at Amber's apartment, and even Tallulah and Ambrose had quit their daily lecture visits.

"Good idea," someone said from the driveway. "Painting the trim will increase your curb appeal a hundred and ten percent. You should plant some flowers in those window boxes, too. Buyers like flowers."

He glanced past the porch, surprised to find Nancy Day standing beside her white Caddy. He must have been too lost in thought to hear her drive up. That wasn't like him at all.

"I *knew* you owned this place," she said, coming closer with her eyes — and her gold jewelry — shining. "No 'handyman' would have worked as hard as you have."

He shrugged, offering her his least paint-splattered palm for a handshake. "It's complicated."

"I don't think so." Making herself at home, Nancy sat on the wide porch railing. She gazed up at him steadily, with unnerving perception. "I think it's pretty simple. You know what you want, and you're going after it. That's an admirable quality. I hope you succeed."

"Right. With six percent commission going to you."

"Maybe. If you decide to let me help you sell this place." She smiled, not the least bit bothered by his blunt statement. "You know, you and my daughter have a lot in common. She's always had that go-getter quality, too. It's what led her to dancing."

Not wanting to hear about Josie — not *ready* to hear about Josie — Luke picked up his paintbrush again. He stroked on a little more Colonial Blue, not speaking.

"One innocent showing of the Radio City 'Christmas Spectacular' with her grandmother," Nancy rattled on cheerfully, "and Josie *knew* she was going to become a Rockette. Nobody was going to stop her."

"But she's not a Rockette," Luke pointed out, not sure why he needed to make that distinction. "She's a showgirl."

"Well, technically, she *was* a showgirl. We both know that's finished for Josie now."

Chastened, he went on painting. He focused on smoothing on an even layer of blue, unwilling to think about Josie as a little girl. Josie sitting in a theater balcony, enchanted, watching a bunch of high-kicking, Santa-suited Rockettes. Josie dreaming of dancing . . . dreaming, as an adult, of teaching dancing. Exactly the way he dreamed of being a mechanic.

"Anyway, that's beside the point." Nancy gave a dismissive wave, her multiple bracelets jangling. "The point is, Josie did it. She achieved her dream."

Luke didn't agree. "If she didn't become a Rockette, she didn't achieve her dream. End of story."

"Some people," Nancy said, "are wise enough to know when their dreams need modifying."

Luke met her gaze. The meaning there was loud and clear.

"If you're one of them," she added, "you'll never need this."

She plucked out one of her business cards and anchored its corner beneath Luke's paint can. She gave Blue Moon one final, covetous look, then clattered down the porch steps.

"Wait." Frowning, Luke fisted his hand. "Does Josie still want her dance school? Or did all . . . this . . . make her give up?"

Graciously, Nancy Day didn't push him on what *this* referred to. It was obvious she already knew. It was equally obvious he'd underestimated her all along.

She smiled. "Give up? Not while there are still Rockettes in the world."

Then Nancy Day drove away in her

Caddy, leaving Luke with the distinct feeling he'd just been outmaneuvered by the QVC jewelry queen. She'd called his bluff, too.

Stymied, he gazed out over the estate's wide green lawn. If holding tight to his pride didn't work, and explaining to Josie didn't work . . . what would?

Browsing through the overstuffed racks at Glenda's Clothing Cache in downtown Donovan's Corner, Josie slid aside another flowered skirt. Her lunch break from her new filing job at her mother's realty office wasn't long enough to allow any waffling. She either liked something or she didn't. Moving on . . .

"Not me, not me, not me," she told Jenna, scraping the hangers aside. "*So* not me. Unless I become a professional hog caller."

Jenna made a face. "How would you know what's not you? You've been impersonating *me* for the past few months."

"Right," Josie agreed, looking her sister over. "And I have to say, our wardrobe swap has done *your* look a world of good. I want those jeans back, by the way."

She leaned over and gave Emily a chin tickle, delighting in her niece's throaty chuckle. Ever since asking her mom to take over Luke's auction of Blue Moon, Josie had felt better. Almost free, strange as it sounded. She'd even cut back on E! TV.

"My point is," Jenna persisted, "when are you going to become *yourself* again?"

"I am myself. A little worse for the wear, but —"

"No, you're not," Jenna interrupted. "You're not 'you' yet. That's my crew neck top, and those are Mom's gold sandals."

"Well, it's my skirt," Josie said defensively. She examined her sister. "What's your problem, anyway? After everything I've been through with Luke, with him *lying* to me, with losing my job, and losing Blue Moon . . . I don't need this today."

"I happen to think it's *exactly* what you need." Pulling a soggy price tag from Emily's mouth, Jenna serenely substituted an animal cracker. The girl munched. "We've all been walking on eggshells around you for days. It's gone on long enough."

"Sheesh. Settle down, Oprah."

"Nope." Jenna shook her head, boosting Emily higher on her hip as she followed Josie to the next rack. "I've had it! You keep whining about 'Luke this,' and 'Luke that,' and complaining about him 'lying' to you. Well, here's a news flash."

Josie gawked. Her sister — her perfect, patient, and sensible sister — was actually going ballistic on her.

"What about *you*, huh?" Jenna asked. "You haven't exactly been a thousand percent truthful about who you are, either."

"Yes, I was! I always was."

"Oh, yeah? Baked any cupcakes lately? Dropped in on any PTSO meetings?" She narrowed her eyes as though sensing her impending victory. "Worn any orthopedic shoes?"

Josie gasped. "You promised you'd never mention those again!"

"Desperate times call for desperate measures."

This wasn't fair. Jenna knew darn well Josie had been *forced* into doing all those things to gain support — and students — for her dance school.

"Did Luke *really* know who you were?" Jenna asked, pushing even harder. "Or did he buy into all that stuff, too? Did you ever give him a chance to honestly know you?"

Josie crossed her arms. "He knew me."

"Oh, yeah? How?"

"Some of that stuff was really me, that's how!" Josie ticked off the specifics on her fingers. "Luke liked my false eyelashes! I know he did. He liked my cleaning. He liked my dancing. He liked my knock-knock jokes." Of which there'd been precious few lately, she admitted. She raised her chin. "He liked *me*."

"Okay. So let me get this straight. One minute you're baking cupcakes. The next minute you're putting on a miniskirt and pinning 'Frank' to your head. How's Luke supposed to know which of those things represents the real 'you'?"

A frown. "He just . . . does."

"Uh-huh." Jenna rolled her eyes. She gave Emily another animal cracker and then stood by, waiting with her usual saint-like tolerance for Josie to catch a clue.

"He ought to know!" Josie said in her own defense. "After all, everybody else in town did. They could tell I wasn't *really* into cupcake baking." She stopped, stunned by the truth. "They *could* tell, couldn't they?"

"Probably," Jenna mused. To her credit, she didn't even gloat about being right. "People have a way of detecting insincerity. Inauthenticity. That's probably why they didn't exactly line up to help you."

Josie had been more than sincere in wanting her dance school. She'd been downright serious. But right now, she had more important things to think about. Like Luke.

"I never really gave Luke a chance," she said, marveling at the revelation. "When it comes right down to it, I never gave *anybody* in Donovan's Corner a chance. Not to know the *real* me."

"I know. I helped you do it."

Josie dismissed that. "I made you help me."

"You're not *that* powerful. But the real you is a good person. Fake hair and all." Jenna grinned. "It's not too late to change things, you know."

"Yes, it is." Feeling like a hypocrite, Josie moaned. "I've lost Luke. My dance school is indefinitely postponed. I'm a filing clerk in Donovan's Corner. And I'm wearing plaid!"

"All those things can be fixed," Jenna soothed.

"That's right," a mysterious voice added. "None of those are insurmountable problems."

They turned, staring at the nearby dressing room.

The curtain moved aside. Tallulah Carlyle emerged, a bow-wearing shih tzu in her arms and a grin on her face.

"We can fix *everything* if we get started right now," she said. "I have just the plan . . ."

Twenty-Two

From the moment Luke decided that things had to change — that *he* had to change — the universe seemed to jump on board. Tallulah and Ambrose ended their self-imposed Luke boycott and started coming to Blue Moon again, full of advice and plans. TJ ditched his silent treatment and actually helped with the scheme Luke cooked up. And even Nancy Day, once he called her, didn't need much persuasion to join in.

His plan was a simple one. First, he had to apologize to Josie for deceiving her — in as big and as public a way as possible. Second, he had to make things up to her — ditto on the "big and public." Third, he had to tell her he loved her.

Accomplishing it wouldn't be easy. Hell, it would probably be terrifying — especially given the "public" part of his plan. But Luke decided he'd rather risk losing everything than go on the way he had been. If it came down to a choice between

proving himself and proving his love —
and it looked as if it did — there was no
contest.

Luke chose love.

He wanted Josie back. Whatever it took.
As long as she was still in town, and so was
he, Luke figured he had a pretty good shot.
So long as his plan didn't fall apart, his estate didn't fall apart, and his accomplices
— Tallulah, Ambrose, TJ, and Nancy —
didn't fall down on the job, he just might
make it.

"Hey, Ambrose." He gestured to the
opened toolbox lying at the attorney's feet.
"Hand me that one-sixteenth's inch drill
bit."

After a moment's hesitation, Ambrose did.
Squinting at the hole Luke had drilled in the
ballroom wall, he wiped his hands on his
new blue jeans. Nearby, Tallulah swooned.

"Oh, Ambrose. You look so macho! You
should build things more often."

Luke grinned. No need to mention that
Ambrose's contribution had mostly consisted of handing over the stud finder and
gazing in the toolbox in mystification. It
was kind of sweet to see his aunt back to
her old self again.

A few minutes later, Luke stepped back
to survey his work.

Brand-new ballet barres lined two of the ballroom's newly mirrored walls. Wires trailed along the floor, leading to the speakers, amplifier, woofer, and other sound system components he had yet to install. Combined with the refurbished floor and the other additions to the room, it would make this place the perfect location for Josie's dance school.

Even if she didn't know it yet.

"Did the furniture get delivered for Josie's office?" he asked, running his hand along the nearest barre. "And the new computer? Once Josie gets here" — God, he hoped she came — "she'll need all that stuff for managing student records and payments and schedules."

"Hmmm." Tallulah nodded approvingly as she petted Crackers, her shih tzu. "Looks like *somebody* was paying attention during all those stints in the corporate office."

Luke frowned. "Was it delivered or not?"

"It's all set up in the downstairs library. Just as you ordered."

Subdued, Tallulah nodded through the doorway toward the nearest room, which overlooked Blue Moon's driveway and front lawn. With that room as Josie's office, she'd be able to see students as they arrived, do paperwork, and take care of her dance school's administrative details — all while enjoying a view of the pansies Luke had planted in the window boxes.

Nancy Day had told him Josie liked flowers.

Feeling unaccountably nervous, Luke strode toward the sound system wiring. His hand trembled as he picked up an input jack. After days of preparation, he couldn't believe it was almost time to unveil his surprise to Josie. The only potential snag in his plan would be if she didn't come to Blue Moon.

"Ambrose, did you call Josie about the 'paperwork' she's supposed to come out here to sign on Saturday?"

"I did. I told her it was regarding the dispersal of the estate, exactly as you requested."

If everything went as planned, Josie would think she was tying up loose ends regarding Tallulah's bungled "gift" of Blue Moon. What she didn't know was that Luke had other plans for the place. Plans that involved Josie.

"She seemed surprisingly amenable to the notion of coming here for a visit," Ambrose went on, straightening the collar of his new golf shirt. "I think she misses you."

Tallulah shot her husband a look Luke couldn't decipher.

He decided his aunt must be trying to protect his feelings in case things didn't work out with Josie.

"Hey, it's all right," he said, following the trail of the speaker wire to the jumbled pile of multicolored connectors, wires, and components. "I know this might turn out to be one gigantic 'gotcha!' If Josie doesn't come, I'll look like an idiot in front of the whole town."

They'd invited everyone they could think of to the event Luke had planned, and word had gotten around pretty quickly to include even more people. Not that communication was a real problem in a place the size of Donovan's Corner.

There'd been talk of the "big shindig at that old Blue Moon place" in the hardware store, in Frank's Diner, and in the warehouse zone of the local Shop 'N Save. If they could just keep the details under wraps for two more days, Luke would be in business.

"You'll look like a *lovesick* idiot," Tallulah corrected.

But Luke didn't care. "If it brings Josie back, it'll be worth it."

He got back to the tangled wiring. While

Tallulah and Ambrose nattered on about floral arrangements, parking accommodations, and the dearth of nightlife in Donovan's Corner, Luke lifted and connected and plugged in. He fit the speakers in their designated positions, tested the connections and controls, then went back to wiring again.

Heavy footfalls sounded. "I should have known I'd find you taking something apart."

It couldn't be. Stopping in mid-connection, Luke glanced over his shoulder. Robert Donovan stood in the doorway to the ballroom, flanked by a grinning TJ.

"Actually," Luke said, "I'm putting this together."

"Then I guess TJ's right. You *have* made some changes."

As Luke rose, his father strode farther into the room. Dimly, he heard Robert greet Tallulah and Ambrose. He heard his aunt give her little brother hell for not telling her he was coming. He heard his own stupid heart, thudding with automatic rebellion and confusion and — damn it — even hope.

He glared at TJ. His idiot friend only grinned wider.

"What are you doing here, Dad? The

boardroom's that way." Luke angled his head to the west, toward L.A. "You're out of your element."

"I'd say I'm right where I belong. Finally."

Stubbornly, unwilling to hope this meant anything at all, Luke stood his ground. His father looked exactly the same as he always had. Business suit. Dark hair tipped with gray at the temples. Severe expression. But there seemed to be a few new wrinkles on the old man's face, and his shoulders stooped a little more than Luke remembered.

"Whatever TJ told you, it's bullshit."

"Hey!"

"Shut up, TJ." Luke skewered him with an impatient glance. "You've done enough already."

But his dad only shook his head. "I knew hanging out with all those mechanics would ruin your language skills."

"Screw language skills."

That earned a full-on chuckle. "Your love of wiring and taking things apart isn't the only thing that hasn't changed."

"Right. My patience hasn't grown overnight, either." Feeling himself weaken, just a little, Luke crossed his arms over his chest. He wasn't giving in until his dad did. "So why don't you cut to the chase?"

Nearby, Tallulah and Ambrose watched, not even pretending they couldn't overhear the drama taking place. TJ waited, too, a dumb-ass grin on his face. Still.

"All right." Seeming to gather his own patience, Robert Donovan gazed at the chandelier overhead, then at his son. "TJ tells me —"

"TJ told you a lot of things," Luke interrupted. "None of them were true. You should've picked a more reliable spy."

"Hey! That's low, dude."

"I wasn't finished." Sternly, his dad went on. "TJ tells me that you're dating a showgirl. That you're *in love* with a showgirl."

Ahhh. It figured. All at once, Luke understood.

"Now I get why you're here. TJ tells you I'm hunting for aliens, hanging out in the local loony bin, and building tree houses out of beer bottles, but it's the news that I might be *dating* someone that brings you here?"

"Dating a showgirl," his father specified, brows knit.

Luke swore. "Maybe you should leave."

"Not yet. Not until I meet her."

"What? Are you kidding me?" Luke moved closer, setting his chin at a screw-

506

you angle. "No. You're not getting any-where near Josie. She's too good for you."

At that, his father looked pained. He glanced backward at TJ. Improbably, TJ gave him a go-ahead signal.

"Luke, that's not all," his father continued. "TJ told me about your mechanic's shop, too. The one you've been running in the carriage house."

"Jesus Christ, TJ! Whose side are you on, anyway?"

"Yours, dude. You don't know the whole story."

Luke didn't believe it. He glared at his father, not surprised to find Robert Donovan frowning at his tattoos.

TJ nudged him. "Tell him, Bob-O," he urged.

Obstinately, Luke's dad remained silent.

"Men!" Tallulah rolled her eyes, then grabbed her husband. "Come on, Ambrose. Let's go make out in the backyard arbor."

They trotted away, Ambrose moving fast in his new sneakers.

Luke squared off against his father and his friend, both of them seeming determined to have a standoff. Right in the middle of his preparations for Josie's surprise. Damn it.

"Look," he began. "I don't have time for this."

"As it turns out," his father said, "neither do I." He cast a regretful look over Luke, then turned. "Sorry, TJ. I tried."

With a sense of unreality, Luke watched his father leave. A minute later he heard gravel crunching in the drive — probably beneath the tires of his dad's sleek BMW.

A wallop from TJ brought him back to earth.

"Dude! What's wrong with you?"

"Nothing. But I can't say the same for you." Luke tightened his jaw. "Looks like you're out one spy job."

TJ only shook his head. "You don't get it. Do you seriously think I'd tell your dad all that crazy stuff about you?"

"You told him about Josie."

"Yeah. But that's it." Looking disgusted, TJ met Luke's gaze in the mirror. "That's *it*. The rest of it never happened. I'm your friend."

"Yeah. My 'friend' who's spying on me for my dad."

"No way. That's where you're wrong."

Luke stared at him, a dawning suspicion growing. Something nagged at him — something about the confusion in his dad's face as Luke had ranted about TJ's alien-hunting stories.

"*Somebody* had to make sure you and your dad didn't lose touch with each other forever," TJ explained. He pointed both thumbs at himself, his beaming smile returning. "Dude! You guessed it. I'm a freaking double *double* agent!"

Unbelievable. Luke released a pent-up breath.

"Your dad just wanted to make sure you were okay after the argument you guys had," TJ said. "When he asked me to come after you, that's what he said. 'Make sure Luke's okay.' So that's what I did. That's what I'm *still* doing."

At his meaningful look, Luke frowned. "I don't need my dad here right now. This thing with Josie —"

"Is *exactly* why you need your dad here!"

Looking at TJ's goofy, optimistic expression, Luke sighed. Why was everyone suddenly determined to meddle in his life?

"Your dad really wants to meet Josie," TJ urged. "I told him all about her. He's happy for you."

"Wasn't that a little premature?" Luke ran his hand through his hair, feeling exasperated, overwhelmed . . . and okay, fine — disappointed things hadn't turned out

509

better with his dad. "What if Josie doesn't come?"

"Dude, she'll come. And when she does, your dad will be there to see it!"

Oh, Christ. "TJ. You didn't."

"I did. I invited your dad to come here on Saturday for the big shindig." TJ chortled, looking pleased. "He booked a room at your aunt's hotel. He already said yes!"

Great. If Josie didn't show, Luke would be humiliated in front of the whole town *and* his dad. And Tallulah and Ambrose and TJ and, probably, Amber. That was just terrific.

Feeling even shakier than before, he went back to his wiring. There was no backing down now. Luke only hoped he could pull off his reunion with Josie better than he had his reconciliation with his father.

On Saturday morning, Josie awoke with a smile on her face and not a stitch on anyplace else. After her showdown with Jenna — and her subsequent strategizing session with Tallulah — she'd reverted to her old ways . . . including sleeping in the buff.

Bare-naked snoozing might not be right for everyone. But to Josie, it felt natural. It felt as much *her* as Frank, her false eyelashes, and the tight pink pants she'd decided to wear today did. That was good enough for her.

More importantly, it was authentic. Powered by the realization that she'd never get anywhere — would never be honestly happy — if she wasn't true to herself first, Josie had returned to her roots. Triumphantly.

Only in the figurative sense, of course. A girl would have to be crazy to give up the advantages of Clairol Sedona Sunset.

But oddly enough, the moment Josie had decided to quit worrying about making a good impression on Donovan's Corner . . . she'd started making a good impression on Donovan's Corner. Almost the same way Jenna had predicted during her "baking cupcakes" lecture at Glenda's Clothing Cache.

As near as Josie could tell, the pro-Josie movement began with her dad's cable-TV campaign. It picked up momentum when he welcomed her back home, and then reached a crescendo when she dared to appear in Donovan's Corner as herself — false eyelashes, short skirts, and all.

The whole experience had been pretty liberating. But what mattered most to Josie was that having the town's support would prove plenty convenient when it came to today's events. . . .

And the surprise she had planned for Luke.

Looking forward to it, she hopped in the shower and then got dressed, adding an improvised shuffle step here and a step-ball-change there. Moving felt good. Anticipating Luke's reaction felt good. Being herself — *really being herself* — felt great. Finally, Josie had her self-respect back.

Next on the agenda was getting Luke back, too.

Flipping her head upside down, Josie squirted styling spray at the roots of her hair and then blow dried for maximum volume. That was her, too. Big hair, big dreams, big risk-taking. Her dreams would be on hold for a while, but that was okay. Postponing her dance school plans — *modifying her plans,* as her mom called it — would be worth it. It would be worth it if Luke came back to her.

With a grin, Josie thought about the scheme she'd cooked up with the help of Tallulah and Jenna and TJ and her mom. Thanks to Ambrose's phone call earlier this week, Josie's visit to Blue Moon today would dovetail with her plans nicely. Luke wouldn't know what had hit him.

At first she'd worried he would bolt, wanting to avoid seeing her. But Tallulah had assured her that Luke was so busy working on Blue Moon — getting it ready for auction, Josie guessed — that he'd stick around. Reassured, she'd decided to go ahead.

Not that it had been easy. She'd had to swallow her pride and ask for help. She'd had to contact the same people who'd turned up their noses at her and ask them to pitch in for Luke. She'd had to organize and strategize and plan ahead . . . none of those skills a strong suit for her. But now that the day had arrived, Josie *knew* it would work.

It had to work. She needed to make things up to Luke. She needed a second chance with him. If she couldn't do that . . .

Well, she *would* do it. She refused to admit the possibility of failure. All the same, butterflies tangoed through her midsection as Josie slipped into her pink pants and a cute halter top. Her fingers trembled as she fastened the straps on her rainbow wedgies. Her smile faltered as she examined her appearance in the mirror and wondered how Luke would react when he saw her.

Would he see her with love? With happiness? Or with the same disdain Donovan's Corner had? She'd left it behind once, too. Regaining its trust had been an uphill battle all the way.

She guessed she'd just have to wait and see.

"It's show time," she whispered to her reflection.

Then Josie lifted her shoulders and — for courage — performed an exemplary showgirl walk, all the way to her car.

Twenty-Three

Somehow, when Josie's back was turned, her simple real estate auction turned into a three-ring circus.

Arriving at Blue Moon, she couldn't even park her convertible in the driveway. Gawking at the crowds of bikers, of running children, of Chardonnay-drinking PTSO members, Josie pulled past the estate house. She followed the handmade signs — where had those come from? — to a sandy improvised parking lot.

As she got out of her car, still confused by the hubbub all around her, a yellow balloon zoomed past her head. Powered by helium, it soared into the clear Arizona sky. Josie watched it disappear, feeling equally set adrift by this change of plans.

Well. She'd just have to get her bearings and go from there. Making her way toward the house, she waved to a few familiar people. She caught a whiff of hot dogs grilling. The citrusy tang of lemonade tickled her nose.

Hot dogs? Lemonade? Gazing across the lawn until she located them, Josie frowned. This was supposed to be an auction. An auction designed to gain Luke the money he needed for his motorcycle mechanic's shop. Not a potluck barbecue.

Something was definitely off-kilter here. Did she have the wrong day? Did Luke have other plans? This sure didn't *look* like the hard work of prepping the place for sale.

On the lookout for Tallulah or Jenna or TJ, Josie continued past the carriage house, feeling a pang as she looked up at Luke's apartment window. Somewhere nearby, a band played. She couldn't quite identify the song . . . probably because of the conversations taking place everywhere.

Visitors dotted the lawn that Luke and TJ had raced their competing mowers across. Laughter wafted from the distant open windows of Blue Moon's estate house. Tallulah's shih tzu barked at the neighbors' curious cat as it streaked into the pine trees, rustling the boughs.

Here and there, Josie spied the well-heeled townspeople, contacts of her mother's, whom she'd invited with the hopes of enticing big bids from them. Feeling mystified by the presence of everyone else — especially the kids and the bikers and the blue-collar families — she circled the house. Now and then she shook hands or passed out auction info sheets.

Where the heck was everyone? She glimpsed Luanne from Frank's Diner, a contingent from the Donovan's Corner ladies' auxiliary, and — for one brief instant — David, with Emily in his arms and Hannah by his side. But Jenna was nowhere to be found, and neither was her mother or Tallulah.

Squinting, Josie checked her watch. The auction was due to begin in just under an hour. If her mother didn't show soon, she didn't see how she could pull this off.

Moving forward, Josie recognized one of the PTSO moms from Hannah's school. On autopilot, she handed her the auction info.

"Hey, cute pants," the woman said. "Where'd you get them?"

A compliment? From the super-judgmental Mommy & Me crowd? Now Josie *knew* something was wrong. She blurted out the name of her favorite discount store, then offered an apology and made her getaway. She felt seriously freaked out. If she could just find Tallulah or her mom . . .

Then, midway between the hot dog–covered barbecue grill and the spot where a clown was making balloon animals — no, scratch that, where *TJ* was making balloon animals — Josie spotted him.

Luke.

Her heart stuttered. A sense of unreality gripped her. Unable to move, she watched him instead. He wore a fitted gray T-shirt, jeans, work boots. His tattoos flashed, and so did his smile. As she watched, he leaned toward someone, talking, his dark head bent in concentration.

In that moment, Josie knew what yearning felt like. What need felt like. Because all she could do was stand there — stand there and wish it was *her* ear Luke murmured into, *her* arm he touched briefly as he spoke, *her* face he smiled at. In a rush, she remembered the sound of his voice, the callused feel of his fingertips, the warmth of his body.

She remembered what TJ had said, the stories he'd shared about "Link." She remembered knowing, with certainty, that she owed Luke more than her usual dodge-and-run routine. More than "pulling a Josie." Which was why she was here today. Why she was coming back, really, for the first time in all her life.

Luke laughed, and Josie felt herself drawn toward him. Gathering her courage, she squared her shoulders and started walking. Groups of people parted as she moved between them, her gaze fixed on the man she loved . . . on the man she'd arranged every moment of this occasion for.

Hazily, she wondered why he wasn't confused by the crowds descending on his estate. Why he wasn't befuddled that his lawn, his house, and his impromptu "parking lot" overflowed with Donovan's Corner residents. But then Luke glanced up and saw her. All rational thought fled, chased by the significance of knowing there was no backing out now.

Surprise registered on his features. His gaze zipped over her halter top, her sexy pink pants, her wedgies. It had been a long time since she'd worn them. As though he'd only just realized that fact, Luke let his gaze linger on her rainbow shoes. A grin kicked up the corner of his mouth.

His attention swerved to her face.

Oh, wow. She'd forgotten the impact of having Luke completely focused on *her*. All at once, Josie felt as though everyone else on the lawn faded away . . . as though someone had pressed a gigantic mute button. All that remained was Luke. And her. And her clumsy, trembling, embarrassingly damp palms.

"Hey," he said when she reached him.

His voice, deep and beloved and familiar, reached all the way inside her. It easily found every lonesome, missing-him molecule Josie had tried to push aside. Faced with Luke, here, now, pushing aside anything — least of all her feelings — was downright impossible.

His smile widened. "You came."

Was it her imagination, or did he look relieved? She couldn't imagine why that would be, but . . . *oh, wow.* Luke touched her hand, tentatively interlaced their fingers, gave her a gentle tug — a tug that clearly communicated *I want you . . . but coming closer is up to you.*

Heart hammering, Josie bravely stepped nearer. At her movement, Luke *definitely* looked relieved. If she hadn't known better, she'd have sworn *he* was the one who'd planned a surprise for today.

"Of course I came."

She had no idea how she managed to string those words together. Her head reverberated with a chant of *Luke, Luke, Luke.* Her hands still hadn't quit shaking. Her knees wobbled. She figured she could pass off her hot, blushing cheeks as a sunburn. Or maybe the result of an over-zealous application of her Cover Girl Wild Raspberry Cheekers. But the overall meaning of those symptoms was unmistakable.

This meant the world to her. *Luke* meant the world to her. That was all there was to it. On the verge of telling him so, Josie was stopped by the strange expression on his face. He looked . . . nervous?

"Josie, I'm sorry," he blurted. Roughly. Sincerely. "Things got out of hand with Blue Moon. I know it's no excuse, but I never meant to hurt you. You've got to understand that. To believe it. I —"

"No, *I'm* sorry!" she interrupted, squeezing his hand. "I should never have cut and run like that. I know you. I should have known you had a reason, a *good* reason, for everything."

It wasn't enough. Not enough to make up for hurting him, for not believing in him. Contrite, Josie shook her head.

"I want to make it up to you," Luke said seriously. "That's why . . . this. All this."

He released her hand and opened his arms wide, indicating the throngs of people. All the hullabaloo.

She didn't get it. "Huh?"

"They're your new dance school students. That's why everyone's here, for a grand opening sign-up party." Beaming, Luke swerved his gaze to her face. "What do you think of that?"

Grand opening? Dance school students?

Stunned, Josie could only gape. She looked at the people, at the running children, at the — holy cow, how had she missed that? — nearby booth labeled *dance school sign-ups.* She looked at Luke's proud, happy expression. His hopeful expression.

"I think they're all here for you," she told him. Despite all evidence to the contrary, there was no *way* her plans were going AWOL. She just wouldn't allow it. Stubbornly, she insisted. "They're here for your auction. To bid on Blue Moon. Luke, I arranged it all for you. You're going to get your mechanic's shop!"

This time it was Luke's turn to gawk. Frowning in confusion, he took in the wine drinkers, the men in business suits, the photocopied auction flyers being passed from hand to hand. He noticed the arrival of Nancy Day with a suspiciously official-looking man by her side. He tilted his head and reexamined Josie.

She bounced on tiptoes on those crazy shoes of hers. Her hair looked fiery red and loose, her eyes bright with excitement. Her sexed-up pants lured his attention again.

Resolutely, Luke fought against succumbing. Something important was going on here. Something almost as big as finding Josie by his side again.

They're here for your auction. You're going to get your mechanic's shop.

Still bopping, she nudged him. "Aren't you happy?"

"Happy?" He looked at her, with her warm smile and her just-Josie va-va-voom look. He remembered the way she'd felt in his arms, the way she'd laughed and danced and pushed him to work when he'd almost given up trying. He thought about loving her . . . and about losing her. "Absolutely. I'm happy."

It was true. With Josie by his side, Luke didn't need anything more. He didn't need to prove anything, didn't need to rebel, didn't need a trust fund or a fancy car or a state-of-the-art mechanic's shop that would prove his dad wrong. All he needed, all he wanted, was Josie. Forever.

"Me, too," she said. "I'm happy. Now."

"It's a good thing you came today," Luke observed, reaching for her hand again. "You would have missed all . . . this."

She grinned. "Whatever 'this' is."

Drawn jointly to the confusion surrounding them, Luke and Josie both frowned. Clearly they'd somehow planned concurrent events, both at Blue Moon. An auction *and* a dance school grand opening. But how . . . ?

A nearby titter caught his attention. His suspicions growing, Luke sought out the source of that sound. He found it almost instantly. His aunt stood nearby, flanked by Ambrose and Jenna and Nancy, along with TJ the clown. Tallulah clutched a wineglass, looking fit to burst.

"Gotcha!" she yelled. "This'll teach you to break up on *my* watch!"

"Ahhh." Josie nodded. "Tallulah. I should have known."

"Me, too."

They looked at each other. Then, simultaneously, he and Josie shrugged. It didn't matter how they'd gotten to this place, Luke reasoned. Only that they had.

"Now go, you two." Tallulah made pushing motions with her arms, an enormous grin on her face. "Go and be in love."

"Wait a minute." Robert Donovan stepped forward. Wearing a stern look, he crossed his arms. "I think giving the familial seal of approval is my job."

524

Josie gasped. "That's your dad!"

Luke couldn't believe it. "How did you know?"

"Identical machismo. Carbon copy bad attitude." She peered closer. "Matching devastating good looks."

For the first time, his father grinned. "I like her, son."

But Josie wasn't acquiescing so easily. She stepped forward, spine straight and proud.

"You might want to hold off on forming an opinion, Mr. Donovan. I have a bone to pick with you."

Bemused, his father raised his brow. "You do?"

"I do!" Josie announced. "Starting with the terrible way you've treated your son."

"Josie!" Luke had to stop her. Nobody went up against Robert "the Crusher" Donovan — not his board members, not his employees . . . no one. No one except Luke. And look at the price he'd paid.

But Josie only shook off his restraining hand. "For your information, Mr. Donovan —"

"Call me Bob-O. Everyone's doing it."

Luke gawked. Bob-O? What the . . . ?

TJ chortled. Aha. That explained it.

"For your information, your son is very

talented," Josie said. "He's an excellent mechanic. Ask anybody. They'll tell you. I don't know why you can't be proud of him for that, but you'd better get ready to change your ways. Because once he auctions off Blue Moon and gets that mechanic's shop he wants —"

"Josie —"

"Hang on, Luke. I'm on a roll." She shot him a loving glance, then tackled his father again. "He'll be a huge success. A *huge* success! You just wait and —"

"Josie," Luke interrupted again. "I'm not auctioning off Blue Moon."

She stopped. Wheeled around, mouth agape.

"I decided to keep the estate," he explained, needing to make her understand. "So I can give it to you. For your dance school. It's yours."

"Luke, no . . ." she breathed. "You can't."

"I want to," he said. This wasn't the way he'd planned this revelation — with half the town looking on and the other half dribbling mustard and kraut on his lawn. But if this was what it took to have Josie in his life, this was what he'd do.

"That's what this whole day is about," Luke explained. "To give you Blue Moon.

To give you a chance to become a Rockette."

Looking confused, Josie tilted her head.

Nearby, Nancy Day grinned.

"The estate is yours," Luke said, cutting to the chase. "And so are these students."

He wanted to smile, to deliver the news with a flourish. But as he gazed into Josie's eyes, as he prepared to make the final part of his offer, Luke discovered this felt too important for that. Too crucial to his future. Swallowing hard, he went on.

"The only question now is . . . Will you stay to teach them?"

"Oh! Oh, Luke . . ."

"Will you stay," he continued doggedly, "to be with me?"

She brought her hands to her mouth, looking stunned. Her eyes glimmered with unshed tears. As far as Luke was concerned, that was a bad sign. A sign that needed to be dealt with and eradicated.

"I love you," he said. "Pretty much, I've loved you since the moment you sashayed onto my lawn and took over my house. I love your smile and your courage and your jokes. I love the way you dance when you think I'm not looking. I love your crazy shoes and your false eyelashes and I love the way you feel in my arms. I know I can never be happy again unless you're beside me."

Josie gave a small cry. Luke stopped. *Oh, crap.* Now she wept openly, gulping for air like the goldfish Luke had owned when he was ten. The one he'd killed with kindness by feeding it too many stinky fish flakes.

"I love you. I love you, and I'll never lie to you again," he blurted, desperate to make her understand. Casting around for proof, he said, "I'll tell you if your pants make your butt look too big. I'll tell you if I don't want you to eat my French fries after you order a salad for lunch. I'll —"

"Shhh." Blinking away her tears, Josie put her palm against his lips. "Quit it before you promise something really radical, like giving up Monday Night Football."

"Mmmmph," he protested against her hand.

She smiled. "I take that to mean you'd do that, too."

"Whoa," TJ said. "That's what I call true love."

There were murmurs of agreement from everyone else. But Josie only went on gazing into Luke's eyes, looking beautiful and beloved and exactly like everything he'd always wanted. She drew in a breath and blinked again.

"Well. I've only got one thing to say to that."

Luke pulled away her hand. "What?"

"It goes like this." Josie smiled. "Knock, knock."

This time, he smiled, too. "Who's there?"

"I love."

"I love who?"

"I love *you* and no one else!" Jubilantly, she flung her arms around him and kissed him. "I love you more than anything, Luke. More than dancing. More than Ding Dongs. More" — she paused for emphasis, her eyes sparkling — "than my Swiffer Duster."

"Now *that's* saying something."

"You bet your life, it is."

Tallulah whooped. Ambrose hollered right beside her. Everyone else looked on and smiled. Warren Day hugged Nancy close. He volunteered the opinion that he'd known all along "the kids" were perfect for each other. TJ agreed.

But Luke didn't care who was watching, and he didn't care who took credit. Because an instant later Josie kissed him again, and he could feel her love in every sigh, in every glance, in every brush of her lips against his. That was all he needed.

That, and a few good knock-knock jokes. For the rest of his life.

"There's only one more thing," Josie announced.

Luke raised his brows in question.

"We have to share everything," she specified. "Everything, like Blue Moon. We can live in the main house together. You can expand the carriage house for your mechanic's shop, right? I mean, your Harley-riding friends already said you'd have all the business you could handle."

She gazed at him in all seriousness. In that moment, Luke loved her more than ever — just for believing in him.

Before he could agree, though, his father butted in.

"That shop of yours is a fine setup," Robert Donovan said. "It'd be a shame to waste it."

He stepped forward, an unfamiliar caring in his expression. He looked straight at Luke. In his eyes, Luke glimpsed all the pride, all the respect, all the *love* he'd ever hoped to receive from his father. The realization left him too shook up to speak. Naturally, the same couldn't be said of Robert Donovan.

"I was never opposed to your having a mechanic's shop, son. TJ will tell you that.

I only wanted to make sure it was really what you wanted to do. Not a knee-jerk rebellious decision you'd regret later on."

Nudged by that comment, Luke flashed on what TJ had said.

Make sure Luke's okay. Damn. His dad really did care.

Saving Luke from speaking around the sudden knot in his throat, Josie stepped forward. She regarded Robert Donovan solemnly, shaking her head with sham regret.

"Oh, Bob-O," she said, "we *never* make knee-jerk rebellious decisions around here."

At that, half the crowd guffawed.

Luke laughed, too. Now that he had the woman he loved, his family and friends, *and* his father by his side, he felt unstoppable.

"No knee-jerk rebellious decisions, huh?" He gazed into Josie's upturned face, unable to hold back an answering smile. "What do you call all this, then?"

Securely and dazzlingly herself, she studied the expectant crowd.

"I call it a party!" she yelled. "Woohoo!"

Grabbing his arm, she tangoed them both across the lawn.

Just as Luke might have predicted, Donovan's Corner fell in step right behind them. Because when it came to dancing — just like when it came to true love — all anybody really needed was the courage to get started . . . and a really good partner to try out the moves with. After that, it was mostly a matter of keeping the rhythm.

About the Author

When she sat down to write her first book, Lisa Plumley expected the process to be easy. Three tries and several years later, she realized it's not easy — but it is the most fun to be had outside of shoe shopping. Now the bestselling author of more than a dozen books, Lisa lives in sunny Arizona with her husband and two children. She invites readers to visit her Web site, www. lisaplumley.com for previews of upcoming books and more.